THE
NAKED
SAVAGES

Fred Mustard Stewart

TOR®

A TOM DOHERTY ASSOCIATES BOOK
NEW YORK

This is a work of fiction. All the characters and events portrayed in this book are either products of the author's imagination or are used fictitiously.

THE NAKED SAVAGES

A Tor Book
Published by Tom Doherty Associates, LLC
175 Fifth Avenue
New York, NY 10010

www.tor.com

Tor® is a registered trademark of Tom Doherty Associates, LLC.

ISBN: 0-812-56685-8
Library of Congress Catalog Card Number: 99-24482

First edition: August 1999
First mass market edition: August 2000

Printed in the United States of America

0 9 8 7 6 5 4 3 2 1

As always, to my beloved wife, Joan.

ACKNOWLEDGMENTS

My thanks to my agent, Peter Lampack, and my editor, Claire Eddy, for their excellent suggestions.

I would also like to thank David and Joanna Samson for their love and counsel.

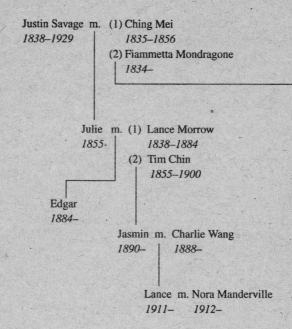

Justin Savage m. (1) Ching Mei
1838–1929   1835–1856
          (2) Fiammetta Mondragone
             1834–

Julie m. (1) Lance Morrow
1855-   1838–1884
       (2) Tim Chin
         1855–1900

Edgar
1884–

Jasmin m. Charlie Wang
1890–   1888–

Lance m. Nora Manderville
1911–   1912–

❈ The Savage Family ❈

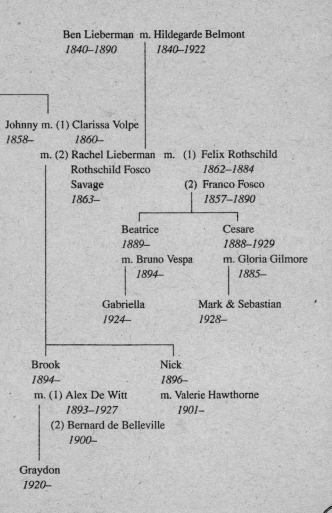

Ben Lieberman m. Hildegarde Belmont
1840–1890   *1840–1922*

Johnny m. (1) Clarissa Volpe
1858–   *1860–*
        m. (2) Rachel Lieberman   m. (1) Felix Rothschild
                Rothschild Fosco   *1862–1884*
                Savage   (2) Franco Fosco
                1863–   *1857–1890*

                Beatrice   Cesare
                1889–   *1888–1929*
                m. Bruno Vespa   m. Gloria Gilmore
                   1894–   *1885–*

                Gabriella   Mark & Sebastian
                1924–   *1928–*

Brook   Nick
1894–   *1896–*
m. (1) Alex De Witt   m. Valerie Hawthorne
    1893–1927   *1901–*
   (2) Bernard de Belleville
       1900–

Graydon
1920–

PART ONE

THE PARTY
OF THE CENTURY

1. "Well, tomorrow's the big day," Rachel Savage said as her butler refilled her wineglass. "Or should I say the big night? With all the publicity this ball has gotten in the tabloids, I just hope it doesn't turn out to be a fiasco."

"Why should it?" Teddy Roosevelt said. He was sitting to Rachel's right in the dining room of the Savages' limestone mansion at Fifth Avenue and Fifty-fourth Street, Johnny Savage having bought the place from his parents when his father, Justin, had moved to Rome to live once again with his mother, Fiammetta. "Personally, I think it will be a bully show."

"An expensive bully show," Rachel said, cutting into her lamb chops. "I can't believe the money the Bradley Martins are spending. It's rather vulgar, and after these hard times the past winter, it seems particularly ill-timed."

"But, darling," said Johnny Savage, who was sitting opposite his wife, "that's why Mrs. Bradley Martin is giving the ball. She told the newspapers she wants to give an 'impetus to trade,' and I quote her."

"An impetus to the wine trade," said Edith Roosevelt, Teddy's second wife, who was sitting to Johnny's left. "I read that she's ordered sixty cases of 1884 Moët & Chandon. That's enough to float a small battleship. I agree with you, Rachel: it's all rather vulgar."

"Yes, Edith," said her husband, who had a high, squeaky voice, "but your nose would have been out of joint if we hadn't been invited."

Edith Roosevelt, who could be chilly and imperious on occasion, gave her husband a look that almost frosted his famous pince-nez.

"Is it true, Teddy," Johnny said to his longtime friend and Harvard classmate, "that you're posting two hundred policemen and forty plainclothesmen on the streets around the Waldorf-Astoria?" Teddy, who had been joined by Johnny in the Badlands of Dakota when they were young men, had become the Commissioner of Police of the City of New York and was considered a rising star in the Republican Party.

"Yes, it's true."

"Then you must be expecting some trouble?"

"The Bradley Martins simply want to insure that there won't be traffic jams. After all, they've invited nine hundred people. That's a lot of carriages."

"Still," Rachel said, "two hundred policemen to handle traffic? If you ask me, the Bradley Martins must be a bit nervous."

"About some sort of Socialist or Nihilist demonstration?" Teddy said. "Well, yes, that's a possibility, I suppose. But I seriously doubt anything will happen. New Yorkers like a good show, the way Londoners like to watch a royal procession."

"Whom are you going as, Rachel?" Edith Roosevelt asked.

"Marie Antoniette, which I now think was probably a bad idea on my part. I can just hear someone say, 'I suppose Rachel Savage thinks we should all eat cake.' "

"Rachel, you're making too much out of all this," her husband said. "Personally, I think costume parties are silly, and so do most people. I know I'm going to feel silly in my costume."

"Which is what, Johnny?" Teddy asked.

"I'm going as Chief Crazy Horse."

Teddy Roosevelt guffawed, his laugh having once been

described by his mother as "an ungreased squeak." "A blond Indian?" he said with a chuckle. "I say, Johnny, that's a bully idea."

"I'm wearing a wig."

"I thought Mrs. Bradley Martin specified costumes from European history?" Edith said.

"I hear J. P. Morgan's daughter is coming as Pocahontas, so why can't I be Chief Crazy Horse?"

"Well, you'd better wear a horse blanket, old man," Teddy said. "The weather says there may be a blizzard tomorrow night."

"Is your Marie Antoinette costume elaborate, Rachel?" Edith asked.

"Yes, I'm afraid it is. It's quite beautiful, actually. I had the final fitting this afternoon, they're shipping it to the Waldorf in a wooden crate that makes it look more like a piece of furniture than a dress."

The butler repassed the crystal decanter filled with 1886 Lafite-Rothschild as the candlelight flickered off the magnificent vermeil candelabra that had belonged to Rachel's first husband, the English Felix Rothschild, whose strange murder—he had been pushed off a cliff into the English Channel—still remained officially unsolved.

However, everyone in New York who knew the story was certain who had committed the murder.

"Well," Teddy Roosevelt said, wiping his lips with his damask napkin, "they say it's going to be the party of the century. And since this century is about over, we might as well go out with a bang."

"Mr. Hearst, you have to let me cover the Bradley Martin ball tonight!"

The speaker was a hulking, twenty-six-year-old reporter for the New York *Journal* named Steve Carson. He was standing in front of the desk of the newspaper's owner, thirty-four-year-old William Randolph Hearst, who had recently bought the ailing newspaper with money loaned by his vastly rich mother, Phoebe.

"Steve, you're one of my finest crime reporters," Hearst said in his high, rather girlish voice, which had been the source of much ridicule from his Harvard classmates before he was kicked out in his junior year for having given members of the faculty chamber pots with their names engraved on the inside. "Why in God's name would you want to cover this ridiculous ball tonight? I'm assigning it to the Society editor."

Steve Carson, who was as tall as Hearst—well over six feet—and who had flaming red hair, leaned on Hearst's desk.

"Mr. Hearst," he said, "you've made the *Journal* a newspaper for the workingman, the little guy, and they love us. Now's the chance for us to toss a journalistic bomb right into the Waldorf! Let me write a rabble-rousing article about all these rich swells, and we can sell thousands of papers tomorrow morning. Every beer drinker in New York will be up in arms about this absurdly extravagant party . . ."

Hearst, who had pale blond hair and a mustache beneath his long thin nose, shook his head.

"No," he interrupted. "It'll be on the Society page, and that's final. But I'll tell you what I will do for you: I'd like you to go down to Cuba for me and see what's going on with the damned Spaniards. Write me a series of articles about Cuba and there's a thousand-dollar bonus in it for you. Of course, you'll make the Spaniards look like the villains they are. I want a war, and I'm going to get one."

Carson, who wore loud bow ties as a sort of trademark, looked impressed.

"Gee, Mr. Hearst," he said, "you make it awfully hard to say no to you. Yeah, I'd love to go down to Cuba. When do you want me to go?"

"How about tomorrow?"

A big grin came over Carson's freckled face.

"You've got a deal, Mr. Hearst. But I'm still going to the Waldorf tonight and see those goddamned millionaires make horses' asses of themselves."

"You can do as you like, Steve. I know you're a Socialist, which is your business. But here's one goddamned millionaire who won't be making a horse's ass of himself tonight. I turned down the invitation."

"Good for you, Mr. Hearst."

"I can't dance worth a damn anyway. Go downstairs to accounting. I'll call down and tell them to get you some traveling money. And have fun! They say Havana's a great party town."

Hearst, who was popular with his employees, picked up his phone as Carson left his office. The *Journal* occupied a rather ramshackle plant on the second and third floors of the Tribune Building at Park Row and Spruce Street on Printing House Square. Across the street was the proud *Sun*, the *Times* was nearby, and a short block north was the glittering Pulitzer Building where Joseph Pulitzer's *World* sold a half million copies a day. Pulitzer was king of the New York publishing jungle, but young Willie Hearst was out to dethrone him, and he had the money and the journalistic flair to do it.

Hearst's father, George Hearst, a big, uncouth, hard-drinking man who publicly boasted (whether seriously or not, no one was quite sure) that he spelled "bird" b-u-r-d, had left Missouri during the gold rush and spent ten years of his life looking for gold. He became so knowledgeable about mining that the Indians called him Boy-That-Earth-Talked-To. When the earth finally talked to George, it wasn't gold he found, but rather silver—part of the fabulous Comstock Lode. The senior Hearst went on to other mines, ending up owning three of the most valuable mines in the West and amassing a huge fortune. He bought a seat in the United States Senate—in California, it was assumed that politicians were to buy their jobs—and moved to Washington to serve with complete lack of distinction until he died.

His widow, Phoebe Apperson, was a petite girl much George's junior in age. She had one child, Willie, whom she lavished love on to the point of momism and whom she raised to be as cultivated as her husband was boorish. Willie was handsome, precocious, wildly extravagant, and amazingly determined to get what he wanted in life. At Harvard, he had been known as a prankster who kept a pet alligator he fed expensive wines to until the poor beast died of alcoholism. But after he was booted for his chamber-pot caper, he went to New York and got a job on a newspaper. It is fortunate for America that he fell in love with journalism, for if he hadn't we probably would never have gone to war with Spain, Teddy Roosevelt might have ended up an obscure politician, Franklin Delano Roosevelt might never have been President, and California would never have had Louella Parsons or a castle, San Simeon.

That evening, February 10, 1897, the beautiful eight-year-old boy stood at the window of his third-floor bedroom overlooking Fifth Avenue and watched through the whirling snow his mother, Rachel Savage, and his stepfather, Johnny, climb into their carriage on their way to the Bradley Martin ball at the Waldorf. The boy's name was Cesare, pronounced *Chay-sar-ay*, in the Italian fashion, and he was the son of Rachel's second husband, the Italian-born Franco Fosco. How many times Cesare had been the butt of jokes and taunts by his classmates at school. How many fights he had initiated—and usually won—when boys would snicker and call his dead father "The Murdering Wop." For everyone knew—or at least thought they knew—that Franco Fosco, a penniless but charming son of Fiammetta

Savage's Roman lover, had insinuated himself into the graces—and then the heart—of Rachel while she was still married to Felix Rothschild. And then, the story went, Franco had conveniently pushed Felix off the cliff so he could marry Rachel and get Felix's fabulous fortune—which he, in fact, did.

But Cesare knew it was a lie. He knew his handsome father, whom he only dimly remembered, was not a murderer. Nor had he been involved in shady loan-sharking, as was also rumored. Even though Franco had been shot to death in Central Park by a young immigrant who called him a "vampire" for charging him exorbitant "vigorish," or interest, on a five-hundred-dollar loan, Cesare was certain that was a lie too.

His father was an honorable man, a gentleman. After all, their family was one of the oldest in Italy—a much better family than these nouveau riche Savages, whose money only dated back to the beginning of the century, when Justin Savage's father had founded a line of clipper ships trading with the Orient. And Justin—what was he? He'd been a pirate! All very exciting, perhaps, but hardly qualifying him as a gentleman.

Cesare had been adopted by Johnny Savage, but he didn't think of himself as a real Savage. He was an outsider. But, he thought, I'll make it my own way. Someday.

When his parents' carriage rattled off down Fifth Avenue toward the Waldorf-Astoria, he thought a moment. Then, putting on his bathrobe and slippers, he let himself out of his bedroom, quietly closed the door, and started tiptoeing down the upstairs hall toward the stairs. His elder sister, Beatrice, and his half sister and brother, Brook and Nick Savage, were all tucked in bed in their own rooms: Cesare had the house to himself, aside from the servants. He felt the knife in his bathrobe pocket, the knife he had "borrowed" from the kitchen that afternoon.

Reaching the stairs, he started down to the second floor.

The house, which had been built some twenty years before, had been modernized with electricity and telephones, and an electric sconce on the wall illuminated the stairs. When he reached the second floor, he went down the broad hallway, hung with gilt-framed paintings, to his parents' master suite at the end. Letting himself in, he turned on the lights. His parents' bedroom, done quite beautifully in the style of Louis XVI, with paneled walls painted a delicate blue, was a thing of beauty that he loved—except for the fact that his mother, Rachel, whom he adored, shared the big bed with Johnny, whom he loathed. He looked around a moment, listening. Hearing nothing, he crossed to the left where, he knew, a door led into his stepfather's dressing room.

He opened the door and turned on the light. The dressing room was long and narrow, the walls sliding mirrored doors. He opened the door to the left, revealing a row of suits beneath which, on slanted wooden shelves, were neatly placed three dozen pairs of shoes, all with custom-made shoe trees fashioned from the same wood used for violins. Cesare knew that his stepfather, Johnny, was considered one of the best-dressed men in New York and was more than a little vain. He also knew that on the opposite side of the room were built-in drawers holding dozens of custom-made shirts, as well as racks of silk ties in bright array.

Pulling the knife from his bathrobe pocket, Cesare took the left sleeve of the first suit and cut it off with a savage slash. Then the right sleeve. Throwing them on the floor, he whispered, "My father was not a murdering Wop!"

He moved on to the second suit and did the same thing.

"My father was not a loan shark!"

Then the third suit.

"My father was a fine gentleman, much better than you, Johnny Savage! My father was better!"

When he had destroyed six expensive suits, he looked at the pile of torn sleeves on the floor and burst into tears.

Then, turning out the lights, he ran back up to his third-floor bedroom, locked the door, threw himself into his bed, and sobbed his heart out as, outside, the winter blizzard blanketed the great metropolis in snow.

"Have I told you lately that I'm madly in love with you?" Johnny asked as he twirled his wife around the ballroom floor of the Waldorf-Astoria Hotel at Fifth Avenue and Thirty-fourth Street.

"Not lately," Rachel said with a smile. "But I like to hear it."

"Well, it's true. And you look fabulous in that outfit. If Marie Antoinette had been as beautiful as you, they would never have chopped her head off."

"And I think you look extremely dashing as Chief Crazy Horse. All the women are gawking at your bare chest. By the way, did you see Otto Cushing when he came in the hotel?"

"I certainly did. He was dressed as a falconer in tights so tight, he left little to the imagination."

"I thought Mrs. Bradley Martin would faint, and she forced him to leave the room. It was very shocking."

"I sometimes get the feeling we're living the decline of the Roman Empire."

They were waltzing to Victor Herbert's orchestra in the ballroom that had been decorated to re-create the Hall of Mirrors at Versailles. Six thousand mauve orchids and hundreds of feet of hanging asparagus vines were festooned around the cavernous room, though what mauve orchids and asparagus vines had to do with Versailles was anyone's guess. When Rachel and Johnny had arrived at the hotel in their carriage, the traffic was so jammed that it took them twenty minutes in line to get to the porte cochere, they were escorted upstairs to individual dressing rooms where hairdressers and fitters waited to help them into their elaborate costumes. In Rachel's case, the costume's designer had been there to help her into the extravagant eighteenth-century dress she had created, made of pink and white silk with a huge skirt adorned with seed pearls and blue silk bows. Rachel had put on a towering white wig, and she was wearing the diamond and emerald necklace and earrings her husband had given her for their fifth wedding anniversary. Then she joined Johnny, who had smeared his torso and face with brown stain and war paint and was wearing leather Indian pants and moccasins, as well as an impressive chief's headdress of eagle feathers. Together, this distinctly odd-looking, if handsome, couple went to the ballroom to wait in line yet again to be greeted by the hostess—who was dressed as Mary, Queen of Scots, presumably oblivious to that unfortunate lady's decapitated end, and who was draped in the French crown jewels formerly worn by Empresses Marie Louise and Joséphine—and her husband, dressed as Louis XV, seated thronelike before a Beauvais tapestry from one of their many homes. The young Savage couple vied for position with such luminaries of the contemporary social scene as "The" Mrs. Astor, wearing her famous $200,000 diamond tiara; Mrs. Cornelius Vanderbilt and her sister, Mrs. Ogden Goelet, the former dressed as a courtier of the court of Versailles; Mrs. Hamilton Fish Webster dressed as Marie Antoinette's mother, the Empress Maria Theresa of Austria; "The" Mrs. Astor's only son, John Jacob Astor, dressed as Henry IV of Navarre (needless to say totally unaware that he would go down with the *Titanic* fifteen years later); Mrs. Herman Oelrichs dressed as an eighteenth-century French dancing girl; and Mrs. O. H. P. Belmont dressed as Tosca.

Johnny, as he had remarked earlier, thought the whole thing was rather silly. But he couldn't help but be impressed by the thought that gathered in that ballroom on that snowy night were people whose total worth was probably well in excess of a billion dollars at a time when the average American family's annual income was less than five hundred dollars and the budget of the federal government was less than a hundred million dollars a year.

As Mark Twain had written a quarter century earlier:

"What is the chief end of man?—to get rich. In what way?—dishonestly if we can, honestly if we must. Who is God, the one only and true? Money is God. Gold and Greenbacks and stock—father, son and the ghost of the same—three persons in one; these are the true and only God, mighty and supreme."

If Mark Twain was right—and he himself was caught up in the scramble for quick bucks—then God that night was at the Waldorf-Astoria Hotel.

But many of the poor New Yorkers, shivering outside on the streets in the howling blizzard, watching this cavalcade of vast wealth, must have thought that the resident of the Waldorf-Astoria that night was not God, but rather the Devil himself. Steve Carson of the *Journal* watched the show from the sidewalks with socialistic disgust, then he went to a saloon to wash down his disdain with a beer.

The next morning, he looked at photographs of some of the guests that Mr. Hearst had printed in the rotogravure section of the *Journal*. He was amused by the picture of thirty-eight-year-old Johnny Savage in his Indian costume. Steve Carson knew that Johnny was blond. He thought a blond Indian was as phony as the entire Bradley Martin ball.

After changing out of their costumes into their "regular" clothes, Johnny and Rachel drove home at four in the morning where they were admitted to their house by a yawning footman.

"I guess it was a 'bully show,' as Teddy said," Rachel remarked as they climbed the stairs to the second floor, "but I'm glad it's over."

"And my feet are killing me."

She smiled and took his arm.

"But you're still the best dancer in New York. And the handsomest. By the way, you have a new admirer."

"Who's that?"

"The girl who designed my costume. She told me at the hotel as she was helping me into the dress that she thought you were extremely dashing."

"Ah well, what can I say? Women just fall all over me."

"But there's only one woman who owns your heart: me."

"Absolutely."

They reached the second floor and went down the hall, going into their bedroom and turning on the lights.

"Thank God tomorrow's Sunday," Johnny said, sitting on a chair to take off his shoes. "I can sleep in. I'm exhausted."

Taking off his tailcoat and pants, he went to his dressing room to hang them up. When he turned on the light, he looked at the floor.

"What the hell is this?" he almost yelled.

"What's wrong?"

"Look: someone cut the sleeves off a bunch of my suits! One, two, three . . . my God, six of my best suits! They're ruined! Who the hell . . ."

He stopped and turned to his wife, who had just appeared behind him at the door and was staring at the torn sleeves.

"Cesare," he said softly.

"Johnny, don't jump to conclusions . . ."

"Who the hell else would do such a crazy thing except that son of yours? By God, I'll spank the living daylights out of him . . ."

"No!" He started past her, but she restrained him. "Not now, it's late and he's asleep. Wait till the morning, when we can talk to him. There must be some explanation . . ."

" 'Explanation'? It's no great secret he hates my guts!"

"It will only make it worse if you attack him! Let's talk

with him, reason with him . . . Believe me, darling, that's
the wiser course. I know Cesare has angry feelings toward
you because of his father, but everything I've read in the
most advanced medical journals say that physical punish-
ment can be counterproductive . . ."

"Did you ever hear 'Spare the rod, spoil the child'?"

"Johnny, please . . . there must be a better way. You
know how much I adore that child, who's been so wounded
at school with his friends saying those terrible things about
his father . . ."

"They happen to be true!"

"Nevertheless, we have to be extra careful with Cesare,
because he's carrying this terrible burden about his father.
Now please, darling. Come to bed and cool off. We'll talk
to Cesare in the morning."

Johnny, who was fuming, began to cool down as Rachel
kissed him tenderly on his mouth.

"Oh, all right," he finally grumbled, taking off his tie.
"But that kid had better straighten up, or I'll know the reason why."

At ten the next morning, Rachel, wearing a light green neg-
ligee, came into the bedroom from the hall and sat on the
side of the bed next to her sleeping husband, whom she
gently shook. Johnny gave a half snore of surprise, more
like a snort, then opened his eyes.

"What time is it?" he asked.

"Ten. I just had a talk with Cesare, and he broke down
in tears and sobbed. He said he's so full of hurt about his
father that he almost didn't know what he was doing last
night. You know, he's a very injured child, and we have
to do everything we can to help him heal his wounds. He's
so beautiful and intelligent. He's outside the door now, and
he wants to apologize to you."

Johnny sat up and rubbed his eyes.

"Couldn't he wait till I had some coffee?" he grumped.

"He's on his way to Sunday school."

"Probably trying to pray that crooked father of his out of Hell."

"Shh! Johnny!" she whispered. "He's right outside the door."

"Sorry. Send him in."

Rachel went to the door and looked outside. Cesare, looking handsome in a dark jacket with matching knickers and well-shined black shoes, his shiny black hair carefully brushed, was standing in the hall staring at his mother with his intense violet eyes that were so much like her own.

"Darling," Rachel said, coming over and taking his hand, "your father will see you now."

"He's not my father," Cesare said in a loud voice. "And I'm not trying to pray my father out of Hell, because he's not there! He's in Heaven!"

Jerking his hand out of his mother's, he ran down the hall to the stairs as Rachel rolled her eyes and sighed. Going back into the bedroom, she said, "He heard you."

"Yes, I gather."

"Oh Johnny, you have to try harder. You have to be more careful with him. Please promise me you'll try."

Johnny, looking sulphurous, got out of bed and started toward the bathroom.

"The damnable thing about this," he said, "is that the kid cuts up my suits, and I come out looking like the villain!"

He went into the bathroom and slammed the door.

2.   IN HIS EARLIER DAYS, WHEN JOHNNY WAS ONE
of New York's most eligible bachelors with a reputation as
being wild, he had encountered in the Dakota Bad Lands a
peculiar French aristocrat named the Marquis de Morès
who rapidly became his nemesis. The Marquis had bought
extensive land and dreamed of raising cattle and butchering
them in Dakota, rather than the long and expensive cattle
drives to the Chicago meat markets. Johnny, ranching with
Teddy Roosevelt, had taken offense at the Marquis's viru-
lent anti-Semitic opinions, and after a misunderstanding
with the Marquis's wife, the Marquis, who had a streak of
murderous violence in him, had almost castrated Johnny,
Teddy saving his friend in the nick of time. Years later,
after Johnny had married Rachel and the couple had moved
to Paris where Johnny was head of the French branch of
the Savage Bank, he encountered the Marquis another time,
this involving the bitter struggle swirling around the Dreyfus Affair. The Marquis had been a leading Dreyfus hater;
and when Rachel had tried to help Madame Dreyfus, the
Marquis became enraged and challenged Johnny to a duel,
which Johnny narrowly won.

Thus Johnny, who was a non-observing Protestant, did
not share the anti-Semitic prejudices of most of his fellow
WASPs, and he had given Rachel carte blanche in the religious instruction of their four children. Rachel, being Jewish, had hoped her two eldest children by Franco Fosco,
Beatrice and Cesare, would opt for Judaism. But both
wanted to remain in the faith of their father—who had gone

to mass less than a dozen times in his lifetime—and so she had given in, if rather reluctantly, to their wishes. Her two children by Johnny, Brook and Nick, were too young yet to make the choice, but she hoped they would choose Judaism.

Two Sundays later, when Beatrice, Cesare, and four-year-old Brook were having Sunday lunch with their parents in the big dining room of the Fifth Avenue house, which was something of a ritual in the family, Cesare said, "Father McGuire was talking in Sunday school today about that ball you went to, the Bradley Martins' party."

"Everyone in town is talking about it," said his mother. "What did he say?"

"He said it had cost three hundred and ninety-six thousand dollars. Is that possible?"

Rachel exchanged looks with her husband at the other end of the table.

"I'm afraid it's true," she said.

"That much money for a party?" Beatrice said, in a disbelieving tone. "There's not that much money in the world, is there?"

"Father McGuire said it was shameful and vulgar to spend money like that when people are going hungry," Cesare said.

"He's right," his mother said. "The whole city is up in arms about the party, and I wish we hadn't gone to it. The city's threatened to double the Bradley Martins' property taxes, and I hear they're fleeing America to go to England they're so upset by all the terrible publicity about them."

Which in fact happened. The Bradley Martins never returned to America. The party of the century turned them into permanent exiles.

After lunch, Brook took Cesare's hand.

"Let's go up and see Baby Nick," she whispered.

"Okay."

They climbed the stairs to the second-floor nursery,

which Rachel had had painted with enchanting murals illustrating fairy tales out of Mother Goose and the Grimm Brothers. Nick, who was almost one year old, was lying on his back in his crib, sucking his thumb.

"Isn't Nick the most beautiful baby in the world?" Brook said, staring fondly at her baby brother.

"I think all babies are sort of funny-looking," Cesare said.

"Oh Cesare, you say the most awful things! All babies are beautiful."

"All right, if you say so. He still looks funny to me. But I remember when you were a baby. You looked funny then, but you've turned out pretty well."

In fact, Brook was a ravishingly beautiful child with wheat-colored hair. Now she turned and smiled at Cesare.

"Do you really think so, Cesare? Do you think I'm pretty?"

"Absolutely. Of course"—he puffed out his chest—"I'm the best-looking of all of us."

"You're awfully conceited."

He grabbed one of her curls and gave it a yank.

"I have a lot to be conceited about," he said.

After he left the nursery, Brook sighed. She thought her big brother was awfully full of himself, and she couldn't understand why he so hated her father. But she had to agree with his own self-estimate.

She thought Cesare was the most beautiful boy in the world.

Cesare went downstairs to the drawing room of the house, which was lavishly decorated with many of the splendid antiques Rachel had inherited from her Rothschild husband, Felix. He picked up a magazine and began to leaf through it when he heard a noise in the next room, his stepfather's study. Putting down the magazine, he walked quietly across the room and peeked through the open door.

"How's Mitzie?" Johnny was cooing as he poured bird

food into his pet canary's cage. "How's my beautiful Mitzie today?"

The next morning, Rachel was just coming downstairs for breakfast when she heard a roar of rage from her husband's study.

"What in the world—?"

She hurried into the drawing room where she almost bumped into Johnny, who looked apoplectic.

"He's killed Mitzie!" he roared. "Where is he?"

"Who?"

"Who else? Cesare! My poor little innocent canary is in her cage, dead!"

"Oh no! I can't believe Cesare could . . ."

"Rachel, you're not going to defend him this time! Cutting up my suits is one thing, but poisoning a sweet little bird—the kid's a monster!"

"But how did he do it—?"

"He put rat poison in her feed! The next thing, he'll put rat poison in my coffee! That boy is a menace! Where the hell is he?"

"He's gone to school . . . But, darling, are you sure he did it?"

"Who else would do it? Listen, Rachel: this is the last straw. I've been asking around town, and I've learned that there's a school out in New Jersey for disturbed children named Longwood Academy . . ."

"But that's a military school!" Rachel exclaimed. "It's terribly strict . . ."

"It's what he needs! I'm calling the Commandant this morning. If they'll take Cesare, I'm sending him out there tomorrow."

Rachel sank into a chair and burst into tears. Johnny frowned.

"Rachel," he said, putting his hand on her shoulder, "I

know you want him here with you. But can't you see we have to do something? It's for his own good, after all. If he has some discipline, he'll begin to straighten out. You're too soft to discipline him, and he's got this war with me. Believe me, darling, it's the best way."

She wiped her eyes with a handkerchief and slowly nodded.

"I suppose you're right," she sighed. "But I'll miss him so."

"It's not as if he's going out of our lives forever. I guarantee you that with a few months at Longwood, Cesare will be a new human being."

Two hours later, Johnny called his wife from his office.

"I talked to the Commandant at Longwood," he said. "Unfortunately, they can't take him until next fall. But we'll enroll him for the new school year."

"Perhaps that's just as well," Rachel said. "I'm going to talk to him when he comes home from school. If he realizes how serious this is becoming, he may change."

"It's fine if he does," Johnny said. "But if he doesn't, it's Longwood. It has an excellent scholastic reputation, by the way. It's not as if we're sending him to some horribly Dickensian orphanage."

"Did you kill that poor little canary?" Rachel said to her son that afternoon when he came home from school.

Cesare looked at her defiantly.

"Yes," he said.

"But why? Why take the life of an innocent creature?"

"Because your husband loved it."

"My husband loves me. Does that mean you'd kill me?"

"Of course not, Momma. I love you. I'd never hurt you."

"I'm glad to hear it. Cesare, you have to change your attitude. Have you ever heard of Longwood Academy?"

"Oh sure. That's where they send rich kids with problems."

"That's where you're going to be sent if you keep up this behavior. Now, I don't want you to go there. I want you here at home, of course. But your father . . ."

"He's not my father! He's my stepfather, and I'd rather go to Longwood than be in the same house with him!"

"Your attitude is totally wrong!" she said, for once her tone becoming harsh. "I love your father very much! He's a wonderful man, and he's been wonderful to you. But you're coming between us . . ."

Cesare smiled.

"Good," he said.

His mother sighed.

"Cesare, you're impossible. But you've been warned: either you behave yourself, or next fall you're going to Longwood. Now, go to your room. And when your father comes home, I want you to apologize to him."

"Never."

"Cesare, I'm not asking you: I'm telling you. Apologize to him!"

Cesare thought a moment. Then he said, "All right, Momma. I'll do it for you. I'd do anything for you, because I love you so much."

She melted into a smile and held out her arms to hug him.

"Oh darling, I love you so much. All I want is for us all to be happy."

"Momma?"

"What?"

"I haven't got any money because he stopped my allowance after I cut up his suits. Would you give me some? There's something I want to buy."

"Of course, darling. Would five dollars be enough?"

"I'd rather have ten."

"I'll give you five."

3.   A FEW WEEKS LATER, CESARE STOOD IN FRONT
of a pawnshop, looking through the window.

It was a bright wintry day, cold enough to cloud his
breath. The pawnshop was in an undistinguished building
on an undistinguished block: this part of the Upper East
Side on First Avenue in the seventies had been farmland
until a few decades before, but now was mainly tenements
as the poor immigrants from Europe filled up lower Manhattan and the second-generation immigrants moved uptown. The windows of the pawnshop were filled with an
odd jumble of objects that had been pawned and not re-
deemed: shirts, shoes, a ratty typewriter, an aged violin, a
clarinet with no reed. Prices were predictably low. After
looking at the windows for a moment, Cesare went to the
door of the shop, opened it, and went in.

The interior was dark and equally as junk-filled as the
windows. Behind a counter, an elderly man was seated on
a stool reading a newspaper. He had garters on his shirt-
sleeves, and there was a yarmulke on his bald head. Hearing
the bell of his door ring, he put down the paper and looked
at Cesare, who came up to the counter.

"Well, young man," the pawnbroker said, "what can I do
for you?"

"I want to pawn these cuff links," the boy said, pulling
an envelope from the pocket of his coat. He opened the
envelope and turned it over. Two platinum cuff links rolled
onto the counter. In the center of each was a large diamond
surrounded by sapphires.

Surprised, the pawnbroker picked one up, aimed a light at it, put a loupe in his right eye, and examined it. Then he removed the loupe and looked at the boy.

"These are real," he said. "Where did you get them?"

"They belonged to my father, Franco Fosco. My mother gave them to him years ago. My father was shot to death in Central Park seven years ago."

The pawnbroker frowned thoughtfully.

"Oh yes, I remember reading about that. Then you're the son of Mr. Savage, the banker. Does he know you want to pawn these cuff links?"

"It's none of his business!" Cesare said hotly. "Besides, he's not my father. He just adopted me when he married my mother, who was born Rachel Lieberman."

"Ah yes, the daughter of the great Jewish banker. You come from a distinguished family, young man. And a very wealthy family. Why would you want to pawn these?"

"That's my business. These belonged to my real father, and they're mine to do with as I please. How much will you give me for them?"

The pawnbroker replaced the loupe in his eye and examined them again, turning them over.

"They were made for Asprey in London," he said. "They're very valuable."

"I know that. How much? And don't try and cheat me because I'm young. I know about business."

The pawnbroker thought a moment.

"I'll give you three hundred dollars. They're worth more, but that's all I'll go for. If you want a better deal, go downtown to the diamond market . . ."

"I'll take the three hundred," the boy interrupted, sticking out his hand.

"But I won't do it unless I have the permission of your parents."

"No!" Cesare almost shouted, his eyes blazing with anger. "My parents mustn't know!"

"Then we don't have a deal."

The boy grabbed the cuff links, stuck them back in the envelope, and went to the door. As he opened the door, he turned back to the pawnbroker and snarled: "You can go to hell, old man!"

Then he slammed out.

The pawnbroker, a slight look of shock on his face, thought a moment. Then he went to his phone at the rear of the shop, picked it up, and cranked the handle.

"Hello, Central?" he said to the operator. "I'd like to speak to the residence of Mr. John Savage. I believe he lives on Fifth Avenue."

"A pawnbroker from First Avenue telephoned an hour ago saying Cesare had been in his shop trying to pawn some diamond cuff links," Rachel said as she paced back and forth in her morning room, wringing her hands. "I sent George out in a cab to find him and bring him home . . ."

"They're my diamond and sapphire cuff links," Johnny said angrily. He had hurried home from the bank when Rachel called him. "He stole them out of my stud box! Dammit, this time he's gone too far . . ."

"There must be some explanation! And, darling, after all, technically they're his. I bought them for his father."

"Rachel, that's not the point! Don't you understand? He's stolen! He's a thief!"

"We mustn't rush to judgment! The child obviously has some sort of problem . . ."

"We know what his problem is, he hates my guts—for no good reason! I've done everything in my power to get him to love me, I've given him God knows what—toys, the finest clothes, the best education, my home . . ."

"Our home."

"Of course, you know that's what I mean. And yet he hates me. When he looks at me with those damned eyes of

his, I know what he's thinking: he wants me dead. I have
no problem with Beatrice! She doesn't hate me just because
I'm not her real father! No, this time it's enough. He's
going to Longwood Academy . . ."

"You might love him!" Rachel interrupted angrily.

Johnny rolled his eyes.

"I do love him—or I did. But it's sort of hard loving a
child who wishes for your death!"

"Sshh—here he is," she said, looking out the window.
"Thank God George found him." She turned back to
Johnny. "Let's try not to have a scene," she went on plain-
tively. "Let's try and behave rationally. You know, Mabel
Lawson had so much trouble with her daughter, Lucille,
who was so moody and nervous. And she told me about
this doctor in Vienna who did wonders with her, a Dr.
Freund, or something like that. Maybe we should take Cesare to Vienna . . ."

"I'm not taking Cesare anywhere but to the woodshed—
if we had one. Unfortunately, we don't."

He paused as Cesare appeared in the doorway. There was
a moment of silence as the boy stared at his father. Then
he looked coolly at his mother.

"Why did you send George after me?" he asked.

"Because I was worried about you!" Rachel crossed the
room and leaned down to hug him as Johnny watched.
"Darling, why did you try to pawn those cuff links?"

"Because they're mine," the boy said, looking at Johnny.
"They're not his."

"You stole them out of my stud box . . ." Johnny said.

"I took them! You have no right to them! They're mine!
It's you who stole them from me!"

"What's the point of giving an eight-year-old cuff links?
I was planning to give them to you on your eighteenth
birthday . . ."

"I don't want any present from you!" the boy shouted,
shoving his mother away from him. Rachel stood up.

"Cesare, you will treat your father with respect."

"He's not my father!"

"A slight technicality, since you live under my roof," Johnny said. "Why did you try to pawn them? What did you want the money for?"

"It's none of your business."

"Cesare, be reasonable," Rachel said. "We love you. We want to help you, but we can't if you persist in being so stubborn. There must have been some reason you wanted the money."

The boy hesitated.

"I wanted to go to Italy," he finally said.

"Italy? Why?"

"I wanted to see my grandfather. You told me he was dying."

"That's not true," Johnny said, "your grandfather has had a slight stroke, but otherwise . . ."

"Not that grandfather. Not your father. My *real* grandfather, Count Fosco. You've never let me meet him because you hate my father, and I wanted to meet him before he dies."

"In the first place," Johnny said, "I didn't hate your father . . ."

"You've told everyone he was a murderer!"

"Well"—Johnny shrugged—"he was."

"It was never proven! Nobody ever proved he pushed Mr. Rothschild over the cliff! And so you've made me a murderer's son—I hate you!"

Rachel and Johnny exchanged looks. Then Rachel turned to Cesare.

"Darling, if you'd told me, I'd have taken you to Italy."

"No! He'd want to go, and I don't want to be with him!"

He pointed at Johnny, who was doing his best to control his anger.

"Look, Cesare," he began in a soft voice. "I want us to try and start over. This situation is becoming intolerable. I don't want to have to punish you . . . I don't want to have to send you to Longwood Academy . . ."

"Darling, don't threaten him!" Rachel exclaimed.

"Well, it's true, I don't want to! I'm no ogre!" Johnny's temper was getting out of control. "But his behavior has to stop! Now, give me back the cuff links. I'll put them in a safety deposit box at the bank until you're old enough to use them."

The boy looked at him, hesitating.

"Is that true?" he said. "You'll admit they're mine, and you'll keep them for me?"

"There was never any doubt they're yours, and your mother is your witness."

"All right."

He reached out and gave the cuff links to Johnny.

"Thank you," Johnny said. "And I truly hope we can get along better from now on."

Johnny looked at his wife a moment. Then he started toward the door.

When he was gone, Rachel leaned down to hug her son again.

"Cesare," she said, "now we're going to have a talk."

"Mother," he said, "why don't you divorce him?"

"Because I love him. And you mustn't talk that way. Now come over and sit next to me and we'll decide what we're going to do."

When Rachel and Cesare returned from Italy a month later, Johnny met them at the dock, kissing his wife and shaking hands with Cesare who, to his surprise, seemed much less hostile.

"I want to thank you," the boy said, "and Mother for letting me see my grandfather before he died. And I want to apologize for cutting your suits and killing your canary."

Johnny, a smile on his face, looked at Rachel, who was

also smiling. Then he turned back to Cesare.

"I accept your apology, Cesare," he said. "And I really think things are going to be better between us from now on."

"I'll try, Father," he said, and it was the first time the boy had ever used that word. "And I'm looking forward to going to Longwood Academy."

"I'm really surprised," Johnny said an hour later as he sat on their bed watching Rachel undress to bathe. "Cesare really seems to have changed for the better."

"I think we should have taken him to Italy long ago," Rachel said, stepping behind a screen to take off her dress. Even in front of her husband, she retained a sense of prudery that rather delighted Johnny. "He was so thrilled to see the country. He told me he thinks of it as his own, which was very sweet. He really enjoyed himself."

"Well, I couldn't be more delighted."

PART TWO

HARVARD COWBOYS GO TO "A SPLENDID LITTLE WAR"

4.   THE SPANISH-AMERICAN WAR, WHICH WOULD
make America a world power and lead eventually to Pearl
Harbor and Vietnam, was a boil that burst after decades of
suppuration. America had managed to push the Spaniards
out of Florida (which the Spaniards ceded in return for a
five-million-dollar purchase, though Spain never saw a
penny of the money) and the vast Spanish-Mexican empire
in the West, including California, Arizona, New Mexico,
and Texas. This didn't leave much of the once-mighty
Spanish-American Empire except Cuba and Puerto Rico.
But America, with an eye on the Monroe Doctrine, wanted
the Spanish crown out of even these two islands; and in
1848 President Polk tried to buy Cuba from Spain for the
then-staggering sum of $100 million. The proud Spaniards
said that they would rather see Cuba "sink into the ocean."

Cuba, which still had slavery, was dominated by *creoles,*
Cuban-born whites, and *peninsulares,* the Spanish-born
elite, most of whom wanted the continuation of Spanish
rule. But for the island's poor, the mulattoes and blacks, as
well as some liberal-minded whites, the dream was for Cuban independence. After the American Civil War, an insurgency was begun in eastern Cuba to try to throw off the
Spanish yolk; but after ten years of bloody fighting, Spain
managed to quell the rebellion. But Cuban refugees in New
York and Florida began to organize, skillfully playing on
American public opinion that disliked the Spanish "dons"
and was usually for the underdog. By the mid 1890s, when
a new insurgency was attempted in Oriente Province in

eastern Cuba (where, six decades later, Fidel Castro would launch his successful revolution), America was eager to help the rebels short of breaking relations entirely with the Spanish government headed by the Austrian queen-regent, Maria Cristina. But Maria Cristina, mother of the boy King Alfonso XIII, miscalculated. She sent as the new Governor of Cuba the teetotaling General Valeriano Weyler y Nicolau, a Spaniard of German descent whose nickname was, ominously, "Butcher." Weyler's contribution to history was to organize the world's first concentration camps. In order to prevent the rebels from infiltrating the poor peasants in the east, he formulated a plan of *reconcentrados,* herding literally all the peasants into huge camps in the various cities. He also dug two huge *trochas* two hundred yards wide that bisected the entire island from north to south. These ditches were lined with barriers of wood and were heavily mined, lit at night by floodlights, creating a no-man's-land.

These two efforts worked: the rebels were almost totally immobilized and dispirited. But they also backfired. The concentration camps had no toilet facilities, little potable water, practically no food, and were rife with disease and famine. Soon word got out to America of the horrible conditions in Cuba—where even the Spaniards admitted the death rate was as high as 400,000—and the American public began to clamor for Uncle Sam to do something about it. The public was egged on by the yellow press; Messrs. Pulitzer and Hearst, no fools they, saw that nothing sold newspapers like atrocities. The business community, whose investment in Cuba was as high as $50 million, also cried out for intervention. The idea of *Cuba Libre!* united the nation as had no other idea since the Civil War.

On January 12, 1898, Spanish loyalists and army officers rioted in Havana, attacking the offices of pro-American newspapers. The American Consul, alarmed, cabled Washington to show the flag. And the American battleship *Maine* was dispatched from Key West to anchor in Havana harbor ostensibly to pay a "friendly" call but in reality to make the Spanish authorities nervous.

For two weeks all went surprisingly well. But at 9:45 on the night of February 15, for reasons which are still argued, the *Maine* was blown up by an explosion so huge that an eyewitness said the 319-foot battleship, which displaced 6,683 tons, rose three feet out of the water before sinking in forty feet of the murky waters of Havana harbor, killing 230 sailors, 28 Marines, and 2 officers. Eight of the survivors later died of their wounds.

After weeks of official inquiries, it was concluded the explosion had been caused by a Spanish mine (although another inquiry six decades later decided the explosion had been caused by the spontaneous combustion of coal dust in a bunker adjacent to one of the ship's magazines, heating the bulkhead sufficiently to ignite the ammunition).

And thus began what the American Ambassador to London would later call this "splendid little war." One of the loudest voices clamoring for action was Theodore Roosevelt who, when his position as Police Commissioner of New York expired, had gone to Washington as Assistant Secretary of the Navy.

"By George, Johnny, we have to teach those damned Spaniards a lesson!" Teddy Roosevelt exclaimed as his fist pounded the dining-room table.

"Theodore," said his wife Edith, "don't pound the table. You'll break a glass."

"Sorry."

"That's all right, Edith," said Rachel Savage, whose dining-room table was the one being pounded. "Teddy's enthusiastic, and I think it's quite wonderful."

"Yes, I think it's wonderful too," Johnny said. The four friends were having dinner in the dining room of the Savage house on Fifth Avenue. "And wouldn't it be fun to be there and see the action?"

"Well, why don't we go?" Teddy said. "I'm sick and tired of all the shilly-shallying in Washington. I'm seriously thinking of resigning as Assistant Secretary of the Navy and raising a regiment to go to Cuba and kick those Spaniards into the ocean. You should come with me, Johnny. We'd have more fun than we had in the good old days in Dakota."

"Johnny couldn't possibly go," Rachel said with a rather nervous laugh. "For one thing, he's too old."

"Fiddlesticks. Johnny's my age. Forty's not old! It's when life starts to be fun. Think about it, Johnny. We'd have a merry time down there. I've talked to Hamilton Fish about it, and he's raring to go."

"Ham Fish is twenty-four," Rachel said. "And he has no children to worry about. What if you two got killed? You have responsibilities!"

"Theodore, you're making Rachel upset," said Edith Roosevelt. "Please change the subject."

"Oh, all right," Teddy said, in a grumbling tone. "But it's going to be a bully show, mark my words."

The butler passed the roast beef and Teddy helped himself to seconds.

"I'm fond of Teddy," Rachel said two hours later as she put on her nightgown in her bedroom, "and in many ways he's a remarkable man. But he's always wanting to rush off somewhere and fight a war! It's rather nerve-racking."

"Teddy believes in action, and in this case I agree with him. The Spaniards should be run out of Cuba. They're terrible to the Cubans, who deserve something better."

Johnny got in the big double bed. Rachel climbed in next to him.

"I'm sure you're right, but you're not going to do the

chasing, and it was irresponsible of Teddy to try and goad you into going with him on some foolish adventure. Soldiering is best left to soldiers. You're a banker, and a darned good one at that."

"It's the bank that's got me worried. We've got several million dollars loaned to various Cubans, in particular Señor Manuel Garcia Flores, who owns one of the biggest sugar plantations on the island. 'Butcher' Weyler, who's running things for the Spanish government, recently arrested Flores and has threatened to burn his plantation."

"Why?"

"He was financially backing the insurgents. He wants to get rid of the Spaniards. If he's wiped out, the bank will be out a lot of money."

"Well, I'm sure the bank will survive."

He took her hand and raised it to his lips.

"You looked so beautiful tonight," he said. "I'm a lucky man."

She smiled and leaned over to kiss him. He put his arm around her and she put her head against his chest.

"And I'm a lucky woman," she said. "By the way, hasn't Cesare been behaving himself lately?"

"He's an absolute angel—who still hates my guts."

"Johnny, don't say that. I really think things are working out between you two. I'm very pleased. Now, if we can only get Brook to stop biting her nails and Nick to stop sucking his thumb, we'll have the perfect family."

"Brook's going to be a stunner one day. She'll be a heartbreaker."

"Not if you don't stop spoiling her!"

"I enjoy spoiling her. As I enjoy spoiling you."

He kissed her on the mouth. After a moment, she gently shoved him away.

"What's wrong?" he whispered.

"Oh darling, I'm just not in the mood. And Teddy talking

about running off to Cuba has given me a headache. Now, turn out the light and let's go to sleep."

"But I'm feeling rutty . . ."

"You're always feeling rutty. We really shouldn't do it as often as we do: I read an article that says too much of that is bad for the health."

"Casanova lived to a ripe old age."

"Well, he was Italian."

"So am I—at least, half-Italian."

"Well, I'm tired. Turn out the light."

He looked at his wife's beautiful black hair spread out on the pillow a moment. Then he turned out the light and thought about Cuba.

Two nights later, when he came home from the bank, to his surprise Rachel had changed her mind.

"I had lunch with Mother," she said, "and I told her about you and Teddy wanting to go to Cuba. She said I should let you go 'to get it out of your system,' as Mother put it. So if you can arrange to have some sort of administrative job that will keep you away from any actual shooting, it will be all right with me if you go."

Somewhat to her disappointment, his face lit up. He threw his arms around her, kissed her, and twirled her around.

"Cuba!" he exclaimed. "What a thrill! You're the best wife in the world!"

5.   A FIRESTORM OF WAR FEVER WAS SWEEPING
America. By April, as dandelions bloomed in the capital,
President McKinley asked Congress for powers to end the
hostilities in Cuba. This was granted, and Spain promptly
declared war on the United States. The next day, the United
States declared war on Spain.

Unfortunately, the country's war machine was woefully
inadequate. The army was limited by law to twenty-five
thousand men, and its actual numbers were less than that.
The nation had been at peace for thirty-three years, and
with the exception of the various Indian wars of the time,
most of the army had seen no actual fighting at all—certainly nothing like the military campaigns fought in Europe.
A call went out for volunteer troops to be organized. Teddy
Roosevelt resigned as Assistant Secretary of the Navy. He
was offered command of one of these so-called cowboy
companies, but with uncharacteristic humility, he declined
on the grounds that he lacked sufficient military experience.
However, he agreed to act as second in command to his
good friend, Colonel Leonard Wood, an army surgeon two
years Teddy's junior. Wood, a graduate of Harvard Medical
School, was a powerfully built athlete, an avid sailor, the
best boxer in the army with fists of iron, blond hair, and
blue eyes.

The troop that he and Teddy started to put together was
a microcosm of America: Indian fighters, cowboys, polo
players, Ivy League millionaires, drifters, house painters,
scions of Society, and hobos. They eventually began train-

ing in San Antonio, but by June they were transferred to
Tampa, Florida—considered the nearest port to Havana
with proper facilities to handle an army. They had a mascot:
a golden lion named Josephine. They had a song: "There'll
Be a Hot Time in the Old Town Tonight." And they quickly
had a name:

The Rough Riders.

Despite Rachel dropping her objections to Johnny going to
Cuba, it was several months before he could join Teddy
Roosevelt. After all, one couldn't simply abandon the leadership of a large bank. A plan was arranged for Johnny's
father, Justin, to return to New York from Rome, where he
had been spending most of his time, especially after suffering a mild stroke. Justin arrived by ship toward the end
of May, and Johnny saw with concern that his father had
aged considerably. However, he retained his faculties; and
after a week's time, during which Johnny brought him up-
to-date with the business of the bank, Justin returned to his
old position of, as he liked to think of it, captain of the
ship.

The night before Johnny was to entrain for Tampa, Rachel gathered all the family in the dining room for a fare-
well. Justin the patriarch was there, his once-famous
red-gold hair now almost entirely white. Rachel, looking
lovely as usual in a white organdy dress. By her side,
Johnny. And then, the children: ten-year-old Beatrice, wearing her new glasses. Nine-year-old Cesare, who, for all of
his recent good behavior, looked at Johnny in a way that
led the latter to think Cesare wouldn't be all that unhappy
if he never returned from Cuba. Then Johnny's two children by Rachel: four-year-old Brook, a ravishing blond; and
two-year-old Nick, still in the charge of his nanny, Mrs.
Peabody. After they all bid their farewells to Johnny, Mrs.
Peabody shepherded them out to eat in their own small

dining room next to the kitchen, and Johnny held Rachel's chair as his father sat between them.

"You have yet to tell me," Justin began as the butler poured the wine, "exactly what you're going to do down there?"

"He's going to stay away from the fighting," Rachel said firmly. "He's given me his word on that."

"Well, if you don't fight, what's the point of going?"

"Teddy has written me he'll find something for me to do," Johnny said. "But he's been so busy trying to turn the Rough Riders into some sort of fighting force, he naturally hasn't had time to think about me. He mentioned something about my helping the paymaster."

"Not exactly a chance for heroics," Justin grumbled. He had made it clear he thought his son was behaving foolishly. "Not that I recommend trying to be a hero. Heroes have a tendency to end up dead. Always remember, Johnny: you have a responsibility to your family—to us. That's always the important thing: the family. Stay alive and come back in one piece."

"Teddy says the whole thing will be over by the fall. The Spanish don't know what they're doing."

"That's what Napoleon said about the Russians."

"Father," Johnny said, "can we be a little cheerier? This is my last night home, after all."

"Sorry."

Rachel forced a tense smile.

"Well," she said, "Maud made your favorite dinner, darling: mutton chops. I doubt you'll get much mutton in Cuba."

"Teddy says the food is ghastly, but look on the bright side: I'll lose weight. Father," he went on, turning back to the patriarch, "you haven't told me much about Mother. I hope she's fine?"

Justin chuckled.

"Your mother's as much a firecracker as ever—with one exception."

"What's that?"

"You know how she used to lie about her age? I think she was twenty-nine for something like eight years."

"Oh, I know."

"Well, now she's turned completely around. She goes around Rome bragging to everyone how wonderful she looks for her age—and she tells her age! She admits it— hell, she brags about it."

"Does she look good for her age?" Rachel asked.

"She looks splendid. What a remarkable woman. I'm more in love with her than ever."

Rachel and Johnny beamed.

"How nice," they both said in unison.

"Isn't your father sweet?" Rachel said two hours later as she lay in Johnny's arms in their bed upstairs. "To still be in love at his age! How old is he, by the way?"

"He was sixty, his last birthday. Yes, it is sweet that he and Mother are getting along so well. I'm very happy for them."

She ran her hand over his chest and kissed his ear.

"Will we be as happy at their age?" she whispered.

"Damned right. Happier, even."

He kissed her a long, tender kiss that was also passionate. Then their bodies merged.

"Oh Johnny," she whispered, "please take care of yourself. Please don't get hurt. I've asked myself a thousand times if I haven't been foolish letting you go to this crazy war, but it's too late to change now, so please promise me you'll be careful."

"I promise. Do you think I want to get hurt? I just want to see a little action before I sink into senility."

"You're not going to be senile!" she said forcefully.

"You're going to be my lover forever, just as your father is to your mother! Our love will last forever!"

"Yes, darling Rachel," he said, kissing her hotly. "Our love will last forever."

The Tampa Johnny arrived at on a blisteringly hot June day was a boomtown of tourists side by side with shanties housing the poor Cuban refugees who had fled their home island years before to escape the Spanish tyranny and work in the Tampa cigar factories. The dynamo behind Tampa's growth was a developer and promoter named Henry Bradley Plant, who had started out as a cabin boy on the ferry between New York and New Haven. During the Civil War, he had managed to buy into southern railroads on the cheap. Clever enough to foresee that eventually America would be doing enormous business with Central and South America, he started buying Tampa real estate. To attract tourism, he first built a strange hotel called the Port Tampa Inn that extended out over the water so guests could fish from the windows. At nearby Port Tampa, he built an enormous wharf with huge warehouses, then two one-way railroads to connect with Tampa itself. He also put up an amusement park called Picnic Island.

As the tourists poured in during the fun- and sun-seeking Gay Nineties, he put up on a sixty-acre tract of land a monstrosity of a hotel called the Tampa Bay that one newspaper correspondent described as larger than "the palace which Ismail Pasha built overnight in Cairo." Built in a garish Moorish architectural style, it had silver domes and minarets, spread over six acres with almost five hundred rooms, and was surrounded by wide porches that stretched like avenues. Teddy Roosevelt had written to Johnny to spend his first few nights at the Tampa Bay, and it was to the huge dark red, five-story hotel that Johnny walked from the nearby railroad station, carrying his one suitcase. It was

steamy, and he could feel the sweat trickling down his spine
as he climbed the steps to the hotel's front porch, then went
into the only slightly cooler main lobby to check in. The
lobby was crowded with tourists and some army officers,
and cigar smoke fouled the hot air as Johnny made his way
to the registration desk.

"Ah, Mr. Savage," said the clerk, flashing a sparkling
smile. "Welcome to Tampa. We have a fine room for you
on the water side with a wonderful view. Oh, by the way,
Colonel Roosevelt has left this note for you."

He turned to reach into one of the letter boxes and pulled
out an envelope that he handed Johnny. Johnny opened it
to read:

My dear Johnny:

*It's fine to have you with us, and I guarantee we'll have
a bully time. When you are rested, come see our troops and
I'll get you a uniform and some equipment. The hotel clerk
will give you directions. Looking forward to a great adventure!*

Yours, Theodore

A bellboy took Johnny's valise and led him to the elevator up to the third floor where, after walking a seemingly
endless corridor with a carpet of flashy Florida flowers woven in it, they finally reached a room marked "Poinciana
Suite." "Colonel Roosevelt booked this for you," said the
bellboy, unlocking the door. "He said you're an important
banker up in New York. Are you one of those millionaire
friends of the Colonel's? The talk of the town is that half
of the Four Hundred are down here with the Rough Riders."

"I think that's a bit of an exaggeration," Johnny said
modestly as he followed the young man into a large room.

"I'll turn on the fan," the bellboy said. "It sure is a
scorcher, but when the windows are open you'll get a nice
breeze from the Gulf."

He flipped a switch, turning on a ceiling fan, then crossed the room to open the windows. Repeating the procedure in the adjoining bedroom, he came back. Johnny tipped him a quarter. The bellboy looked rather scornfully at the coin. Then he said to Johnny: "Guess you must be one of them millionaires. They're tight as ticks with tips."

Johnny sighed and coughed up three more quarters, which brought a smile to the young man's face.

"The dining room's open in a half hour for lunch," he said, going to the door. "And welcome to Tampa. Hope you get a chance to kick them Spaniards in the ass! They sure deserve it!"

When he was alone, Johnny took off his coat and hat. Seeing that his shirt was soaked clear through with sweat, he went to the bathroom and turned on the tub. Waiting for it to fill, he went to one of the open windows and looked out at the water.

"Well," he said to himself, "I wanted an adventure, but I might as well start with a bath."

He began to undress.

A half hour later, dressed in clean linen, natty white duck slacks, a blue blazer, and a straw hat, he went downstairs to the main dining room that was beginning to fill up. As a dozen ceiling fans churned the air, the maître d' led him across the large room to a seat by one of the open windows. After Johnny had ordered a shrimp cocktail, a cold tuna salad, and a white rum on the rocks, he heard a voice behind him exclaim: "Hey, it's Johnny Savage, the blond Indian!"

Surprised, Johnny turned to see a tall young man with red hair coming up to his table. He wore a khaki hunting outfit. He smiled and extended his hand, saying, "You don't know me, Mr. Savage, but I know you. Read all about you at that ridiculous Bradley Martin ball at the Waldorf where you dressed up as an Indian. My name's Steve Carson, and Mr. Hearst sent me down here to report what's going on. Would you buy me a drink? I know you're rich as God."

"Hardly," Johnny said, rather coolly, after shaking his hand. "But sure: sit down."

Steve had already taken the seat across the table.

"So what brings you down to this hellhole?" he asked, signaling to a waiter. "Looking to make a few bucks off this war? I'll have a Coca-Cola, lots of ice, and a shot of rum on the side," he told the waiter. Then he pulled out a pack of Sweet Caporal Cigarettes, then a favorite in the nation, and offered one to Johnny. "Cigarette?"

"No thanks, I don't smoke."

"Smart man. Personally, I think they're coffin nails, but I'm hooked." He lit one and exhaled.

"Actually, I'm down here to join up with my old friend, Colonel Roosevelt."

"Aha, you're going to be a Rough Rider! Well, bully for you, Mr. Savage. Say, can I call you Johnny? And I'm Steve. Now, I think there's a helluva good story in your family, and maybe you can help me out a bit. Lots of colorful material—your father being a Chinese pirate when he was a kid, shacking up with another Chinese pirate—great stuff. You have a half-Chinese sister, am I right?"

"Yes, Julie Chin. She lives in Hong Kong."

"Wow, great stuff. Then there's the murder of your wife's first husband, that Rothschild fellow over in England. Pushed over a cliff, wasn't he? And they said it was some anarchist group protesting his millions, but lots of people say the murderer was actually the young man who married your wife and got all those millions. Now, do you have a comment on that?"

"The murder was unsolved," Johnny said, his tone and expression becoming deadly. Steve chuckled.

"Well, I can see you don't like to talk about it," he said, "and I suppose that's natural. Besides, you millionaires all stick together. Sort of like a clan of exploiters. I bet you don't agree with the idea of an income tax, do you? You see, I think it's the only way to level all the inequalities in America. People like you paying hardly any tax at all on enormous incomes, going to ridiculous circuses like that Bradley Martin ball—you don't give a damn that people go to soup kitchens while you stuff yourself on Millionaire's Row in your fancy mansions . . ."

"Steve," Johnny said as the waiter brought the Coke and rum, "I didn't come down here to be lectured to about my life. I came down here to try and help my country . . ."

"Then why are you staying in this fancy Dan hotel? Why aren't you out in the pup tents with the other Rough Riders?"

"I just got here!" Johnny almost exploded.

"You don't like me, do you?" Steve said with a grin.

"Frankly, sir, no."

"Good. The feeling is mutual. I hate fat cats. I grew up in Lawrence, Massachusetts, where my old man was a postman, and I've had to scratch for everything in my life. Had to work as a soda jerk to put myself through college. Where'd you go, Johnny? Princeton? Yale?"

"Harvard, actually."

"Well, you're what I hate, you overprivileged bastard. I'm down here to write up this war, and I can guarantee you I'll give you the worst publicity you've ever had." He tossed off his drink and stood up. "Well, glad to have met you, Johnny. And if you get killed by a Spanish bullet, I'll write you one helluva obituary. See you."

Giving him a little salute with two of his fingers at his forehead, he walked away from the table as Johnny watched him with an expression of intense dislike.

After he had finished lunch, he left the dining room and went to the reception desk in the lobby.

"I'm checking out of the hotel," he told the clerk, "but I'll pay for my suite for tonight."

"Mr. Savage, I hope there's nothing wrong with your room?" the receptionist asked anxiously.

"No, it's fine. It's just that I've changed my mind. I think I should be staying with Colonel Roosevelt and the others. I'd appreciate it if you could tell me how to get to the Rough Riders."

6.   ASIDE FROM THE EXTENSIVE GROUNDS OF THE Tampa Bay Hotel, which had been lavishly planted with flowers, trees, and shrubs as well as decorated with stately live peacocks to give the place a setting as exotic as its architecture, the town of Tampa was a bit of a letdown. Although the streets had been paved and electrified, whole blocks sat empty except for brambles and weeds, and the prevailing architecture was less than inspiring. Furthermore, since thousands of troops had started pouring into the town in preparation for the great invasion, the prevailing mood was one of mass confusion. The town was connected to the north by only two one-way railroads, and so miles of boxcars holding food and equipment were backed up as far north as Columbia, South Carolina. Furthermore, the town's post office was woefully inadequate to handle the huge volume of mail pouring in, and days would pass before packages and letters could be sorted and delivered. To cap the madness, bills of lading failed to be forwarded, so that the consequence was that the freight trains that managed to get through to Tampa were filled with crates that no one knew to whom they belonged. Rifles, ammunition, food, equipment, and uniforms remained stuck under the broiling sun while sweating officials tried to sort out what was what.

"Pandemonium!" groaned Teddy Roosevelt as he sat in front of his pup tent in the shade of a tree. "To think I was once a high-ranking member of this government! What an embarrassment. If the Spaniards saw this, they'd probably invade Florida instead of us attempting to invade Cuba."

"Yes, I must admit it's somewhat disappointing," Johnny said. He had moved into a tent next to Teddy's and had been one of the lucky ones to have been issued a Rough Rider uniform, brown fatigues of light cloth that in the tropical heat were much preferable to the heavy uniforms of the regular army. To complete the uniform, Johnny had bought a blue and red bandanna from two street vendors and tied it around his neck. The bandannas had become a fad and a symbol of membership in the Rough Riders. But the sad fact was that because of the pervasive confusion and traffic jam of the railroads, many of the volunteers were still in their civilian gear.

"Johnnie," Teddy said, turning to his old friend, "Edith has arrived from New York and is staying for a few days at the Tampa Bay. Let's go greet her and you'll be my guest at dinner. She has a letter for you from Rachel."

"Oh, señor, you make me feel so good!" squealed the Cuban-born whore Carmelita as Steve Carson plowed his midsection against hers.

"Do I get it for free?" Steve grunted, sweat pouring down his haunches.

"You're not that good, beeg boy!" Carmelita snapped, and even though Steve was coming close to an orgasm, he laughed in her face. They were in a tiny, filthy back room in the shanty called "Noah's Ark." The room was dimly lit by a bare bulb hanging from the ceiling, and glistening roaches rambled gaily on the board floor. Outside, at the canteen, or bar, a fair cross section of the proud American Army was getting roaring drunk on nickel beer.

"Aieeee!" squealed Carmelita as she and her lover reached a suitably steamy climax. Then Steve climbed off her, pulled up his underwear and pants, and gave her five dollars.

"Hey, I charge seven!" she said, buttoning her sweat-stained blouse over her truly monumental breasts.

"I'm a little short today," he said, leaning down and giving her a kiss.

"Hah! You weren't five minutes ago!"

He laughed as he left the room to join the soldiers at the bar.

Teddy's second wife, Edith Carow Roosevelt, was a stately, handsome woman who had been Teddy's childhood play-mate. It had been widely assumed in their patrician circle that the two would one day marry. But in 1880, when Teddy married the beautiful Alice Lee, Edith kept her dis-appointment—if she had any—to herself and maintained a dignified silence. Four years later, when Alice Roosevelt died of Bright's disease, a bereft Teddy vowed he would never betray her memory by marrying again. He underes-timated his own romantic impulses, as well as Edith's charms, for when he met her at the house of his crippled sister, Bamie, Teddy began writing the initial "E" in his diary—and nothing else. They were married in London in 1886, and Edith produced over the next eleven years five healthy babies, all of whom Teddie adored as much as the child of his first wife, who was in turn adored by his niece, the young Eleanor Roosevelt—at least while they were young.

Edith was a woman of many moods. She could be kind

and tactful; she could be ruthless. She was extremely bright with an excellent taste for literature and a deep love of poetry. She also suffered from neuralgia and could, at times, be short with a sharp tongue. She had more influence than any other person over her multifaceted husband, but she knew enough not to involve herself with the politics of the day except on rare occasions. However, when Edith spoke, Teddy listened.

Edith had overcome a slight initial prejudice against Rachel Savage's Jewishness to become very fond of Johnny's wife, and the two couples were close. Thus, when Johnny and Teddy joined her that evening in the dining room of the Tampa Bay Hotel, Edith, who was wearing white in the sizzling heat, smiled and gave her husband a kiss and Johnny a hug.

"My, how dashing you both look in your uniforms!" she exclaimed as the fussy maître d' escorted them to a table by one of the open windows. "I've brought you mail," she said to Johnny as the maître d' seated her. "Here's a letter from your wife."

"That's very kind, Edith," Johnny said, taking the envelope. "Do you mind if I read it?"

"Please. Do you have any lemonade?" she asked the waiter as Johnny tore open the envelope. As he read the letter, Theodore took a menu and said:

"This hotel is an eyesore and it has a big casino, which I don't approve of. But the food's the best in town—which isn't saying much. I've instructed my men who have independent incomes to rough it the same as those who don't, but tonight I'll make an exception for myself. Rank hath its privileges, eh, Johnny?"

But Johnny wasn't listening. He was reading the letter from Rachel, in which she told him she was taking the children to Newport for the summer, and that they all missed him, herself in particular.

I pray every night for your safety, my sweet Johnny. You know you are my life. Please take care of those horrid Spaniards quickly so you can come home to me soon.

Your adoring wife,
Rachel

He put the letter in his pocket, thinking how lucky he was to have such a wonderful woman in his life.

The dining room was full, Saturday night being the big night of the week when every soldier who could get a pass and had the money went out on the town. Johnny and the Roosevelts had a pleasant dinner, during which they caught up on gossip of mutual friends back home, and Teddy discussed the latest rumors about the impending Cuban invasion, the conventional wisdom being that the American Army would land on the southern coast of Cuba opposite Havana, then march across the island to storm the capital.

After dinner, Teddy suggested they walk to the Oriental Annex of the monstrous hotel where every evening a band played beneath palm trees. Edith said she was tired and complained of a headache, so she asked to be excused: she wanted to go to bed—she was known to leave a dinner abruptly. She went to the elevator while Teddy and Johnny strolled through the hotel to the Annex, passing the popular casino where men and women, dressed in bulky bathing suits that exposed a minimum of flesh, were splashing happily in the cool waters of the new swimming pool.

When they reached the Oriental Annex, they sat at a small round table and ordered rum and ice as they watched the beautiful young ladies, many of them recently fled from Havana, dance habaneras in the moonlight while above them, atop the silver minarets of the bizarre hotel, artificial crescent moons represented the months of the Muslim year. Johnny lit a Tampa cigar, and as the rum dulled his brain, he thought the great Cuba adventure—at least so far—was not half-bad—except for Steve Carson.

Shots rang out in the hotel. Screams. Johnny and Teddy sat up, Teddy muttering, "What in damnation—?" The shots grew louder, as did the screams and calls for "Get the police!"

Johnny got to his feet. "Let's go, Teddy," he said, starting back toward the hotel lobby.

"I pray it's not my Rough Riders!" Teddy said as he followed Johnny through the tables. "By God, if some of them create a brawl, I'll have them locked up!"

When they reached the casino, they saw a half dozen of the regular army soldiers standing by the swimming pool, taking off their clothes. They were all drunk, and several of them were firing their guns at the ceiling as, in the pool, the terrified bathers cringed.

"You!" Teddy bellowed, coming at them. "Put down your guns and stop this nonsense! Go back to your tents immediately! I'm Lieutenant Colonel Roosevelt, and that's an order!"

The men, stunned by the appearance of someone they all knew, stopped firing their guns. They stood uncertainly, half-naked, staring at Teddy.

"All we wanted to do was take a swim," one of them slurred. "It's so damned hot, and we're scared of the ocean. They say there's sharks in it . . . people drown, step on jellyfish and die of the sting . . ."

"Nevertheless," Teddy shouted, "you will go to your tents at once! And I will report this to your commanding officer in the morning!"

"And who the hell are you to prevent these boys from cooling off?" said a familiar voice, and Steve Carson stepped out of the shadows. He was wearing a white panama suit with a red bow tie, smoking a cigar, carrying a gun, and he was drunk. "Why can't these brave men who may soon give their lives so you stinking millionaires can romp around in swimming pools—why can't they have the same privilege?"

"I don't know who you are, sir, but if you think I'm a millionaire, then you are sadly unacquainted with the state of my personal finances."

"Perhaps so, Colonel, but your friend there—he's a millionaire, aren't you, Johnny, my old buddy? A millionaire many times over, eh, Johnny?"

"Who is this man?" Teddy whispered to Johnny, who was standing beside him.

"It's Steve Carson, one of Mr. Hearst's reporters."

The people in and around the swimming pool had fallen silent as the crowd watched Steve start walking toward Johnny.

"So, Johnny, we meet again," he said. "I was told you had moved out of the hotel to rough it with the boys, but I see you came back soon enough with your fancy pal, Colonel Roosevelt. Can't keep away from the sweet life, can you, you rich bastard?"

"Carson, mind your language," Johnny said. "There are ladies present."

"Ladies? What a laugh. I was with a whore two hours ago that was as much a lady as any of this riffraff."

Gasps of shock from the crowd.

"You're drunk!"

"Damned right, and feeling like making trouble. Every time I look at you, I want to make big trouble. Like this!"

He aimed his gun at the stars and fired. Screams. Yelling "You idiot!" Johnny tackled him, bringing him to the ground. As the soldiers and hotel guests watched, Johnny and Steve wrestled, Johnny punching the reporter hard in the gut and face as he tried to wrest the gun from his hand.

"Give me the gun, you fool!" he kept yelling.

Suddenly, the gun fired. Johnny howled with pain and rolled over on his back, clutching his right thigh where he had been hit.

"Johnny!" Teddy cried, running up to him as Steve staggered to his feet, a look of fear on his face. "Someone get a doctor!"

"It was an accident!" Steve panted. "I didn't mean to fire, the gun went off . . ."

"Yes, yes . . . a doctor! Johnny, my dear friend . . . Good God, you're bleeding like a stuck pig . . ."

Johnny, whose pants leg was sticky with blood, forced a weak smile.

"Looks like," he whispered, "I'll be the first casualty of the war. But what a place to get it . . . in the Tampa Bay Hotel . . ."

Then he passed out.

"Johnny, Leonard Wood's in South Carolina trying to break the logjam on the trains and get the medical supplies down here, he won't be back for several days," Teddy said ten minutes later. "This doctor was in the hotel, he's also a surgeon." Dr. Rufus Haines, an elderly gentleman who had been at the hotel bar when he was summoned by Teddy Roosevelt to assist Johnny, pulled the bullet out of Johnny's right thigh as Johnny groaned with pain. He had been taken to the hotel laundry room where he had been laid on a steel folding table and his bloody pants pulled down to reveal the wound, copious amounts of blood matting his yellow hair to his thigh. Dr. Haines, a Tampa resident, had cleaned the wound with alcohol, then pulled the bullet out, which had penetrated Johnny's right thigh. Teddy, standing nervously by watching the procedure, said, "Did it hurt his thigh bone?"

"No, he's lucky," said the white-haired doctor, "he'll recover all right, but right now you might go to the bar and get him a good stiff drink."

"Yes, of course," Teddy said, looking anxiously at Johnny, whose face was drenched with sweat. "You're sure he'll be all right? I know nothing about surgery . . ."

"Oh yes, I'll dress the wound and stitch him up. He'll be right as rain. Have the dressing changed in a few days."

Teddy still stood staring nervously at Johnny. "Johnny, old boy," Teddy said, squeezing his hand, "the doctor says you'll be fine."

"I don't feel fine," Johnny whispered. "In fact, I feel awful."

Dr. Haines turned to Teddy. "He doesn't need you holding his hand, he needs a good stiff drink!"

"Oh my God!" Rachel gasped as she read the telegram Teddy had sent her from Tampa.

"Mommy, what's wrong?" her daughter Brook asked. The children and their mother were all seated in the dining room of the rented ten-room Queen Anne-style "cottage" overlooking Narragansett Bay at Newport, Rhode Island, eating lunch on a rainy day.

"It's your father," Rachel said. "He's been shot by some drunken maniac at a hotel!"

"Is he dead?" Cesare asked hopefully. To please his mother, he had tried to appear less hostile to his stepfather. But he disliked the discipline at Longwood Academy so much that his old hatred of Johnny had rekindled to a slow burn.

"No, of course not. They got the bullet out and he'll be fine in a few days. But the poor darling lost a lot of blood and is terribly weak. They arrested the man who shot him, but Mr. Hearst pulled strings in Washington, and they let him go scot-free! How shameful!"

"Why would Mr. Hearst do that?" Cesare asked.

"Because the man is one of his ace reporters, and of course everybody in Washington kowtows to William Randolph Hearst, who started this foolish war in the first place with his newspapers. Oh, I find the whole thing shocking."

"Will Daddy still be going to Cuba?" Brook asked.

"Yes, next week, according to Mr. Roosevelt."

"Is he going to be a hero?" the little girl asked.

"I sincerely hope not," Rachel said, refolding the telegram. "Your father promised me he'd stay away from the fighting."

Cesare put a piece of bacon into his mouth and chewed it.

"Is he a coward?" he asked.

His mother frowned at him.

"Of course not," she said, rather sharply. "He's a very brave man. It's just that he promised me he'd be careful. And, Cesare, don't pick your bacon up with your hands."

"They say there are a lot of deadly snakes in Cuba," Cesare went on in a calm voice. "And I read they have a lot of diseases down there, like malaria, that can kill people. Wouldn't it be terrible if he got bitten by something?"

"Oh, Cesare," said his little sister, "you sound like you want it to happen to Daddy!"

"Do I? Sorry about that."

"Cesare," said his mother. "You must learn to think positive thoughts about everything."

Cesare gave her a smile that always melted her annoyance.

"Of course, Mother," he lied, "I'll try my best."

If the American forces were ill-equipped and badly led—the commander, Major General William Rufus Shafter, was a Civil War veteran with a lackluster record, weighed over three hundred pounds, and suffered numerous ailments in the tropical heat—the Spaniards were even worse. A Spanish squadron under the command of Vice Admiral Pascual Cervera sent to beef up the Cuban defenses looked formidable on paper, but the reality was woefully different. All the ships experienced engine troubles—the destroyers had to be towed most of the way—the ships' guns had significant mechanical troubles, much of the ammunition was faulty, and before reaching the Caribbean from the Cape Verde Islands the armada, if such a word could be used, practically ran out of coal. And this was the naval force that many New York tabloids were trumpeting might well descend upon New York and bombard the city! Admiral Cervera's final gloomy dispatch to the Ministry of Marine in Madrid said tersely, "Disaster is upon us!" At least the Admiral was realistic.

Meanwhile, in Tampa the Americans were desperately trying to launch a fleet of transports and gunboats for Cuba, but snafus had delayed the June fourth departure for a number of days. The one dock at Port Tampa, nine miles from Tampa, could handle only nine ships at a time and had limited, if not primitive, loading facilities. The army had managed to charter thirty-one small freighters to transport General Shafter's twenty-five thousand troops to Santiago de Cuba, the port on the southeastern coast of Cuba—for it had been finally decided that this city would be the soft underbelly of the island from which, presumably, the American forces could march westward to Havana. But the loading and victualing of the ships had to be done by manpower, the troops carrying the supplies fifty feet from the railroad, the heavier equipment such as guns and horses being loaded onto the transports by ships' hoists. When the fleet finally embarked on June seventh, Steve Carson, who was one of the reporters aboard the flotilla, cabled a dispatch to his New York newspaper that was almost as gloomy as Admiral Cervera's dispatch to Madrid.

But the major cause of griping was the main staple of diet for the American troops, which was a canned so-called fresh beef that even Teddy Roosevelt, who tried to keep up the morale of his Rough Riders, admitted was "nauseating."

Johnny's thigh wound was healing and despite occasional pain, he had regained his strength to the point that Teddy deemed it safe for him to join the flotilla for Cuba. He had been assigned the position of Assistant Paymaster for the Rough Riders and given the rank of Captain. When finally, on the fourteenth of June, the flotilla got under way, Johnny, standing beside Teddy in one of the troop transports, felt a real thrill of excitement as the adventure tardily began. There were some forty-eight crafts all in three columns, the black hulls of the transports setting off the gray hulls of the men-of-war. There were a dozen naval warships, two water tenders, three lighters, and an assortment of newspaper tugs carrying such famed reporters as Stephen Crane and Richard Harding Davis, eighty-nine in all, representing newspapers from all over the world. There were 819 officers, 15,058 enlisted men, 30 civilian clerks, 11 foreign military observers, 272 teamsters, and 2,295 horses and mules. There were four light artillery batteries, four seven-inch Howitzers, four Gatling guns, two hundred wagons, seven ambulances, and one observation balloon. The weather was benign, and the flotilla sailed through a sapphire sea under a cloudless sky. It was the greatest armada ever sent from the shores of America, and it made a grand sight.

That night, Johnny, Teddy, and some other officers stood on the bridge of the transport and watched the sun set in a splendid bloodred sky while the band on another transport played "The Star-Spangled Banner" and "The Girl I Left Behind Me."

"If we fail," Teddy said, "we'll share the fate of all who fail. But if we succeed—and God willing, we shall—we'll put our great country in the front rank of the nations of the world."

Johnny's heart filled with pride and excitement. He felt twenty again; he knew the throb in his leg would be gone soon.

7. A WEEK LATER, THE FLOTILLA ROUNDED THE eastern tip of Cuba and steamed westward along the southern coast of the island. A contingent of Marines had taken the city of Guantanamo ten days earlier. But, despite its magnificent harbor, it was decided to go farther west toward Santiago. The leaders of the Cuban insurgents recommended the army embark at the small ore-loading town of Daiquirí.

At daybreak on June 22, the flotilla stood in toward the little town, which had no harbor, but it had been concluded that the landing could be made with small boats. There was a strongly built steel pier extending out some distance from the shore, but as its purpose was to dump iron ore into ships, it was too high to be of any use. However, nearby was a smaller wooden dock that extended some twenty yards from the shore, and it was decided this dock could be used.

At 9:40 in the morning, the naval warships began a bombardment of the shore, their turrets bursting into vast billows of smoke as they scanned the hills with their fire. Johnny watched with fascination as shells exploded in the jungle, sometimes the shells hitting one of the ancient Spanish forts that actually seemed deserted. After a half hour, the bombardment stopped. Teddy came up to Johnny and shook his head in disbelief.

"What a rum show," he said. "We've been bombing the jungle and killing nothing but birds and monkeys. We just got word that the Spanish evacuated the town at five this morning."

"Even so, it was splendid to watch," Johnny said. "Now they know we're here."

"Yes, but it's going to be a jolly mess trying to off-load everything. The word is, they're going to just push the animals into the water and let them swim ashore."

"Look, Teddy! Some of our men have just landed on the beach!"

"By jingo, we're on Cuba!"

Two boats had pushed through the surf to the beach, and several dozen men scrambled out. In an instant, a cheer rose faintly from the shore and more loudly from the warships. It was caught up by every ship in the fleet and was carried for miles over the ocean. Carried away by excitement, the men waved their hats, jumped up and down, and shrieked like kids at a football game.

Soon the rough sea was dotted with rows of white boats filled with men carrying white blanket rolls and holding their guns at all angles. As the boats rose and fell on the water, and the newspaper yachts and transports crept closer and closer, Richard Harding Davis, the dashing reporter, thought the scene was strangely suggestive of a boat race.

But in the case of the swimming animals, it was a rather macabre regatta. Many of the mules and horses that had been dumped from cargo ports into the water became confused and swam out to sea instead. Others, unused to the rough surf, became exhausted and drowned; and soon death, rather than coming from the Spaniards, became evident instead by the bobbing bodies of the dead mules.

But death was not far away for the men, either. One boat, carrying men of the Tenth Cavalry, an all-black unit, suddenly capsized in the increasingly rough seas. Johnny and Teddy, who had made it safely ashore and were standing at the end of the wooden dock, saw what had happened. As Teddy yelled for help, Johnny tore off his shirt and

boots, and dived into the water swimming toward the cav-
alrymen, many of whom were experiencing difficulties,
burdened as they were by their equipment. Johnny, who
had swum on the Harvard team, was still in good shape
despite his thigh wound, and he quickly reached the first
soldier who was desperately trying to keep afloat.

"I can't swim, Cap'n!" he yelled. "I can't swim!"

"Hold on to me," Johnny yelled. "You'll be all right . . ."

He was only a few yards away when the young man went
under.

"Damn . . ."

Taking a deep breath, Johnny dived beneath the water.
He could see the young black man struggling to get out of
his equipment. He swam to him, grabbed him around the
waist, and with all his strength, pushed himself and the
soldier up. As they broke through the surface, the soldier
was gasping.

"Hang on to me," Johnny said. "Hang on. We're going
to make it."

"I'm scared, Cap'n," the soldier gasped. "Scared of water
. . . always have been . . ."

"We're all scared. Let's go."

As the soldier clung to his back, Johnny started swimming toward the shore. They reached the beach safely but
exhausted, both men lying on their backs to catch their
breath. The soldier, whose parents had been slaves, finally
sat up, still panting.

"I gotta thank you, Cap'n," he puffed. "That was mighty
close. I won't forget this."

Johnny sat up and grinned.

"Hell, it's so hot," he said, "I was wanting a swim anyway. What's your name?"

"Private Leroy Collins, Tenth Cavalry, sir. My God, I
was scared, and I'm not ashamed to admit it. But that was
a wonderful thing you did, sir. I owe you my life, and
you're a white man."

Johnny frowned.

"Well, what does that have to do with it?"

"Everything."

The pithy answer seared a memory into Johnny's brain.

"Look, sir," Collins said, pointing to Johnny's trousers. "You're bleeding."

Johnny looked down at his right thigh. In fact, blood was spreading on his trousers. He reached down and felt his leg.

"My dressing must have come off in the water," he mumbled.

"What dressing?"

"I was shot in the leg back in Tampa. I guess when we were swimming, the damned thing came off."

"Well, sir, you better go see the doctor. That looks bad. Does it hurt?"

"No. Well, a little. I've been having some pain the last couple of days, but I'm sure I'll be all right."

Private Leroy Collins had been lucky, but two members of the Tenth Cavalry weren't. They drowned. Thus, the first fatalities of the Spanish-American War were black.

Johnny asked directions to the ambulance, but he was told it hadn't been brought ashore yet. He went behind a tree and took down his trousers to inspect his wound, which he hadn't looked at for several days, there not being much privacy on the crowded transport. Now he saw that his thigh had swollen and the bullet wound, which was still oozing blood and some pus, had become discolored. It had also started to throb enough to make him uncomfortable.

Realizing he had no choice but to wait to see the doctor, he untied his bandanna, which was dirty, and tied it around his thigh to contain the bleeding. Then he pulled up his pants and went around the tree to look around.

The off-loading of men and equipment continued through the rest of the day. Johnny, with nothing to do for the time being, strolled around the tiny town that the Spaniards had so abruptly abandoned, favoring his right leg, which was continuing to ache. One building, a shop belonging to the ore company, had been set fire and was still smoldering. Johnny looked in to see the burned-out hulk of a Baldwin locomotive, which had been used to haul ore from the interior over a narrow-gauge railway. The town was seedy and run-down, but, Johnny reflected, not for the first time, if Cuba, so rich in resources, could ever be freed politically so it could develop economically, it could become a very rich island indeed.

In the late afternoon, Teddy had his bugler sound assembly, and the Rough Riders gathered on the beach. A roll call was taken, and every man was accounted for. About five in the afternoon, one man pointed toward a bluff above the village. Outlined against the sky, the Rough Riders saw four tiny figures scaling the sheer face of the mountain up a narrow trail to a blockhouse on top. When they reached the abandoned Spanish fort, they raised the American flag above it and the sailors on the men-of-war, the Cubans and Americans in the village, the soldiers in the longboats, and those still hanging on the ratlines of the ships shouted and cheered. Every steam whistle on the ocean for miles around shrieked and tooted and roared in a pandemonium of delight.

Johnny thought it was the most thrilling moment of his life.

After the roll call, Teddy marched his Rough Riders a quarter mile inland where they pitched camp on a dusty, brush-covered flat, with jungle on one side and on the other a shallow, fetid pool fringed with palm trees. Johnny put up his small tent, then joined Teddy and some other officers to cook some canned beans over a fire. The night was hot and buggy, swarming with mosquitoes, and Johnny's right thigh was by now aching so badly that he sat on the ground next to Teddy and began rubbing it.

"What's wrong, old man?" Teddy asked.

"My leg's hurting. I lost my bandage when I jumped in to save that private, and the damned thing started bleeding."

"You should see Colonel Wood."

"Yes, I intend to in the morning."

"By the way, Johnny, that was a damned bully thing you did, saving that young man. But I've always known you had grit. I remember when you shot that charging bear back in the Bad Lands, years ago. You saved my life, and I'll admit I thought my number was about up." He started snickering.

"What's so funny?" Johnny asked.

"I remember what you said at the time. It was so wonderfully vulgar, but it still makes me laugh."

"I've forgotten: what did I say?"

"You said, 'I was scared shitless.' And this from a Harvard man!"

Teddy Roosevelt doubled over with choking guffaws.

That night, Johnny couldn't get to sleep. Not only was the air a steam bath, but his leg was hurting him more and more. Around midnight, he sat up and with some difficulty pulled down his pants and felt the bandanna on his thigh. Alarmingly, it was wet and sticky. He lit a match and saw that it was soaked with blood and pus. Carson's bullet had gone through his thigh a few inches above his knee, narrowly missing his thigh bone. The doctor in Tampa had told him the wound would heal without complications.

But obviously, the doctor in Tampa was wrong.

He lay back down again and tried to go to sleep.

But by three in the morning, he was feeling feverish. And his thigh was hurting him so violently that it was all he could do not to groan out loud.

"Good Lord, Captain, who dressed this wound for you in Tampa?"

It was the next morning. Johnny, by now in excruciating pain, had limped to the ambulance that had finally been set up near the beach and showed his wound to Colonel Leonard Wood, who had removed the bloody bandanna and gently probed the suppurating wound with a steel instrument.

"Some old geezer named Haines," Johnny said, wincing with pain. "I think he might have been a bit tipsy . . ."

"Tipsy? He must have been dead drunk! He didn't properly debride you!"

"What do you mean?"

"He didn't clean the wound properly. He left dead tissue in the wound and it's become badly infected. I'm going to have to open this up again. How are you when it comes to pain?"

"How much is this going to hurt?"

By now, Johnny was becoming frightened.

"I'm afraid a lot. I'll give you some morphine. Here, lie down on this table. Good God, man, you're swollen and there's serious discoloration . . ." The morphine put Johnny into a semidrugged state that made him feel as if he were in a bad dream. But the dream quickly became a nightmare when Dr. Wood said to him words that seemed unreal: "Captain, I have bad news for you. Your leg has become gangrenous, and blood poisoning has set in. I'm afraid we're going to have to amputate."

Drugged as he was, Johnny sat up, leaning on his left elbow.

"Amputate?" he said disbelievingly. "You're not serious . . . ?"

"I'm very serious, and the sooner the better. It's either your leg or your life."

Johnny started whimpering.

"Oh, please, Doc, there has to be some other way . . ."

"There's no other way, Captain." He turned to a young orderly. "Let's give this man ether. And prepare me a saw."

When Rachel received the telegram in Newport, she became hysterical.

"Mommy, what's wrong?" little Brook asked in alarm as her mother sank onto a chintz-covered window seat and started sobbing. Cesare was outside on the front lawn throwing a football through a fork in a tree and Beatrice was at the beach.

"It's your dear father," Rachel sobbed. "They've amputated his right leg."

"You mean, they cut it off?"

Rachel nodded as she wiped her eyes with a handkerchief.

"It became infected from that gunshot wound. Oh, my poor darling, my poor sweet darling . . ."

Brook, who had never seen her mother so upset, backed quietly out of the room as Rachel continued to sob. She hurried out of the house and ran over to Cesare, who was wearing a bathing suit in the hot summer sun.

"Cesare," she said excitedly, "guess what? They cut off Daddy's leg!"

Cesare, who had just retrieved his football and was preparing for another shot at the tree fork, looked at his sister and grinned.

"Good," he said.

Many of Johnny's friends and co-Rough Riders came to the recovery tent to pay him their sympathies, particularly Teddy, who squeezed his old friend's shoulder and said, "Johnny, old man, you've done honor to yourself and your family."

"Oh, come on, Teddy," Johnny said bitterly. "Honor? For what? For getting in a brawl in a hotel and having the bad luck to be treated by a drunken quack?"

"Never mind. You didn't have to come down here. Whatever glory we manage to achieve in Cuba, part of it will be shared by you."

"That's kind of you to say, Teddy, and I appreciate it. But the fact remains, for the rest of my life I'm a damned cripple."

To his surprise, even Steve Carson came to the tent and apologized. Johnny had the grace to exonerate him from blame, telling him he knew the gun had gone off accidentally.

But the person who moved him the most was Private Leroy Collins, the black cavalryman he had saved from drowning. Collins came in the tent and stood beside Johnny's bed, holding his hat in his hands.

"Cap'n," he said, "if I thought they could sew you on a new leg, I'd gladly give you mine, though you might not want a black leg."

Johnny, who was sitting up in his cot, reached out his hand and shook Collins's.

"I'd be honored to have your leg," he said, "and I don't care if it's green."

"God bless you, Cap'n. You're the nicest white man I ever met. If they ever figure out how to sew you on a new leg, you just give Leroy a call. I mean that, now."

Johnny, who was terribly depressed by the loss of his leg, had to fight back the tears. He truly appreciated what the private was saying, which was obviously heartfelt.

"I certainly will."

"I hear that you're a very rich man, Cap'n, an important banker up in New York City."

"Well, I'm not that important . . ."

"Anyway, you certainly helped me, and if you're ever in a position to help any of my people, the Good Lord would bless you, and so would I. Because you see, my people need all the help they can get. Will you remember that, Cap'n?"

"Yes, I'll remember."

"You're a good man, and God bless you."

After Collins had left the tent, Johnny considered what he had said. Johnny shared most of the prejudices of his time, which was the apex of Jim Crow days. But in light of meeting Leroy Collins, whom he truly liked, he decided he would have to reexamine his biases.

Private Leroy Collins was killed the next week during the successful charge up San Juan Hill.

As was Steve Carson, the mailman's son from Massachusetts, who was only twenty-seven years old.

"Darling, the children bought you this present out of their allowances," Rachel said, handing Johnny a box wrapped in gift paper. "They even tied the bow themselves."

Johnny was sitting up in his bed on the second floor of his Fifth Avenue house. After the amputation of his right leg, he had been transferred from Daiquirí to Tampa on a battleship, then sent to New York on a private train that Rachel had chartered. He had been home two days now and his strength was almost completely restored. However, his mood was still bitter. Now he tore off the gift wrapping, revealing a big box of chocolates.

"How sweet of them," he said, taking off the lid and removing one chocolate from its paper setting. He put it in his mouth and bit. "Um, it's good. Filled with caramel. Here: have one."

"No, I'm trying to lose weight."

"I have a quick diet for you: have your leg amputated. You'll lose about twenty pounds at once and you won't even go hungry."

Rachel took the candy box and put it on the bed table.

"I don't think that's very amusing, darling," she said.

"Sorry, but I'm short of laughs these days. Did Cesare contribute to the candy?"

"Yes."

She sat in a chair next to the bed.

"I bet it hurt him to do it."

"Oh darling, you're really so wrong about Cesare."

"Yes, I know. He's an angel. Well, I guess you all can be really proud of me, the great hero of the Tampa Bay Hotel. I'm surprised the Mayor didn't organize a parade to welcome me back to New York."

She took his right hand.

"You're a hero to me, Johnny. You always have been, and you always will be."

He looked at her.

"At least you won't have to worry about me chasing other women. Cripples aren't very good at running, and what woman would want to go to bed with me?"

She raised his hand to her lips and kissed it.

"This woman does," she said softly.

"Come on, Rachel, you must be disgusted to look at me. I can't even look at it myself. This hideous . . . stump." His face winced slightly as tears formed in his eyes. "I used to be so proud of my body," he whispered. "And now . . . and for what? Some damned drunk Socialist reporter . . . My God, every time I think of it, it's as if a knife were stuck into my guts. To lose a leg for your country is one thing. But to lose a leg for nothing . . ." He shook his head wearily. "That hurts. That really hurts."

"Time will heal this hurt," Rachel said. "And you're alive and healthy and still beautiful."

"You must have an odd concept of male beauty."

"Darling, let me see it."

"What?"

"I want to see the stump."

"Don't be disgusting, Rachel. It's revolting to look at."

"Johnny, you've been home two days. I've tried to bathe you, but you refuse to let me. Don't you understand that your body is part of me? That I desire you, no matter what? Or are you trying to tell me we can never make love again?"

He turned his head away from her on the pillow.

"I don't know . . ." he finally said. "I don't know . . ."

"Of course we can. We'll be just the same as before. We'll even be closer than before. Now, remove your sheet. I want to see it. It's not revolting or morbid, it's just that I want to see my husband."

Johnny said nothing for a moment. Then, slowly, he removed his sheet, then pulled up his nightshirt to his waist. Rachel winced slightly as she saw the stump, which was scarred: the leg had been amputated just below the hip.

Then she stood up, leaned over him, and kissed the stump with her lips. Johnny stared at her with amazement as she straightened.

"My God," he whispered, "you could do that? It didn't make you sick?"

"How little you know me, Johnny Savage. How little you realize how deeply I love you. I'd love you if you had no legs or arms. Don't you understand? We're not just husband and wife. We're soul mates."

She leaned over and kissed his mouth.

PART THREE

A NEW CENTURY IS BORN: THE AMERICAN CENTURY

8.   AT 12:01 A.M., January 1, 1900, a young
German-American couple in Jersey City, New Jersey,
named William J. Witt and Anna Waddilove, became the
first couple to be married in the twentieth century—
although technically, the twentieth century wouldn't begin
for another year. As pundits and pedants had repeatedly
observed, the first century hadn't ended until the year 100,
so the nineteenth had to end in the year 1900. But as
churchbells rang in the year 1900, everyone felt in their
bones that they had moved into the twentieth century. As
the New York *Tribune* wrote, "By writing the date '1900,'
everyone felt something momentous had happened to the
calendar."

Some were fearful of the new century, others were excited by it. Everyone tried to peer into the future to see
what would come. What most people were pretty sure of
by now was that the new century would be dramatically
changed by the automobile. The first American automobile
had been bought on April 1, 1898, but now, only two years
later, over eight thousand of them were driving around the
country, and even the horses were getting used to them. In
New York, automobiles had to stay under nine miles an
hour, carry a gong, and stay out of Central Park. Despite
these annoying restrictions, there were already over one
hundred taxis in the metropolis. Telephones and electricity
had already transformed people's lives; the automobile was
going to revolutionize them.

Other miracles of technology were either already being

used, or just over the horizon: Caterpillar tractors, X-rays, Victrolas, vacuum cleaners. Predictions were being made that by the year 1950, there might even be a machine that could fly. This at a time when, in Dayton, Ohio, the Wright Brothers were already building their first successful glider and in a mere three years would fly their first airplane at Kitty Hawk.

And then, there were the movies.

Johnny Savage's beautiful half sister, Julie Chin, celebrated the new century by throwing a big party in her brand-new mansion on the Peak high above Victoria Harbor on the island of Hong Kong. Although Chinese were excluded from buying property on the Peak—which was fast becoming the most desirable real estate on the island—Julie and her husband, Tim, had managed to sidestep the exclusionary regulations by a combination of financial muscle and Julie's devastating charm. The Chin department store was now the second largest on the island, pushing Jardine, Matheson Company, the greatest of the hongs, into a state that could politely be termed "nervousness." Tim, the former political revolutionary, had turned out to be something of a business genius, and Julie herself was no mean promoter of the store's clothes, housewares, and other merchandise: her sensational figure, which looked good in both European-style dresses as well as the increasingly seen slit-skirted Chinese cheong-sam, was the best advertising possible for Chin's fashions. Though the stuffier British in the colony maintained a stubborn racist disdain for the Chinese in general—and it was undeniable that Hong Kong's Chinatown was about as dirty as any ghetto in the world—those of more liberal and sophisticated bent had come to accept the Chins at most social gatherings not only because Julie, after all, was half "white," her father being Justin Savage, and also an American, which by the convoluted rules of British snobbery made her somehow "different" and exempt from the normal bigotry; but the Chins were also enormously rich and, thanks to Tim's aggressive property buying, the biggest landowners on the island; and nothing crumples bigotry like big money. There were even rumors afoot that the Governor was petitioning London to give Tim a knighthood (Tim had acquired British citizenship and also astutely made large contributions to important English politicians), and if that happened, Sir Timothy and Lady Chin might even someday get into that social Mount Everest, the Hong Kong Club.

It was the Governor's friendship (there were those that whispered he was half in love with Julie) that had enabled the Chins to buy their property on the Peak. And although there had been howls from the most conservative property owners, since there was no specific anti-Chinese rule written in any of the regulations governing the Peak—the exclusion was implied and "understood"—nothing could be done to keep the Chins out. And as their handsome, pillared mansion went up on a promontory that everyone agreed had one of the best views of the harbor and city below, the howlers began to shut up, albeit sulkily, and Tim and Julie felt with intense satisfaction that some sort of historic landmark had been achieved.

To some, this all might seem trivial and a bit petty. But Julie remembered the snubs and insults she had endured growing up in New York City; she would never forget that snowy night so long ago when Norman Prescott, the young man she was so desperately in love with, had proposed to her, only to have the proposal called off the next morning because Norman's father objected to his son marrying a half-Chinese. Julie was determined that her children—sixteen-year-old Edgar and the ravishing ten-year-old Jasmine—would never go through what she had when she was young. Thus, being the first Chinese couple to live on the Peak was no minor achievement.

Though the American side of Julie's makeup discounted the many and confusing Chinese superstitions, she and Tim had nevertheless taken into account the principles of *feng shui* when they built their twenty-room mansion, and on the last night of the old century the house blazed with light and filled with the strains of a Western-style orchestra as Hong Kong's Chinese elite and not a few *gweilos* (literally "ghost" or "devil man," hence a foreigner) waltzed in the new century and grazed at a buffet that combined Western food with the best Chinese food in the colony—even the Chins' enemies agreed Julie had the best chef on the island. And at the double hour of the rat, as fireworks paid for by Tim and Julie went off in the black night air and the orchestra played "Auld Lang Syne," Tim put his arms around his wife and kissed her tenderly.

"Happy New Year, darling," he said. "I'll love you all through the new century."

"And I'll love you forever."

Old China hands in Peking had sensed for some time that trouble was coming. But most of the foreign diplomats living in the small, isolated world of the Legation Quarter between the Imperial Palace on the north and the great Tartar Wall on the south went on about their business secure in their sense that they were perfectly safe from the millions of Chinese surrounding them, that white Europeans and Americans were inherently superior to the Chinese "heathens" whose vast empire had been systematically sliced up by the English, Germans, Russians, and French for over sixty years. Hadn't the impotent government of the corrupt old Dowager Empress as short a time as two years before given the English a ninety-nine-year lease to Hong Kong that wouldn't expire until the year 1997, at which point the English, presumably still owning the greatest empire on earth, would undoubtedly renegotiate the lease for another

ninety-nine years? In the view of the diplomats, their wives
and children, the Chinese were rather quaint, but hopelessly
out-of-date in the fast-moving modern world. Their only
hope lay in conversion to Christianity and adapting to the
new civilization the West had created since the Industrial
Revolution.

But there were signs the Chinese were increasingly
unhappy about being treated with such condescension by
what they regarded as "Barbarians," a term still used by
the court when referring to non-Chinese. While the Barbarians shopped at Imbeck's, dined at the Hôtel de Pékin,
or attended Mrs. Conger's Wednesday afternoons when the
wife of the American Minister would entertain with her
homespun Iowa hospitality, outside the Legation Quarter
the price of knives was rising, the phrase "foreign devil"
was snarled at the few Barbarians who ventured beyond the
walls of the Legation Quarter, and posters were going up
proclaiming: "The will of Heaven is that the telegraph wires
first be cut, then the railways torn up, and then shall the
foreign devils be decapitated." The native patriotic society
called Boxers—literally "Fists of Righteous Harmony"—
was spreading to Peking from the south.

And inside the Forbidden City, Julie Savage's old nemesis, the aging Dowager Empress Tz'u-hsi, the wily woman
who had risen from being one of the Emperor's concubines
to supreme ruler of the Celestial Kingdom, during whose
corrupt reign more and more concessions had been granted
to the Barbarians whom she loathed, smiled when she heard
that the Boxers were growing stronger.

Perhaps, she thought, these Boxers will drive the long-
nosed roundeyes into the sea and China will once again be
mine.

She also had a number of old scores to settle. The Dowager Empress had a very long memory.

"What extraordinary things are happening in China," Rachel said one night at dinner. It was the following June, 1900, and she and Johnny were eating alone in the big dining room in the Fifth Avenue house. "I read this afternoon that the Chinese are trying to throw all the foreign diplomats out of Peking. Do you think they can do that, darling?"

Rachel was wearing a pale blue chiffon dress. She was leaving the following morning with the children for Newport for the summer. Johnny cut his mutton chop.

"It seems they think they can get away with it," he replied. "But I daresay the European governments will make a stink."

"Do you think there might be a war?"

"As to that, who can tell? That crazy old Dowager Empress should know better than to try and take on the whole world, but one never knows. I'm just glad Julie and Tim are safe in Hong Kong."

"Yes, I am too. Well, I suppose even if there is a war, it shouldn't involve us, so I'm not going to worry about it. Have you decided when you'll be coming up?"

"To Newport? Probably the end of next week."

"I'll be looking forward to seeing you, darling. And this summer is going to be wonderful, I just feel it."

9.   ON JASMINE CHIN'S ELEVENTH BIRTHDAY, AT least a dozen of the boys whom her parents invited to her party at the mansion on the Peak were in love with her. Jasmine's rather unusual genetic pool had produced a beauty that even prepubescent boys found dazzling. Though she was three-quarters Chinese, her maternal grandfather, Justin Savage, had contributed his red-haired, blue-eyed genes, so that Jasmine's hair was an entrancing auburn color, and her eyes were a fascinating green. Her skin was flawless, and already she was developing a figure that would leave absolutely no doubt about her gender. Fourteen-year-old Reggie Pope-Hennessy, the grandson of a former Governor of Hong Kong, one of the handful of non-Chinese children at the party, couldn't take his eyes off her.

Tim and Julie, the proud parents, stood on the pillared verandah of the big white house watching the fifty children on the lawn below who in turn were watching a magician perform tricks, currently pulling a live rabbit out of a top hat, which sent the kids into squeals of rapture. It was a blazingly hot early August day, but a slight breeze cooled the Peak somewhat, and attached to the ceiling of the verandah, a number of electric fans churned the humid air. Julie, wearing a white cheong-sam, had her right arm crooked into Tim's left.

"It's going well, isn't it?" she said.

"Oh, yes," Tim replied. "And wait till we serve the ice cream."

"Jasmine loved the pony you bought her."

"And the new dresses you bought her. Let's face it: we both spoil her."

"It doesn't matter: she's turning out to be adorable."

"I think some of these fresh-faced boys are having lecherous thoughts about her."

"Tim, honestly! They're too young."

"You'd be surprised how early lecherous thoughts creep into the male mind."

"Oh Daddy and Mommy, that was the best birthday party anyone ever had!" Jasmine exclaimed that evening as she, her parents, and her seventeen-year-old half brother Edgar sat down at the mahogany dining table in the big dining room overlooking Victoria below. Two enormous silver candelabra with tall, etched-glass hurricane lamps protecting the candles from the twirling electric fans above, illuminated the room as the fierce summer sun finally sank over the hill above the house. Three white-jacketed Chinese servants began to serve the chilled shrimp soup as Jasmine babbled on about her party. As was customary, the family conversation was in English. "And I just love Vicky," she went on, Vicky being the name she had given her pony. "And now that we belong to the Jockey Club, I can go every morning to Happy Valley to ride! Won't that be wonderful?"

Happy Valley was the setting for the racetrack, one of the most wildly popular diversions on the island, the gambling-loving Chinese as well as the *gweilos* swarming to its three o'clock races; and the Royal Hong Kong Jockey Club, which only recently had begun to admit Chinese as members, the Chins being one of the first, was considered to be one of the most powerful establishments in the colony.

"Yes, it will be wonderful," said her white-suited father with a smile.

"And, Mommy, I adore all the dresses! Thank you so much!"

"You're welcome, darling. I'm glad you like them."

"And the new shoes, and the gold bracelet . . . Gosh, I feel like a princess!"

"You are a princess, Jasmine," said her father.

"She's also a pain in the neck," Edgar growled. He was seated opposite Jasmine. "Can't you talk about something beside your presents?"

"You're just jealous because it wasn't your party," Jasmine said, sticking out her tongue.

"Jasmine, behave yourself," snapped her mother. "And Edgar's right, you mustn't talk about yourself so much. It sounds conceited."

"Well, she is conceited," Edgar said, "and spoiled rotten. I'd hate to be her husband, she'll bankrupt him in a week."

"Reggie Pope-Hennessy asked me to go riding with him Saturday," Jasmine went on, unable to change the subject from herself. "He's very handsome, don't you think, Momma?"

"Yes, very."

"I think he's in love with me."

"Jasmine, really: that's enough. Edgar's right."

The young Chinese waiter, who had just been hired by the Chins the previous week, passed around the table, pouring white wine into the crystal Baccarat goblets imported at great expense from France. Then he placed the decanter on a silver tray on the Chinese-style sideboard behind Tim (the house was furnished throughout with a pleasing mixture of Chinese and Western-style furniture). As the family chatted away, he pulled a dagger from his right sleeve, came up behind Tim, and plunged it into his back. Julie screamed as the young Chinese yelled, "Death to the Foreign Devils!" and ran out of the room onto the verandah, where he leaped over the railing onto the lawn and ran down the hill into the night.

Tim was dead of blood loss before the doctor even got to the house. Julie, sobbing hysterically, threw herself on his body, which had been placed on a couch in the drawing room.

"Oh Tim, my darling, come back to me," she kept repeating. Jasmine, stunned by the sudden loss of her beloved father, sat in a corner of the room, tears running down her cheeks as she confronted death for the first time in her young life. While Edgar was truly shaken by the assassination—Tim was not his biological father, but he had come to love him as if he were—he felt that as the new man of the family, it was incumbent upon him to keep control of his emotions. It was he who put in the telephone call to the police; and when Sir Roger Llewellen, the chief of the Hong Kong police, arrived at the house on the Peak, it was Edgar who gave him an account of the murder as well as a description of the murderer, whose name was known only as Ho—undoubtedly fake—and who had been hired on the week before after the somewhat mysterious disappearance of another servant. Ho had spoken Cantonese, as did the vast majority of Hong Kong Chinese, and had a letter of recommendation from a wealthy Mandarin in Canton.

The efficiency of the Hong Kong police was demonstrated by the fact that the young assassin was captured in Chinatown within twelve hours. To no one's particular surprise, he turned out to be a Boxer—the siege in Peking of the Foreign Legation was now in its sixth week, causing headlines around the world. But what surprised many— although not Julie Chin—was that he confessed to being paid by an agent allegedly of the Dowager Empress herself to assassinate Tim. The same ruthless woman who had extracted a million-dollar ransom from Julie's family for Tim.

The British police dismissed this as a drug-induced fantasy—the young assassin turned out to be an opium addict.

But Julie knew that her husband had been secretly financing the Chinese revolutionary movement for years, in particular a group led by the son of a village watchman near Macao who had been educated in Hawaii, where he learned English and converted to Methodism, and was a graduate of the College of Medicine for Chinese in Hong Kong named Sun Yat-sen. For some time, Tim had been receiving veiled death threats, and Julie knew that the Dowager Empress, who once had imprisoned and tortured Tim in Peking, was aware that he was financing Sun Yat-sen.

Julie had no doubt at all that the Dowager Empress, whose memory was indeed long, had used the Boxer Rebellion as an excuse to pay back Tim Chin for the heresy of wishing to drag China into the twentieth century.

Eleven-year-old Jasmine Chin, who had never even thought about death, was so traumatized by seeing her beloved father's assassination that she vowed that somehow, someday, she would avenge his murder.

PART FOUR

BIRTH OF
THE MOVIES

10. THE NAKED YOUNG MAN WITH THE THICK BLACK hair and the striking good looks finished making love to the blond girl who clerked at the local Woolworth's, then rolled off her, sat up, and lit a cigarette.

"I thought you were in training?" said the girl, whose name was Mabel and who had extremely large breasts.

"I am—enough in training," said Cesare Savage, striking a safety match on the edge of the steel mattress. "A couple of cigarettes a day won't hurt my speed. I'm the fastest man on campus, you know."

"Oh, I know," Mabel said, standing up and going over to the cheap dresser to run a comb through her blond hair. "You've told me often enough. Isn't there a game tomorrow afternoon?"

Cesare inhaled the smoke as he watched her buttocks, which were slightly dimpled.

"That's right," he exhaled. "One o'clock. My mother's coming down from New York to see her son, Princeton's best football player, score another triumph for Old Nassau."

"Sometimes your modesty overwhelms me. I don't suppose you'd ever introduce me to your mother? Or is she too big a swell for a floozie like me?"

Cesare smiled slightly.

"I'd be delighted to introduce you," he said, scratching his left knee. "I'll bring her over to Woolworth's after the game. You'll like her. She's beautiful and has a real sweet disposition."

Mabel turned around and looked at him. He was

stretched on the rumpled bed, lying on his left side, his left arm propping up his head, the cigarette dangling lazily from his right hand, a rather insolent smile on his thin lips. She looked at his smooth torso. He had an almost feminine beauty that, paradoxically, made him all that much more attractive to her. He was without a doubt the sexiest man she had ever seen, but she told herself for the hundredth time not to fall in love with him. Mabel might have been poor, living in a one-room boardinghouse on Witherspoon Street four blocks from Nassau Hall in a neighborhood that was largely black, but she wasn't dumb. She knew she'd never have a chance to catch Cesare Savage.

"You know something, Cesare?" she said. "You're one mean son of a bitch."

His smile widened, showing his white teeth.

"Yeah," he said. "I know."

It was a chilly October day in 1907, and Rachel was wearing a mink coat as she got out of her silver Rolls-Royce. There were cheers from the nearby field where Princeton was playing Brown. She couldn't see the crowd or the action because the field was surrounded by parked automobiles, those fashionable toys of the rich.

"We must be late," she said to George, her chauffeur. "The game's already started."

"I'll be waiting for you here, Mrs. Savage."

"Thank you. After the game, I'll be taking my son to dinner."

She started walking toward the stadium.

"I hope he wins," George called.

Rachel smiled back at him.

"Oh, he will," she said. "He's the best, you know."

George, whose personal opinion of Cesare was rock bottom, made no comment. He knew that the mother was blind to her son's many faults. As he often whispered to the other servants in the Savage household. "It's almost as if she was under his spell . . ."

Which, in a way, she was.

Now she was at the field, trying to elbow her way through the crowd of excited undergraduates and alumni to be able to see the action. Football, which had been developed in the 1850s, was becoming wildly popular. It not only had the attraction of gladiatorlike violence—and the game was rough from the beginning—but it was the first sport available to female spectators; before football, Victorian dictates of decency had forbade women from witnessing anything more strenuous than tennis or croquet. But now, the "fair sex" could scream their heads off as the young men on the field tackled and, in those more free-wheeling days, often punched and wrestled each other as well—no game was considered really successful unless there was a good deal of broken bones. As Rachel finally pushed her way through to a spot near the forty-yard line, the crowd went wild yet another time.

She saw Cesare, Princeton's left end, run down the field, the Brown line in hot pursuit, and catch a long pass, running into the Princeton end zone to score a touchdown.

"Cesare, Cesare, Cesare!" howled the crowd as two Smith undergraduates next to Rachel went into hysterics.

"He's so CUTE!" one of them screamed.

Rachel purred with pleasure.

"We'll have a bottle of the Châteauneuf du Pape," Cesare said that evening, handing the wine list to the tall, lanky proprietor of the small French restaurant on the outskirts of town called Le Bon Coin. The restaurant, a cheerful place with Paris-styled white lace curtains hanging from brass rods over the windows and big framed French posters on the walls, was filled with jubilant parents and alumni.

Princeton had trampled Brown 29 to 0, two of the winning touchdowns having been scored by Cesare.

"Darling, you were wonderful today," his mother said. She was sitting opposite him under a poster for Hermès saddles. "I was so proud of you. There were two very attractive young ladies standing beside me who about swooned over you. But you mustn't let all this adulation go to your head."

"Of course not, Mother. I'm still the sweet, unspoiled boy I've always been."

" 'Unspoiled' is hardly *le mot juste*," his mother said. "But why didn't you ask one of your adoring female fans to come to the game?"

He reached across the table and squeezed her hand.

"Because you're the best date a fellow could have. And the prettiest. Besides, the best Wellesley girl I asked— Abbie Farnsworth, you know her parents—caught a cold at the last moment, so here I am with you, and I couldn't be happier. Now: how's Beatrice?"

"She's fine. She sends her love."

"And Brook and Nick?"

"As naughty as ever."

"And my dear stepfather?"

Rachel's smile faded at the slightly snide tone that entered his voice whenever he mentioned Johnny.

"Well, he's very busy right now. You know, they're having a bit of a crisis on Wall Street."

"Yes, I've been reading about it. What's going on?"

The maître d' brought the bottle of wine and presented it to Cesare, who inspected the label.

"Yes, that's fine. And you can bring my mother a glass of Lillet. By the way, Mother, this dinner's on me."

"Don't be silly. I'll pay, as always."

"Nope, it's on me. Since your husband refuses to give me a decent allowance, I put together a little betting pool on the game this afternoon and I won almost three hundred dollars."

"But, darling, isn't that against the school regulations?"

"Not that I know of. And if it is, what they don't know can't hurt them." The waiter had uncorked the wine and poured a sample into Cesare's glass. He twirled it professionally, sniffed it, then took a sip, swishing it in his mouth a moment, then swallowing it. "It's all right," he said. "Not exactly a Lafite-Rothschild, but what can one expect in New Jersey? Now, Mother: Wall Street. What's going on?"

"Well, several banks are in trouble—in danger of failing—and Mr. Morgan is trying to save the situation. You know he's always been fond of your father . . ."

"Stepfather."

"Yes, of course. He's always been fond of him even though he's so close to President Roosevelt, and Mr. Morgan can't stand President Roosevelt because of his attitude toward the Street in general."

"Teddy thinks Wall Street are a bunch of crooks," Cesare said with a mischievous grin. He loved to tweak his mother and, as always, she responded by looking slightly shocked.

"Well, of course that's an overstatement," she said, rather primly. "Naturally, not everyone on Wall Street has the character of your stepfather. At any rate, Mr. Morgan has asked your stepfather and several other bankers to his library to discuss the financial situation and try to save the country from banks failing and creating a panic."

Cesare let out a slow whistle.

"A panic? So it's that bad?"

"It's that bad. What with one thing and another, suddenly no one seems to have any cash. It's got everyone quite nervous."

Seventy-year-old J. P. Morgan, unquestionably the most powerful financier on the planet, was an interesting set of paradoxes. Though a Connecticut Yankee, born in Hartford, he was educated abroad and was fluent in French and German. Though an undoubted financial genius, he failed to invest in the early days of General Motors and formed the maritime trust that built the Titanic (on whose fateful maiden voyage he almost sailed). Though a devout Episcopalian, he broke all but one of the seven sins. Though he shared the bias of his class and time against Jews, he wrote a million-dollar check to save the Jewish art dealer, Lord Duveen, from going to jail. Though he had been a handsome young man, he had inherited from his maternal grandfather a pronounced nose that, in later life, contracted a severe case of *acne rosacea*, an uncurable disease. As his wealth and power increased, his nose slowly grew larger and more hideous until it resembled a huge, ghastly strawberry, as if an evil fairy had decided to punish him for his success. This real-life Pinocchio was so ashamed of his nasal deformity that he became a crusty bear of a man, hating the press that swarmed around him whenever possible, and becoming as much of a recluse as his financial position permitted. Though an undoubtedly masculine man who sired four children and had a long line of mistresses, most notably the beautiful Broadway star Maxine Elliot, he had a feminine side that prompted him to rule on all the clothes bought by his wife and three daughters and to insist on final say on the decorations of the many fetes, galas, and banquets his princely lifestyle entailed. Though never so much as a hint of homosexuality was whispered about this much-gossiped-about man, he surrounded himself at his bank at 23 Wall Street with junior partners all of whom were extremely handsome athletes, so much so that one waggish broker quipped, "When the angels of God took unto themselves wives among the daughters of men, the result was the Morgan partners." Undoubtedly, Morgan's self-consciousness about his hideous nose—which, as he once remarked, he couldn't go outside without—led him to surround himself with exceptionally good-looking subordinates whose dependence on his power helped soothe his bruised ego.

This was certainly one reason he liked Johnny Savage who, even without one leg, was still a handsome man. The other reason was that Johnny and his family controlled an extremely successful bank, not far from Morgan's own on Wall Street. So when, in the autumn of 1907, overextended banks began to teeter on the brink of financial failure, J. P. Morgan summoned Johnny and other "responsible" bankers to his newly opened marble library on East Thirty-sixth Street to set about devising a way to save the nation from financial ruin.

The purpose of the library was to house the huge collection of invaluable paintings, incunabula and rare books and prints, tapestries and art objects that Morgan had collected at vast expense over the preceding quarter century. And once again perhaps to provide a setting so princely that his bulbous nose would be overlooked, he proceeded with a damn-the-expense attitude that dazzled even the architect, Charles McKim, whose clients were some of the wealthiest men in the country. Noting that the Erechtheum in Athens had been built from blocks without the use of mortar, Morgan ordered the same for the construction of his marble temple, even though McKim warned him it would balloon the price by $50,000—no small sum at the time—or perhaps even more.

The result of years of construction and millions of dollars was a classically handsome building on the north side of the street between Madison and Park Avenues. One entered through massive bronze doors imported from Italy into a vaulted entrance hall surrounded by green Cipolino columns. Two enormous rooms took up the bulk of space: the East and West Room. The former was decorated in the Florentine style, its lofty walls holding Circassian walnut shelves filled with volumes bound in gold, gems, enamel,

and ivory. The monumental fireplace was framed by columns of lapis lazuli.

But the great banker's favorite retreat was the West
Room. On its walls, lined with crimson damask from the
Chigi Palace in Rome, hung rare paintings by Botticello
and Raphael, among others; its elaborate gilded ceiling
came from a cardinal's palace in Lucca. Here, seated in his
plush armchair, smoking one of his twenty daily cigars, he
would receive privileged visitors or, when alone, play sol-
itaire on a folding table, accompanied by his pet Pekingese,
Chun, who snored on a pillow in front of the huge fireplace.

And it was here one night the next week that Johnny and
a number of other influential bankers gathered to be addressed by Jupiter, as Morgan was nicknamed on the Street.
He lost no time getting to the point.

"Gentlemen," he said, "you all are aware of the situation.
Due to financial mismanagement on the part of several
large institutions, these banks are almost without funds.
Frightened depositors were lined up around the corner this
afternoon, trying to get their money out: the city is panick-
ing. If we don't save these institutions by providing them
with new infusions of capital, they will collapse, and I can
guarantee you that the stock market will collapse soon after.
We must restore trust. I will expect each of you to pledge
funds which we will lend interest-free until this panic is
over. I need ten million dollars. You may all adjourn to the
East Room where brandy and cigars are available. I'll await
your decision here. But gentlemen: I've locked all the
doors. None of you is leaving tonight until I have the
money I need."

He glared at the bankers, who looked cowed and awed
by the great man's presence. There was a long moment of
silence.

Then Johnny stood up, propped by his two crutches.

"Mr. Morgan," he said, in loud tones, "the Savage Bank
pledges two million dollars."

J. P. Morgan, who was also known as The Great Stoney Face, smiled.

"Happy birthday to you, happy birthday to you, happy birthday dear Brook, happy birthday to you!"

Brook Savage took a deep breath and blew out the fifteen candles on her lemon cake. The thirty or so children of both sexes in the dining room of the Savage house on Fifth Avenue applauded.

"Did you make a wish, Brookie?" asked her older half sister, Beatrice, who, like Brook, was wearing a white dress, though Brook's had pink bows.

"Yes, and I know it's going to come true," Brook said.

"Tell us the wish!" said one of the boys present.

"That Princeton beats Yale this Saturday and that my brother makes all the touchdowns."

"Aw, Yale's gonna cream Princeton," said another boy, who had high hopes of going to Yale, as his father had. Rachel, hoping to avert trouble with these high-spirited kids, signaled the butler to start serving the ice cream.

After J. P. Morgan, with the help of bankers like Johnny, managed to avert the fiscal crisis on Wall Street, the nation settled back into a holiday mood, and intense interest focused on the Yale-Princeton football game, the two teams being considered the best in the country. Though football was still considered a rich man's game since few people could afford to go to college, still sports mania was beginning to catch on with the general public and many workers earning a dollar a day were placing bets on the outcome of the great game, most bookies giving odds on the Princetonians mainly because of Cesare's reputation.

But to the intense disappointment of the Princetonians, Cesare failed to make one touchdown. He failed to catch all but two of his passes, and Yale won the game handily.

"He must have had a bad day," a sorely disappointed Brook told her mother, who had brought both her and Beatrice to New Haven to see the game.

"I don't understand it," Beatrice said—she was as disappointed as Brook. "I've never seen him play so badly—he could have easily caught most of those passes."

"Well," Rachel said, patting Beatrice on the shoulder, "we'll not say anything to him. I'm sure he's as disappointed as we are."

"Nineteen hundred, two thousand," said the bookie known as Trenton Joe as he finished counting out the cash onto the table. Cesare, a smile on his face, picked up the money and put a rubber band around it. The two men were in a small room at the back of a bar in Trenton. Trenton Joe was puffing a cigar.

"So, you college kids are hard to figure out," he said. "I thought you guys were all rah-rah for the old school tie and all that shit, and here you throw the biggest game of the year. What's your angle, kid?"

"My angle's money, Joe. I love money, the more the merrier."

"Yeah, but your old man's rich."

"I'm going to get rich my way. And my way's going to be the fun way. You see, most of the guys in my class figure they'll go work for their old man and wait for him to die so they can get their hands on the big money. I say to hell with that. Life's too short to wait. Look me up next season, Joe."

He started out of the room, but turned as he put his hand on the doorknob.

"By the way, my price will be going up. Next year it's three grand."

11. THE LARGE BROWNSTONE AT **11 East Four-**
teenth Street had once been a grand mansion; but on the
warm spring day in 1910 when Johnny's chauffeur parked
in front of it, Johnny, sitting in the backseat of the Rolls-
Royce, could tell that the house, and the neighborhood, had
seen better days. Fourteenth Street, once the heart of Manhattan's theater district, had steadily gone downhill since
the theater moved uptown to Times Square and Broadway.
There was a plaque beside the front door of the house that
proclaimed "Biograph Motion Picture Studio."

Tim, the chauffeur, came around the car and opened the
door, helping Johnny get out onto his crutches.

"Wait for me, please," Johnny said, starting toward the
front door, which was open on this warm day. He went into
what once must have been a rather grand foyer but which
was now slightly dingy, the parquet floor scraped in many
places. The only furniture was a number of plain benches
lined up against the wall. Several young people were sitting
on the benches. They looked at Johnny as he crossed the
room to a desk, behind which a woman in a white blouse
and dark skirt was sitting. She wore pince-nez and was
rather formidable looking.

"My name is Mr. Savage," Johnny said. "I have an appointment with Mr. Griffith."

"Oh yes. Mr. Griffith is shooting a scene right now, but
he should be done in a few minutes. In the meantime, if
you'll wait over there."

She indicated one of the benches.

"Thank you."

Johnny hobbled across the room and sat down next to a young girl with golden hair in long curls that reminded him of an actress who was becoming quite popular in the movies, Mary Pickford. Except this girl was larger than "Little Mary" seemed in her pictures. She was wearing a gray skirt and jacket with a white blouse and a small feathered hat. She looked at Johnny as he sat next to her.

"Are you a character actor?" she asked.

"No. Why?"

"Well, I thought maybe they were casting for a one-legged man."

"I'm not an actor at all," he said.

"Then why would you be here? I mean, Biograph is pretty hot right now, but this place is sort of a dump. And they work you hard all day for a lousy five dollars. You don't look like you need the money."

"Well, you see, I'm a banker."

"Oh."

"And I've been asked by the owners of Biograph to loan them some money. So I came down to see what the place is like. Mr. Griffith, the director, is going to show me around. I like the few movies I've seen at nickelodeons, but I really don't know much about how they're made, or the business in general."

"Oh." She thought a moment, then lowered her voice. "Say, if you could put in a good word to Mr. Griffith about me, I'd certainly appreciate it. My name is Gloria Gilmore, and I've had some stage experience, but I've never done movie work. You know, stage people look down their noses at the movies. They think they're cheap and vulgar, and of course the nickelodeons don't get the kind of customers that go to Broadway plays, but I think the movies have a future, and if you could tell Mr. Griffith that you've seen my work and that you think I'm talented, I'd be ever so grateful."

"But I haven't seen your work."

"Oh"—she shrugged and gave him her best smile—"you could say you did."

Johnny was charmed by her casual disregard of the truth.

"Well," he said with a slight smile, "I don't like to make a habit of lying, but I'll see what I can do. You say your name is Gloria . . . ?"

"Gilmore. Gloria Gilmore. Here's my card." She opened a small purse and rummaged around it. "I live in a theatrical boardinghouse on West Forty-fourth Street, in case Mr. Griffith wants to get in touch with me. My address and the phone number's on the card." She handed it to Johnny.

"Oh, here he is now," she said in an excited tone. "They say he's the best director in the business."

A tall man had come through two doors behind the receptionist. Now he said something to the woman, who pointed to Johnny. D. W. Griffith crossed the room, extending his hand.

"Mr. Savage, I'm D. W. Griffith. Sorry to have kept you waiting."

Johnny stood up, leaning on his crutches, and shook the tall man's hand. He was nattily dressed and had a prominent hawk-beak of a nose.

"Not at all, Mr. Griffith," Johnny said. "I've had a most interesting conversation with this attractive young lady, whose stage work I've seen. Mr. Griffith, Gloria Gilmore."

Gloria, flushed with excitement and surprised by Johnny's introduction, stood up and shook Griffith's hand. The director looked at her with interest.

"Glad to meet you, Miss Gilmore," he said. "And you're very pretty. Perhaps I can give you a screen test later this afternoon. In fact, come back at five. My cameraman will take a look at you. Come this way, Mr. Savage. We're shooting a little comedy called *The Preacher's Daughter*. I think you'll enjoy watching us do a scene or two."

He led Johnny to the double doors, which he had closed and which led to what had been the ballroom of the house.

He slid the doors open again and motioned for Johnny to go in. Johnny obeyed, taking a last look back at Gloria Gilmore.

"Larry, I have the most sensational news!" Gloria exclaimed five nights later as she met her boyfriend, Larry Gordon, at a cheap diner in the theater district, a favorite hangout for out-of-work actors. "Mr. Griffith liked my screen test and he's hired me to play a big part in a new one-reeler he's shooting next week."

Larry, a handsome blond who specialized in drawing-room comedies, lit a cigarette and said, "I've told you not to work for the movies. You'll ruin your reputation."

"Oh, come on, it's work! And he's paying five dollars a day. It's not much, but in case you haven't heard, I'm not exactly rolling in money. And I met this sweet one-legged banker named Johnny Savage who's invested a lot of money in Biograph. It never hurts to know rich bankers who back movies. When are you going to offer me a drink?"

"What do you want?"

"A gin and French. I'm feeling celebratory."

They were seated in a wooden booth. Larry signaled the waiter, who came over and took the order.

"Anyway," Gloria went on, checking her reflection in a pocket mirror, "this Mr. Savage may help my career."

"Listen: if you go to bed with this guy, I'll make sure you never get a part in a legitimate play again."

"Oh, stop threatening me. And he's old enough to be my father."

"That wouldn't stop you."

"Honestly," she sighed, "you're being a bore. I'm not trying to be a vestal virgin, I'm trying to be a star!"

"Tell me about yourself," Johnny said to Gloria two weeks later as they were eating sandwiches on the set of her second one-reel comedy, directed by Griffith. "Where are you from?"

"Oh, a little town in upstate New York. You've never heard of it—nobody has. My father's a judge. He's a sweet man, but he's horrified that I'm an actress. Happily, there's no nickelodeon up there, so he won't see me in a movie. But isn't it exciting? To be in a movie? And I do appreciate your help so much, Mr. Savage."

She gave him her warmest smile.

"It was my pleasure, and Mr. Griffith tells me he thinks you have a real future in movies."

"That's so thrilling! It gives me goose bumps to hear."

"By the way, the company is talking about expanding the length of the movies to two reels. Of course, that means higher production costs, but Mr. Griffith feels the audience is out there for longer movies with more complex stories, and I tend to agree. Of course, that means higher ticket prices in the long run, but from several surveys I've read, it seems that the middle class is becoming interested in movies, so it's not just your immigrants and kids who are going these days. It's people who can afford to pay more than a nickel for a ticket. The future of the business seems to me to be truly exciting."

"I read in the paper about your daughter's coming-out party tomorrow night. That sounds exciting too."

"Yes, my wife is pulling out all the stops."

"They say your daughter is very beautiful."

"Yes, she is. I can say that without sounding immodest, because she takes more after her mother than me."

Gloria smiled at him.

"Oh, but, Mr. Savage, as I've told you several times, you're very handsome."

After having lost his leg, Johnny had to admit he liked being told he was handsome. And while it bothered him to realize he enjoyed being with the beautiful young actress, nevertheless he did enjoy it.

Then he thought of his beautiful wife, Rachel, whom he adored so much, and with whom he still had a wonderful love life. But then, why was he so attracted to this Gloria? Of course, she was beautiful. And she was flattering him, something that was most pleasurable to him after losing his leg. And then, there was his age. Johnny would be fifty soon. Fifty! It seemed inconceivable to him he could be that old!

His attraction to Gloria made no sense, it ran counter to all rational thought, to all loyalty, in fact it ran counter to everything that he admired and loved in life.

Maybe that was why it was so irresistible.

12.	NO MATTER HOW MUCH RACHEL LOVED CESARE, she wasn't so blind as to be unaware of his antisocial tendencies, especially regarding his detested stepfather. So it came as a great relief to her when Cesare not only was graduated at the top of his class at Princeton, but also announced that he wanted to go to medical school and become a doctor. This thrilling news Rachel attributed to the fact that her dashing son had finally fallen in love—head over heels, judging from what she could tell—with a lovely redheaded Smith girl named Amanda Cartwright whose father, Whitney Cartwright, was one of New York's leading physicians. Cesare had even confided to his mother that he was going to propose to Amanda. Again, Rachel couldn't have been more pleased, for in her opinion Amanda had everything: beauty, brains, breeding, and charm. Of course, it would have been nice if she were Jewish, but you couldn't hope for everything, and Cesare, though technically a Jew because of his mother, had, since his Sunday school days, shown little interest in religion at all.

Despite Woodrow Wilson's—then the President of Princeton University—warning that nothing was spreading socialistic feeling in the country more than the automobile, as a graduation present from that institution, Rachel had bought Cesare a sleek red Pierce-Arrow with leather-upholstered seats. At $4500, the Pierce-Arrow was the *ne plus ultra* of sporty, snobby glamor. And since Cesare couldn't care less whether he was inciting socialism (in fact, he found that the reaction of most poor people was exactly the opposite: they ogled the car with adoration), he was thrilled by the gift.

The next night, dressed in impeccable tails, he drove to Madison Avenue and Eightieth Street, where the Cartwrights owned a large brownstone, parked the car in front of the house, leaped out over the door, and went up the steps to ring the doorbell. An Irish maid opened the door, admitting him to the fern-filled foyer, then took him to the drawing room where Dr. Cartwright, a tall, distinguished man with a white Vandyke beard, was sitting before the fireplace reading a book.

"Ah, Cesare, dear boy," he said, standing up to shake his hand. "Amanda will be down in a few minutes. I fear she is not the most punctual of people."

"But she's the most beautiful, Dr. Cartwright," Cesare said with a winning smile.

"You're too kind. Might I offer you a sherry?"

"No thanks. Sir, while we have a few moments together, I wanted to ask you something—though perhaps this isn't the most appropriate time. As you know—in fact, in many ways thanks to you—I'm almost through my first year at Harvard Medical School . . ."

"And doing quite well, the Dean informs me. In fact, he says he thinks you have the promise to be a brilliant doctor. I'm most pleased."

"Thank you, sir. I know that doctors don't make much money in their first years of practice, but happily, my mother has volunteered to supplement my income, and I've managed to save a fair amount of capital myself." He didn't inform the good doctor that his savings had come from throwing football games. "What I'm leading up to is, I, ah . . . well, I'm deeply in love with Amanda, and I have the great good fortune to feel that she returns my affection. I want to ask her to be my wife, but I wanted to inform you of this first, to see if you had any objections."

Dr. Cartwright smiled and placed his hands on Cesare's shoulders.

"How could I possibly have any objections, Cesare? I would be honored to join my family with one as distinguished as yours. Tell me: when do you intend to propose?"

"Tonight. There's even a full moon. What could be more romantic?"

"Ah, to be young and in love again!" the old man sighed. "Well, dear boy, I hope my daughter says 'yes.' And I appreciate your asking me beforehand. I fear that's becoming a rather old-fashioned custom these days. Ah: here she is!"

Cesare turned to see Amanda in the doorway. She was tall and slender, wearing a beautifully simple pearl satin gown that flared becomingly at the knees, the dress being held over her bare shoulders by thin straps. She carried a matching stole around her arms. A necklace of seed pearls was around her long throat, and a diamond star was in her strawberry-blond hair. Her full, luscious mouth was slightly colored by lipstick—by then becoming fairly acceptable in more sophisticated circles—and she had put a touch of rouge on her satin cheeks. But her big blue-green eyes needed no cosmetics to enhance their beauty: Amanda Cartwright was a natural knockout.

Cesare extended his hands and came to her, taking her gloved hands in his.

"You take my breath away," he said softly. Then he raised both her hands to his lips and kissed them.

What an attractive young couple! her father thought. They could be on the cover of the *Ladies' Home Journal.*

Back on Fifth Avenue, Brook Savage was having an argument with her mother, Rachel.

"Amanda's mother lets her wear lipstick!" she was saying. "Why can't I? All the really smart young women are wearing it these days!"

"Brook, Amanda is four years older than you and out of college, so she can do what she wishes. You're barely eighteen and you're being presented to Society tonight: we want you to make a good impression, and we don't want people to start saying, 'Brook Savage is fast.' "

"Oh, Mother, how could anyone call me 'fast'? I'm hardly ever allowed to be alone with a boy, much less be kissed by one! I'm about as slow as a girl could possibly be! Enid Whitney told me she allows boys to kiss her all the time, and one of her brother's classmates actually put his hand on her knee!"

"Brook, that's shocking!"

"Mother, you're being prehistoric, like a dinosaur. Now, I know the whole point of this silly ritual tonight is to try and nab me a husband, so I want to look pretty, and without lipstick I look like an old dishrag!"

She was standing in front of a full-length mirror in her second-floor bedroom. Her mother looked at her stunning daughter, who was wearing a rather low-cut white ballgown with a pale blue sash.

"For what I paid for that dress," Rachel said, "I'd hardly

call it a dishrag. Now there'll be no more arguments: lipstick is forbidden."

"Oh, Mother . . ."

The door opened and Johnny hobbled in. He smiled when he saw Brook.

"Darling, you look so beautiful!" he exclaimed, starting across the room on his crutches.

"And she had the nerve to tell me she thought she looked like a dishrag," Rachel said.

"Some dishrag. Now, Brookie, I have a little present for you." He pulled a black velvet box from his tailcoat pocket and handed it to her.

"Oh!" she gasped. She opened the box, which was marked Tiffany. Inside was a diamond and pearl brooch. *"Oh!"* she repeated, her blue eyes sparkling. "It's beautiful! Oh, thank you! Mother, pin it on, will you?"

"It's also from me," Rachel said, taking the jewel and pinning it on the neckline of Brook's dress.

"Oh, thank you both!" she exclaimed, hugging her mother, then her father. "It's almost as nice as lipstick!"

Rachel rolled her eyes.

Brook reflected the confusion her generation of girls had about love and men. While Brook, like all of her friends, devoured romantic novels and magazine articles that throbbed with unrequited love and pulsed with unrequited passion, when it came to the real thing in the presence of real men, the social conventions were only beginning to unfreeze from the Victorian ice age. In an article in the March, 1908, edition of the *Ladies' Home Journal,* a female author wrote that such a seemingly harmless act as a girl allowing a boy to hold her hand "acts directly . . . on the nerves of the body, renders them morbidly sensitive, rouses the emotions and passions which it is physically harmful to have aroused . . . it wakens and stimulates feelings and desires that should not be wakened . . . by allowing these liberties that she thinks so little and harmless, her nerves and forces and powers are almost certain to become diseased, and her strength undermined."

With stern advice like this from one of the most popular and respected magazines in the country, was it any wonder that girls like Brook were confused about men?

With the memory of the disastrous Bradley Martin ball still fresh, not to mention the lavish ball thrown at Sherry's by the insurance heir James Hazen Hyde that caused such a public outcry against the extravagances of the rich that the young Mr. Hyde was forced to resign his position and flee to France for the rest of his life, Johnny and Rachel had wisely decided to "pull all the stops" for their daughter's coming-out party, but to do it with discretion and as little publicity as possible. Johnny sternly forbade any leaks to the press; and while of course a total blackout was impossible, there was no orgy of speculation about what was involved in terms of cost as there had been at the earlier bashes.

Nevertheless, the affair on the evening of June 15, 1910, was catered by Mr. Sherry, the champagne was vintage Veuve Clicquot, and the music was provided by Victor Herbert.

Cesare was feeling on top of the world as he danced a fast two-step with Amanda.

"Your sister looks so beautiful," Amanda was saying.

"Yes, Brook's a pretty girl, but not half as pretty as you."

Amanda smiled.

"Cesare, you're sweet."

"Sweet? Well, it's the first time I've been called that. The fact is, I'm crazy. Crazy about you." He stopped dancing and took her hand. "Come on: I have something I want to show you."

He led her off the crowded floor of the ballroom on the ground floor of the Fifth Avenue house and took her into the adjacent library, which was empty. He closed the door, then took her in his arms and kissed her, hotly. After a moment, she pushed him away.

"Cesare, this isn't a good idea . . ." she began.

"It's the best idea in the world!" he interrupted. "Amanda, I'm so crazy in love with you, I . . ." He hesitated, then pulled a small velvet box from his coat pocket. "Here: this is what I wanted to show you. And because I want you to know that I swear all my heart and love to you and want you more than anything in the world and . . ." He sighed. "I rehearsed this speech all morning, but I'm getting it mixed up. What I'm trying to say is, will you marry me?"

Amanda, looking a bit surprised, opened the box to reveal a ruby ring surrounded by diamonds.

"Oh," she said. "Cesare, it's beautiful. I'm very flattered and . . . and I'm honored that you've proposed to me. But . . ." She closed the box and handed it back to him. "Cesare, I like you a lot and I'm very attracted to you . . . I certainly wouldn't lie about that . . . but you're the last man in the world I'd ever marry."

He took back the ring box, a look of stupefaction on his face.

"You mean," he whispered, "you're not in love with me?"

"I never thought I'd suggested I might be. The truth is, Cesare, you're so much in love with yourself, you can't imagine anyone else not being in love with you too."

A storm cloud passed over his face.

"That's a damned thing to say!" he snorted. "Why don't you love me? What's wrong with me? I'm smart . . ."

"Very."

"Good-looking . . ."

"You're a god."

"I've got plenty of money! My mother's one of the richest women in the city!"

She put her finger on his starched shirtfront.

"Cesare," she said, "you've got nothing in there. You've got no heart. Oh, you can fool people because when you want to you can charm the birds off the trees. You've charmed my father, who thinks you're wonderful—and he's got a good sense of character. But, Cesare, darling, as wonderful as you are, you haven't fooled me. There's something wrong about you—something twisted. There have been times when you say things that are so hateful to hear, and yet you say them without so much as a shrug of the shoulders, no sense of shame whatsoever. Oh no, Cesare: I'll dance with you and have fun with you. If I weren't such a damned lady, I'd love to have you make love to me—and don't think I haven't fantasized about that. But marry you? Oh no. I'd rather marry Cesare Borgia—whom you rather remind me of."

He slapped her, hard.

"Get out of this house, you bitch," he whispered. "I never want to see you again. No one ever says no to Cesare Savage."

Holding her cheek, she stared at him a moment. Then she said, "Now I've seen the real you."

As she walked out of the room, softly closing the door behind her, Cesare's face went red with anger. Then, he closed the ring box, sat down on one of the chairs, buried his face in his hands, and began to sob.

PART FIVE

JASMINE AND THE WARLORD

13. FOR A LONG TIME, JULIE SAVAGE CHIN HAD BEEN itching to open a branch of her highly profitable department store on the mainland of China, more particularly in Shanghai, which was becoming an enormously important international port, hot with money. At the end of 1911, political events in China enabled her to start turning her dream into reality.

In November of 1908, Julie's long-time nemesis, the Dowager Empress, who she was convinced had ordered the murder of her husband, Tim, appointed a two-year-old child to be the next Emperor of China, which, she believed, would allow her to remain in power until her death. On the next day, the actual Emperor, Kuang Hsu, who had been held a virtual prisoner by the Dowager Empress for ten years, conveniently died—rumors swirled around Peking that he had been murdered by eunuchs at the order of the Dowager Empress. Whether that was true or not, the very next day, the Dowager Empress herself died and the two-year-old Pu-i climbed the Dragon Throne.

China was so exhausted by years of corrupt government, the failed Boxer rebellion, and the nibbling away of its territory by Japan and the Western powers that a revolution of some sort was almost inevitable, and it happened three years later in 1911 when the Regent, the new Dowager Empress, terrified by rebellions in the south of China, abdicated for the child Emperor and four thousand years of various ruling dynasties came to an inglorious end. The man Tim Chin, and later his widow Julie, had financed for so many years, Dr. Sun Yat-sen, was chosen to be President of the new Republic of China. Julie, rejoicing at these events that she and Tim had for so long dreamed of, began immediate plans to travel to Shanghai and buy real estate to build a branch of the Chin Department Store. She felt that her beloved husband's murder had, at long last, been vindicated.

Leaving the management of the Hong Kong store in the hands of her capable son, Edgar, she took the ferry to Canton and then the train to Shanghai where, within a week, she had negotiated the purchase of a prime block of real estate on the Nanking Road, the principle shopping street in the growing metropolis. Then she returned to Hong Kong where she hired a young Chinese architect to design her a four-story building.

But as usual in China, nothing went smoothly. Julie's principle ally, Dr. Sun, was replaced in power by a general named Yuan Shih-k'ai who moved into the Imperial City in Peking, although he allowed the child Emperor and his court to continue to live in the Forbidden City. Dr. Sun was made Director of China's railroads, the new and more dictatorial Yuan hoping this job, with its big salary, would keep Sun happy and out of his way. With the loss of her political influence with the deposed Dr. Sun, Julie encountered the usual corruption in Shanghai and was forced to pay off numerous bribes to allow the construction of her store to continue.

But finally, in January of 1914, the store was ready to open. And Julie brought her son, Edgar, and daughter, Jasmine, from Hong Kong to witness the gala event.

Unfortunately, the great day was cold and snowy, so that Julie had to install several electric heaters on the wooden platform she had put up in front of the handsome stone store building. She had had a paper red ribbon with a huge bow wrapped around the building, giving it the festive look of a big Christmas gift, and had run ads in the local papers saying that a buffet and free champagne and beer would be offered on the ground floor after the opening ceremonies; so despite the cold, a large crowd gathered to watch local dignitaries make long-winded speeches about the glowing commercial future of Shanghai and the Chin Department Store. Julie, looking as pretty as ever in a mink coat, sat on the platform, surrounded by Edgar and Jasmine, who was now twenty-four, a graduate of Wellesley, and at the peak of her exotic beauty.

A young Chinese man in a Western-style suit standing in the crowd looked at her with fascination. She's the most beautiful girl I've ever seen, he thought. He had an angular face with a long scar on his right cheek.

Like her mother, Jasmine was equally fluent in Chinese and English. Having spent a total of nine years being educated in American schools, she was in many ways more American than Chinese, a fact that many of her friends in Hong Kong disapproved of, Chinese being by nature suspicious of foreigners as at the same time they are fascinated by them. Having spent many vacations in New York with her Savage cousins, Jasmine also knew and loved that city. She was passionate about America and all things American, and she desperately wanted China to become as much like America as possible, particularly in politics. Having witnessed the murder of her father, she knew that Chinese politics were passionate and confusing, and had a long way to go before an American-style democracy could be securely institutionalized.

At Wellesley she had majored in English literature, particularly loving the fiery passions of Arthurian romance, and minored in philosophy. She studied French, music, astronomy, history, botany, English composition, biblical history (the Chins were Christians), and elocution. She was on the swimming team and played excellent tennis; in her junior year she was elected a member of Tau Beta Epsilon. She was popular with her classmates and in her senior year was named a "Durant Scholar," the highest academic distinction conferred by the college.

Jasmine was a remarkable young lady at a remarkable time in Chinese history.

That night, shortly after midnight, Jasmine was asleep in her room in the Cathay Hotel when a window slowly slid open and a man climbed in from the fire escape. He was wearing a shaggy fur coat and he carried a rag soaked in chloroform. He tiptoed up to Jasmine's bed and looked at her sleeping face a moment. Then he placed the rag over her nose, putting his right knee on her stomach to prevent her from moving. Jasmine's eyes opened, staring with terror at the man standing over her. She could barely make him out in the darkness of the room, but enough light came in from the city so that she could see he had a long scar on his right cheek. She struggled for a moment, trying to force his hand away from her face, but he was as strong as steel.

After a half minute, her hands dropped to her side and she slipped into unconsciousness. The man with the scar removed the rag and picked her up in his arms.

Then he carried her to the open window and out onto the fire escape and disappeared into the night.

Julie, asleep in the adjoining bedroom of the hotel suite, woke up a few minutes later aware that an icy wind was blowing into her room beneath the door to Jasmine's. Getting out of bed, she put on a peignoir, went to the door, and opened it. Seeing the open window, she crossed the room and closed it. Then she looked at her daughter's bed. She turned on a bed lamp to confirm that the bed was empty.

"Jasmine?"

She looked around the room, then looked at the window.
"Oh my God . . ."

She reopened the window and looked out. The fire escape was empty. Dreading what she might see, she looked down. But the alley four floors below the window was empty.

She hurried to the telephone and called down to the reception desk.

"This is Mrs. Chin in suite four-A," she said in Chinese. "Call the police. Something terrible has happened to my daughter."

14. WHEN JASMINE REGAINED CONSCIOUSNESS, SHE found that she was lying on her back in a bed of straw with a blanket over her. Her hands were tied behind her back, her ankles were tied, and her mouth was gagged. She was in some sort of covered wagon, bumping along a road in the cold night. She tried to sit up, turning to look toward the front. A man in a shaggy fur coat and a black hat was sitting in the front, driving a horse. She started making noises with her throat. The man turned to look at her.

"So you're awake," he said in Shanghaiese, the local dialect. "I trust you're comfortable? I put a blanket over you so you wouldn't be cold. We have another few hours to go, so you might as well go back to sleep. Pleasant dreams. By the way, my name is General Wang. Terribly pleased to meet you, even if the circumstances are somewhat unusual and probably not what you're used to. Sorry the road's so bumpy, but we're in a rather out-of-the-way place."

Then he turned back to his driving and became silent.

Though she was frightened and shivering with cold despite the blanket, Jasmine stopped twitching and moaning and lay back in the straw, trying to relax. She had absolutely no idea who General Wang was, though from the little she had seen of his face, he looked awfully young to be a General.

She wondered if he meant to rape her.

Or kill her.

Or both.

"I found this note in the newspaper outside my hotel room this morning," Julie said the next day, reaching across the desk of Sir Phillip Stanhope, the British Consul in Shanghai, to hand him a folded piece of paper. She was sitting in Sir Phillip's office in the British Consulate, a pleasant Colonial-style building surrounded by a garden, situated on the shore of the muddy Huangpu River on the Bund. "It has me terribly worried."

Sir Phillip, a distinguished man in his early sixties with graying hair, dressed in a well-cut frock coat, unfolded the note.

"It's in Chinese," he said. "I'm embarrassed to admit I can't read it, even after ten years out here."

"It's signed by someone named General Wang," Julie said, "who says he has kidnapped my daughter, Jasmine, and that if I don't get him one hundred thousand American dollars in cash by Saturday, he'll send me Jasmine's head." Julie opened her purse, pulled out a handkerchief, and wiped her eyes. The British diplomat looked at the beautiful woman in the mink coat with compassion as he handed back the note.

"I've heard of this General Wang," he said. "He's a

young peasant from near Soochow who's organized himself a small army and proclaimed himself a warlord—though these days, half of China is filled with warlords. One sometimes wonders if China is governable. The situation in Peking is pure chaos."

"But what can we do?" Julie wailed. She was trying to remain composed, but the note had terrified her. She adored Jasmine, and the thought of her being killed made her almost physically ill. "Should I pay the money?"

"Well, we have six days. I wouldn't do anything precipitous right now, although you might start getting the cash together in case of an emergency."

"What does he want that much money for? It's a fortune!"

"Undoubtedly to buy weapons and ammunition. Without weapons, this Wang chap can't operate very effectively. You're a very well-known woman here, Madame Chin, and you've been doing a great deal of advertising these past few months about the opening of your new store. I'm sure Wang read your adverts, and knowing you are wealthy, the idea must have popped into his warped mind to kidnap your daughter."

"But where could he be?"

"Ah well, that's difficult to answer. From what I've heard about him, he's smart and he keeps moving about out in the countryside. We don't have enough men to cover the entire province. No, I think our best bet is to entice him back into Shanghai."

"How?"

"He has to send you instructions about where and how to get him the money. Obviously, he has some sort of contact working at your hotel, which is how he got the ransom note to you. I've sent our chief detective, Mr. Hooper, over to the hotel to sniff around. I don't have too much hope about his succeeding because the hotel staff is easily bought, but one never knows what he may find out. Meanwhile, our people will be asking around Shanghai: I'm certain there are people in the Chinese city who can help us out with General Wang."

"Is he dangerous?" Julie asked nervously.

Sir Phillip stood up. She was surprised to see how tall he was—well over six feet.

"My dear Madame Chin," he said, "I'm sure this Wang chap is a lot of sound and fury signifying nothing."

He was too worried himself to tell her the rumors he had heard: that General Wang was said to horribly mutilate his enemies.

Despite the bumpiness of the ride, despite her cold and fear, Jasmine had fallen asleep in the straw-filled wagon. But when the bumps stopped, she woke up to realize the wagon was still and it was dawn. The driver appeared at the rear of the wagon and grabbed her ankles.

"We're here," he said, pulling her body down across the straw toward him. Then he drew a bandanna from one of his pockets and started to blindfold her. "Sorry to have to do this," he said, "but it's for your own safety. We wouldn't want you leading the police to us—if we send you back alive."

She let out a little squeak of fear as her vision was cut of. Then she felt him pull her halfway out of the wagon and hoist her over his shoulder. She tried to kick and pummel her fists against him, but it was useless—and, she realized, pointless. She could tell he was a man of enormous strength, and she was totally in his power.

She heard some metallic clicks—perhaps those of rifles being cocked?—then the squeak of hinges as a door was being opened. She was carried into a room that was warm: she could smell the smoke of a fire. Then she was deposited, rather gently, onto a thin mattress.

"Don't move," the man's voice said. "I'll free you."

He began untying the blindfold. When he removed it, she saw that she was in a small room with a dirt floor. The walls were made of mud bricks, and there was a thatched roof. In one corner stood a squat Chinese stove that radiated welcome heat. Three windows admitted the cool winter light, and there was a wooden table and two wooden benches.

Now General Wang, whom she judged to be in his twenties, untied her gag.

"So, Jasmine," he said when the gag was off, "welcome to your new home. Have you ever been kidnapped before?"

"Of course not."

"But your father was kidnapped, years ago before you were born. He was kidnapped by the old Dowager Empress, which gave me the idea of kidnapping you. It's sort of a family tradition for you people. Are you hungry?"

"Starving."

"I'll get you something to eat. There's really no reason why this can't be a pleasant experience for you, as long as your mother pays your ransom."

"You're too kind," she said bitingly. He coldly looked at her a moment and she thought that his scarred face and high cheekbones, sharp nose, and cold, slanted eyes could be frightening. Then he relaxed into a smile, and she thought his face could also be attractive, even handsome in an offbeat way. He took off his hat and coat, tossing them onto the table. Then he went to the open door and called out, "Bring our guest some food and a beer . . ." He turned to her, adding, "You do like beer?"

She shrugged sullenly.

"Beer," he called outside. "And hurry."

He closed the door and came back to the bed, pulling a knife from his belt. He wore fur-lined Chinese boots of cow hide decorated rather gaily with red and green stitching around the tops. He leaned over her, reached around her, and cut the rope holding her wrists, in so doing bringing his face close to hers. She recoiled slightly. Again, he grinned.

"You're shy," he said. "Ever been alone with a man before?"

"That's none of your business."

"Are you a virgin?"

She brought up her newly freed right hand and slapped him, hard, so hard he looked surprised and angry.

"Listen," she said, "whatever you may think of me, I'm a lady, and you'll treat me with respect!"

He laughed.

"All things considered with your present situation, my treating you like a lady seems a bit absurd. But, to keep you happy, I'll do my best to treat you well."

"You probably have never met a lady," she said.

"If it makes you feel better to think that, then do so."

"I hate you!"

"I'm sure." Then he smiled. "Put the food on the table."

A young man carrying a rifle over his shoulder had come into the hut with a tankard of beer and a plate filled with dumplings and pork. He set it on the table, then tossed a rag beside the plate.

"This is one of your guards," Wang said, stooping down to cut the ropes on her ankles. "They'll treat you well as long as you don't give them any trouble. If you do give them trouble, they have orders to shoot you."

"Is that your idea of a pleasant experience?"

"Oh, I don't want to have to shoot you. Far from it. Dead, you're worth nothing to me. Alive, you're worth a hundred thousand dollars. There's a chamber pot under the bed, which the guards will clean twice a day. You'll be well fed and given anything you want within reason."

"I want some decent clothes!" she exclaimed.

"I'll send you something. In the meanwhile, sit down and eat. The food here's good. And if you behave . . ." Again, he smiled as he started toward the door, "I may join you for lunch."

15. "ALL RIGHT, GLORIA, WE'RE BRINGING THE CAM-era in for a close-up on your face," D. W. Griffith was saying as he indicated to his cameraman, the German-descended Billy Bitzer, to move the bulky camera closer. "I want you to look dreamy, as if you've just met the man you're falling in love with."

Gloria Gilmore had a secondary role in a potboiler called *The Battle of the Sexes* that Griffith was filming on a shoe-string budget in a loft off Union Square. The plot was creaky for even then—an older man is seduced by a young gold digger, which drives his wife to the brink of suicide—and the tight budget left scant money for glamorous costumes or lavish sets. But Gloria had bought her own clothes and she was wearing a glamorous and shockingly diaphanous chiffon dress that showed her curves to advantage. With her lovely complexion almost invisible because of the heavy white makeup necessary for the camera, she looked something like a vampire on the set; but both Griffith and Bitzer knew she photographed like a dream, and with her angelic features and long, curly golden hair, she was already being favorably compared to Mary Pickford, who was fast emerging as the movies' first megastar. Gloria was sitting at a dresser, gazing dreamily into a mirror. Bitzer's camera approached at a diagonal so he could get not only her face but its reflection as well—a double whammy for the audience.

"Gloria, can you give us a tear?" Griffith prompted, watching the actress like a hawk, trying to milk the scene for everything it was worth without the luxury of retakes: the shooting schedule for the whole movie was only five days.

Gloria, who had an amazing ability to create emotion on cue, obediently came up with a tear, which rolled lusciously down her chalk-white cheek.

"Beautiful! Cut!"

"And how is your good friend, the one-legged banker?" D. W. Griffith said that evening in his slow, Kentucky-bred drawl as he exhaled a cloud of cigarette smoke.

"You mean Johnny Savage?" Gloria asked, sipping her gin and French. Griffith had asked her out for a drink.

"There aren't that many one-legged bankers in New York."

"Johnny's fine, as far as I know. And what are you insinuating by calling him my 'good friend'?"

"Come now, Gloria, let's keep pretense at a minimum. It's no secret that you and Johnny are . . . close. Besides, I know what I pay you. And what I pay you couldn't possibly let you buy expensive baubles like that diamond bracelet on your left wrist."

"That?" Gloria shrugged. "It's fake."

"I choose to believe otherwise. I think the diamonds are real, and of extremely good quality. I had an uncle back in Kentucky who was a jeweler."

She took another sip of the gin, watching him carefully.

"What are you getting at, Mr. Griffith?" she finally said.

"I like to take an interest in the private lives of my actors. I rather think of myself as a sort of father to you, my children. I like to know what's going on." He carefully removed a small piece of tobacco from his tongue. "Is he your lover?"

She leaned back against the booth they were in.

"Not yet. He's really crazy about his wife."

"Tell me: does Johnny approve of your acting career?"

"Oh yes. Why wouldn't he? Johnny's a man of the world. He's not like all those farmers out there who think actresses are all whores. Well, of course, some are, but you know what I mean."

"Oh yes, I know very well." Another long, luxuriant drag on the cigarette. "Does Johnny Savage think your career is advancing satisfactorily?"

"Well, he'd like me to get better parts. So would I."

"That could possibly be arranged."

Gloria sat up again, an interested look on her face.

"What do you mean?"

"Have you ever heard of a book by a man named Thomas Dixon called *The Clansman?*"

"Wasn't it a play on Broadway a few years back? I seem to recall it got ghastly reviews."

"Yes, the critics didn't like it—they seldom like anything unless it agrees with their preconceptions—but it was quite successful commercially. It toured in the South for almost five years. I happen to know the author personally. Mr. Dixon is an unusual man, quite brilliant in some ways, but he has definitely peculiar theories about colored people. He wants to send them all back to Africa, which even I, as a Southerner whose father fought for the South in the great war, find bizzare. At any rate, I'm thinking quite seriously of making a movie out of *The Clansman*. It has many elements that would transfer brilliantly to the screen. Of course, it would have to be a big movie."

"How big?"

"It might run as long as three hours."

Gloria's pretty mouth opened slightly with astonishment.

"Three hours?" she repeated. "Would people sit still that long?"

"They would if they were entranced by the story, which I think they would be. It's very moving, emotionally, and there are stupendous battle scenes. Of course, a movie of this scope would require a lot of money to make."

"How much?"

"Perhaps forty or fifty thousand dollars. Perhaps even more. But there's a role in the movie that it struck me would be perfect for you. It's quite a big role, and a very sympathetic one."

Gloria's look of interest segued into a look of hungry desire. She leaned forward, her elbows on the wooden table between them in the booth.

"What's the role?" she asked softly.

"More about that later," Griffith said suavely, putting out his cigarette in the black ashtray. "In the meantime, you can do me a great favor."

"Anything, Mr. Griffith. Just ask."

"You might speak to Johnny Savage about this project of mine. You might see if he'd be interested in investing some money in it. A colossal movie about the Civil War."

Gloria smiled slightly at Griffith's circuitous way of getting to what he wanted.

"How much?" she asked.

"Well, that would be up to you, my dear. Up to your powers of persuasion, which I think are probably considerable." He smiled. "Another gin and French?"

"No thanks," she said, standing up. "I have a dinner date."

"Might I ask with whom?"

She pulled on her gloves, giving him a suggestive look.

"With a one-legged banker."

"My dearest daughter, I have some rather bad news for you," said the old woman in the black bed jacket sitting in the huge Victorian walnut bed in her second-floor bedroom overlooking Fifth Avenue. The speaker was seventy-five-year-old Hildegarde Lieberman, Rachel's mother, who was suffering from a nervous disorder her doctors were totally confused by, but which they privately believed was terminal.

"What's that, Mother?" Rachel asked. She was seated in a chair beside her mother, sipping tea. Rachel was wearing a light yellow suit trimmed with black.

"I have it on good authority that your husband has taken a mistress."

Rachel set her teacup so abruptly into her saucer, she almost spilled the tea.

"On what authority?" she said tersely.

"Esme Levine told me she has seen Johnny on three separate occasions dining out at restaurants with an extremely attractive young blond woman—rather careless of him, I must say. Now you know I'm terribly fond of Johnny, but I remember when he was a young man he was wild with women. He's no longer young—he's approaching middle age—and I think we must not be foolish about this. I think we can only infer that he has taken a mistress. Or are you going to tell me you think that's impossible? That he's so much in love with you he couldn't betray you with another woman?"

With trembling hand, Rachel set the saucer on the bed table. She was enormously upset by the news, but in her heart she thought it might be true.

"No," she finally said, "I suppose I'd be a fool to think there'd never be another woman. He's so terribly attractive, and since he lost his leg, he's felt somehow undesirable, which of course isn't true at all."

"Do you still love Johnny?"

"Oh yes, Momma, very much. He's my whole life to me! This is why this . . . if it's true . . ."

She suddenly started crying. Her mother held out her hand and patted her.

"There, there, child," she said. "We must realize it's in the nature of men to roam."

"But he told me our love would be forever!" Rachel

wailed, pulling a lace kerchief from her purse. "Forever doesn't seem to last very long, does it?"

"I'm sure he still does love you, Rachel. But you must realize that lust is something few men can control. That thing between their legs—which I've always thought was extremely unattractive—has a mind of its own."

"Oh Momma, what am I to do?" Rachel wailed again.

"Do nothing, my dear. Don't lower yourself to get into a vulgar brawl with him. Keep your dignity at all costs. He'll tire of this woman soon enough, then he'll come back to you, crawling with guilt. Then you'll have him under your thumb!"

Rachel wiped her eyes.

"Well, I'll try, Momma. I know you're right. I'll try. But it will be difficult. If this is true, he's broken my heart."

"Hearts can always be mended," the old woman said. "Life goes on. We live and learn. And then"—she smiled rather sadly—"we die and forget it all."

"Who's that kid over there, losing at the craps table?" asked Arnold Rothstein, New York's most successful gangster. He was standing at the ornate bar of his casino in midtown Manhattan, smoking a cigar and nursing a Scotch on the rocks. "The good-looking one in the well-cut tuxedo?"

He was standing with Julius Fleischmann, the yeast king, whose family would a decade later finance *The New Yorker* magazine. Fleischmann looked across the big main room of the lavish casino, through the smoke-hazed air.

"That's Cesare Savage," he said. "Johnny Savage's step-kid."

"No kidding? I read somewhere he was going to med school."

"He did, for a year. Then he dropped out. They say it was because he broke up with his girlfriend, old Dr. Cartwright's daughter. He got fed up with medicine. Now he's just a playboy—quite wild, I hear. He and his stepfather can't stand each other."

"Interesting," Rothstein said. The son of a wealthy Jew who owned a dry goods store and cotton processing plant, Arnold, known all over town by his initials, A. R., was pronounced dead by his ultra-religious father when he married a gentile. Old Abe Rothstein covered his mirrors and read the Kaddish, setting his son free to do what he really wanted: become a successful gangster. "I like the kid's style. He's already dropped fifteen hundred bucks, but I guess he's good for it."

"Are you kidding? His mother's as rich as God. Rothschild money, and she dotes on him."

"I think I'll introduce myself."

Stubbing out his cigar, he started toward the craps table, making his way through the well-dressed crowd, many of whom smiled when they saw him and shook his hand or clapped his back. A. R., tall, beautifully dressed in his custom-made dinner jacket, had saturnine good looks with a mole on his left cheek. Defying the stereotype of the gangster, which at the time was that of a slum-crawling thug, Rothstein was suavely elegant and oozed charm when he wanted. He came up behind Cesare, who had just rolled snake eyes.

"Damn!" he said. "My luck is shit tonight."

"Mr. Savage," Rothstein said, putting his hand on Cesare's shoulder. "My name's Arnold Rothstein, and I'd like to buy you a drink."

Cesare turned and looked at the already infamous gambler. His face broke into a smile as he shook A. R.'s hand.

"Well, I'm certainly pleased to meet you, Mr. Rothstein," he said. "And since I've lost my shirt tonight, I'll gladly accept a drink. Several, in fact."

"Good. Let's go back to my office where we can talk."

"Just a minute, I want to tip your man."

Cesare pulled his wallet from his jacket and extracted a

twenty-dollar bill, tossing it on the craps table.

"Thanks for a lousy evening," he said.

"What'll it be?" Rothstein said five minutes later, standing at the private bar in his paneled office. "Whiskey? Gin? Rum? Champagne? You name it."

"I'll have some champagne," Cesare said, looking with interest at the many framed photographs of well-known New York types that festooned the walls. "You seem to know everybody, Mr. Rothstein. Everybody, that is, worth knowing."

A. R. popped the cork of a bottle of Moët & Chandon.

"I get around," he said, filling two glasses. He carried them over, handing one to Cesare, who took it.

"Tell me, Mr. Rothstein," he said, "have you ever killed a man?"

"If I had, do you think I'd be stupid enough to admit it to you?"

"Well, perhaps not. Except I don't see much point in being in your line of business if you don't kill people. Do you see what I mean? Cheers."

He clicked A. R.'s glass, then sipped the champagne.

"Mmm," he said, "good stuff."

"I don't serve bad stuff in my casino. But I don't understand what you're saying about killing people?"

"Well, it must be the most exciting thing in the world, don't you think? To actually take someone's life? I can't think of anything more thrilling. I'd certainly envy you if you had killed someone, and if you hadn't, well, I think I'd recommend you try it at the first opportunity."

Rothstein stared at him a moment. Then he laughed.

"You're one fresh kid," he said. "And you've got nerve. I like your style, Mr. Savage."

"Call me Cesare, Mr. Rothstein. The Italian pronunciation: *Chay*-sar-ay."

"Well, *Chay*-sar-ay, I think we may become good friends. Tell me: would you like one of the most beautiful girls in New York tonight? She's in the new Ziegfeld Follies and she's a dream. All it takes is a phone call, and it will be on me—to help make up for your losses tonight."

Cesare raised his champagne glass and smiled.

"Mr. Rothstein," he said, "the evening is definitely beginning to improve."

"I think, Cesare, that you and I probably have a lot in common."

"D. W. Griffith has asked me to invest in a new movie he's planning to make," Johnny said to his wife. He and Rachel were seated opposite each other in the dining room of the Fifth Avenue house. Two tall Georgian silver candelabra held four flickering candles apiece. "It's to be a sort of epic about the Civil War. He says it may go on for as long as three hours."

"Are you going to invest?"

"Yes. There isn't any screenplay yet so I don't know what the story is. But I trust Griffith's instincts. I committed myself this afternoon for fifteen thousand dollars. He's quite pleased."

"I can believe it. From what I understand, that's at least five times what it takes to make one of those two-reelers they show at the nickelodeons."

"Well, the price even of those is going up. Movies are expanding in scope. Griffith even talks about them becoming an art."

"An art?" Rachel's tone was somewhat scathing. "I can hardly believe that will ever happen."

"He plans to shoot it on the West Coast, in a little town near Los Angeles called Holly-something-or-other. Hollywood, I think. Apparently, the weather out there is gorgeous, quite suitable for moviemaking. I plan to go out

there when he begins shooting, which won't be until sometime this summer. I'm rather curious to see southern California."

Rachel finished her soup and rang for the butler, who
came in to serve the next course, mussels in white wine
sauce, one of Johnny's favorites. After he had left, Rachel
said, "I wanted to talk to you about Cesare."

"I have nothing to say about him." Johnny's tone was
cold.

"I know, darling, but you have to help me. I'm terribly
worried about him. He's fallen in with a very bad crowd,
I fear. He told me he's been going to Arnold Rothstein's
casino and gambling. He's even become friendly with
Rothstein, who really is nothing but a common criminal, as
I understand it."

"He's anything but 'common.' He's got his hand in half
the rackets in New York. I'm sure that Cesare finds him
fascinating. And Rachel, if you want to bring that son of
yours to heel, stop giving him money. If he had to work
for a living, he might straighten up."

"That's what I wanted to talk to you about. I know how
you feel about him, and you may have your reasons. But
couldn't you find him a job at the bank?"

Johnny rolled his eyes.

"That would be like inviting the fox into the chicken
coop," he said. "What you don't seem to understand about
him is that he has no morals at all! He's just like his father . . ."

"That's so unkind . . ."

"But it's true!" Johnny roared, throwing down his napkin. "I will do anything in the world for you, Rachel, you
know that. But I will not bring Cesare into the bank. And
I don't want to hear another word on the subject."

Rachel remained tight-lipped as the butler came back in
to refill the wineglasses. When he had left, she said, "I have
to give him money because you won't, nor will you give

him a job. You're so unfair. He deserves a chance."

Johnny closed his eyes a moment, then sighed.

"All right," he said, "I'll see what I can do."

Two mornings later, Glenda O'Brian, Johnny's new secretary (and his first one of the opposite sex, going along with the increasing trend of working women), came into his paneled office at the Wall Street bank. Glenda was a tall and attractive brunette, who wore crisply ironed white blouses and skirts that had inched their way up to her ankles.

"Your stepson is here to see you, Mr. Savage," she said.

Johnny looked up from his desk.

"Yes, show him in, Glenda."

"He's very dashing," Glenda added with a mischievous smile. "If I weren't married and were about fifteen years younger, I think I'd be very attracted to him."

"Yes, I'm sure." Johnny sighed. He was not looking forward to this.

Moments later, Cesare came into the office. He was wearing a dark blue pin-striped suit, beautifully cut, and dove-gray spats. He closed the door and crossed the big room to Johnny's desk.

"Mother told me to come see you," he said in a quiet voice. "I don't have to tell you I objected strongly to doing it, but she insisted. What did you want to see me about?"

"Thank you for the filial warmth and respect in your voice," Johnny said coolly.

"I'm not your son."

"And you delight in that fact, I know. Sit down, Cesare. We might as well try to make this as pleasant as possible."

Cesare sat down in a chair before the desk.

"Your mother," Johnny began, "is very worried about you. She feels you've gotten in with a rather nasty crowd."

"If she's referring to Arnold Rothstein, he's one of the

most brilliant, interesting men I've ever met."

"I'm sure he is interesting. Nevertheless, he's not exactly the type of friend one of your social position should have."

"I'm no snob."

"Yes, that's one of your better traits, Cesare. You'd lie down with pigs."

"I didn't come here to be insulted!" he said hotly.

"No, of course not. I retract that remark. But to get to the point: your mother, who was extremely disappointed when you left medical school, has asked me to find you a job, and I have. A very interesting job, in fact, and one that will pay you extremely well."

"I don't want to work in your damned bank."

"The job is not here. The job is in a most interesting place, a place that I think would intrigue your youthful, exuberant high spirits. By the way, I understand you better than you think. When I was your age, I went out west with Teddy Roosevelt, and it was one of the most exciting times of my life. At any rate, to get to my point: the bank has acquired a large sugar plantation outside Havana, Cuba. It belonged to a Señor Flores to whom we had made several large loans before the war with Cuba. During the war, he was tortured by the Spaniards and, unfortunately, the wounds he suffered ultimately killed him, leaving his family destitute. Now, you may know what the situation in Cuba is—that is, assuming you read the newspapers from time to time . . ."

"I read the papers every day!" Cesare interrupted hotly. "You don't have to condescend to me, damn you!"

"I'm delighted to hear you're so well-read. Then you know that after we routed the Spaniards, the American flag flew over Cuba until 1902 . . ."

"And then the Platt Amendment was passed by Congress which let the Cubans run things their own way, with the proviso that we Americans could intervene if they started to mess things up."

"Exactly. Since then, in the past twelve years, American investments in Cuba have ballooned. So: Señor Flores's sugar plantation is some of the most valuable land on the island, but it's terribly run-down now and needs capital and good management to make it productive again. Since Señor Flores's family defaulted on our loans, the plantation is now under the bank's control. It occurred to me that you might be the very person to go down there and get the place on its feet. We could provide you with all the capital you'd need, and your salary would be very generous, with travel and entertainment allowances. I understand that Havana is one of the most colorful and fun cities in our hemisphere. Since you'd be something of a duke down there—by which I mean you'd have absolute control of everything on the plantation—it seems to me you might have a damned good time."

Cesare stared at him a moment.

"And of course," he said, "you'd get me out of your hair."

"That, too, had occurred to me. But most importantly, it would give you a chance to do something constructive with your life. I say this with no personal animus, Cesare, but the direction you're headed so far is one that seems to me to lead to ruin. You're old enough to start building your life in a positive way."

Silence. Johnny could almost hear Cesare's brain whirling. Then, Cesare said, "How much salary are you thinking about?"

"Twenty-five thousand dollars a year, plus generous allowances."

"Twenty-five thousand's nothing. My mother gives me all the money I want."

"You may find that no longer is the case. Your mother has told me that if you refuse this offer, she will cut off your allowance entirely. The party's over, Cesare. You're going to have to go to work."

Cesare glared at him.

"You're hoping I'll fail, aren't you?" he said softly.

"On the contrary, I'm hoping you'll succeed. For your mother's sake, as well as yours."

After a moment, Cesare stood up.

"All right," he said, "I'll take the job. And I'll make that place the best damned sugar plantation in the world! Just to make you miserable."

16. "WHY ARE YOU CRYING?" GENERAL WANG asked as he came into the hut, closing the door behind him. It was raining heavily, and the rain was dripping through the thatched roof in several places. Jasmine, wearing crude peasant clothes and a woolen jacket, was sitting on her small bed sobbing. She looked up.

"Why?" she said. "Why do you think? I'm cold and miserable, I've been stuck in this terrible place for I don't even know how long, I'm afraid, and I hate these clothes. What do you expect me to do, laugh and sing?"

Wang, who was wearing a gray uniform consisting of a buttoned tunic and slender pants going into the tops of a pair of leather riding boots, came over to her.

"You've been here six days," he said quietly. "I have been in Shanghai, in disguise of course, making arrangements. Your mother has been informed how to ransom you, which she has till tomorrow to do. If all goes well, by tomorrow you can be back in Shanghai and on your way home."

She sniffed and wiped her eyes.

"And if all doesn't go well?" she asked. "You'll kill me, won't you?"

He said nothing for a moment, looking down at her. Then:

"I will not lie to you. I would find it difficult to kill you."

"But you'd do it?"

"We mustn't think of evil things. The evil spirits must be kept at bay with positive thoughts. You're very beautiful."

He sat on the bed beside her.

"I look awful," she said. "I haven't had a bath in a week, these hideous clothes . . ."

"You have been corrupted by your great wealth. Clothes are only superficial. Cleanliness can be less arousing than filth."

She studied his face.

"Are you trying to be romantic?" she asked. "If you are, it's certainly a new approach, though I don't think it's going to be very successful."

"I only want to learn something about you before you leave tomorrow, one way or another. I know you went to school in America. Where was that?"

"In Boston. A place called Wellesley."

"Is America beautiful?"

"Yes, very."

"So you speak their language?"

"Of course. English."

"Did you know many men in this place called Wellesley?"

"Oh yes. I mean, Wellesley admits only women, but there are several universities near it—Harvard, for example—and the men took us out to parties and football games."

"What is this 'football'?"

"It's a game. They kick a ball around a field."

"It sounds foolish."

"Well, I guess it is, in a way. But it's exciting."

"Did you find these men exciting?"

She shrugged.

"Some of them."

"Did you make love to any of them?"

She gave him a cool look.

"As I already told you, that's none of your business."

"But I make it my business. Do you find me exciting?"

She hesitated.

"I'm terribly hungry," she said. "It must be near lunchtime. Can't we have something to eat?"

"You change the subject, but I shall return to it. In the meanwhile, we will eat." He got up, went to the door, opened it, and called out into the rain: "Bring the food for two! And the wine I bought in Shanghai." He turned back to Jasmine. "You see, while I was in Shanghai, I went to something called a 'motion picture.' Have you ever seen one of them?"

"Oh yes. I'm quite fond of them. I'd heard they'd opened one in Shanghai."

"They're very interesting. This was something made in New York. It was about a man trying to seduce a woman. Very interesting how roundeyes seduce women. They give them much wine. So I bought some wine for us."

She gave him a cool look.

"So you're trying to seduce me?" she said.

He smiled slightly, causing the scar on his cheek to crease.

Two of his men came in, carrying several bowls, which they set on the table. A third carried in a bucket in which rested a bottle of wine. The bucket was set on the table. Then the men left, closing the door.

"Come sit down," Wang said, rather gruffly. He pointed to one of the benches.

Jasmine needed no urging. She got off the bed and hurried to sit down at the table. Wang sat opposite her.

"First, the wine," he said. "I had my men take out the cork and chill it. The wine is from a place called France. It was very expensive."

He filled two cups and handed her one.

"I see you're already beginning to spend my mother's ransom money," she said. "I thought the idea was to buy your army weapons?"

"There will be plenty of money for weapons. Meanwhile, you are my guest, and I must keep you pleased."

"You've done a miserable job so far."

He frowned.

"You will drink the wine and make me happy!" he snapped. "It's a woman's job to make a man happy! A woman is inferior to a man!"

"Not in America. Women will even have the vote some-day soon."

"What is this thing, a 'vote'?"

"It's something called democracy. People have votes so they can elect their rulers."

Wang's face sneered.

"What a stupid idea."

"It's not stupid at all. It's the best form of government, and one day all of China will have regular elections. You should read a book about democracy. Better yet, go to America and see how it works for yourself."

He stared at her a moment.

"I do not think it's a good idea that women go to college. They get foolish ideas in their heads, as you have in yours. Drink your wine."

She obeyed. The wine, nicely chilled, was dry and excellent.

"So tell me, General," she said. "What are you going to do with your little army?"

"Take territory, then make little army a big army and take more territory. Take perhaps all of China! You see, now that the Manchus are gone and there is no more Emperor, China is helpless and strong men like me will replace the Emperors and bring good rule to the country. You'll see: I'll be a great Emperor. But no 'votes.' Stupid idea."

She drank more of the wine. She was surprised how mellow she was beginning to feel, and how fascinated she was by his face. She leaned forward and lowered her voice, smiling mischievously.

"And when you're Emperor, will you have many concubines?"

"Of course, but none that went to college. And no eunuchs. Eunuchs are all thieves. I see you are beginning to smile. The movie must have been right: wine makes women happy."

"A little food would make this woman happier."

"Yes, of course." He removed the covers from the bowls. "Eat! Eat, eat, eat!"

Chopsticks had been provided. Now Jasmine took one of the bowls and began eating.

"Ningpo oysters," Wang whispered, with a lecherous smile. "Food of love!"

She giggled. My God, she thought, he's really funny! But I actually sort of like him.

When they had finished eating, Wang let out a loud burp, which Jasmine knew was a Chinese sign that the meal had been enjoyed, but nevertheless it sent her into another fit of giggles. Wang looked at her.

"What is funny?" he asked.

"Well . . . I know it's correct to belch in China, but still . . ." She went into another fit of giggles. Wang's face became stormy.

"You think I'm an ignorant peasant!" he exclaimed. "Yes, you're right, I am! But don't you dare laugh at me, you rich, spoiled girl, for tomorrow I may kill you!"

At which point, he stood up and left the hut, slamming the door behind him. Jasmine, her giggles dying quickly, stared at the closed door and wondered if she had just signed her death warrant.

An hour later, the door burst open and two of General Wang's soldiers came into the hut carrying a five-foot diameter canvas tub, filled with water. They set it down on the dirt floor, then left as an aged amah came in.

"Take your clothes off," she said. "General Wang has ordered that you be bathed."

Jasmine, totally surprised, stood up and began to undress.

The morning after her bath in the canvas tub, Jasmine awoke to see that the sun was out, promising an unusually warm day after the chilly rains of the day before. She reflected that if this were to be her last day on earth, at least it was going to be a pretty one.

At ten o'clock, she was surprised to see the old amah who had washed her come into her prison hut carrying a long box marked "Chin Department Store."

"General buy this for you in Shanghai," the amah said, putting the box on the table. "He say for you to put it on and stop complaining about your clothes."

She left the hut. Jasmine hurried to the table and opened the box. Inside was a beautiful green silk cheong-sam, embroidered with silver thread. She took the dress out of the box and held it up, admiring it and, at the same time, wondering how Wang could have the nerve to shop in the very department store whose owner's daughter he had kidnapped. Never mind: the dress was beautiful. She quickly took off the dirty clothes she had been wearing for a week and slipped the green cheong-sam over her head. She wished she had a mirror so she could see how she looked.

Her mirror came through the door a few minutes later in the person of General Wang. He still had on his gray tunic and leather boots, but now he wore no hat. He stood for a moment looking at her.

"You like the dress?" he finally said.

"Yes, it's very beautiful. Thank you. But you certainly have a nerve to walk into my mother's store!"

He grinned, and she saw that he had good teeth.

"Yes, that gave me much amusement," he said. "I walked past two guards who didn't even give me a second look. As long as you have money, you have respect: a great lesson for all of China."

"I don't suppose you saw my mother?"

"No."

She asked nervously, "Has she sent my ransom?"

"Yes. Tonight I will take you back to Shanghai, and you will be free."

"So that's why you bought me this dress? So I wouldn't go home in rags."

"That's one reason."

"What's the other?"

"I wanted you to have something to remember me by."

He said it softly, almost tenderly.

"I would never forget you," she said.

"Do you still hate me?"

She looked embarrassed.

"I never hated you," she said.

"You said that the first day."

"Well, I didn't know you very well then."

"And now that you know me better?"

"I . . ." She hesitated, uncertain of her own feelings. "I like you very much, I think. And I hope you do well. I mean, with your army."

"I bought a book about America, written by a Chinese who lived in San Francisco for a number of years. The book is very interesting. Perhaps you were right about America, although the place has faults."

"Oh yes, many faults. No place is perfect. For instance,

black people are not treated well in America, though that seems to be changing for the better—at least, a little."

"I read that there are two political parties called Democrats and Republicans, and they switch back and forth in power. That seems rather confusing to me. Could you explain to me a little how that works?"

"Gladly, except it would take time . . ."

"How much time?"

"I suppose several days. I'm not even sure where to begin . . ."

He frowned.

"Will I be able to see you in Shanghai?" he asked. "I mean, would you talk to me if you weren't my prisoner?"

"Oh, I'd like that very much!" she exclaimed sincerely. "Except, of course, you'll have to hide from the police, won't you? I mean, kidnapping is a crime."

He continued to glare at her, and she could tell he was furious about something. Then, suddenly, he exploded. "Damn!" he yelled. "Damn, damn, damn!"

"What's wrong?"

"Everything's wrong!"

To her amazement, he hurried out of the hut, leaving her alone and totally perplexed.

An hour later, he came back. He was smoking a cigarette and he looked cross.

"You!" he said, pointing a finger at her. "Your father was murdered many years ago. Am I right?"

"Yes, when I was a child. The murderer was a Boxer, and he'd been hired by the Dowager Express. It happened right before my eyes."

"It must have made a terrible impression on you, am I right?"

"Oh yes. I've never gotten over it. That's why I've always had a great dream for China, because my father wanted China to be a democracy—"

"That word," he interrupted, almost with a sneer. "Votes!

Votes for women, who then become like you, with fancy ideas."

"I don't think wanting people to be free is a particularly 'fancy' idea. I just think it's a good one."

"You talk too much. Women should not talk, except about love. If a man married you, he'd be better off being deaf." He studied her a moment. "I suppose you have some fat, rich young man in Hong Kong who wants to marry you."

"In fact, there are several who are interested in me."

"And you? Are you interested in them?"

"Perhaps." Her voice took on a rather coy tone.

General Wang scowled and snorted.

"Huh," was all he said. Then, again, he left the room, slamming the door behind him.

The next morning, he came back into the room without even knocking. Jasmine, who was still on her mattress, sat up and stared at him.

"You!" he said. "Get dressed. I'm taking you back to Shanghai. I've made a mistake. I, General Wang, have made a stupid mistake, and it's all your fault."

"My fault? What did I do?"

"I'll send you back to your mother with the ransom— except for the dress! I'll keep the money I spent on the dress—it was expensive! Come: I'll take you back now. Damn, damn, damn!"

Utterly confused, Jasmine got dressed, then followed him out of the house. He had mounted a horse. Now he pointed to another.

"Get on," he said. "I'll lead you back to Shanghai, then you can take a taxi to the hotel. Here." He tossed a leather bag to her. "There's the ransom money. Give it back to your mother. Damn!"

Amazed, she put the pouch in a saddlebag, then mounted the horse.

"He sent back the ransom money?" her mother said four hours later after Jasmine had returned to the hotel. "But why?"

"I don't know. He just said he had made a stupid mistake and brought me back here."

"Where is he now? I must call the police . . ."

"You'll do no such thing!" Jasmine said hotly. "He didn't commit any crime . . ."

"He kidnapped you!"

"Yes, but he's set me free, and he treated me very nicely. He even bought me this dress in your department store—and so much for your guards! He told me he walked right past them."

Julie looked confused.

"He went in the store? He certainly has nerve!"

"Oh, he's brave as a tiger. And quite intelligent. He was asking me about America and I tried to tell him how democracy works. He didn't much like the idea of votes at first, but who knows? Maybe I converted him. And he's quite attractive physically."

Her mother looked nervous.

"He didn't try anything?" she asked.

"No. I'm telling you, he was really quite nice. Actually, a real gentleman."

"Preposterous! The British Consul told me he's a peasant."

"So what? Mother, don't be such a snob. Actually, he really was one of the most interesting men I've ever met. Much more interesting than Sammy Wu, whom you're always trying to push on me."

"Sammy Wu is the most eligible bachelor in Hong Kong and he's crazy about you! You should take my advice and encourage him a little. Speaking of which, now that you're back, I think we should return home. Edgar's staying here to run the store for the first few months—he's looking for a house to rent—and I want to see how things are going at the Hong Kong store. But I'll have to phone Sir Phillip Stanhope and tell him you're safe."

"Remember: no police! The General didn't commit any crime, and if he's brought to trial I'll testify that he was a perfect gentleman."

Her mother shook her head.

"Jasmine, sometimes you truly baffle me. But all right: no police."

She picked up the phone.

That evening, Jasmine and her mother and brother were all eating in the hotel dining room, Jasmine still wearing the green dress that General Wang had bought her. Edgar was describing a house he had found to rent when Jasmine looked at the door of the dining room.

"Oh my God," she muttered. "It's he!"

Standing in the door, wearing a well-cut Western-style blue suit, was General Wang. When he spotted her, he made his way across the room to the table, avoiding the maître d'. He bowed to Julie.

"Good evening, madame," he said. "I am General Wang."

Julie stared at him.

"Does he have a gun?" she stammered.

"Mother, don't be silly," Jasmine said. "Of course he doesn't have a gun. General, this is my brother, Edgar."

Edgar, looking as amazed as his mother, shook the General's hand.

"How do you do?" he gulped.

"Please," Jasmine said, "join us for dinner."

"Jasmine, are you mad?" her mother exclaimed.

"Thank you," the General said, taking the empty fourth chair at the table. He smiled at Jasmine for a moment. Then he said to her mother:

"I have decided I want to marry your daughter."

Julie's mouth dropped open.

"You what?" she sputtered.

"I want to marry your daughter. Jasmine," he said, turning to her, "I am in love with you. That's why I said it's all your fault, but I forgive you. Will you marry me?"

Jasmine was staring at him.

"General," Julie said, "this is totally unacceptable behavior. My daughter is practically engaged to another man . . ."

"Mother, be quiet," Jasmine interrupted. "I'm not going to marry Sammy Wu. Yes."

"Yes what?" the General said.

"Yes I'll marry you. But I don't even know your name."

"Hsueh-liang. But now that I've finished the book on America, I've decided to give myself an American name. You give me an American name."

Jasmine's smile was dazzling.

"Charlie," she said. "I've always liked that name. I baptize you Charlie Wang. By the way, are you a Christian?"

"No."

"Then the marriage is off!" Julie snapped. "Jasmine, this is absolutely mad! You can't marry this man! How can you marry a man you just baptized?"

"I'll take him to get baptized tomorrow. And, Mother, you're wrong. I'm marrying Charlie."

She reached out and took his hand. He took it and stood up. Then, as everyone in the dining room watched in hushed awe, he pulled Jasmine to her feet, put his arms around her, and kissed her on the lips.

"Jasmine!" her mother gasped. "You can't do this in public!"

But neither Jasmine nor General Wang paid any attention at all.

Julie, always pragmatic, was determined to contain the damage. She said, "At least wait three months. If you still feel the same way, I will give you my blessing."

Three months later, Jasmine and Charlie were married in one of the most lavish weddings ever seen in Hong Kong. As was usual in China, the bride wore red; Jasmine looked indescribably beautiful. Charlie was somewhat uncomfortable in his cutaway coat, but everyone agreed he looked dashing.

For their honeymoon, Jasmine and Charlie went to New York to meet the rest of the family and for Charlie to see democracy. Johnny was somewhat dazed by his niece marrying a warlord who spoke no English—Jasmine translated for him—but Rachel and the children were dazzled by this glamorous man who didn't know how to use a knife and fork, but who was learning fast. And Cesare, who was about to embark for Cuba, was floored by him, awash in admiration.

"Have you ever killed someone?" he asked one night as the family ate dinner in the Fifth Avenue mansion. Jasmine translated.

"Oh yes," he said calmly, trying to pick up some peas with a spoon, but finally giving up and popping them into his mouth with his hands.

"Was it exciting?" Cesare was practically breathless.

Charlie Wang shrugged.

"The first time," he said, "but then it becomes routine. Torture, though, is more fun."

"Torture?" Cesare practically fell off his chair. "Have you tortured people?"

"Many times. Torture in China is an art."

"Gosh!"

"Cesare," his mother said, "I think we can change the

subject. Jasmine, dear, have you taken Charlie to the Metropolitan Museum of Art?"

"Why did you say those things to Cesare?" Jasmine said to her husband 'later when they were alone. "About murdering people and torture?"

Charlie smiled at her.

"Because it's what he wanted to hear," he said. "And he believed every word of it. By the way, I think he's a very dangerous young man."

"Dangerous? Cesare? Why?"

"I just feel it. I think he's going to bring his family great trouble."

Charlie and Jasmine spent a week in New York, Jasmine showing him all the sights of the great city and explaining to him as best she could how democracy worked.

He came away impressed and converted.

"Someday," he said to Jasmine as they drove down Fifth Avenue, "China will look like this."

17. CESARE STOOD UNDER THE HOT CUBAN SUN and looked at the weed-grown front garden of the rather dilapidated plantation house five miles outside of Havana.

"No one's lived in it for five years?" he asked the young, Havana-based, Yale-educated architect he had hired, Carlos Flores, a distant cousin of the family that once owned the Santa Isabel plantation.

"No. After my cousin died, his family was practically

destitute. They couldn't even afford a caretaker. The last time I was out here, there was an old man living in it. I had to chase him away. But the building is basically sound, and it used to be one of the most handsome *palacetes* in Cuba."

" '*Palacete*'?" Cesare asked, looking at the dark-haired young man in the white suit.

"That's the word for plantation house."

"I see." The building was a one-story yellow stucco with a red tile roof, fronted by a handsome columned gallery that wrapped around the two sides of the house. "What's that building over there?"

He pointed to a small structure some hundred feet from the main house.

"That's the *Ingenio,* where the sugarcane used to be milled. Beside it is the old slave quarters, although of course there haven't been slaves working this place for fifty years. Shall we go inside?" He was holding a ring of keys. Now he led Cesare onto the tiled gallery and unlocked the elegantly carved wooden front door. He opened it and went into a large entrance hall with wooden doors on either side.

"The doors lead to the two *aposentos*," he said, opening one door to reveal a small room in which stood an iron bed with a mosquito netting hanging from a canopy. Otherwise, the house was devoid of furniture. There were two shuttered windows. Everything was incredibly dusty. A rat scurried across the room and ran out the open door.

"Charming," Cesare said. "Can we get an exterminator out here?"

"Yes." Carlos led him back out into the hallway, then into a large room with a handsome wooden ceiling from which hung glass oil lamps. The room, with white plaster walls and a tiled floor, was pleasantly cool on the hot day.

"This is the *saleta*, the main living room of the house. It was also the dining room on cool days, though most of the time the family used to eat out on the gallery. Over there is the storehouse and kitchen, and opposite it is the office of the plantation."

"That's it?"

"That's it."

"What about plumbing?"

"None. There's a privy."

"All right. I want you to design me an addition with a modern kitchen, a proper dining room, and a master bedroom and modern bath. Put in two other bathrooms somewhere. I want electric wiring, and this place brought into first-class condition. Get in some landscape people and fix the gardens. Oh, and build me a two-car garage. Can you do it in a month?"

Flores looked at him in disbelief.

"A *month*? Señor, this is Cuba!"

"I'll give you two months."

"I'll try, señor, but I can't guarantee it. And the budget?"

"There isn't one. Whatever it takes. Now let's get out of here and go back to Havana. I hear it's a fun town. You're going to show me some fun."

A little over a year later, on the evening of February 8, 1915, Johnny, dressed in a tuxedo, escorted Gloria Gilmore through a huge crowd milling about in front of Clune Auditorium in Los Angeles to see the premiere of the most talked-about film ever made to date, D. W. Griffith's *The Birth of a Nation*, which had formerly been the subtitle of *The Clansman*. However, Griffith had been persuaded to change the order, making the subtitle the movie's main title, because of angry rumblings from the young National Association for the Advancement of Colored People, who were objecting strenuously to the public showing of the movie that, they had heard, portrayed blacks in an unfavorable light; in fact, they had managed to obtain an injunction against the matinee showing of the film that day on the grounds that it might incite a race riot.

However, none of this seemed to have dampened the excitement of the crowd milling about in front of the 2500-seat auditorium owned by W. H. Clune, who had watched some of the movie's scenes being shot and had invested in it. Of course Johnny had invested too and was looking forward to seeing the longest, most expensive film ever made—something so unique that it threatened to make all movies made before totally obsolete in concept, as steamships had made sailing ships obsolete in the previous century. Most of the well-dressed crowd, which was being photographed by countless press people (this was the first of the Hollywood premieres on a big scale), were associated in some way with the film, so suspense was high about whether Griffith's huge opus would be a hit or a flop of monumental proportions.

"I hope it lays an egg," Gloria growled to Johnny as they entered the theater. "That bastard, Mr. Griffith, practically cut my part out."

"They'll love what they see of you, darling," Johnny soothed, hobbling on his crutches. Gloria looked glorious in a heliotrope evening dress, wearing diamond and sapphire earrings Johnny had given her for the occasion.

They were met in the auditorium by usherettes dressed in Civil War dresses who led them down the crowded aisle to their seats. They were also handing out petitions addressed to the Los Angeles City Council urging it to take no action that would prevent the exhibition of the film—a countermove against the action of the N.A.A.C.P. Johnny, who had only recently heard of the building brouhaha about the film's depiction of blacks, was more than a little disturbed to read the petition; it had never occurred to him that he might have invested in a film that might turn out to be a diatribe against blacks, whose standing in Jim Crow America was only just beginning to improve slowly.

But there was little time for reflection, because shortly

after eight o'clock, the conductor Carli D. Elinor took his place in the pit (Clure's orchestra was considered the best west of the Mississippi), the houselights dimmed, and the opening fanfare thrilled the audience as the titles appeared, at first blurrily against the house curtain, then clearly on the big screen as the curtain rose. When the titles were ended and the action began, the audience sat enthralled, swept along by a narrative so big in scope that there was literally nothing to compare it with. Griffith's Southern prejudices had certainly portrayed the black characters—or at least most of them—in a bad light, but the force of the film was overwhelming (even members of the N.A.A.C.P. who later saw it admitted they had been carried away by the story).

At the end of the film, the audience arose cheering, clapping, even screaming: it was a first night success like nothing before and very likely nothing since.

"Goddammit," Gloria shouted over the din, "it's brilliant!"

But Johnny, though he had been absorbed by the action on the screen, saw why the N.A.A.C.P. was complaining. And as he hobbled out of the theater, he remembered the promise he had made to Private Leroy Collins, the young black soldier whose life he had saved back in Cuba. "My people need all the help they can get," Leroy had said to him in the hospital tent where Johnny was recovering from his amputation. Now, he thought, is my chance to keep that promise to Leroy. I'll give every penny I make from this movie to the N.A.A.C.P.

The movie turned out to be such a box-office bonanza that Johnny's profits amounted to over $100,000, all of which he donated to the National Association for the Advancement of Colored People. In fact, the opening night of *Birth of a Nation* not only put D. W. Griffith on the map, it can be argued it did the same for the N.A.A.C.P.

"Daddy," Gloria said later as they drove from the theater in their rented Locomobile limousine, "Wittle Gworia is having a wonderful idea." She was snuggled up against Johnny in the backseat, their conversation sealed off from George, their chauffeur, by a glass panel.

"Gloria," Johnny grumped, "you know when you talk baby talk, I want to 'fwow up.' What's your idea?"

She straightened, adjusting her golden hair.

"Well, I'm getting nowhere in Hollywood, and I think it's because I look too much like that bitch, Mary Pickford. I'm thinking of cutting off my curls and acquiring a more sophisticated look."

"What do you mean, 'sophisticated'?"

"Sexy."

"A bad idea. It's too much for the audience. If they come to think of you as a 'bad' woman, your career could be over in a week."

"Theda Bara's doing all right. Everyone loves the idea that she's a vamp. And I've found a screenplay where the heroine is a wicked woman, but at the end she gets religion and becomes a nun."

"How wicked is she?"

"Well, she starts out as a chorus girl on Broadway and then she becomes the mistress of a very rich businessman who's old enough to be her father."

He turned to look at her.

"That sounds familiar."

"What do you mean?"

"It's us."

"I never was a chorus girl. Anyway, what if it does resemble our lives? Besides, there are all sorts of differences in the plot. And I certainly am not going to become a nun."

"I'm glad to hear it."

"Anyway, I can buy it from the writer dirt cheap. He's

a starving reporter who dreams of writing the Great American Novel or something—you know, all writers are idiots—and I want you to read the screenplay and tell me what you think, because you're so smart about these things. Will you?"

He sighed.

"You know I hate reading screenplays, but all right."

She curled her arm in his and kissed his cheek.

"You're so sweet," she cooed. "Did you know I'm just crazy about you?"

The limousine pulled up in front of the two-story Spanish-style mansion Johnny had rented for her in the Laughlin Park subdivision, down the street from Cecil B. De Mille. While the new-rich movie people had not yet begun building the extravagant palaces they would later on, they were using their sizable, low-tax salaries to rent homes that had been built by rich Los Angeles businessmen. Jesse Lasky, the pioneer producer, lived in a Spanish-style mansion at 7209 Hillside Avenue near the Hollywood Hills, his house boasting one of the first private screening rooms as well as a tennis court, swimming pool, and terraced gardens. Pickford herself was living at Western Avenue near Sunset Boulevard in a rather modest bungalow, and Charlie Chaplin, who had an advanced case of the cheaps, was living in the Los Angeles Athletic Club despite his enormous film earnings.

But as movies caught on more and more with the great American public and movie fortunes began mounting into the stratosphere, mad extravagance was just around the corner.

Cesare's twenty-sixth birthday cake, when it was brought in from the new kitchen of Santa Isabel plantation to the spacious new *comedor* where he was entertaining a dozen of his friends from Havana, caused a roar of laughter. When the curvacious mulatto *puta* from Havana—one of the dozen Cesare had hired for the "orgy," as he had dubbed the evening on the invitations—set the silver tray on the table, the guests, most of whom were by now drunk, stood up to see that the large cake was in the shape of a big erect penis with a smidgin of whipped cream coming out of the operative end and twenty-six candles burning cheerfully around it. The guests burst into applause, yelling: "Perfect, Cesare! It's you!" "Bravo!" Et cetera. Cesare's friends were the cocky young blue bloods of Havana, the fast set that splurged its youth at the racetracks and at exclusive clubs like the Centro Asturiano and the Centro Gallego on the Parque Central or at the huge Hotel Nacional on the beautiful seaside boulevard called the Malecón. As Cesare ended his first year in Cuba, he had not only done a remarkable job getting the Santa Isabel plantation back on its feet and actually turning a slight profit, but the dashing American had become one of the stars of this *jeunesse dorée*. The men loved his wild antics, and the women loved him, period.

But tonight was a stag party. The *putas*, all of whom were gorgeous, came in a rainbow of colors. And they were all naked as they served the five-course meal, a gimmick that had proved as popular with the guests as the penis-shaped birthday cake.

Cesare took a deep breath and blew out all twenty-six candles to wild applause and cheers. Then, as the naked girls passed around trays of champagne, Carlos Flores, the young architect Cesare had hired to redo the plantation, stood up and raised his glass.

"Gentlemen," he said, "I want to propose a toast to our host, Cesare Savage. Of course, since he was my boss—and he paid all his bills on time, which you must admit in Cuba is a genuine miracle"—the guests laughed—"what I am now saying could be considered biased, but I'll say it anyway. Cesare has done a remarkable job, turning the

Santa Isabel plantation totally around from an abandoned ruin to one of the best-run sugar plantations in Cuba. Not only that, he pays his workers a good living wage and, as you all know, he has built a small hospital next door to give them decent medical care, something that is practically unheard of on this island. For that, and many other things, I think we all should salute this remarkable young man from New York. And so I say, God bless you, Cesare Savage, and happy birthday!"

The guests all stood up and cheered their host. Cesare, who was also a bit drunk, stood up and untied his bow tie.

"I thank you, Carlos, for your very kind words. And now—orgy time!" he yelled in his not-bad Spanish. "Everybody get naked! Orgy time!"

Howling with more drunken laughter, the male guests proceeded to take off their clothes, tossing their dinner jackets in a pile in a corner of the room. Cesare put a record on his state-of-the-art wind-up Victrola, and hot Latin music filled the room as the orgy commenced.

"Cesare writes me that he wants to volunteer as an ambulance driver in Italy," Rachel said to her husband one snowy night a month later as they sat down to dinner in the Fifth Avenue house, the butler holding her chair. "I'm going to write him that he must stay in Cuba. I don't want him anywhere near that dreadful war."

"Much to my surprise, Cesare's done a damned fine job down there," Johnny said as the butler came around to hold his chair and take his crutches. "It's certainly possible the responsibility we gave him has straightened him out. But I must say, if he wants to go over there, it's his life."

"His life he might well lose!" Rachel retorted.

"Not as an ambulance driver. From what I read, that's pretty safe. Besides, with a year of medical school under his belt, he might be really helpful. Thank you, Redmond. What's for dinner tonight?"

"Roast beef, sir, and Yorkshire pudding."

"Excellent. I adore roast beef."

"And to start, sir, some turtle soup."

"Lovely."

"I'll pour the wine, sir."

After he had poured the wine and served the soup, Rachel said, "But isn't Cesare needed at the plantation? After all the money the bank has invested in it, wouldn't it be irresponsible for him to run off to Italy?"

"No, his manager could run the place till he comes back. I don't think Cesare is being irresponsible. This war is turning out to be much bigger than anyone would have thought, and I could understand why a young man like Cesare would want to see it firsthand. Happily, he can't volunteer to fight because that's illegal, since America isn't in the war—and I certainly hope it won't get in later on. But as a noncombatant ambulance driver, I can see that it might be a useful experience for him, and an exciting one. If you want my advice, I'd say let him go. But he's your son, not mine."

Rachel sipped her wine, a worried look on her face.

"I don't know," she said. "Something might happen to him. Look what happened to you when you went down to Cuba."

"Rachel, as a noncombatant, Cesare wouldn't even be carrying a weapon."

"Still, I worry. And now that, as you say, he has finally straightened out and is doing so well." She sighed. "I just don't know."

PART SIX

CESARE IN LOVE;
HEMINGWAY
IN PAIN

18. RACHEL HAD TAKEN A SHIP TO HAVANA TO
spend a week with her son, see the Santa Isabel plantation
with her own eyes, and implore him not to volunteer as an
ambulance driver in Italy. Cesare had argued with her, saying that he wanted to see the action and help Italy, which
he considered as his second country because of his father,
but Rachel finally won out by the simple device of writing
him a "bonus" check for $15,000: Cesare's love for money
had hardly abated with his time in Cuba.

However, when America entered what had become
known as the Great War in April, 1917, Cesare wrote his
mother he felt he had a patriotic duty to enlist. He sailed
for New York only to find out, to his amazement, that he
wasn't physically fit for active duty because of his flat feet.
Stymied, he returned to Cuba. But as the war in Europe
dragged on, the carnage mounting to terrifying heights, his
idea of volunteering as an ambulance driver recurred to
him.

In May of 1918, he returned to New York and was accepted by the International Red Cross as an ambulance
driver in Italy, which was an ally of France, England, and
the United States against the Central Powers of Germany
and Austria. While he waited for his group to be transported
to Europe, Cesare went downtown to Greenwich Village
where young men from all over the country were being
housed by the Red Cross in a small residential hotel on the
north side of Washington Square called the Hotel Earle. He
drilled with the others on the roof of the hotel during his

first afternoon there. And it was there that he struck up an acquaintance with a sturdy, good-looking young man from Oak Park, Illinois, who had been turned down by the army because he was too nearsighted.

"So you're a New Yorker?" the young man said as they took the elevator down from the roof to have a drink in the bar.

"That's right, born and bred," Cesare said. "Though I've spent most of the past couple of years down in Cuba."

"Cuba? No kidding. I hear that's pretty wild."

Cesare grinned knowingly. "Some very hot señoritas down there."

"I hear we have a couple of days before we sail. Could you show me around New York?"

"Love to. Actually, why don't you come uptown and have dinner with me and my folks? My father's a pill, but you'd like my mother."

"That sounds swell. Say: we haven't really met. What's your name?"

"Cesare Savage. And yours?"

"Ernest Hemingway."

"Glad to meet you, Ernie. And since you're an out-of-towner, these drinks are on me."

"Fine by me. I'm almost broke."

A half hour later, the two young men left the Hotel Earle and walked down Washington Square to where Cesare had parked his red Pierce-Arrow.

"This is yours?" Hemingway almost gasped as Cesare cranked the engine.

"Yep. My mother gave it to me when I graduated from college."

"You've got to have the most generous mother in America, not to mention pretty damned well-heeled."

He climbed in beside Cesare, who was at the wheel. They

drove around the square, then started up Fifth Avenue, where traffic policemen stood on wooden towers at the major intersections.

"Where did you go to college?" Cesare asked as they went uptown.

"I didn't. I went to work on a newspaper in Kansas City instead. I'm going to be a journalist. Maybe someday I'll even try to write books."

"Hey, that's great! I wish I could write, but the only thing I can write are checks."

Hemingway, who had an infectious grin, said: "I wouldn't mind being able to do that."

"Where are you from?"

"Oak Park, Illinois, outside Chicago. My old man's a doctor. What's your father?"

"A banker. Except he's really not my father. My father was Italian, which is why I want to help Italy."

"Ever been there?"

"Yes, several times. I speak it pretty well."

"I figure I'll pick some of it up. I'm really looking forward to seeing Europe."

"You've never been?"

"Nope. I'm a virgin."

"Not with women, I hope?"

"Oh, hell no." Another infectious grin. "I'm pretty good in that department. You ever been in love?"

"Yes, once. I proposed, but she turned me down. She said I had no heart. How about you?"

"Nope, never been in love. But I'm really looking forward to it. I expect it might happen any day now."

When Cesare parked in front of his parents' house on Fifth Avenue, Hemingway gaped at the imposing limestone mansion.

"Is this where you live?" he asked.

"That's right. Come on."

He got out of the car.

"Gosh," Hemingway said as he climbed out the other side, "your folks must really be loaded!"

"They do all right."

As Cesare led Ernest Hemingway up the steps to the front door of the mansion, the young would-be writer from Illinois thought: It pays to have rich friends.

"You'll like my kid sister, Brook," Cesare was saying as he rang the bell. "She's twenty-four and engaged to a Lieutenant in the army who's over in France. She's a real stunner. She's also a major flirt, so watch out." Redmond opened the door. "Good evening, Redmond. This is Mr. Hemingway. I asked him to dinner. Can you put on another place?"

"Of course, sir. Good evening, Mr. Hemingway."

An English butler, Hemingway thought as he came into the entrance hall. Just like in the movies!

"Cesare!" cried the beautiful slim strawberry blond in the white dress who was coming down the main staircase. "Did you get your uniform yet? Oh . . ."

She stopped at the bottom of the stairs and stared at her brother's companion.

"Brook," Cesare said, "this is my new friend who's going to Italy with me. He's from near Chicago and is going to be a writer someday. Brook, meet Ernest Hemingway."

"Oh . . ." Brook smiled as she came to Hemingway and extended her hand. "I'm so pleased to meet you, Mr. Hemingway. But I thought writers were supposed to be old and stuffy. You're anything but old and stuffy, I can tell right off." She turned to Cesare and whispered, "He's dreamy-looking!"

Cesare turned to the butler.

"You'd better seat Mr. Hemingway next to my sister."

"Do you believe in free love?" Brook asked Hemingway twenty minutes later. They were seated next to each other across from Cesare, while Johnny and Rachel sat at the ends of the table.

"Brook!" exclaimed her mother. "What a shocking thing to ask."

"Oh Momma, really, all the advanced thinkers are talking about it, and I assume Mr. Hemingway is an advanced thinker because he's going to be a writer. Do you?" she repeated, turning back to him. She could hardly take her eyes off him, and the attraction was mutual.

"Well, uh . . ." Hemingway rather nervously wiped his mouth with the damask napkin. "I think it depends on the circumstances. I wouldn't recommend trying it in my hometown, but I suppose in Greenwich Village . . ."

"Oh, no one gets married in Greenwich Village," Brook interrupted airily. "One of my best friends from college is down there living with another girl. They're lesbians."

"Brook!" Again, her mother looked apoplectic. "How could you possibly use such a word at the dinner table?"

"Momma, there's nothing wrong with the word! There were quite a few lesbians in my class at Smith, and they couldn't have been nicer. Several of them propositioned me on numerous occasions, and I was mightily tempted. But alas," she sighed melodramatically, "I'm old-fashioned. I like boys." She smiled warmly at Hemingway. "Have you ever had a sexual experience with a man?"

"Brook, that's enough!" roared her father. "I know you're doing this to seem sophisticated, but you've gone too far! Now, talk about something else!"

"What? Curtains? Shopping? Dresses? That's all so boring. I want to live life to the fullest! I want every moment of my life to be a memorable experience! I'm sure you know what I mean, Mr. Hemingway, since you're going to be a writer. Do you?"

Hemingway looked at her with fascination.

"Actually, I think I do," he said.

"Is that why you left your hometown to go to the war? So you could experience life to the fullest and drink the cup of ecstasy to the last drop?"

"Yes, I guess that's pretty accurate."

"I hope both of you are wounded horribly!"

"Brook!" her mother exclaimed yet again. "I can't believe you'd say such a horrible thing to these fine young men!"

"Mother, pain enriches the soul," she said patiently, as if talking to a three-year-old. "Everyone knows that. Cesare and Mr. Hemingway are both beautiful young men, but if they come home all twisted and deformed, their personalities will be so much deeper. I'm sure it would help your writing, Mr. Hemingway."

Johnny looked aghast, as did Rachel.

"Brook," the latter said, in an even firmer tone, "I will remind you that your father was terribly wounded in the last war."

Brook had the grace to blush. "I'm sorry, Father. And I really didn't mean that I hope you both get wounded. I was just speaking . . . well, metaphorically, I guess. Father, couldn't we have some more wine? I feel like getting tight."

"I'll ring for Redmond," Rachel said, pressing the electric floor buzzer with her foot. "But, Brook, I'm deeply displeased with you. You seem to have forgotten all your manners, not to mention the fact that you're an engaged woman."

"What's that have to do with my conversation? Just because I'm engaged surely doesn't mean I have to be boring."

"I'm beginning to have second thoughts," her father said darkly, "about the value of college educations for women."

"Daddy, honestly," Brook sighed. "You're an absolute troglodyte."

Redmond appeared with the wine.

"Mr. Hemingway and Cesare would like some more wine," Rachel said, shooting a stormy glare at Brook, "but my daughter's had quite enough."

"Your sister's quite something," Hemingway said an hour later as Cesare drove him back downtown to the Village.

"Isn't she?" Cesare said. "I thought you'd get a kick out of her."

"Who's she engaged to?"

"Just what you'd expect: a rich, good-looking Yale man who'll probably bore her to tears a week after their wedding. I'm sure she'll cheat on him."

Hemingway guffawed.

"Oh boy," he said, "what a thing to say about your own sister!"

"Well, she will. Brook's a hellcat. Always has been and always will."

"But you love her?"

"Oh sure. Crazy about her. In fact, maybe a little too crazy. Of course, I'd never do anything. And speaking of which, it's such a fine evening, why don't we go get laid?"

Again, Hemingway laughed.

"What a great idea!" he said. "You know something? I really love New York!"

19.   ON THE EVENING OF TUESDAY, MAY 21, Cesare hugged his mother and sisters, all of whom were in tears despite Brook's wicked jest about him coming back wounded, coolly shook hands with Johnny, then taxied downtown to the Hotel Earle where he, Hemingway, and the other volunteers climbed into Red Cross buses for the mile drive to the French Line terminal on West Fifteenth Street. Each of the men either wore or carried in duffel bags the regular Army issue of an officer's overcoat, one raincoat, one cocky field service cap, one dress cap, four suits of heavy underwear, buckskin driving gloves, one pair of cordova leather aviator puttees, two pairs of officer's shoes, one knitted sweater, six pairs of heavy woolen socks, two khaki shirts, and one woolen shirt. Cesare also carried a suitcase with some civilian clothes. It was a warm evening with a full moon. When the buses arrived at the French Line dock, the men boarded an old tramp steamer called the *Chicago* that had been leased to the French Line for the duration of the war.

"Do you think this tub will make it to France?" Hemingway mumbled as he climbed up the gangway behind Cesare.

"I sort of doubt it will make it out of New York harbor," Cesare said. "The damned thing lists to starboard already."

"I hear there hasn't been any U-boat sinkings since March."

"Who'd bother to waste a torpedo on this? I wonder if there's a bar?"

"Let's stow our bags and go find out. I could use a drink."

To no one's surprise, the ship was anything but immaculate and the quarters to which they were assigned was an airless compartment filled with double-decker wooden bunks bolted to the rusty steel deck. When Cesare thought of the luxurious first-class accommodations he had traveled to Europe in with his mother, he was amused; but part of this adventure in his mind was not only to test himself in war, but to get the feel of real life his pampered youth had denied him.

But the *Chicago* did have a bar with a French barman

named Girard, who spoke English with a cockney accent. Cesare and Hemingway ordered a bottle of cheap, but surprisingly good French wine, and decided to celebrate their last night in America by getting drunk.

"I surely liked your family," Hemingway said with a slight slur after they had started on their second bottle. "And your sister . . ." He shook his head with admiration. "What can I say? Never met a girl like her. Or as pretty as her. Liked your parents too."

"They're both hypocrites," Cesare said coolly as he lit a cigarette and exhaled.

"What do you mean?"

"My stepfather plays the role of the great banker, the pillar of the community, who's shocked when anyone says something off-color. But he's a phony. Ever hear of Gloria Gilmore?"

"The movie star? Sure. I love her movies. She's gorgeous."

"You know how she got to be a star? My father bankrolls her movies, just like Mr. Hearst bankrolls Marion Davies."

"You mean, Gloria Gilmore is your father's tootsie?"

"That's exactly what I mean. She's been his mistress for years. He's rented her a big, gaudy pseudo-Spanish mansion in Hollywood, and he goes out there whenever he gets the chance to fuck her through the floor."

"No kidding. Does your mother know about it?"

"Oh sure. She's no fool."

"Doesn't it bother her?"

"Of course. But she pretends Gloria Gilmore doesn't exist. I love my mother dearly, but I have to admit she's a bit of a hypocrite too. So, Ernie, my friend"—he took a final drag on the cigarette, then put it out in the ashtray—"it's a wicked world we live in."

"Amen to that."

"But we'll be heroes and make the world good and clean."

"Do you believe that?"

Cesare smiled slightly.

"Of course not. Let's finish the bottle."

When they had, Girard, the bartender, brought them another.

"This one's on the house," he said. Then he lowered his voice. "I thought you chaps might be interested in a little inside information. There's a girl on board."

"No kidding?"

"Her name's Gaby. She's supposed to be the daughter of one of the officials of the French Line. She's not bad-looking, and it's said she'll fuck anything in pants. Thought you might like to know. The Captain's taking us on the southern route to Bordeaux to avoid U-boats, so we'll be at sea at least nine or ten days. Wouldn't want you chaps to be bored."

Giving them a knowing wink, he took the empty wine bottle back to the bar.

"Interesting," Hemingway said, refilling his glass.

"Very interesting," Cesare agreed. Then he laughed. "We'll fuck Gaby and make the world safe for democracy!"

"Hey! Let's drink to that!"

Which they did.

The *Chicago* steamed down the Hudson River on the morning tide, passing Battery Park as it moved into New York Bay. Cesare, feeling a bit hungover, made his way to the galley to get some hot coffee, then went out on the deck where Hemingway joined him.

"Forget breakfast," Cesare said as the two young men leaned on the starboard rail watching the Statue of Liberty. "I took a look at it. It looks like dog food."

"I don't feel much like eating anyway," Hemingway said. "So that's the Libber of Goddessty."

"Huh?"

Hemingway pointed to the giant green statue.

"I saw it when I went up to see Grant's Tomb," he said. "There were a bunch of bums hanging around the tomb. They offered to give me a blow job for seventy-five cents, but I politely declined. Sort of shocked me, though."

"Welcome to New York," Cesare said with a laugh. "Hey, look."

He pointed forward to the bow where a young girl in a white middy blouse and brown skirt had just appeared. She had brown hair tied back with a dark green ribbon.

"As I live and breathe," Hemingway said in a low voice, "that must be the notorious Gaby!"

"Shall we go introduce ourselves?"

"Why not? It's practically our patriotic duty."

"Let me get rid of this coffee mug."

Cesare took a final sip, then hurried to the galley to return the mug. When he got back out on deck, he saw that Hemingway had gone to the girl and was already talking to her.

"Pushy bastard," Cesare muttered to himself as he went forward. "You might have waited for me," he groused to Hemingway. Then he smiled at the girl. *"Vous êtes Gaby?"*

The girl, who was rather pretty with hazel eyes, smiled at him.

"Vous parlez français?" she said.

"Assez bien."

"Hey, this isn't fair," Hemingway said. "I don't *parlez*. Speak English. She speaks it."

"My name's Cesare Savage. I guess this big lug has already introduced himself. We're going to save your country from the Huns."

"How very nice," she said, with a heavy French accent. "You two big, strong soldiers I'm sure will kill many nasty Germans. We French will owe you a big debt, so let me pay back a little of it right now."

She came up to Cesare and kissed him on the lips, at the

same time surprising him by gently squeezing his genitals. Then she did the same to Hemingway, who literally gaped.

"Tonight," she said, "I'll be in that lifeboat." She pointed to the nearest starboard lifeboat. "See you then. Bye bye."

Smiling, she gave each of them a coy little wave, then went to the nearest door and disappeared inside.

Hemingway grinned at Cesare.

"Can you beat that?" he whispered. "She actually goosed me! Boy, they don't do that back in Oak Park!"

"Ernie, old boy, I think we've hit pay dirt. I'll flip you to see who goes first."

He pulled a quarter from his pocket.

"Heads, I go first," Hemingway said. "Tails, you."

Cesare flipped the coin.

"Tails!" he announced. "Sorry, Ernie, but you get sloppy seconds."

"I'm glad this isn't the *Titanic*."

"What do you mean?"

A wide Hemingway grin.

"Plenty of lifeboats."

Among the seventy Red Cross volunteers on the *Chicago* was a young man who wore steel-rimmed glasses named Bill Horne. That night, Bill, Hemingway, and several others were shooting craps in the ship's bar when Cesare, who had known Bill Horne at Princeton, came in, looking a bit disheveled. He came up to Hemingway, who had just rolled a lucky seven.

"It's your turn," Cesare said, smoothing his hair.

"How was it?" Hemingway asked.

"She smells like a goat, but she knows her business."

The other young men started peppering them with questions. Cesare explained about Gaby as Hemingway went out on deck to find love in a lifeboat.

After two days of beautiful weather, as the *Chicago*

neared Bermuda it encountered a terrible storm. The rusty tub wallowed and rolled in the heavy seas, giving Hemingway a first-class case of seasickness. As he vomited into a steel bucket, filling the sleeping compartment with a horrible stench, he groaned and said to Cesare, "I think I've just smelled death."

Brook Savage had also just smelled death.

"Brad Dexter's been killed in France," she said to her mother, hanging up the phone in the drawing room of the Fifth Avenue house. "That was his mother. She got a telegram from the War Department. Oh Momma, I feel so terrible."

She sank into a sofa and burst into tears. Her mother, looking distressed, came over and sat beside her, hugging her.

"Oh darling, I'm so sorry," Rachel said. "How did it happen?"

"Some artillery shell just blew him up into pieces. And he was only twenty-two. Oh God, I hate this damned war! All these wonderful young men being killed, and for what?"

Rachel squeezed her affectionately. "I know," she said, thinking of Cesare.

"Brad wanted to get married last summer before he shipped out, but I said, 'Let's wait.' It was so damned selfish of me."

"Why selfish?"

"Oh, in the back of my mind was the thought that he might get killed and I didn't want to be a widow. And now, he has been killed, and I'm not even his widow. I'm . . ." She shrugged. "What? His ex-fiancée, I guess. But he so wanted to make love to me, and I held out so I could be 'pure' for him. How stupid of me. We wanted each other, and now he's dead. I just feel sick about it."

"Darling Brook, you did the right thing . . ."

"No I didn't, Mother! The one thing I could have given Brad I didn't because of some silly convention that's totally out-of-date, and now it's too late for him. He'll never know how I really felt about him. That beautiful young body gone . . . Oh, it's such a terrible, terrible waste . . ."

She began to cry her heart out.

"Brook, I didn't realize how deeply you felt about him," her mother said.

"I didn't either until now," she sobbed. "Now that he's gone." After a while, she sat up and dried her eyes. "I thought I was in love with him," Brook sighed. "I certainly was attracted to him, you know, physically, and I liked him and had fun with him. But I don't know if I loved him. I just didn't think about it much. He asked me to marry him, and you and Father were thrilled because he was, you know, from the right kind of family and all that, so I just said yes. But now, I'm not sure. I think I was just a silly, vapid debutante, which I don't really want to be."

"The only objection I had to Brad was his religion. I mean, you know I'd much prefer your marrying someone in the Jewish faith." She paused. "What do you want to be, Brook?"

"Do you think I know?" she said bitterly. "Oh, I rattle on about wanting to live life to the hilt, but I don't know what that means. And now that I think about it, all those silly things I said to Cesare and that sweet Hemingway boy, you know, about getting wounded so they'd feel things more deeply . . . I mean, that was just junk that I got out of a poetry class at Smith, and I must have hurt Daddy as well as them."

"It wasn't the most tactful thing to say."

"But I don't want to be tactful! I want to be me, whatever that is. I want to be desperately in love with someone. But I don't think I was desperately in love with Brad. Now I think all I was trying to do was the conventional thing by marrying Brad and being a mother and all that, but trying desperately to be unconventional at the same time. And I suppose that's impossible. And now that he's dead, I think maybe I really did love him much more deeply than I supposed." She looked at her mother rather defiantly. "But I'll tell you one thing: I'm through with all this phony 'staying pure' stuff. Brad's dead, and life's too short. The next man I want and who wants me I'm going to bed with. And if that shocks you, Momma, I just can't help it."

20. LETTER FROM ERNEST HEMINGWAY TO HIS FAther, Dr. Clarence Hemingway, in Oak Park, Illinois.

June 5, 1918

Dear old Dad,

The Chicago finally made it to Bordeaux on Sunday, June 1. A beautiful city with mist on the surrounding vineyards—it was hard to believe France was at war. We were given a twelve-hour leave, and Bill Horne, Cesare Savage, and I went sightseeing, ate some great food, and drank a bit too much of the fabulous local wine. Bill is a great guy, a Princetonian like Cesare. Both have become great pals. Cesare's family entertained me at dinner in New York. His father is a big banker on Wall Street. They live in a fancy mansion on Fifth Avenue.

Hemingway went on to describe how they had taken a train to the Gare du Nord in Paris where they began to feel the war. Soldiers were everywhere in the great city, and

Parisians could hear the German artillery in the distance. At times, the Huns even lobbed shells into the city, which put everyone on edge. The Americans were billeted at the Hotel Florida on the Boulevard Malesherbes, which was run by the Y.M.C.A. The young men went sightseeing, and Hemingway was starting to pick up some French, though he reported that Cesare was fairly proficient at the language. He also noted that Paris was overrun with French policemen in capes on bicycles who were called hirondelles, which meant swallows. In closing, he said they were scheduled to leave by train for Milan the next Thursday night. He closed it:

> Your old kid,
> Ernie

The long, silver Rolls-Royce limousine with the gray-uniformed chauffeur pulled over to the side of the Boulevard Malesherbes and the rear window rolled down. A beautiful and very soignée lady in a smart feathered hat called out to the two young men in the brown uniforms with strapped puttees on their lower legs: "You! Americans! Come with me."

Cesare and Hemingway, who had been strolling on the tree-lined avenue after a rather drunken lunch, stared at each other.

"Who's she?" Hemingway asked.

"No idea," Cesare responded. "But I think we've hit pay dirt again. Come on."

He walked to the curb. The woman had opened the door. Cesare gave her a mock-gallant salute and climbed in.

"Bonjour," he said. "Where are we going?"

The lady gave him a Sphinx-like smile.

"You'll see."

After Hemingway had climbed in beside Cesare and

closed the door, the chauffeur pulled away from the curb.

"My name's Cesare," he volunteered. "I'm from New York. And this is my friend, Ernest Hemingway."

"I have no interest in your names or where you're from," the lady said. She was dressed in an extremely smart gray suit with small white feathers around her neck. She wore elegant, tight-fitting gloves and spats on her shoes.

"Then what are you interested in?" Cesare asked.

"What do you think?"

Hemingway and Cesare exchanged looks. They both shrugged slightly, then leaned back in the leather seats and remained silent.

Fifteen minutes later, the limousine pulled up in front of an elegant eighteenth century mansion in the faubourg Saint-Germain. The chauffeur hopped out to open the rear door. The lady said to them: *"Suivez-moi."*

Then she got out of the car and walked to the front door. Hemingway and Cesare got out of the car and followed her. A liveried butler had opened the front door of the mansion. The woman went inside, removing her hat and giving it to the butler. Hemingway and Cesare followed her inside, looking at the butler but saying nothing. They came into an elegant, marble-floored entrance hall with a gorgeous balustraded staircase that the lady began to climb.

"Montez," she said to them.

Again, they obeyed. When they reached the second floor, they followed her down a corridor lined with oil paintings to an elaborately carved door that she opened. She led them into a large room lined with pale yellow silk and furnished with antiques. After they had followed her into the room and closed the door, she stood in the center of the room and began to take off her clothes. They watched her, barely able to believe what they were seeing.

She removed the jacket of her suit with the seductive expertise of a stripper and dropped it on the scarlet and gold Savonnerie rug. Then her blouse. Sitting in an elegant chair, she removed her spats, then her shoes. Standing up again, she unbuttoned her skirt and let it drop down her legs. Stepping out of the skirt, she unlaced her corset and dropped it on the floor.

Totally nude, she stood for a moment as the two young Americans ogled her voluptuous flesh. Then she said, "Well? I don't have all day. My husband will be home soon."

Hemingway and Cesare again exchanged looks. Then they started to take off their uniforms. When they were both buck naked, the lady examined them with her cool eyes.

"Very nice," she said. "You are both *bien montés,* well hung. Very good-looking. I have always been curious about how Americans make love. We will do a *trio ardent.*"

She walked to the Louis XV bed and turned down the yellow silk spread. Lying on the satin sheets, she spread her legs and opened her arms. Her armpits were hairy.

"Come," she said. "Both at once."

Hemingway and Cesare went to the bed and climbed on. She pulled them both down against her body.

"I don't know what to do," Hemingway muttered.

"Just follow your instincts," said the lady, "and thank your lucky stars."

"This is my kind of war," Hemingway exclaimed an hour later when they had returned to the Boulevard Malesherbes. The butler had shown them out the back door of the mansion. They had found a taxi and driven to a bar near the Hotel Florida where they ordered drinks on the sidewalk. "Do you have any idea who she was?"

"Nope, but who cares? It was fabulous," Cesare said, sipping his red wine. "Like the orgies we used to have in Cuba."

"But it was all so impersonal, so unromantic!"

"That's the idea. Nothing but sex."

Hemingway finished his wine and signaled the waiter for a refill.

"Do you remember her address?"

"No. Do you?"

"No, but I'd sure like to see her again."

"You won't."

"She must have a rich husband. That house was gorgeous."

"She's probably married to an impotent banker. This is how she amuses herself."

"*Vive la France. Vive les* impotent husbands."

They spent the next few days sightseeing: Napoleon's tomb, the Eiffel Tower, the Arc de Triomphe, Montmartre, the Folies Bergères. On their last night before leaving for Milan, they hired a guide the hotel concierge recommended to show them "the real Paris," not the tourist Paris.

"For a hundred francs," the guide said, "I'll take you to the most famous *maison de passe* in the city."

"What's that?" Hemingway asked Cesare.

"Whorehouse. Let's do it."

"I can't afford fifty francs."

"It's on me." The guide drove them to the historic Chabanais beside, of all places, the Bibliothèque Nationale. They got out of the car and followed him to the front door, where an attendant admitted them. They were taken down a short hall to a room that was dimly lit. The room was unfurnished. On the opposite wall were a series of slits from which light emanated.

"Look through the slits," the guide said.

They went to the slits and peered through.

"Goddamn!" Hemingway whispered. "Will you look at that!"

On the other side of the slitted wall was a large room filled with men and women in various stages of undress.

Most of the men who still wore anything had on uniforms:
French, English, and Italian. The women, obviously
whores, were drinking champagne and fucking.

Cesare started laughing.

"What's so funny?" Hemingway asked.

"Look at the woman over there on the left. The one the
English guy is screwing. Does she look familiar?"

Hemingway gasped.

"Oh my God," he whispered. "It's our friend, the lady
in the silver Rolls-Royce!"

The Red Cross volunteers left the Gare de Lyon for the
overnight trip to Milan on the *Paris Lyon Mediterranée*
train, which passed through the French Alps, passage
through neutral Switzerland being forbidden. At noon the
next day, the train entered the great Garibaldi Station in
Milan, and the volunteers were taken to the Hotel Victoria
in the heart of the city. They were told they would have
thirty-six hours before leaving for the town of Schio, near
Lake Garda, where Cesare, Hemingway, Bill Horne, and
almost two dozen other volunteers had been assigned.

Then they were briefed about the war situation. Eight
months earlier, in the previous October, German and Austrian troops had invaded northeastern Italy, attacking the
Italian Army at a small hill town named Caporetto. After
savage fighting, the Italians were driven almost seventy
miles back to the banks of the Piave River, just north of
Venice. Italy's chief allies, the British and the French, were
so alarmed by this defeat that they sent six divisions of
Allied troops to join the defeated Italians and hold the
line—for if the Germans and Austrians could cross the
Piave River, there would be nothing to stop them from taking Venice and the whole industrial center of Italy would
be in danger. Since then, the Allied line had held. But there
was frequent shelling from the Austrians, as well as sniper

fire, so that Allied injuries were high. It would be the job of the ambulance drivers to get the wounded to hospitals.

Meanwhile, Cesare, Hemingway, and others were given a gruesome introduction to carnage when they volunteered to help clean up the remnants of an exploded munitions factory outside Milan. Both young men were repulsed by what they saw and smelled—body parts of the munitions workers who had been blown apart impaled on distant trees and fences—but as Cesare said, "We'd better get used to blood and guts."

Early Sunday morning, the men assigned to Schio returned to the Garibaldi Station in Milan and climbed aboard a train that took them across the Lombardy plain to Vicenza. There they boarded six of the gray, top-heavy Fiat ambulances they would be driving and were taken as passengers northwest into the Dolomite foothills to the town of Schio where they were put up in a limestone building with a paved courtyard that had formerly been a woolen mill. They were taken to the second floor where, in a long, narrow room, two rows of cots had been put up in front of casement windows and beneath a raftered ceiling that sported an American flag. By now, it was night. And since it had been a long day, the men stowed their gear and went to bed.

In the morning, the volunteers were instructed that every other day a new recruit would make the ten-mile ambulance drive with a veteran to the front in the mountains where injured men would be picked up, taken back to clearing stations called *smistamenti*, and then driven to their assigned hospitals. Cesare made his first trip that day with a chain-smoking driver from Chicago named Dave Casati who had been there six months and was bored to distraction.

"So, what brought you here to this stupid war?" Dave asked as he drove up the pebbled, twisty mountain roads toward the beautiful, sun-dappled Dolomites.

"My father was Italian, and I had a year of medical school, so I thought I could be of some help," Cesare said. "How's the food in the barracks?"

"Pretty good, actually," Dave said. "Spaghetti every night and lots of stews—the rabbit stew's pretty damned good. They give you plenty of red wine that isn't bad. Once a week they give us Americans fried eggs for breakfast so we won't get homesick—although I already am. Then there's a restaurant in Schio called the Due Spadi where they have great antipasto."

"What's the girl situation?"

"Hah: that's a laugh. The girl situation is that there aren't any except the whores at the Villa Rosa."

"Sounds sort of grim."

"Oh well, this stupid war can't last too much longer. They're running out of people to kill. I have yet to figure out what this fucking war is trying to prove."

"To make the world safe for democracy."

"Oh yeah, I forgot."

21. CESARE SAW HER ONE WARM SUMMER'S EVENING as he and Hemingway were eating dinner at the Due Spadi in the center of Schio. She was a tall blond, very young and beautiful, well dressed, and she was walking past the restaurant.

"Look at that," Cesare said, putting down his fork and staring. "Isn't she lovely?"

"Yeah, not bad."

"Not bad? You big lunkhead, she's a Botticelli in the

flesh. And Dave told me there weren't any women in this town! He just doesn't have eyes. Be back in a minute."

He got up from the table, wiping his mouth on his napkin, then dropping it on his chair, and hurried out of the restaurant onto the street. It was their second week in Schio and both of them were getting used to the routine. Now he hurried down the street, which was almost deserted, and came up behind the girl.

"Scusa," he said, speaking Italian. "Can you tell me what time it is?"

She looked at him a moment with the most enchanting blue-green eyes. Then she looked down at his wristwatch, a new development that had become popular during the war.

"Is your watch broken?" she said.

"I forgot to wind it."

She looked at the jewelry shop directly across the street. Above its door was a large round clock. She pointed at it. He looked at it, then smiled at her and shrugged.

"I'm a terrible liar," he said. "The truth is, I just wanted to meet you." He removed his cap. "My name is Cesare and I'm from New York."

"So you're an American?" she said, in lightly accented English. "I thought you might be by your accent. I knew you certainly couldn't be from around here."

"Would you join me and my friend for a drink? He's a most delightful fellow, wants to be a writer."

"You're very kind, but I really couldn't. I'm meeting my aunt. Good evening, Cesare from New York."

She started down the street again. He hurried after her.

"Perhaps some other evening?" he said. "I'd love to take you to dinner."

Again, she stopped and looked at him.

"I'm afraid I couldn't. I'm returning to Rome tomorrow."

"Rome? You live there?"

"Yes. I was just paying a visit to my aunt. My cousin's rather ill."

Again, she started down the street. Again, he hurried after her.

"Won't you at least tell me your name?" he asked.

"Antonia. Now, please don't bother me."

They looked at each other a moment. Then she walked away. Cesare watched her until she turned a corner.

Then he went back to the restaurant and sat down.

"So?" Hemingway said, refilling his wineglass. "Did you make a conquest?"

"No. But I'm going to see her again."

"Why?"

"Because she's enchanting."

"Did you get her name?"

"Yes. Antonia, and she lives in Rome. I'll find her."

Hemingway laughed.

"There's probably only about fifty thousand Antonias in Rome. Besides, you're stuck here, which isn't exactly Rome."

"It doesn't matter. I have family in Rome, and my grandmother knows everybody in the city. I'll find her. And someday, she's going to be my wife."

Hemingway laughed again.

"You'd better lay off the vino. I think you're losing what few wits you have."

"I'm not drunk. I'm dead sober. Sometimes, magic happens in life. And Ernie, old boy, magic has just happened to me."

"Brook, you know I'm so very much in love with you," said the clean-cut Lieutenant in the uniform of the Army Air Corps. "Couldn't we get married before I go back to France?"

Brook, who was wearing a pale aquamarine chiffon

dress, toyed with her champagne glass. The young couple was sitting in the Palm Court of the Plaza Hotel.

"Alex, I'm very fond of you . . ." she began.

" 'Fond'?" he interrupted, grimacing. "Is that all?" He had dark brown hair and his name was Alex De Witt.

"Listen: you know I was engaged to Brad Dexter, who was killed in the war. That was a terrible blow to me, and I still haven't gotten over it. Now, from what you tell me, the war can't last much longer. So why don't we wait till it's over before we talk about marriage? And meanwhile, why don't we rent a room upstairs and just go up and make love?"

Alex stared at her as she puffed on her cigarette, a new habit she had taken up to shock people. Alex looked around the crowded room, then leaned close to her and lowered his voice.

"But, Brook, you're a lady!"

"Oh for God's sake, so what? Most of the ladies I know are going at it like bunny rabbits. I should have gone to bed with Brad when he wanted to, and now he's gone, and don't think I don't feel guilty about that. You're going back to the front in a few weeks, and what if you get shot down? I don't mean to sound gruesome, but it's certainly possible. This way, we'll both have something to remember."

"But I'm not doing any more flying. I've got a desk job. And I want to think of you as . . . well . . ."

"As what? A lady? The little wifey? Alex, grow up. That's out of style these days. I'm very attracted to you, and I'd love to go to bed with you, so let's do it."

"You make it sound like, I don't know, washing one's socks."

"Well, you're supposed to supply a little of the romance."

"But what would your parents say?"

"They won't know."

She stubbed out her cigarette and drank some more champagne.

"Have you done this before?" he whispered, again glancing nervously around.

"Would it matter to you?"

"Frankly, yes. I don't want my wife to have been shopped around."

"Really, Alex, you sound like something out of some dime romance. Now, you're not going to tell me that you haven't been catting around over in France."

"But that's different . . ."

"Oh yes, it's always different for the man. Alex, you're a sweetie and, as I said, I really am awfully fond of you. If you want to have a love affair, fine by me. I think it would be fun. If not, well, we're just wasting each other's time. So, how about it?"

"I've never seen you like this before . . ."

"You haven't been looking."

"I can't believe you'd cheapen yourself this way . . ."

"Darling, no one has ever said Brook Savage is cheap. I'm bloody expensive. So."

She picked up her blue beaded purse, stood up, and leaned over to kiss his forehead. He was too astonished to stand.

"Thanks for the drink. If you change your mind, call me."

As he continued to stare at her, she walked out of the Palm Court as a violinist and pianist began to play "Fascination."

Two hours later, Brook was stretched out on a chaise longue in her bedroom of her parents' Fifth Avenue house reading the latest issue of *Photoplay* when the phone rang. She picked it up.

"Hello?" She listened a moment, then smiled. "Oh Alex,

you are a darling! This sounds so much fun! You order up some champagne, and I'll be there in a half hour. Bye bye."

She hung up the phone, then got up and went to her bathroom door to check her reflection in a full-length mirror. The door to her room opened and her elder sister, Beatrice, came in.

"Who was on the phone?" she asked.

"Alex De Witt. Oh Bea, it's so exciting: he's rented us a room at the Plaza and I'm going over to spend the night with him!"

Beatrice closed the door, a look of shock on her face.

"You're going to spend the night?" she whispered.

"Well no, I'll come home after we've had a wonderful romantic evening, but isn't it exciting? He really is so good-looking! Of course, it was like pulling teeth to get him to do it, he really is so stuffy, like his family, but here we are!" She smiled and hugged her sister. "I'm off to become a fallen woman!"

"Brookie, do you think this is a smart thing to do? I mean, if he tells people, it could ruin your reputation . . ."

"Oh pooh, I haven't got any reputation to ruin. If Mother asks where I went, tell her I've gone to see a movie with Alex. She's dying for me to catch him, even though he's not Jewish, so she won't say anything."

"But this way, you may not catch him! You know what they say about buying a cow when the milk is free?"

"Sweetie, the rules have changed. This is the new way to catch a man. He'll marry me, you'll see. And if he doesn't, there's plenty more where he came from. Bye."

She blew her a kiss and left the room. Beatrice, who was very shy and bookish and still wore glasses, sighed and shook her head.

22. FIRST THERE WAS A COUGH, THEN A STRANGE
sound of *chuh, chuh, chuh*, then a whiny roar that decreased
swiftly, and then a huge white flash. "As when a blast fur-
nace door is swung open, and then a roar that started white
and went red and on and on in the rushing wind," Hemingway wrote later. "I tried hard to breathe but my breath
would not come and I felt myself rush bodily out of myself
and out and out and out all the time bodily in the wind. I
went out swiftly, all of myself, and I knew I was dead and
that it had all been a mistake to think you just died." But
then, he went on, he floated back to himself and realized
he was still, after all, alive.

It was a steamily hot night, July 8, 1918, shortly after
midnight at a place called Fossalta on the lower Piave
River. Hemingway had bicycled to a town called San Pedro
Novello to celebrate the Fourth of July holiday with his
pal, Bill Horne. Three days later, the Austrians had started
an offensive across the Piave River. The Italians had retal-
iated by arching 350 artillery shells across the river; the
Austrians sent back volleys from machine guns and boom-
ing fieldpieces—75s or 149s—along with burning phos-
phorous star shells that blazed the night sky.

One Austrian artillery shell, a Minenwerfer, had exploded next to Hemingway, killing the man next to him,
blowing off his legs, the stumps of which still twitched
even though the man was dead. Hemingway, who thought
he had been killed, his legs full of shrapnel and shrieking
with pain, had bravely picked up yet another soldier beside

him, whose chest had been riddled with shrapnel from the Austrian shell, and carried him, fireman style, back to the trenches. An Austrian searchlight blinked on. Hemingway pitched forward to the ground as an Austrian machine gun rat-tat-tatted, sending a barrage of bullets over his head. Gasping with pain, fading in and out of consciousness with shock, the would-be writer from Oak Park, Illinois, managed to stagger fifty yards back to the safety of the trenches carrying his wounded comrade, whose name he didn't even know.

"I ordered your favorite champagne, Veuve Clicquot," Lieutenant Alex De Witt said as Brook Savage came into the fifth-floor suite he had rented at the Plaza Hotel. The twenty-three-year-old Harvard graduate, who had proven himself an ace in the Army Air Corps in France, having shot down sixteen German Fokkers, was bursting with lust as he looked at the gorgeous Brook in her aquamarine chiffon dress and beaded bag. He had been shocked by her casual attitude toward sex earlier that day in the Plaza's Palm Court. But when she challenged him to sex first, marriage, perhaps, later, her attitude had been so truly revolutionary to a young man who had grown up with the conviction that "nice" girls didn't do anything more than, perhaps, necking, that he simply couldn't handle it. But when Brook left him, his lust and hormones triumphed. He didn't care about anything except having her. And, he thought, since Brook's mother was Jewish, maybe "they" did these things differently.

And here she was: the defining moment of feminine sexuality, standing in the doorway of the Plaza suite, his without any struggle. She had forced herself on him. It was so different from what she had experienced in his young life, he could hardly cope with it: before this, it had been he fighting to touch the young debutantes he lusted after.

But Brook had offered herself up on a silver platter.

He had loosened his tie and unbuttoned his collar. Now he stood up. Room service had brought up a round, wheeled table with a bottle of champagne in an ice bucket and toast and caviar. Alex had truly conventional ideas of seduction, not improved after two years in France. He was feeling much more awkward than Brook.

She closed the door and smiled.

"I'm so glad you called."

"You know, I . . . well, I feel a bit like a fool. You truly surprised me."

"Oh, come on, darling, I shocked the pants off you. Speaking of which, why don't you take off your pants? I'm dying to see what you look like."

"I thought we should have some caviar first . . ."

"Boring. Let's do it naked."

"Brook, you amaze me!"

"Good. Alex, you're not being in the least bit modern. If you read Sigmund Freud . . . you have heard of Sigmund Freud?"

"Isn't he that Viennese Jew?"

"That's one way of describing him. Perhaps not the best way. But he has shown us what life is really all about, and what life is really all about is sex. We desire each other, and there's no earthly reason why we shouldn't have each other. Don't you agree?"

"Yes, I suppose . . . Except . . ."

"I know. Oh, Alex, you're so damaged by all the garbage from the past. That I should be a virgin and that sex is dirty and all that baloney . . . We're two extremely attractive young people, blessed by the fact that we also happen to be rich and social, and we should just enjoy everything we were born with. Don't you agree? Oh, *do* take your clothes off. I so want to see you naked."

He stood up and started unbuttoning his shirt.

"Brook, you're so different . . . !"

"Thank God."

"I've never heard anyone talk the way you do . . ."

"You haven't been listening."

"This will be our secret."

"Of course, darling. Do you think I want to tell your mother I've seduced you?"

"Is that what you're doing?"

"Well, if it isn't, I don't know what it is."

"I want you so much!"

"Good. And vice versa."

"We'll still have a proper wedding?"

"Oh for God's sake, stop talking about weddings! Such a bore!"

Uncertainly, he started taking off his clothes. Brook came into the room and pulled her chiffon dress over her head, tossing it in a corner.

"Pour me some champagne," she said, "while you're disrobing."

"The waiter uncorked it. I hope it's not flat."

"Darling, I hope *you're* not flat."

Shirtless, he filled one of the tulip glasses with the Veuve Clicquot.

"How do you know so much about sex?" he asked.

"You'd be amused if you knew the truth."

"Amuse me."

"This is my first time."

"Oh no—really?"

"Really."

"You mean, you're a virgin?"

"Yes."

"My God, you intrigue me."

"Good."

"But you talk such a big game—I mean, you sound so sophisticated!"

She laughed.

"Alex, haven't you figured out yet that I can be, on occasion, absolutely full of horse manure?"

She accepted the tulip glass, sipped the champagne, then got nude. As did he. Naked, the two beautiful young people stood, examining each other.

"I like the fact that you don't have a hairy chest," Brook said. "I like smooth young men. And I adore the way your chest narrows down to that lovely vee of your waist. You're sort of like Michelangelo's *David*. I think he must have been in love with whomever his model for that statue was. Don't you?"

"I never thought about it. But I love your body. You really are gorgeous, Brook."

"We're both gorgeous. So, don't you see that it would have been criminal if we didn't make love?"

His impressive penis erect, he came to her and took her in his arms, planting a hot kiss on her lips.

"You'll never guess who was the first person who might have taken my virginity," she whispered mischievously.

"Was it someone I know?"

"I don't think so."

"Well then, tell me."

"It was my roommate at Smith, Lydia Ashley."

"A woman?"

"Yes. She propositioned me down in Greenwich Village. Of course I said no, being a proper young lady—or, at least, proper enough. But I'm glad I saved it for you."

"Do you mean that?"

"Yes."

"Brook, you've made me the happiest man in the world. I adore you."

"Hem, you're going to be all right," Cesare said as he helped transfer the mutilated young man into his ambulance.

"Oh God, Cesare . . . the pain . . ." Ernest Hemingway groaned. He was being carried on a stretcher. His right leg had been bandaged.

"I'm going to give you some more morphine the moment you're in the ambulance."

"Don't give me too much . . . I don't want to be addicted . . ."

"Don't worry, old man, we're going to take the best care of you and you're going to be doing the turkey trot before you know it . . ." He turned to the three other orderlies carrying the stretcher. "Okay, let's lift him into the ambulance . . . take it easy . . ."

"Cesare, the pain . . . it's killing me . . . the pain . . ."

"You're going to be fine, Hem. Just leave it to me."

At which point, yet another Austrian shell exploded above their heads in the sultry night sky.

23. THE EIGHTY-YEAR-OLD LADY IN THE SILVER DRESS with the many diamond rings on her fingers was elegant and beautiful despite her great age. She sat in a gilded chair upholstered with red silk in the *gran salone* of her palazzo on the Corso in Rome and looked at the young man in the rather shabby uniform standing before her.

"So, Cesare," Fiammetta Savage said, "you have been given a week's leave and you have come to see your old grandmother in Rome. You have done well to volunteer to come to Italy and drive ambulances. You didn't have to do it."

"I consider this my other country," the young man said. "You knew my grandfather."

"Your grandfather was a man of great charm and beauty. I remember him with great fondness. Even though you are not my flesh, you will stay with me here and I will do everything in my power to make you happy."

"You are very kind, Grandmomma—if I may call you that."

"Of course you may."

"Why," asked the silver-haired old man sitting next to Fiammetta, "do you so dislike my son, Johnny?"

The speaker was Justin Savage, who for many years had lived in Rome with Fiammetta, his wife.

"Because he called my father a murderer, which was never proven," Cesare said. "However, that wound is old. I suppose it is slowly healing."

"You say that your friend, Mr. Hemingway, has been badly wounded and is in a hospital in Milan."

"Yes, his right leg was hit with scrapnel, and they've operated on his right knee. He's in a great deal of pain, but I think he'll be all right in the long run. He was very heroic." Cesare grinned. "I think he's fallen in love with one of his nurses."

Fiammetta looked at Justin and smiled.

"Ah, youth," she said. "And you, my handsome Cesare: you say that you are in love?"

"Yes, Grandmomma. With a beautiful blond woman who lives in Rome and whose name is Antonia. She has an aunt in Schio. I would give anything if you could help me find her."

Fiammetta thought a moment. Then she said, "It must be Antonia Barberini. She has an aunt in the north. She's a charming girl from a distinguished family—the Barberinis have a Pope in the family, Urban VIII, and a number of Cardinals—but her branch of the family doesn't have much money. However, that would present no problem to you. Would you like me to invite her to dinner?"

Cesare's face lit up.

"Oh yes, Grandmomma! That would be splendid! And the sooner the better."

"The impatience of youth," Fiammetta said, with a slight smile. "Would tomorrow night be soon enough?"

The shiny black 1914 Fiat pulled up in front of the handsome brown building on the Via Ludovisi, a half block west of the Via Vittorio Veneto, and a chauffeur in a smart taupe uniform got out to deliver a note to the second-floor five-room flat rented by Claudia Barberini and her daughter, Antonia. The note was accepted by a maid, who took it to the drawing room where Claudia and her daughter were drinking post-breakfast coffee. Claudia, a handsome woman whose graying hair was piled on top of her head, opened the envelope and read its contents.

"How odd," she said to her daughter. "We're invited to dinner tonight by Mrs. Savage."

"Do you know her?" Antonia asked.

"I've met her several times, but I certainly don't know her well. She says she wants us to meet her grandson, Cesare, from New York."

"Cesare? From New York?" Antonia looked startled. Then she smiled.

"You know him?" her mother asked.

"It must be that American soldier who chased me down a street in Schio last month."

"Chased you?"

"Well, he introduced himself to me. I think he was trying to start a little romance. I had no idea his grandparents live in Rome."

"Would you prefer not going tonight?"

"Oh no, Momma. I'm dying to go. He's very good-looking."

And very rich, her mother thought. This might turn out quite interesting.

"I'm sure Mrs. Savage will have a piano," she said aloud. "You should be prepared to play something. Some Chopin, perhaps. Your Chopin is so good."

That evening, Cesare stood behind Antonia as she sat at Fiammetta's Steinway and played the E-flat Nocturne. When she finished, he applauded enthusiastically.

"That was lovely!" he exclaimed. "I've never heard anything so beautiful!"

"You're very kind," Antonia said, standing up.

"Please play something else!"

"I don't want to hold up dinner."

"There's plenty of time," Fiammetta said. She, Justin, and Claudia were seated in the gilt-swirling *gran salone*. "I'm sure we'd all love to hear something else."

"Well . . ." Antonia thought a moment. She was wearing a beautiful aquamarine dress with a string of pearls around her slender neck. Then she smiled rather mischievously at Cesare who was wearing a tuxedo. "This is for our American friend. I just learned it from a phonograph record. It's very catching."

She sat back down at the piano and started banging out "Alexander's Ragtime Band."

"Hey!" Cesare exclaimed, clapping his hands in time to the music. "That's my favorite song!"

When she was finished, there was another round of applause. Then the butler announced dinner, and the guests started for the dining room. Fiammetta took Antonia's arm.

"There's so little nightlife in Rome," she said, "especially since the war began. But I have a Victrola and some dance records. After dinner, you and Cesare can dance in here.

And I'll keep the old folks in the dining room."

To Antonia's surprise, the old woman winked at her.

"My grandson," she added, "tells me he's a very good dancer."

Two hours later, Cesare put the Victrola needle on a record of Jerome Kern's hit song from several years back, "They Wouldn't Believe Me." Then he took Antonia in his arms and started dancing to the dreamy music.

"It was nice of your grandmother to turn her drawing room into a dance hall for you," she said. "She's such a wonderful lady. I hope I can look like her when I'm her age—if I ever get there."

"You'll get there," he said. He pulled her closer to him and put his cheek on hers. She didn't resist him. "I'm the luckiest man in the world," he said.

"Oh? How so?"

"Because I'm dancing with the most beautiful girl in the world, and I'm in love with her."

"Really? You hardly know me. I have all sorts of bad habits."

"I don't care. I loved you from the first moment I saw you walking past the Due Spadi. You and I are going to be together for a long time. In fact, forever."

She closed her eyes, not sure of what to say, but thrilled by what he was saying.

"Could you love me?" he whispered.

"I . . . I don't know, I . . ."

"Then don't say anything. You will love me, I know. I'll make you love me."

"Perhaps . . ."

"Perhaps what?"

"Perhaps I already do."

The record ended. Cesare stopped dancing, put his arms

around her, and put his lips against hers. They kissed for almost a minute. Then Cesare released her.

"You're the best thing that's ever happened to me," he said. Then he walked to the Victrola to put on another record.

"Cesare's engaged to be married!" Rachel said, putting down the letter that had just arrived at her Fifth Avenue home. "To a Roman girl named Antonia Barberini. He says she's beautiful and sweet and he's wildly in love with her! Isn't that marvelous?"

She was eating breakfast with Johnny, who was buttering a piece of toast.

"When are they getting married? And where?"

"He's gone back to Schio now, but they're planning to get married in the fall in Rome. Your mother loaned him the money to buy the engagement ring. Oh, how I wish we could be there, but I suppose it's impossible unless the war ends."

"Yes, I don't think it's easy to get to Italy just now."

"But I'm so pleased for Cesare! You see, he's turning out to be a fine young man after all, isn't he?"

"I suppose." Johnny didn't sound too enthusiastic.

"Darling, you have to admit he did a good job in Cuba. And he's been so brave in the war . . . I wish you could say a good word for him just once."

"If I can think of the word, I'll say it. But I'm glad he's engaged, and I hope he'll be very happy. That doesn't mean I have to like him."

"You know, Johnny," she said, throwing down her napkin, "sometimes you make it very difficult for me to have any feeling for you at all." She was about to confront him about how hurt she was by his Gloria Gilmore escapades but her mother's voice stopped her.

She looked at him sadly for a moment, then left the room.

Johnny saw the hurt in Rachel. He was awash in guilt over Gloria. Alone, Johnny buried his face in his hands.

"God," he whispered to himself. "Why can't I give Gloria up? Why am I so damned weak? Rachel is ten times the woman she is—twenty! Why am I so goddamned weak?"

It began in the middle of September, 1918, like Poe's Red Death.

The first American case of Spanish influenza, as it came to be called, appeared in Camp Devens, an army camp thirty miles west of Boston. No one knows how or why, but on the very same day, the flu also reached Bombay. The epidemic spread around the world with incredible speed and ferocity. It was as if the four years of warfare that now swept all the way from the trenches in France across Europe and Asia to Vladivostok, four years of men killing and maiming other men, had caused a biblical reaction of deadly disease that swept the world, with only a few remote Pacific islands to escape it. The death toll in New York City was forty-five hundred a week; in Philadelphia, it was a thousand a day. Corpses piled up all over the world, and there was a severe shortage of coffins.

In Camp Devens, where it first broke out, raw recruits, instead of training for action in France, spent all day disemboweling the seventy to eighty corpses that came each day, carrying the intestines in steel slop buckets to be burned as far from the camp as possible. Then name tags were tied to the toes of the corpses and they were placed on the ground beneath canvas until coffins could be made.

Before it ran its course, this pandemic would kill twenty million people all over the world, as many as died in the Great War and the Russian Revolution combined. In the

United States, twice as many died from the flu as were killed in the war.

In the middle of October, two weeks before his marriage to Antonia in Rome, Cesare drove his Fiat ambulance back to the barracks in Schio. It had been a hard day; working by himself now, he had driven a dozen wounded men from the front to various hospitals. He was hungry and tired, sick of death and wounds, and sick of the war that, if it had had any point in the beginning, which was doubtful, now was nothing but totally meaningless slaughter. He had seen things during his months in Italy that were nauseating: the bloated, week-old corpse of a German pilot in a crashed biplane, the Mercedes star on its tail, the body swarming with flies. Fields strewn with bodies from both sides twisted by death into grotesque postures. Bomb-blasted farmhouses, dead defoliated trees, mud-filled bomb craters buzzing with mosquitoes. Total waste, meaningless and ugly. He longed for it all to be over, and he dreamed of his impending marriage and the joy of being with Antonia.

Parking his ambulance in the paved courtyard, he walked into the former woolen factory to be greeted by Captain James Gamble, a thirty-six-year-old Main Line aristocrat and Yale graduate, who was in charge of the ambulance unit.

"Savage, there's a telegram for you," he said, handing him an envelope. "It's from Rome. Must be from your fiancée."

Eagerly, he opened the envelope and pulled out the wire. As Gamble returned to his desk by the front door, he heard Cesare moan. He looked back to see him doubled over, holding his stomach as if he were in great pain. The moan grew to a howl.

"Good God, man, what's wrong?" Gamble cried.

"Antonia's got the Spanish flu!" he cried. "She's very

sick . . . her mother's afraid she may die . . . Oh, God, oh, God . . . Captain, I've got to go to Rome . . . You have to give me leave . . . Oh God, she can't die . . ."

"She has a very high fever," Claudia Barberini whispered to Cesare the next afternoon. "The doctor says you must be warned, that if you go in there you may catch it yourself . . ."

"I don't care," Cesare whispered back. They were standing outside Antonia's bedroom in the flat on the Via Ludovisi. "I have to see her . . . I can make her well. I know that sounds crazy, but my love will help her pull through. She can't die, Signora Barberini. She can't. I won't let her."

Claudia squeezed his hand.

"You're very sweet, Cesare," she said. "And very brave. Go in. But stay only a few minutes. She's very weak."

"Yes, yes, I understand."

Cesare opened the door and went inside the bedroom. It was a warm October afternoon, but the windows were closed and curtains had been pulled over them so that the high-ceilinged room was plunged into a penumbra. In the gloom, Cesare saw an elderly nun sitting beside the big bed in which Antonia was lying. He crossed the room, coming up beside the nun, who looked at him and put her finger to her mouth.

"She's sleeping," the nun whispered.

Cesare nodded, staring down at the beautiful, pale face of the woman he adored so much. There were beads of perspiration on her forehead, and her golden hair was spread out on her pillow like a halo. As he stared at her, his heart in agony, her head turned toward him and she opened her eyes.

"Cesare," she whispered. "My darling Cesare . . ."

The nun stood up and whispered, "Only a few minutes, my son."

"Yes, Sister."

As the nun went to the door, Cesare took Antonia's hand and raised it to his mouth to kiss.

"How did you get away from the front?" she whispered.

"They gave me leave to come see you. You're going to be all right, my darling. I'll be here with you until you're well again."

"You're so sweet, Cesare. What a good, kind heart you have."

Cesare thought briefly of Amanda Cartwright, who had told him he had no heart.

"My heart is good because of you, Antonia," he said. "I'm not a very good person or a very kind one, but loving you has made my whole world different. I'm a better person because of you."

She smiled up at him.

"What a nice thing to hear," she whispered. "And you've made me different too. I've never been so happy before . . . loving you has made my life so sweet and wonderful. Oh, Cesare, I can hardly wait till our wedding . . . And my dress is so beautiful . . . I think you'll be very proud of me . . ."

She started coughing, a terrible hacking cough that filled him with dread. He turned to the nun in the corner.

"Sister," he said, "is there some medicine?"

The nun hurried back to the bed and filled a glass with water from a crystal carafe. Then she leaned over and gently propped up Antonia's head, putting the glass to her lips.

"Take a sip," she said.

Antonia tried, but the coughing made her spew the water onto her sheet. The nun turned to Cesare and motioned for him to leave the room.

Cesare, a look of anguish on his face, went to the door and opened it. He looked back at the bed a moment, where Antonia was still coughing. Then he left the room and quietly closed the door.

"The coughing is getting worse," her mother said nervously.

"She's going to be all right," Cesare said grimly. "God won't let her die. He couldn't be that cruel."

Claudia took his hand.

"My dear Cesare," she said, "we must be prepared for the worst. In the meantime, I think we must pray."

"Yes, that's a good idea. I'm not very religious, but let's pray."

Holding hands, they both closed their eyes. Claudia said, "Our Lord in Heaven, we beseech Thee to come to the aid of our beloved Antonia, who is a good daughter of the church . . ."

She stopped as the bedroom door opened. They looked at the nun, who shook her head sadly.

"No!" Cesare cried. *"No!"*

He pushed past the nun and ran into the room.

"No!"

He ran to the bed and looked at Antonia, who seemed to be asleep.

"Antonia . . . !"

Frantically, he held her wrist. There was no pulse.

"Oh no!" he cried, bursting into tears as he knelt on the bed and held her in his arms, covering her dead face with kisses. "Antonia, come back . . . Please come back . . . You can't leave me . . . Without you, I'm nothing . . . Oh please come back . . . please . . ."

He held her in his arms, shaking with sobs, as the nun and Claudia came into the room. After a moment, the nun came up to him and put her hand on his shoulder.

"My son," she said, "she's now with God in Heaven."

"There is no God!" he cried. "And if there is a God, I hate Him for taking my love!"

The nun, a shocked look on her face, crossed herself.

Corporal Roger Gates was firing his fifty-caliber machine gun at a clump of trees from where sniper fire was coming when an ambulance pulled up from behind him. Gates stopped firing and looked back to see Cesare Savage jump out.

"Get back!" he yelled as Cesare ran toward him. "There're Hun snipers in the wood!"

Gates knew Cesare, who had been there many times picking up the wounded. He knew he wasn't armed.

"Give me your gun!" Cesare yelled as he jumped into the machine-gun nest on his belly. His face was red, covered with sweat. His bloodshot eyes looked manic.

"You're a noncombatant!" Gates yelled. "Get the hell out of here!"

"Give me your gun!" Cesare screamed, pushing him aside. As Gates stared in amazement, Cesare grabbed the machine gun and started shooting at the trees.

"Kill!" he screamed over and over. "Kill, kill, kill! Fuck this war! Fuck the flu! Kill, kill, kill!"

As the machine gun chattered maniacally, Gates and two other soldiers finally managed to subdue Cesare and drag him back to his ambulance.

They took him to a hospital in Treviso, because he had gone completely out of his head. It wasn't until three days later, when his mind returned to some sort of normality, that he learned he had killed fourteen Austrians.

To his amazement, an officer of the Italian Army visited him in the hospital and told him he had been awarded the Silver Medal for Valor for his courage under fire.

Cesare had become a war hero without even remembering what he had done.

In December, 1918, a few weeks after the Armistice that ended the Great War that had caused revolution in Russia and Germany and did not make the world safe for democracy, Captain Alex De Witt, who had been promoted and decorated for his gallantry, returned to New York on the battleship Florida, one of the first troop ships to return from France. Standing on the dock, part of the cheering crowd, was Brook Savage, looking beautiful in a mink coat with a matching mink hat. In the past few months, Brook and Alex had exchanged letters; and while Brook had been wildly attracted to Alex physically, it was his passionate love letters to her that made her fall in love with him. She was so excited that when she actually spotted him at the rail of the battleship, standing with hundreds of other returning troops, she jumped up and down like a little girl waving at him and shouting with excitement. When he spotted her, he waved and shouted back as a band played "Over There," "When Johnny Comes Marching Home," and "America the Beautiful."

Twenty minutes later, when he finally managed to come down the crowded gangway to the dock, Brook saw him embrace an elderly and rather fat woman in a sable coat, then hug a tall man in a black overcoat trimmed with Persian lamb who wore a top hat. Brook made her way through the crowd to Alex, who looked at her with a rapturous smile.

"Brook!" he exclaimed, hugging her and kissing her on the lips.

"Welcome home, darling," she exclaimed.

"Gosh, you look beautiful!" he said with endearingly boyish gush. Then he turned to the older couple behind him.

"Mom, Dad," he said, "I want you to meet the girl I'm crazy about who I hope will be my wife."

The elder De Witts looked somewhat less than enthusiastic.

Two nights later, after a romantic dinner at Delmonico's, Alex proposed in earnest, presenting Brook with a beautiful diamond and emerald engagement ring. Brook, thrilled and wildly in love, accepted him with unmistakable ardor.

It was all like a fairy tale.

But two days later, as they lunched at the Plaza to discuss wedding plans, a tiny cloud appeared on the horizon.

"Brook," Alex asked, "you've never told me: are you particularly religious?"

"Not as much as my mother wishes," she said, sipping a martini. "She raised me in the Jewish religion. But the fact is, I'm an atheist, although when I get older I'll probably start believing in God just as an insurance policy. Why?"

"Well, my mother has asked me where we plan to get married. She wants St. Thomas on Fifth Avenue, which is our church. But of course, I know that your mother, being Jewish and all that, might want us to get married in a . . . you know"—he looked a bit uncomfortable—"synagogue."

She looked at him rather coolly.

"Would that bother you?" she asked.

"No, it wouldn't bother me," he said, almost too quickly. "But I think it would bother Mother. She's pretty, uh, religious."

"Does that mean she doesn't like Jews?"

"Oh, no! And of course she doesn't think of you as being Jewish, since your father isn't."

"Yes, but I am Jewish, if you want to get technical," she said. "So what do you want?"

"I want whatever will make you happy, of course. But it would make my parents happier if we did, you know, get married in a church rather than . . . you know. And Father has promised me that he'll build us a big house on Long Island and pay for it himself if we . . . well, you know . . ."

He looked rather miserable as he dived into his martini.

"In other words, he's bribing us?"

"Oh no!"

"Come on, Alex, let's face facts: that's exactly what he's doing. If I agree to get married in St. Thomas, he'll build us a dream house on Long Island. Well, my mother has a helluva lot more money than even your father, and I can tell you one thing is certain: she's not going to be happy if we don't get married in a synagogue. So where does that leave us? I mean, we could start a bidding war between your parents and mine, but I think that would be rather tacky, don't you?"

"Oh, definitely. Definitely. Oh dammit, I never even thought about this until Mother brought it up. I mean, it makes me furious. Why don't we just go down to City Hall and have a civil ceremony?"

"We can't."

"Why?"

"It would hurt my father. I know he wants me to have a real wedding with all the frills. And frankly, I want it myself. I mean, a girl dreams about her wedding all her life. Why should I be cheated?"

"You shouldn't, of course. But the decision's up to you. Whatever you want, I'll be happy with."

She ordered another martini thinking.

"All right," she finally said. "St. Thomas it is. I know it's what you really want."

He broke into a smile and squeezed her hand.

"Thanks, darling," he said. "That's really swell of you. And our honeymoon—! Well, I'll take you anywhere in the world!"

"Is that a promise?"

"Absolutely."

She smiled slightly.

"Then I want to go to Jerusalem."

His smile faded, and he looked rather shocked.

"Jerusalem?" he said, making it sound like a dirty word. "Why in the world would you want to go there?"

"My mother had given money to fund some Jewish settlements, and I'd like to see Palestine. I'd also like to see Jerusalem, being Jewish. You know, it's a rather important city. A lot of things happened there, like Christianity."

He shrugged.

"Well, if you want to, we'll go. But I hope you're not going to wear a prayer shawl or something."

Brook eyed him rather coolly.

"Alex, I think we'd better get something straight right now, before it's too late. Are you an anti-Semite?"

He looked shocked.

"No!" he exclaimed. "As you said about yourself, I'm really not very religious at all. Except"—he frowned and paused—"Well, during the war, there were several times I thought I was about to get killed, and once my plane's engine caught on fire. I guess I started thinking about God then. But I have nothing against Jews, really."

Brook sucked on a cigarette, eyeing him.

"But your parents have tried to talk you out of marrying me, haven't they?"

He squirmed rather uncomfortably.

"Well, to be honest, my mother's not happy about all this. But I don't care! I love you! To hell with Mother!"

"So your family is anti-Semitic, but you're not?"

He looked annoyed.

"Dammit, Brook, why are you harping on this?" he said.

"Because I've turned my back on what should be my religion, and I guess I'm feeling a little guilty about it. And that crack you made about a prayer shawl . . ."

"It was just a joke. A stupid joke."

"I wonder."

They looked at each other. Then he smiled and raised her right hand to his lips to kiss.

"We're going to be the happiest couple in the world. You'll see."

Am I making a horrible mistake? she thought. Is Mother right?

Brook Savage married Alexander Chapman De Witt III in St. Thomas Church on Fifth Avenue in February, 1919. Over seven hundred people attended the lavish reception in the nearby University Club; newspapers, glad to report something beside war news, called it the wedding of the season. The bride was beautiful. Her sister, Beatrice, was her Maid of Honor.

One of the few positive things to emerge from the horrible war was that, because of the enormous number of amputations, there had developed great advancements in the technology of prosthetics. Johnny, wishing to be able to walk down the aisle with his daughter, had in January acquired an artificial leg so that, for the first time in years, he was able to walk without crutches. Consequently, the wedding was an occasion for him of double joy.

But Rachel, sitting in the front pew on the bride's side, was not quite so happy. She had reluctantly acquiesced in the St. Thomas decision. But she knew that the senior De Witts were telling their friends around Manhattan they couldn't understand why their son was marrying "that Jewess."

"Brook, stop staring at that sailor," Alex snarled two weeks later. He and his bride were sitting at an outdoor café near the King David Hotel in Jerusalem. It was a balmy late afternoon.

For three days they had seen the settlements and the sites of the holy city. Rachel had even arranged for them to have tea with Sir Herbert Samuel, the civilian High Commissioner; all of which had thrilled Brook and driven Alex to drink.

"What sailor?" Brook said.

"Don't give me that malarkey. That young Greek sailor over there at that table. You've been ogling him for the past twenty minutes."

"Alex, you're drunk. I haven't been 'ogling' him, though he is good-looking, and I certainly have the right to look at good-looking men if I want to."

"The hell you do. And there was that waiter in Rome. You practically drooled over him. And two nights ago at the hotel that young American Jew from New York you insisted on buying a drink at the bar. You're a goddamn flirt, and I don't like it."

"Alex, you're doing your best to turn this honeymoon into a nightmare. If you persist in this ugly behavior, I'll take the next boat back to New York—and I'll go alone."

"You try that and you'll be sorry."

"Don't you dare threaten me!"

"I mean it: you'll be sorry! Let's get one thing clear: in this marriage, I'm the boss. You do what I say, you understand?"

Brook, who was wearing a smart white suit with a matching white hat, looked at him a moment. Then she stood up from the table.

"I'm going back to the hotel," she said. "When you sober up, I'll expect an apology."

She walked away from his table, going through the crowded café. When she reached the table where the young sailor was sitting by himself, sipping a coffee, she leaned down, took his face in her hand, and kissed him on the lips. As the sailor gaped with surprise, she straightened and looked back at Alex defiantly. Then she walked down the street toward the hotel.

A half hour later, she was sitting in the bathtub in their suite when Alex slammed open the door and stumbled inside the bathroom.

"You slut," he slurred, weaving over to the tub. "You goddamned slut."

As she screamed, he reached down and grabbed her neck with both hands, starting to choke her.

"Alex!" she gasped, pounding his arms with her fists, then trying to pry his hands loose from her throat. But his hands were like steel.

"I'm going down!" he yelled. "My plane's on fire . . ."

He pushed her head down under the water. She was about to lose consciousness when he suddenly released her, pulling her up out of the water. As she gasped for breath, he stumbled back from the tub.

"I'm sorry . . ." he said. He looked in shock, as if the knowledge of what he had just done had sunk into his drunken brain and truly frightened him. "I . . . forgive me . . . Oh Christ, I thought I was back in my plane over France . . ."

As Brook rubbed her sore neck, he stumbled back out of the bathroom, saying, "I need a drink . . ."

It was not the first time he had thought he was back in the war.

Brook wondered if it was the alcohol or if he was going mad.

PART SEVEN

BOOTLEGGERS

24. "CESARE, THERE'S MONEY TO BE MADE FROM THIS crazy new Prohibition law. I mean, big money. And you're in a great position to make it."

The speaker was Arnold Rothstein. He and Cesare were having dinner together at the elegant Hotel Nacional in Havana. Both men wore tuxes. It was a week before Christmas, 1920, and Rothstein was taking a short vacation that was also part business.

"Tell me how," Cesare said.

"You've been down here since the war, so you probably have no idea how Prohibition is changing things. Those damn fool Temperance people think they can change people's habits by passing a law, but of course all they've done is change how people drink. And ironically, the poor man is the one who's getting really screwed, because he hasn't got his saloon to go to anymore and booze is so expensive, he can't afford it. But the rich are drinking plenty—hell, if anything, they seem to be drinking more. And I should know, because I'm bringing in illegal booze across the Canadian border and making a bundle doing it. I'm also bringing it in from the Bahamas. But it occurred to me that we could bring it in from Cuba too. Which made me think of you. You know, I always said you and I had a lot in common."

Cesare signaled the waiter to bring another bottle of the excellent pre-war Carton-Charlemagne that they were drinking with their fish and *moros y cristianos*. During his years running the Santa Isabel plantation, Cesare had become passionately fond of Cuba's spicy cooking.

"I'm not so sure breaking the law is something I want to share with you," he said to the elegant gangster.

Rothstein smiled.

"Come on, you know crime fascinates you. I remember when you used to come to my casino, you loved all the colorful types that hung around there. I always thought, this kid would make a first-rate gangster if he weren't so damned rich. I even remember your telling me you thought the most exciting thing in the world would be to kill a man."

"That was before I saw the war. I've had enough blood and guts to last a lifetime."

"Well, you wouldn't be doing any killing. Besides, what I have in mind is perfectly legal for you. I'd be doing the bootlegging."

"What's that mean?"

"Bootleggers is what they're calling the guys like me who get the booze into the country. There's a huge market for the good stuff, which you can buy here in Havana perfectly legal. Then you and I buy ourselves a boat on a fifty-fifty partnership. You fill the boat with legal booze and bring it up to New York, say, once every ten days. You stay outside the three-mile limit and I send my boys in with small boats to ship the booze into town. You don't break any law, I break the law. But I've already paid off all the right people, so there's no problem. Think about it. You'd make a fortune, there'd be no risk for you, and it would be fun. Besides, you can't tell me running a sugar plantation is exciting."

"Well, I'll admit you're right there. Except, I like Cuba, and as you know, I don't get along well with my stepfather, so I don't want to live in New York. What kind of boat are you talking about?"

"A yacht big enough to go fast and hold plenty of booze. I hear you've taken up sailing down here?"

"Yes, I have a yawl. There's great sailing around here. Havana harbor is ideal."

"So, take a step upward and become a yachtsman. Think about it, Cesare. Here's an opportunity to make millions—I mean it."

As the waiter poured the wine, Cesare began thinking about it.

"A boat as big as what you're talking about would cost at least half a million," he said after the waiter left.

"I know. Then we'd need the start-up capital to buy the first shipment of booze. Let's say we'll both put up three hundred thousand dollars. Another reason I came to you is that I know you'd have no trouble finding the money, being so rich."

"I'm not so rich," Cesare said. "My parents are."

"So, would your stepfather loan you the money?"

"No, and I wouldn't ask him for it. But my mother would."

The two men eyed each other.

"Then," Rothstein said, "are we in business?"

"Let me think about it."

"I'll need an answer soon. I'm leaving Havana in two days; I'll be back by Christmas."

"I'll tell you tomorrow."

"Excellent. You'll never regret it, Cesare. Now: are you going to show me around this town? I wouldn't mind seeing a little action, and I know there's plenty of action in Havana."

"Alex, I'm going to town."

Brook Savage De Witt was lounging in a white wicker chaise longue in the garden room of her twenty-eight-room mansion overlooking Long Island Sound at Oyster Bay. She was sipping a brandy alexander. Her husband was standing at one of the window-doors of the room looking out at the Sound, which was whitecapped by a lusty December north wind.

"Don't you think eleven in the morning is a little early for cocktails?" Alex said. He was wearing a custom-made tweed jacket and gray slacks.

"Oh, don't be so damned stuffy. You're beginning to sound like your father. And just because you can't drink without becoming a mean, ugly drunk doesn't mean I have to be a teetotaler. Anyway, I think I'll drive into the city and do some shopping."

"It's the last Saturday before Christmas. The stores will be packed."

"So what? I like crowds." She finished her drink and got off the chaise longue. "Everything's set for tonight, and I'll be home by five."

"When are the guests coming?"

"Seven-thirty. What are you going to do with yourself?"

"I thought I'd lunch at the club, then take in a movie."

"What's on?"

"Tom Mix's new western. It's called *Rough Riding Romance*."

"What does he do, fall in love with his horse? I hate westerns. I want to see love stories with a lot of hot kissing. Anyway, have fun, darling. I'm going to check with Miss Pringle, then I'm off."

She came over and kissed his left cheek.

"Good-bye," he said, looking at her rather oddly. "Have fun."

"I will."

She was wearing a smart suit she had bought in Paris the previous summer from a young designer named Chanel. The skirt was daringly halfway up to her knees, and her legs were encased in daring flesh-colored silk stockings. The previous year, after her honeymoon in Jerusalem, she had surprised Alex by having her strawberry-blond hair cut short and bobbed. He was furious with her, accusing her of looking like a "goddamned boy," but in time he got used to it, although he had yet to get used to her outrageous behavior. Their marriage, which had had such an ugly beginning in Jerusalem, had become a war when Alex was drinking and a strained truce when he wasn't. He was as jealous of her as Othello was of Desdemona; and Brook was well aware that Alex had within him a streak of violence as dangerous as the Moor of Venice's.

After Brook had left the plant-filled room, Alex went to the extension phone and picked it up.

Brook went into the spacious entrance hall of the mansion and started up the stairs. Alex's father, the multimillionaire owner of the American National Life Insurance Company, had, as promised, given his son as a wedding present ten acres of the choicest waterfront real estate in Oyster Bay and a half million dollars to build his dream house. Alex had hired the fashionable society architect William Delano, who designed a handsome brick house in the Georgian style with surrounding English-style gardens and a large swimming pool with an adjacent poolhouse pavilion. The place was generally considered one of the most handsome estates on the fashionable North Shore, but Brook thought the place was boring. She had wanted to hire a young architect who designed "modern" houses. It had caused a screaming fight between them, but this one Alex had won.

When she reached the top of the stairs, she walked down the hall to the master bedroom and took a chinchilla-trimmed mink coat out of her capacious closet. Putting it on, she chose one of her collection of forty hats, then went to check herself out in a full-length mirror. Freshening her lipstick, which was called "Dragon Red," she picked up a purse, put on a pair of fine leather gloves, left the room, and went next door to the nursery where Miss Pringle, the English nanny, was feeding one-year-old Graydon. Brook loved her beautiful baby boy. He was the only positive thing to come out of the marriage, Brook mused sadly. After kissing the top of his head, she told Miss Pringle she was going into New York.

Returning downstairs, she went through the house to the enormous kitchen, which was filled with the latest appliances including a six-burner gas stove and a huge, double-door stainless-steel refrigerator. Her butler, chef, and two maids were sitting at a zinc-topped table drinking coffee when she came in. They started to stand, but she held up her hand.

"No, please, stay seated," she said. "I just wanted to check that everything's ready for the party tonight. I'll be gone till this afternoon. Mr. Farnwell, the flowers should be here shortly after noon. You'll take care of them for me."

Mr. Farnwell was the very dignified English butler; following the English custom, he was always addressed as "Mr."

"Yes, of course, madame."

"Has Cooper finished polishing the silver?"

"I believe he has, madame."

"Would you tell him to bring the Cadillac around in front? I'm going into New York."

"Very good, madame."

"I'm sure everything will go beautifully tonight. Please go on with your coffee."

She left the kitchen and returned to the entrance hall. After a few minutes, a black, four-door Cadillac pulled up in front of the house and a uniformed chauffeur jumped out to hold the rear door as Brook left the house.

Watching her get in the car from the garden room was her husband.

"Well, I thought the evening went quite splendidly, didn't you, darling?" Brook said. She was standing in front of a mirror in her bedroom taking off the diamond earrings Alex had given her on her last birthday. It was two in the morning, and Alex, wearing impeccable tails and white tie, had just come upstairs. "Of course, Bunny Vandergriff got drunk, but she always does. It seems such a shame when we have to pay so much for the best wines to the damned bootleggers, and she swills it down. It could be furniture polish and she wouldn't know the difference . . . what the hell—!?"

Alex had come up to her, grabbed her left arm, pulled her around, then slapped her, hard.

"You bitch," he whispered.

"How dare you?" she yelled. "I thought you weren't drinking?"

"Keep your voice down. I don't want the servants to hear. Where did you go today? Who lives in 610 Park Avenue?"

She was holding her cheek.

"I don't know what you're talking about! I went shopping . . ."

"Don't lie to me!" He grabbed her with both hands and shook her violently. "Do you think I'm a complete fool? I hired a detective to follow you today. Cooper drove you into Manhattan. You got off in front of Lord & Taylor except you didn't go inside. After Cooper had driven away, you took a taxi and went to 610 Park Avenue. You went into the building and didn't come out for an hour. Then you went back to Lord & Taylor, where Cooper picked you up and brought you home. Who was in 610 Park Avenue? Who were you making love to?"

Angrily, she shoved his hands away.

"Hiring detectives," she sneered. "How cheap."

"Answer my questions!"

She looked at him coolly.

"I wasn't making love to anyone. I was having my regular appointment with Dr. Morgenstern, my psychoanalyst."

"What the hell are you seeing a psychoanalyst for?"

"To try and save this miserable marriage! And the reason I don't tell you and sneak away from the chauffeur is that I don't want anyone to know that I'm so unhappy with you that I have to go to a damned doctor to try and save my sanity!"

"A psychoanalyst," he said in a sneering tone. "Only a mixed-up, crazy Jew like you would go to one of them."

"Yes, I'm a Jew, and proud of it! I should never have given in to your deal about being married in St. Thomas—my poor mother has never gotten over that! But I'll remind you, darling Alex, that your son is a Jew too, so you'd better get over your vicious anti-Semitism if you want to have any sort of peace in this family."

"What do you tell this Dr. Morgenstein?"

"It's Morgenstern. And I tell him that you're an angry man with a streak of violence that actually frightens me— maybe you got it from the war, I don't know. And that I really don't like you very much."

"You don't look like you don't like me when I pay those incredible bills you run up!"

"You can't buy me," she snorted. She picked the diamond earrings off the chiffonier, went to the nearest window, opened it, and threw them outside.

"Brook!" he practically gurgled. "What the hell are you doing? Do you know what those things cost?"

"I couldn't care less. Coco Chanel says fake jewelry is more chic anyway. Listen, Alex: let's get a few things straight. First, never hit me again. I mean never. The next time you lay a hand on me in any way except your apelike attempts at making love, I'll walk right out the door. Second: I don't consider this marriage a prison. I want our marriage to work because of the baby. But I won't be a prisoner. Is that understood?"

He glared at her a moment.

"And third?" he finally said.

"I think we should have separate bedrooms. I don't want to sleep with you anymore. If you want physical relief I'll give you satisfaction."

"This isn't a marriage you want, it's a whorehouse."

"You can call it whatever you please, but those are my terms. Now get out of here. I'm tired and I want to go to bed."

"I don't agree to your stinking terms. I'm your husband and I have my rights."

"That's what you think, buster."

"What a fool I was to ever have fallen in love with you. I should have known that first time at the Plaza that you're nothing but a whore. Any woman who would go to bed with another woman is even worse than a whore. You're a pervert."

"That word!" she snarled. "I'm sick of it! In the first place—in case you've forgotten—I never went to bed with Lydia, so don't try to label me a lesbian. Although after what I've gone through with you, I could make a damned good case that perhaps lesbianism is better than this hell called marriage! I'm a woman who considers her body her own to do with as I please. I'm your wife, not your concubine. Those are the rules of the game, Alex, and if you don't like it, you can lump it."

"I could have you divorced like that," he said, snapping his fingers. "And you wouldn't get a penny of alimony."

"You don't seem to understand that I have no interest in your money except spending it! I have my own money. And if you want the scandal of a divorce which would not be good for our child, fine. You won't even have to hire a lawyer. I'll have my bags packed and I'll leave. But, darling, I take the baby with me."

He stared at her.

"I'm finally beginning to realize I hate you," he said

softly. "My mother was right: she told me I was a fool to marry a Jew."

"Oh? You know, Alex, your anti-Semitism is really loathsome."

"You've made me an anti-Semite."

"Come on, Alex, it's been in the back of your wormy little mind from the very beginning. I remember before we got married and I asked you straight out if you were an anti-Semite and you looked at me with those big baby blues and said, 'Oh no.' What an idiot I was to have believed that. And what an idiot I was to get into this rotten marriage."

"God, I wish you were ugly."

"You're the ugly one, Alex. Now get out of here."

He hesitated, then went to the door.

"I'd be very careful if I were you, Brook," he said. "You're very accident-prone."

"Is that a threat?" she snapped.

He smiled slightly.

"Maybe."

He left the room, closing the door quietly behind him. Brook stared at the door a moment, thoughtful and sad. And a bit frightened.

25.   FIFTY-YEAR-OLD FILM DIRECTOR CLIVE FLYNN was walking up the sidewalk of his comfortable rented bungalow in Brentwood. It was near midnight. The only illumination was a distant streetlight: Los Angeles was still a city that went to bed early, especially movie people who

often had to report to the studios at six in the morning to
be ready for shooting in the early sunlight.

As the English-born Flynn approached his front door,
feeling in his pocket for his house key, a dark figure
stepped out from behind a bush. Flynn, surprised, said,
"Who are you?"

The dark figure fired twice, hitting Flynn in the chest
both times. As Flynn crumpled to the sidewalk, dead, the
figure fled into the night.

The next morning, Johnny Savage was seated in his office
at the Wall Street bank when his secretary told him he had
a phone call from Los Angeles.

"Daddy!" It was Gloria Gilmore, and she was sobbing.
"Daddy, the most horrible thing has happened! You have
to come out here right away! Oh, I'm so frightened . . ."

"Gloria, calm down," Johnny said. "What's happened?"

"It's Clive Flynn . . . He was murdered last night outside
his house . . ."

"Clive Flynn? You mean that English director, the one
who directed *Hearts on Fire*?"

"Yes . . . Someone shot him . . . the police don't have a
clue yet, but . . . Oh Daddy, please come out! You simply
must! The police are going to be asking me questions . . ."

"You? Why? Did you know Flynn?"

"Oh yes, of course I knew him! We were . . . well . . .
friends . . . oh, please come out, I need you desperately."

"Yes, I'll try. But listen, Gloria, are you in trouble?"

"Well of course, Daddy! Why do you think I'm so
afraid? This could ruin everything!"

She burst into new sobs. Johnny, who was totally confused, said, "Gloria, listen: get yourself a good lawyer.
Don't talk to the police or anyone until you've gotten a
lawyer. I'll get to the coast as fast as I can, but you have
to tell me what this is all about!"

"Oh Daddy, I can't! Not on the phone! Please hurry!"
And she hung up.

Johnny, rolling his eyes, summoned his secretary.

"Glenda, get me a drawing room on the first train to Los
Angeles."

"Yes, Mr. Savage."

By the time he reached Los Angeles five days later, Johnny
was in as agitated a state as Gloria had been on the phone.
Newspapers all over America had started a hue and cry,
calling for a crusade against the cesspool of Hollywood
vice that the murder of Clive Flynn was uncovering. Met
at the train station by a car and driver, Johnny was driven
first to the Ambassador Hotel where he checked into his
suite. Then he was driven to Highland Avenue and Sunset
Boulevard where, near the intersection of the two streets,
stood the palatial, Spanish-style mansion he had bought for
Gloria from the Russian-born star, Alla Nazimova. The
house, set in grounds planted with orange and lemon trees,
was made of stucco with a red-tile roof. Johnny got out of
the car and walked to the front door, which had already
been opened by Gloria, who was expecting him.

Johnny hadn't seen her for several months, and as always
he was excited by her beauty, although on this warm, sunny
day, she looked rather pale. She was wearing a white skirt
and a white-and-peppermint-striped blouse, with white
shoes. Her blond hair was tied in a peppermint scarf.

"Daddy!" she said, opening her arms to embrace him.
"Thank God you're here."

They kissed, but Johnny was in no mood for romance.

"Let's go inside," he ordered. "We have a lot to talk
about. Did you get a lawyer?"

"Yes. His name's Brett Harris and he's very smart.
Daddy, you're not mad at me?"

"I'm sure as hell not happy."

He went into the front hall, which was paved with soft pink Mexican tiles. A Spanish-style wrought-iron curved staircase led to the second floor, and a life-size oil painting of Gloria in a slinky white evening gown hung on the wall. From the ceiling depended a Mexican-style iron and glass lantern, and big clay pots of red geraniums lined the wall. Gloria closed the door as Johnny went into the large living room, the floor of which was also tiled. The room was two stories high, the ceiling was elaborately carved and painted wood, and framed photos of Gloria were everywhere. Johnny sat down in a high-backed Spanish chair.

"Why did you have an affair with Flynn?" he asked.

"Daddy, that's all wrong! The newspapers are just making it up because my name sells papers and . . ."

"Gloria, the police found a pair of your silk underpants in Flynn's bedroom. Your initials were on them, and Flynn had tacked a note with them saying, 'Gloria Gilmore. I scored on Saturday, November 12, 1920. She's great in bed.' "

Gloria looked at him a moment, then burst into tears.

"I couldn't help it," she sobbed. "It was wrong of me, I know that now, but . . ."

"The newspapers are saying Flynn was selling drugs as a sideline to pick up extra money. Were you buying from him?"

"Oh no, Daddy! Oh God, you mustn't think that about me! God knows, I have my faults, but I don't take drugs— though there are plenty of people in the business who do! Wallace Reid is totally hooked on morphine, and Barbara La Marr shoots heroin like it's candy . . ."

"Then why the hell did you go to bed with him?" Johnny shouted angrily. "After everything I've done for you, why did you betray me? Now my name's been dragged into the tabloids! I've been made to look like a dirty old man, I'm terrified even to look at my wife . . . Damn you, Gloria! Damn you! Damn you!"

He pounded his fists on the arms of the chair in total frustration. Gloria had never seen him so furious. Frightened, she hurried to his side and knelt on her knees, taking his right fist and kissing it.

"Please, Daddy, I'm so sorry, but try to forgive me . . ."

"I can't! Was this Flynn so attractive you couldn't stay away from him? All these years you've been telling me you love me, but obviously you don't love me that much."

"I do love you, Daddy—how can you doubt that?"

"Easily!"

"It's just that . . . Well, you know my last two pictures haven't done well and the talk in the business is that I'm slipping, and Clive had this part that would have been so perfect for me, and . . . oh God, I was weak and stupid . . ."

"Damned stupid! Don't you know this publicity can end your career? I've read all the papers on the train, the public is up in arms about this! Because Flynn didn't just have your underpants as a trophy in his room! The man was screwing half of Hollywood! You know, the public out there likes to think you people have a few morals. They're not asking for total abstinence, but leaving your underpants as a souvenir seems to be going a bit far!"

"It was foolish of me, I know, but he begged me for them . . . I think he had some sort of—what's the word? 'fetish' I think they call it—about underpants."

"How classy. How elegant. Do you know who your public is? Your public is people who scrape by on maybe two thousand dollars a year. Your public is poor housewives who slave over a washing tub all day. How do you think they feel when they read how much you movie people make? When Mary Pickford makes two thousand bucks a day? They resent you—that's how they feel! And now when they read you're all sleeping around, they're going to hate you!"

"Oh Daddy, please, don't say any more! I'm scared enough as it is!"

"Have the police questioned you?"

"Yes."

"Was your lawyer with you?"

"Yes, and you were so right to warn me about that."

"What did you tell the police?"

"Everything I knew, which wasn't much. I have no idea who murdered him, though everybody seems to think it had something to do with his drug dealing. I mean, Daddy, I only went to bed with him once! It's not as if we were intimate friends."

"I think going to bed with a man qualifies as intimacy."

"Oh Daddy"—she burst into tears again and started kissing his hand—"tell me you forgive me! I won't be able to stand it if you're angry with your Gloria for long. I love you so much . . . You're breaking my heart!"

He sighed, but said nothing for a moment. Rather stealthily, Gloria put her right hand on his crotch and rubbed his pants gently. "Does my big friend forgive me?" she whispered. "I know he likes me even if Daddy doesn't. And it's been so long since we've had fun. Daddy sits in his big old bank on Wall Street and leaves poor little Gloria all alone out here. Is it any wonder I get in trouble?"

"Oh Gloria, I don't know . . ." Another sigh.

She started unbuttoning his fly.

"Gloria will make Daddy feel happy again," she whispered. "Just as she's done so many times before."

Johnny stared at her a moment. Then he pushed her hand away.

"It's not going to work, Gloria," he said. "I've finally learned my lesson. We're through."

"What do you mean?"

With some difficulty, he stood up.

"I've been infatuated with you. I've cheated on my wife, which I never should have done because she's a fine woman whom I love. I've acted like a besotted old fool, and maybe that's the best way to describe me. But no more.

I'm going home and try to be a good husband."

He started toward the entrance hall as Gloria stood up.

"You can't do this!" she wailed. "Not now, when I need you! Not now, when my career's in danger . . ."

"You should have thought of that sooner. Or you should have picked better pictures to be in. You can keep this house, Gloria. As you know, the deed's in your name. But I won't be financing any more of your movies. Good-bye, Gloria. In some ways you're a wonderful woman, but unfortunately, you're a whore."

He started across the room to the entrance hall. Gloria put both hands to her head.

"You can't leave me!" she screamed. "You can't! I need you!"

"You'll find someone else. The world is full of suckers."

"You bastard!" she screamed, picking up a china vase and throwing it at him. She missed: the vase crashed against the wall. "You cripple!" she howled. "You miserable one-legged cripple!"

Johnny winced. But he didn't stop. He got in the car, and the chauffeur drove him to his hotel. When he got in his room, he picked up the phone and called his wife in New York.

"Rachel," he said when she answered, "I'm coming home tomorrow. I want to spend the rest of my life with you."

Rachel, in New York, could hardly believe her ears.

"What do you mean?" she said.

"I'm leaving Gloria. I was a fool to have ever touched the damned woman. I know I've hurt you over the years, and I wouldn't blame you if you never spoke to me again. I apologize from the bottom of my heart, Rachel. You've never said a word, you've been a perfect lady about this whole thing, for which I admire you extravagantly. I've behaved like a rotten cad, but if you'll take me back, I'll do my best to spend the rest of my life making it up to you."

Rachel closed her eyes a moment. How right her late mother had been: "Do nothing, my dear," she had said. "Don't lower yourself to get into a vulgar brawl with him. Keep your dignity at all costs. He'll tire of this woman soon enough, then he'll come back to you, crawling with guilt."

How right she had been, even if Rachel hadn't been able to totally hide her hurt. But in the end, when it counted, she had won.

Rachel opened her eyes.

"I'll be waiting for you, my darling," she said.

Then she hung up, a smile on her lips. She sat in a chair and started crying with joy.

Four-thirty A.M. Broome Street in lower Manhattan. A tank truck marked "Callahan Dairy Farm" is lumbering across town on the dark street.

Suddenly, a four-door black Buick turns onto the street and roars up behind the milk truck. The Buick passes the truck. A Thompson submachine gun, the newest (invented just the previous year) and most lethal weapon *du jour,* juts out of the rear window and sprays the side of the truck with bullets. As the Buick roars off into the night, a liquid starts gushing out of the many bullet holes onto the pavement. Except the liquid isn't milk.

It's whisky.

Farther uptown at a speakeasy called the Purple Parrot on East Forty-eighth Street located in the basement of an elegant brownstone town house, the owner, Arnold Rothstein, was sitting at a table drinking a final highball for the night. As usual, the dapper gangster was wearing an impeccably cut dinner jacket. The smoke-filled club was beginning to empty: in Prohibition New York, people partied all night, to the frustration of the dwindling number of dries who still believed the Volstead Act would sober America up.

Rothstein checked his watch, then lit a cigarette with a gold lighter. After a moment, two men wearing suits instead of tuxedos pushed their way through the exiting crowd of evening dresses and dinner jackets and came up to Rothstein's table.

"How did it go?" Rothstein asked.

"The Callahan Dairy Farm is out of the booze business," one of the men said.

"Good. Sit down and have a drink."

The men obeyed as Rothstein signaled a waiter. After drinks had been served, Rothstein said, "The *Half Moon* should be offshore tomorrow night. This will be its first trip, and I want things to go off without a hitch. You'll need at least four boats. There's five hundred cases aboard, and it's the best stuff, the absolute best. Gordon's gin, Johnnie Walker, Black and White, Peter Dawson, Bacardi rum . . . the works, plus a hundred cases of fine wines and champagne."

One of the men, known as Little Hymie Weiss, who was a sadistic killer, let out a whistle.

"Five hundred cases!" he said in awe. "Jeez, Boss, that's a big haul."

"Yeah, and it's only the beginning," Rothstein said. "This Cuba connection is going to be a gold mine. And, boys, you'll treat my new partner with respect. Cesare Savage isn't your ordinary bootlegger. He's Park Avenue all the way. He's class."

He ground out his cigarette in a Purple Parrot ashtray.

"Brook and Alex are practically not talking," Rachel said the next night at the Marlboro Club, an elegant speakeasy at 15 East Sixty-first Street. When Johnny returned from Hollywood, he had taken her out for dinner to celebrate their "new start," as he called it. Prohibition had shut down most of the town's better hotels and restaurants, which couldn't survive without serving liquor; speakeasies like The '21' Club and the Marlboro had quickly filled the gap. The best, like the Marlboro that catered to the rich, served good food as well as the best wines and liquors. Rachel and Johnny were dressed to the nines, Rachel looking gorgeous in a smart lavender evening dress. "Brook told me Alex had actually threatened to hurt her physically."

"Dear God, what brought all this on?" Johnny said, carving into his steak.

"Well, I'm afraid a lot of the fault is Brook's. You know Brook: she writes her own rules. But she told me she's trying to keep the marriage afloat, for the baby's sake. I do so hope it works out, although young people today don't seem to be bothered too much by the idea of divorce."

"Our marriage has survived, so maybe theirs will too." He reached over and squeezed her hand. "It's good to be home again. That is"—he looked around the crowded room—"if you can call a speakeasy a home."

She smiled. "It's so good to have you back, darling. Oh: Beatrice is going to Europe in the spring. She particularly wants to go to Rome to see your parents."

"Good. We'll send her in style. Has she gotten any boyfriends yet?"

"Oh yes, several, but I don't think she's very serious about any of them. You know how shy she is. But I think one day soon she'll meet the right man and fall in love, and I have the feeling that when it happens to her she's going to fall desperately in love. Don't ask me why, it's just a mother's instinct. But it may also be wishful thinking."

"Well, I hope she'll be very happy."

"Darling, I . . ." She hesitated. Johnny looked at her. "What is it?"

"I didn't want to tell you this. I mean, Cesare asked me not to, but I think you should know."

"Now what? What's he done now?"

"Oh nothing. I mean, nothing that I know of. But he did ask me to loan him a rather large sum of money, which I did."

"How large?"

"Three hundred thousand dollars."

Johnny put down his fork.

"Three hundred thousand?" he repeated disbelievingly. "What in the world did he want that much money for?"

"I don't know. He just said it was an investment he was very eager to make, and so I lent it to him. He has been such a darling, and he's done so well in Cuba. I felt the loan was part of what I'll leave to him after I die."

Johnny shook his head slowly.

"Well, it's your money, of course, and he's your son. It's only that that's a helluva lot of money to be lending to someone, even one's son, without knowing where it's going."

"I realize that. But I'm his mother, and I so desperately want him to be happy."

"Rachel, you're a wonderful woman and a very strong woman. But . . ."

"I know." She sighed. "Cesare."

The murder of Clive Flynn, like the murder of his friend and fellow film director William Desmond Taylor two years later, was never solved by the Los Angeles police. But everyone in the picture business knew that he had been killed for his drug dealing; and that the studios, anxious to protect their public image, covered the crime up, just as, two years later, they would cover up the murder of William Desmond Taylor, who was a predatory pederast.

Hollywood, the city of trends, actually never changes much at all.

26. "YOU KNOW, IT'S INTERESTING," BROOK DE Witt said as she sipped a martini at The '21' Club. "I actually think my husband's considering murdering me. Isn't that delicious fun?"

"It won't be such fun if he succeeds," said her good friend Bunny Vandergriff, who was lunching with Brook at the wildly popular speakeasy on West Fifty-second Street after a morning of shopping. It was almost exactly a year later, and retailers during this Christmas season of 1921 were understandably nervous about sales: the economy had suffered a serious recession the previous year. "But surely you're exaggerating? Alex wouldn't really try to murder you?"

"I don't think he has the nerve, but you never know. He murdered a lot of Germans during the war."

"Well, that's a bit different, darling. Alex was a hero."

"Yes, I know. Men love to kill as long as it's considered patriotic and is legal. But when it comes to murdering wives, which isn't legal, they get scared. On the other hand, he tried to strangle me in the bathtub on our honeymoon, and God knows when he's drunk he's attacked me enough times. But this is somehow different. I mean, I think he's plotting something murky. It's a bit nerve-racking."

"But why is he being so Macbeth-ish? Haven't you been good lately?"

"I've been a saint, which is boring beyond belief, but Alex doesn't trust me. I don't think he's still hiring detectives to follow me, but he might have. He lurks around the house and is extremely moody. He's also started to drink like a fish again, which is frightening."

"So much for Prohibition. Speaking of which, I'm ready for another martini. You know, there's really much to be said for booze," she went on, signaling for a waiter. "One is never bored when drunk."

"You have a point," Brook said, lighting a cigarette. "It's a rather stupid one, but it's a point. Another ugly thing is that he's getting more openly anti-Semitic."

"Alex? I don't believe it. Of course, his family is . . ."

"Yes, there's the rub. It comes with those Protestant genes."

"But, darling, you're no more Jewish than I am."

"Yes I am. I may act like a nice little Smith debutante— up to a point—but Mother is Jewish, which I'm quite happy with. Unfortunately, Alex isn't." She sighed. "It's a real mess."

"But he knew this before he married you?"

"Yes, but then we were in love. Odd how quickly love can fly out the window."

The speakeasy was packed almost solid and the noise level was high. Brook and Bunny were seated near the bar on the main floor. Now, as Bunny gave her drink order to the waiter, Brook noticed a young man in a rather rumpled suit with wheat-colored hair standing at the bar, drink in hand, looking at her.

"Don't look now," she said to Bunny, "but there's this absolutely dreamy-looking young man at the bar who I think is trying to get up the nerve to come over and join us. Should we encourage him?"

"If Alex finds out you're picking up strange men at The '21' Club, he really will murder you."

"To hell with Alex: let's have some fun. He looks inter-esting."

"Darling, you're asking for trouble—I'm warning you."

"It doesn't mean I'm going to jump in bed with him: I just want to meet someone new."

She smiled at the young man and beckoned him to come over, which he did.

"I have the distinct impression," Brook said to him, "that there are naughty thoughts in your pretty head."

The young man smiled rather awkwardly.

"Well, I've never been to an uptown speak, and I was feeling sort of lonely. I didn't mean to be obvious."

"You're forgiven. Please join us, My name is Brook, and this delicious brunette is Bunny."

"Hi," he said, sitting down between the two women. "My name is Lance Fairfax, and I'm a writer looking for romantic experiences to put into my first novel."

Brook and Bunny exchanged looks, Brook sucking on her cigarette.

"This may be your lucky day," she said, eyeing him with appreciation.

Bunny gave her a frowning "no" look, shaking her head negatively.

"Bunny, darling," Brook said in her flutiest, birdsong tones, "you'll be late for your hair appointment. This young man will drink your martini."

"I think," Bunny said, getting up and taking her purse, "that's my exit cue. Brook, I'll pay you for my drinks later. So glad to have met you, Mr. Fairfax. When it comes to romantic experiences, Brook is a veritable research library."

She made her way through the crowd to the door, thinking, My God, Brook is really going too far!

"Brook what?" Lance asked, resuming his seat.

"Brook De Witt."

"I see by the ring that you're married."

"That's right. To a rather neurotic husband. Where are you from, Lance?"

"Nebraska. My father's a farmer. But I live in Greenwich Village."

"Oh, how wonderfully Bohemian. I imagine you live in a tiny room, barely getting by, struggling to write the great American novel."

"Actually, I have a garden apartment. You see, my father's a big farmer—I mean, in the sense of his acreage, not his waistline—and he's told me he'll support me for three years. Then, if I haven't gotten anything published yet, I've agreed to come back and help run the farm. So you see, I can't waste time, and I really have to experience things so I can write about them."

"I think it's wonderful. I've always wanted to experience everything, or at least as much as I can, so we have that in common."

"Would you like to see my apartment?"

She laughed.

"You certainly don't waste much time. Yes, I'd love to. Let me get the check, then we'll go downtown."

When Cooper drove her back to Oyster Bay from Manhattan, it was already dark and had begun snowing lightly. The Georgian mansion glowed cheerily with light. Brook let herself in the front door, rubbing the snow off her shoes on the mat first. Giving her fur coat and hat to the butler, she went upstairs to dress for dinner. It was now five in the afternoon; she knew Alex would be home from the office soon.

Getting undressed, she went into the capacious marble bathroom and turned on the tub, pouring bubble bath into the water. When the tub filled, she stepped in, lowering herself into the lilac-scented suds, luxuriating in the warmth of the water, thinking with intense pleasure of her afternoon with Lance Fairfax. The young Nebraskan had been a wonderful lover who had the knack of making her burn with pleasure, like one of Edna St. Vincent Millay's candles, although not at both ends. But she had also liked the Vil-

lage, filled with artists and writers. She had been there before, of course, but always as a sort of tourist in a foreign
land. But that afternoon, lying in Lance's strong arms in
his small apartment, she for once felt that she was, no matter how briefly, part of that wonderful world of Bohemians,
and she liked the feeling. Her whole life had been spent in
the structured world of New York Society and wealth, a
world she had always rebelled against.

In Lance's arms, she suddenly felt like a rebel no longer.
She had felt at home.

The bathroom door opened and Alex came in.

"Don't you bother to knock anymore?" she asked, annoyed at the intrusion. "I've told you to stay out when I'm
in the bathtub—it gives me bad memories of our revolting
honeymoon."

"Farley Vandergriff called me at the office. Bunny came
home drunk and told him what happened at '21.' How you
picked up some young man. Or are you going to deny it?"

She took her big sponge and ran it over her sudsy shoulders.

"No, I won't deny it," she said. "His name is Lance Fairfax, he's a young writer from Nebraska, and he's very
sweet. We went down to his apartment in the Village and
made love. It was a wonderful experience."

"At least you're honest. I suppose, in a strange way, I
sort of admire you for that. You feel no shame, do you?"

"No. None whatever."

"Are you going to see him again?"

"I may. We didn't talk about it."

"Are you in love with him? That is, assuming you know
what love is."

"I know what love is. I loved you, once. Before you
turned into this clichéd jealous husband."

"My view of marriage may strike you as boring and
stuffy, but I'm a conventional man. I have no intention of
having an unconventional marriage."

He reached into his jacket and pulled out a revolver, which he aimed at her. Brook stared at it, then at him.

"You don't have the nerve," she said scornfully.

"Don't I?"

He pulled the trigger. There was a click, nothing else.

"The next time," he said softly, "I'll load it."

He walked out of the room.

Lance Fairfax was tapping the keys of his Smith-Corona typewriter on a plain wooden desk overlooking his small garden when the doorbell rang. Getting up, he crossed his living room—which was on the ground floor of an old brownstone—unlocked the door, and opened it. Standing outside was Brook. She was holding a wicker basket.

"I've brought us lunch," she said. "Cold chicken, the best cole slaw in New York, ham sandwiches, and some really wonderful white wine, properly chilled. We can eat on the floor and pretend it's June and we're having a picnic."

"What a swell idea! Come on in."

Which she did, setting the basket on a table and taking off her hat and coat.

"I heard a typewriter," she said, tossing her hat on a chair and throwing her fur coat over it. "Were you writing some inspired prose?"

"As a matter of fact," he said, closing the door, "I was trying to get down on paper what happened to us yesterday."

"Oh—may I read it?"

"Absolutely not."

"Why? Isn't it any good?"

"No, it's damned good—at least, I think it is—but I wrote some fairly unflattering things about you."

She looked at him. He was wearing a rather ratty sweater and dark corduroy trousers.

"Let me guess," she said. "You wrote that I'm a wicked,

brazen woman with no morals whatsoever. A whore, a Jezebel, et cetera."

"Well, I didn't give you very high marks in the morals department, but I didn't say you were a whore."

"Then what did you say? Do you have a corkscrew? I'll open the wine."

"I said you were a spoiled rich girl looking for pleasure." He went to the door of the tiny kitchen and reached in for a corkscrew, which he brought to her. "I said you were one of the by-products of our rotten capitalist system and that you'd probably be much happier the wife of a farmer in, say, Nebraska."

"Oh dear me. Something tells me you're a Democrat."

He laughed.

"I'm way past that. I'm a Nihilist. Actually, politics bore me. I'm just an old-fashioned romantic."

"I like that." She pulled a bottle of Chablis from the basket and started working the cork. "Well, maybe you're right. Maybe I'd be happier a farmer's wife—at least, for about a week, and if you were the farmer. Do you have some plates and glasses? I brought a tablecloth."

"Oh . . . of course. Just a minute. Nothing very elegant, I'm afraid."

He went into the kitchen as Brook pulled a red-and-white-checked cloth from the basket and spread it on the floor. Then she sat on the floor, cross-legged. Lance came back with glasses, plates, and utensils. He sat on the floor opposite her and handed her a plate and glass.

"My husband fired a gun at me last night," she said, filling the glasses with the wine.

"You're joking!"

"Oh no. The gun wasn't loaded, but he threatened the next time I saw you, he'd load it. So you can see, this might be a very expensive lunch for me." She handed him the wine bottle.

"Is your husband crazy?" Lance asked.

"It's certainly possible. He's behaving very oddly lately. Were you in the war?"

"I was drafted in the summer of 1918, but the war was over before I saw any action."

"Well, my husband was. He was a bit of a hero—Air Corps ace, and all that—so perhaps things he saw in France might have unhinged him a bit. Anyway: cheers. To us." She clicked his glass and took a sip. "Mmm, that's good."

Putting down her glass, she took a cold chicken from the basket and tore off a leg and thigh.

"Let's eat Henry the Eighth style," she said, putting the chicken back in the basket and biting into the leg. "You know, I really truly enjoyed yesterday. Meeting you has been wonderful. I'm sure you have lots of girlfriends. Do you?"

"Oh, quite a few, but nothing serious. Girls seem to like young writers."

"Especially ones that look like you."

"I don't understand you, Brook," he said, tearing off his own chicken leg. "Why are you slumming down here in the Village? What do you want? I mean, I'm not exactly thrilled at the idea of becoming some rich woman's toy."

"Don't underestimate the rich. I could help you a lot. Right now you're a nobody, but I could make you a somebody."

"I don't need your help."

"I know quite a few important publishers."

She said it casually, so casually that, to her surprise, he took offense.

"For God's sake, what do you think I am?" he said. "Some male whore? I'll make it on my own, or I'll go back to Nebraska."

"Lance, don't take it that way!" she exclaimed, putting down her wineglass. "I want to help you . . ."

"Why?"

"Because I like you! It's that simple. This is a very tough

city, and you should take advantage of all the help you can get. You want to be a writer, and it's a difficult profession. Let me introduce you to publishers—believe me, they wouldn't publish you if they didn't like what you write, but just getting them to read a manuscript is difficult." She reached over the basket and took his hand. "It's wonderful that you're proud and idealistic—I admire that! But be a little practical too."

He looked at her a moment. Then he smiled rather sheep-ishly.

"Well, I guess you're right," he said. "You see, the trouble is that I'm scared. I'm terrified that I'm really not very good, and that if some publisher told me that . . . well, it would shatter all my dreams."

She smiled at him.

"Dear Lance," she said, "we're all scared. Life is a shooting gallery, and we're the targets. More wine?"

An hour later, a naked Brook was lying in a naked Lance's arms on his small, rumpled bed in his small, messy bedroom when she suddenly exclaimed: "Good God, I just realized you have no Christmas tree!"

"No, I don't bother."

"But you have to have a Christmas tree! At home we always had a menorah and a tree. Christmas Eve is only five nights away!"

"Brook, really . . . I don't have any ornaments, I just don't bother with Christmas trees."

"Come on: let's get dressed and go out and buy one. And I'll buy you some ornaments, then we'll come back here and trim it. It'll be fun, and you simply have to have a Christmas tree, I won't allow you not to." She kissed him, then got out of bed. "Good Lord," she said, shivering, "it's freezing in here."

"My landlord's not great about heat. You know, I think you may be as crazy as your husband."

"That's certainly possible."

Forty-five minutes later, they were back with a five-foot tree and boxes of Christmas ornaments Brook had bought at a local Woolworth. Lance fit the tree in a stand in a corner of the living room while Brook opened the boxes.

"This is going to be the most beautiful tree in New York," she announced. "You'd better put some water in the stand. By the way, what are you doing Christmas Eve?"

"I don't know. I'll probably go to a restaurant."

"On Christmas Eve? No you don't. You're having dinner with me. I want you to meet my baby, who's adorable."

He stared at her as she began hanging balls on the branches.

"Excuse me, but if you think I'm going to your house when your husband's packing a pistol, you really must be crazy."

"I'm not talking about my house. I'm talking about my hotel suite. I've decided I'm leaving my husband in the morning. After all, he really might take a potshot at me— but next time with a loaded pistol. So I'm leaving him. I've rented a suite at the Plaza. We'll have the most wonderful Christmas Eve there and make love while Santa climbs down our chimney."

"Brook, you amaze me."

Brook smiled. "Do I, darling? Good. I like to be amazing."

27. THE 120-FOOT-LONG, WHITE-HULLED STEAM yacht *Half Moon* bobbed in the icy waters of the Atlantic just beyond the three-mile limit off Provincetown, Massachusetts. It was a cold, dark night, and the sea was rough. Four small power launches banged against the hull of the yacht as Little Hymie Weiss and his crew of a dozen bootleggers struggled to off-load another five hundred cases of whiskey and fine wines from the yacht to the launches. The operation was illuminated by searchlights from the *Half Moon*; and though the sea was choppy, the men had by now sufficient experience that the transfer was made without incident.

On the *Half Moon* bridge, Cesare, wearing a fur-lined parka to protect against the icy weather, stood with Little Hymie who was similarly garbed.

"A. R. is raising the prices," he said to Cesare, referring to Arnold Rothstein. "We should all make a real bundle with this shipment—just in time for Christmas bonuses."

"That's good news," Cesare said.

"You going directly back to Havana?"

"No, I'm going to New York for a couple of days. Shopping for some real estate."

"I thought you didn't like New York?"

"You got it wrong. I love New York. It's my stepfather I don't like, but what the hell"—he laughed—"I'm getting so rich off booze, I don't have to see the old fart."

❖

"I see Cooper has piled your luggage into the Cadillac," Alex De Witt said the morning after Brook's picnic lunch with Lance Fairfax as he came into his wife's bedroom at Oyster Bay. "He tells me he's driving you, Miss Pringle, and Graydon to the Plaza. I assume you're leaving me?"

Brook, who was wearing a dark blue suit, was standing in front of a mirror brushing her hair.

"You assume correctly. I've had enough of you and your guns. Frankly, Alex, I think you should see a psychiatrist. It's not normal going around aiming guns at people—particularly your wife. I'll have my lawyers contact yours after Christmas."

Alex closed the bedroom door.

"So it's that simple?" he said. "You just waltz out of my life, taking my son with you, and expect me not to do something to stop you?"

"You can't stop me," she said, picking her mink coat and a purse off the bed. "Let's try and do this as amicably as possible, Alex. I don't want to hurt you, and for the baby's sake, the less ugliness the better. Surely you must agree to that?"

"No, I don't." He pulled the gun from his pocket and aimed it at her. "This is a .38-caliber Smith & Wesson, darling, and this time, it's loaded. And in case you don't believe me . . ."

He aimed the gun at a window and fired. The bullet shattered one of the windowpanes.

"Alex, stop it!" she screamed. "Put that damned gun away!"

"Why?"

He turned the gun on her again.

"Because you're going to hurt someone! Do you want to go to the electric chair? Do you want to destroy us all? Our marriage isn't working out, so let's end it! Can't you see that?"

"You were with that writer yesterday, weren't you?" he

said softly. "Down in the Village. Are you in love with him?"

"Yes, I think I am—and it's none of your business!"

"Oh? I'm just the husband, but it's none of my business? What a weird sense of priorities you have, Brook. I loved you once. I was crazy about you. But I've come to hate you. It will give me great pleasure to destroy you, you cheating bitch."

She stared at his trigger finger. For the first time, she was truly frightened.

"Please, Alex . . . don't do this . . ." she whispered, backing away from him.

Suddenly, to her surprise, he moaned and started crying.

"I can't," he sobbed. "I can't kill you, dammit. Here: take the damned gun . . . you kill me, if you want, but please don't leave me, Brook . . . Let's try and work this out . . ."

Turning the gun around, he came to her and thrust it into her hand.

"I don't want it," she sputtered.

"Kill me! Go on! I deserve it, I suppose . . ."

She tossed the gun on the bed.

"I'm not going to kill anyone, and neither are you. All right, maybe we can work something out, but I'm still going to the Plaza. I have to get away from you for a while. It's better this way, darling, believe me." She crossed the room and opened the door. Turning, she looked back at him, rather sadly. "Good-bye, Alex."

She left the room, closing the door behind her.

Alex pulled a handkerchief from his pocket. Wrapping it around his right hand, he went to the bed and very carefully picked up the gun by its muzzle.

She arrived at the Plaza Hotel shortly before noon and moved into her suite on the seventh floor, overlooking Cen-

tral Park, where it was beginning to snow. After she un-
packed with the help of Miss Pringle, who had her own
bedroom off the living room to share with the baby, Brook
ordered up a light room-service lunch. Then she called
Lance. "We're all ensconced, darling," she said when he
got on the phone. "We're on the seventh floor, suite seven-
fourteen. I'm going to get my hair done this afternoon, and
you be here at seven this evening. We'll have a cocktail,
then dinner. I brought some wonderful wine. It'll be such
fun!" It was the Saturday before Christmas.

"So you really have left Alex?" Lance said.

"Oh yes. He pulled a gun on me again—and this time
the thing was loaded—but just as I expected, he didn't have
the nerve to do anything. He started blubbering like a
schoolboy. I actually felt rather sorry for him. Now, I don't
suppose you have a dinner jacket?"

"Are you kidding? I'm a Nihilist."

"Well, put on your best suit tonight, darling. I want all
the women to be green with envy."

Sending him a few phone kisses, she hung up. Going to
the window, she looked out at Central Park, which was
turning solidly white. She felt absurdly happy.

I think I really am in love with Lance, she thought.

She returned to her hotel suite from her hairdresser at two-
thirty in the afternoon. She was about to lie down for a
short nap when the phone rang. It was Alex.

"Brook," he said, "I've talked to my lawyer. Can you
meet me at my office in a half hour? I think we can work
out a lot of our problems."

"Alex, it's Saturday, for heaven's sake! We can talk after
the holidays."

"No, it's very important I see you this afternoon. It won't
take long, and when you hear what I have to say, you'll
agree it was worth it."

"But your office building is closed, isn't it?"

"Yes, but Jerry, the old night watchman, will let you in and take you up in the elevator. The office is unlocked. I'm here now."

She sighed.

"This is such a bore . . ."

"Please, Brook. I ask it as a favor. After all, you didn't give me much warning about leaving."

"Well . . . no guns?"

"No guns. You saw this morning I couldn't harm you. I was only bluffing."

"Oh, all right. I'll be there as soon as I can."

The American National Life Insurance Building was a thirty-story pseudo-Gothic skyscraper on lower Broadway, not far from the Stock Exchange and the Savage Bank. When Brook got out of her taxi in front of the building, the snow was coming down heavily and the wind was blowing it through the canyons of the deserted financial district. Hugging her mink to keep warm, she went into the handsome lobby of the building, whose high arched ceiling was painted with a mural representing the Triumph of American Business over poverty and ignorance. She walked down the lobby, her heels clicking on the marble floor, to a desk where an old man in a blue uniform was reading The Police Gazette.

"Good afternoon," she said. "I'm Mrs. De Witt. Is my husband upstairs?"

The old man put down his magazine and stood up.

"No, he went out for cigarettes, but he'll be back in a few minutes. He told me to take you up."

He led her to a bank of elevators with elaborately carved bronze doors and went in the first one. Brook followed him. He took her to the executive suite on the thirtieth floor.

"The office is unlocked," he said as the elevator door slid silently open.

"Thank you."

She left the elevator and walked into the paneled reception room, which was empty. Going down a hallway, she went into Alex's office, which was also empty. She looked out the windows a moment at the swirling snow, then sat down in a leather sofa and lit a cigarette.

"Where the hell is he?" she said, twenty minutes later, looking at her watch. She stood up and went back to the reception room. It was still empty. "Damn him," she mumbled. She looked through some magazines, then picked out the latest copy of *The Saturday Evening Post* and sat down to leaf through it.

After forty-five minutes had passed, the phone rang. Getting up, Brook answered it.

"Yes?"

"Brook, it's me." It was Alex.

"Where the hell are you?"

"I slipped on some ice and twisted my ankle pretty badly. I'm sorry. Listen, we'll have to wait till next week."

"Dear God, you drag me out in this weather on a fool's errand . . ."

"I said I'm sorry. Anyway, Merry Christmas."

He hung up. Brook slammed down the receiver and went to the elevator to ring the bell.

Annoyed with her husband, she took a taxi back to the Plaza and returned to her suite to take the postponed nap. Then, at five-thirty, she woke up and went into her bathroom to fill the tub. After she had bathed, she started dressing for dinner. It was a time when strict dress codes were in effect at the city's better restaurants and speakeasies, and she knew that Lance would never have been able to get in most of them without a tuxedo, so she had decided to eat in her suite. Nevertheless, she fully intended to dazzle him, so she chose what she considered was her most seductive evening dress, a black peau de soie with a lace trim that she had bought at Chanel's and which exposed almost all of her back as well as her shoulders and a good part of her breasts. The hem in front came up almost to the knees, though in back it made a slight nod toward convention by descending to the heels. She put on four diamond bracelets on her right wrist and three on her left, as was the current custom ("if you got 'em, wear 'em"), the diamond earrings Alex had retrieved when she threw them out the window, then she sprayed on perfume. Checking her reflection, she thought she looked fabulous—which she did. Then she went into the living room of the suite where she had put a bottle of Dom Perignon in an ice bucket, and sat down to wait for love and romance to enter in the form of the fair Lance Fairfax.

When he hadn't arrived by seven-thirty, she phoned his apartment. A man with a rather crude accent answered the phone.

"Yeah, Falco here."

"I'd like to speak to Lance Fairfax, please."

"Who's this?"

"I'm Mrs. De Witt."

"Oh yeah, are you the broad he was supposed to have dinner with tonight uptown at the Plaza?"

Brook stiffened slightly.

"I'm the lady he's having dinner with," she said, a bit icily. "Is he there?"

"Not anymore."

"Who are you?"

"Lieutenant Falco, Homicide. His landlord told me he was havin' dinner with you. Maybe you'd better wait there—you're at the Plaza now?"

"Yes . . ."

"Wait there, please, ma'am. I'll be there in about a half hour. I'd like to talk to you."

"About what?"

"Your boyfriend was found shot this afternoon."

"Shot?" she gasped. "Is he all right?"

"Sure he's all right. There ain't no safer place than the morgue."

"You mean he's dead?"

"They don't come no deader. See you in a while, ma'am."

He hung up. As did Brook, so dazed she couldn't believe what she had heard. But then, after the tears, she began to believe.

Lieutenant Mario Falco was thirty-four years old, the son of first-generation immigrants who had come to America from Naples via Ellis Island and who still, after thirty years in America, spoke in Italian at home, though they had learned English. Falco was a rather rumpled character who grew up on the mean streets of Brooklyn. He had been with the police twelve years and was well respected, even though his thick black hair was rarely combed. He was tall and rather good-looking despite his lack of sartorial splendor. He had a wife and two children, and wished like hell he was with them this cold night rather than investigating a murder.

As he rang the bell of Brook's suite, he took off his hat. He wore a dark suit under a black overcoat that was missing two buttons. When the door opened and he saw Brook in her Chanel and diamonds, he wondered why a poor unpublished writer in the Village would be spending Saturday night with a knockout society blond wearing a fortune in diamonds—as, at the same time, he knew the answer.

"Good evening, ma'am. I'm Lieutenant Falco, Homicide."

He also noted that Brook was slightly drunk.

"Yes . . . please come in . . . I can't believe what has happened . . ."

He came inside, looking around the luxurious suite. Brook closed the door, then, weaving slightly, went to the chair where she had just poured herself a third glass of champagne. "May I offer you a drink, Lieutenant?"

"No thanks, ma'am. I never drink on duty."

"Please sit down. This has come as such a shock to me. Who could have wanted to kill Lance?"

"That's what I'm hopin' you may be able to tell me, ma'am. How well did you know Fairfax?"

"Not very well. I only met him the other day . . . when did this happen?"

"Sometime this afternoon. We think about three-thirty. Fairfax had been taking a bath. Apparently someone rang the doorbell. Fairfax got out of the tub, wrapped a towel around him, answered the door and was shot dead. We have the murder weapon. It was left on the floor by the door. It's a .38-caliber Smith & Wesson."

"I know nothing about guns . . . wait . . ." She took another gulp of champagne. "My husband has a gun like that."

"Who is your husband, ma'am?" Falco had taken out a small black notebook and a pen.

"His name is Alex De Witt. We live out in Oyster Bay."

"That's on the North Shore?"

"Yes."

"What does your husband do, ma'am?"

"He's President of the American National Life Insurance Company."

"Uh huh. Might I ask what your relationship with Mr. Fairfax was, ma'am? I mean, not to get personal, but . . ."

"No, that's all right. We were friends. I was interested

in his . . ." She hesitated. "Excuse me. His career."

"So interested you were spending Christmas Eve with him rather than with your husband?"

"My husband and I are . . . we're separated, at least for the time being."

"Uh-huh. Now, ma'am, could you tell me where you were this afternoon?"

"Certainly. I went to my hairdresser shortly after noon, then came back here to the hotel about two-thirty. Then, shortly after that, my husband called and asked me to meet him at his office in the American National Life Building downtown. I went down and was in his office for about forty-five minutes. My husband had slipped on some ice."

"Could anyone verify you were there, ma'am?"

"Well . . . let me think . . . the building was empty except for the night watchman . . . He could verify I was there."

"I see." He closed the notebook and stood up. "Well, I won't bother you any more tonight, ma'am, and I appreciate your cooperation."

"If there's anything I can do . . . You see, I was terribly fond of Lance and wanted to help him . . . I just can't believe anyone would murder him . . ."

"It's a tough city. Goodnight, ma'am. And merry Christmas."

"Some merry Christmas," she said, in bitter tones, as she escorted Falco to the door. When he had gone, she finished the bottle of champagne, then threw herself on her bed, still fully dressed, and cried herself to sleep.

Christmas Eve day, Johnny and Rachel were eating breakfast on the terrace of the ocean-side villa they had rented in Palm Beach for the holidays.

"I got a letter from Julie in Hong Kong," Johnny said, drinking his orange juice as the surf splashed lazily onto the nearby beach.

"Oh? And how is she?"

"Everyone's fine. The stores are doing great business."

"And how's our dashing warlord, Charlie Wang? Is he still military attaché to Dr. Sun Yat-sen?"

"Yes, and Julie writes that he and Jasmine have become very friendly with a young soldier who's President of the Whampoa Military Academy, a man named Chiang Kai-shek. Apparently, Charlie, Jasmine, and Chiang Kai-shek sit up all hours of the night talking about how to build a strong army for China."

"It sounds terribly exciting. You know, darling, it's wonderful being part of a family that has warlords and pirates in it. I wouldn't dream of missing any of it."

He smiled and reached across the table to take her hand.

"It is fun, isn't it?" he said. "And I'm damned lucky to have you as a wife." He turned to see the maid come out of the house. "Yes, Molly?"

"There's a phone call for you from New York, sir," she said.

Excusing himself, Johnny got up from the glass-topped table and went inside the large, Spanish-style house. Rachel continued eating her breakfast of grapefruit, soft-boiled eggs, and orange juice as the ocean continued to lap lazily on the beach. It was another balmy day in Florida, which was enjoying something of a real-estate boom.

Fifteen minutes later, Johnny returned to the terrace, a troubled look on his face.

"Who was it, darling?" Rachel asked.

"Brookie," he said. "She's been indicted for the murder of someone named Lance Fairfax. We'll have to return to New York immediately."

28. "ALEX FRAMED ME!" BROOK SAID TO HER mother and father. It was the next afternoon. Johnny and Rachel had come up from Palm Beach on the train. After going to their house to leave their luggage, they had gone on to Brook's Plaza suite where they found her in a state bordering on hysteria. She was out on $50,000 bail. "Oh, he was clever, I suppose. He got my fingerprints on his gun by staging this little scene, and then he lured me to his office so I wouldn't have any alibi at the time of the murder . . ."

"Wait a minute," Johnny interrupted. "You said there was a night watchman who took you up in the elevator."

"Yes, an old man named Jerry O'Toole. Well, guess what? Jerry O'Toole took early retirement, thanks to my darling husband, and is now somewhere in Ireland so he'll never testify for me—and even if he could be found, he probably still wouldn't testify for me for fear of Alex canceling his pension. Oh, he's got me right where he wants me, the dirty, rotten . . ."

She sank into a chair and started sobbing.

"I can't imagine Alex being so vicious," her mother said. "And I can't believe he would murder anyone!"

"Oh Momma, you're so good yourself you can't see evil in others," Brook said, wiping her eyes. "Alex hates me—"

"But why?" her mother interrupted. "You were so in love once!"

"He hates me because I'm Jewish, among other things."

"I can't believe that," said her father.

"Well, believe it!" Brook shot back. "It's come out since we got married. You know his mother is a rabid anti-Semite . . ."

"That's true," Rachel said.

"And she works on Alex when I'm not around, turning him against me, and it's worked! His mind is twisted enough against me to get rid of me this awful way. Why in the world would I want to murder Lance Fairfax? I loved him! But the police have the murder weapon, which has my fingerprints on it, so I'm caught!"

"In fairness to Alex," Johnny said, "you did provoke him. After all, you weren't faithful to him."

Brook sniffed.

"I don't think you're in much of a position to preach to me," she said.

Johnny and Rachel exchanged looks.

"I'm not preaching," her father said. "I'm the last person in the world to do that. We want to help you, Brook. I'm in the process of hiring Cory Dillon to defend you. I'm told he's the best criminal lawyer in the city. I'm fully confident we'll beat this. As you say, you had absolutely no motive to kill this young man, and I think any jury would see that."

"Oh, Daddy." She got up and came across the room to hug him. "I love you so. Thank you for being so supportive."

"Of course we're supportive," her mother said. "But I hope that this terrible experience will lead you to rethink your life, my dear. You've behaved in a terribly irresponsible fashion. And while I don't like preaching, I intend to anyway: you have a responsibility to your family and to your child."

Brook sighed.

"All right," she said, "I guess I had that coming. I'll try to do better from now on."

"You've had every advantage, Brook. You might think about giving something back to a society that has given you so much. There is more to life than just a mindless search for pleasure."

Brook looked at her mother with perplexity.

"Yes, but what is it?" she said.

Cory Dillon was an enormously fat man—he weighed 350 pounds making him, at five feet seven, almost a sphere—who dressed flamboyantly and wore a big diamond ring on one of his pudgy fingers. As he waddled into Johnny's office on Wall Street, Johnny reflected that his physical appearance might resemble an elephant, but he had been told by people who knew such things that his mind was as agile as a fox's. After greeting the renowned lawyer and offering him a cigar, which he refused, Johnny offered him a seat before his desk.

"Well, sir," Dillon wheezed after squeezing into the chair, "I've had a long talk with your daughter, and I think she'll make an excellent witness. Mind you, I don't often put my clients on the witness stand. But Brook comes across as sincere, and I think a jury would react favorably to her, despite all this damned publicity. But then, one has to expect the publicity. You're a well-known family in this town, and when a Savage is charged with murder, that's news."

"Yes," Johnny said sadly, "I'm well aware of that. Do you think the publicity will bias the jury against her?"

"Possibly. But we'll have to take every precaution to prevent that, or at least minimize it. Of course, what would really cinch this case would be if we could find out who in fact did kill Fairfax."

"I've assumed my son-in-law did it."

"Perhaps. However, a man with his social and business position would be very rash to risk committing a murder, and from what I've found out about Alex De Witt, he's a very conservative man. Plus, we must remember that he's a war hero, and if we so much as hint that we think a war hero committed this murder, it could do us more harm than good. It could—what's that new word?—backfire. Yes, that's it. It could backfire, just like a Model T."

"Then what can we do?"

"The police and the prosecution are convinced Brook committed the murder, so I want your permission to hire a private investigator to work on this. I've worked with this man on several other cases, and he's proven to be extremely effective." He pulled a wallet from his jacket and extracted a business card, which he placed on Johnny's desk. "He's expensive, but I think he'll be worth it."

Johnny looked at the card. "Do it," he said. "I don't care what it costs, I don't want my daughter going to the electric chair."

"Well, sir, we won't even think that. We must think positively. We will save Brook."

"There's a gentleman to see you," Johnny's secretary said four mornings later as she came into his office.

"Who's that, Glenda?"

"It's Arnold Rothstein."

Johnny frowned.

"The gangster?"

"Yes."

"What in the world does he want to see me about?"

"I have no idea. Shall I send him away?"

"No, no . . . I'm curious to meet him. Send him in."

Glenda left the office. Moments later, the door was opened and a tall, distinguished-looking man in a dark blue pin-striped suit with a diamond stickpin in his gray tie entered. He came over to the desk.

"Mr. Rothstein," Johnny said, extending his hand.

"It's a pleasure to meet you, Mr. Savage."

Arnold Rothstein shook Johnny's hand, then sat down in front of his desk.

"Now: what can I do for you?"

"Nothing, thank you," Rothstein said. "But I can do something for you. Of course, I've read all about your daughter being charged with the murder of this young writer in the Village. I happen to know who really committed the murder."

Johnny sat forward, rapt.

"That's very good news, Mr. Rothstein. Who did it?"

"It was a professional killer who was hired by your son-in-law. I won't name him, as that would be, shall we say, a breach of professional ethics. But I have enough influence at City Hall that I can arrange for the prosecution of your daughter to be dropped, which I will be glad to do for you."

Johnny was stunned.

"Mr. Rothstein," he said, "you overwhelm me. But why are you being so kind to me?"

"I was asked to do this by your daughter's half brother, Cesare."

"Cesare? Ah, yes, of course. I remember that you and he were acquainted."

"Cesare is very upset about Brook getting in trouble, so he asked me to help as a favor, which I am delighted to do. This whole thing should be resolved in a few days. So." Rothstein stood up and again reached over the desk to shake Johnny's hand. "It's a great pleasure to have met you, Mr. Savage, being, as I am, so very fond of Cesare. Good day, sir."

He started to leave.

"Mr. Rothstein," Johnny said.

"Yes?"

"My wife tells me Cesare has bought a duplex penthouse on Park Avenue and is spending a fortune fixing it up. He's told his mother that when he moves in, he'll be giving up the management of the Santa Isabel plantation in Cuba. Do you have any idea where Cesare is getting all this money? What investment did he make that's paid off so spectacularly? Of course, as you know, we barely speak, and he's been rather secretive with his mother."

Arnold Rothstein's face assumed a look of angelic innocence.

"I'm afraid I can't help you there, Mr. Savage. Cesare and I are friends, but he doesn't tell me much about his business dealings, as I don't tell him much about mine. Good day, sir."

"Good day. And again, my heartfelt thanks. I am eternally indebted to you, Mr. Rothstein."

He doesn't think I know where Cesare's money comes from, Johnny thought after Rothstein left the office. My own stepson a bootlegger! Dear God! And yet, he's saved Brook.

Alex and Brook were divorced two months later. Brook gained custody of Graydon along with a five-million-dollar trust fund in his name. The real killer was convicted but on the way to prison miraculously escaped. Part of the settlement was that Brook would never reveal what she knew about Alex's involvement with the murder of Lance Fairfax.

"We're a family," she remarked to her father after the divorce, "with a lot of secrets."

"Unhappily, you're right," Johnny said. "What are you going to do now, Brookie? Your mother's right, you know. You brought a lot of this on yourself. It's time you settled down."

"Yes, I know. I've been giving it a lot of thought. I think I probably should get out of the country for a while until all this publicity is sort of forgotten. I've been thinking it would be interesting to move to Paris for a few years. That way, Graydon could learn French, which would be useful for him. And maybe I'll find something I can give back to the world, as Mother put it. Maybe I can find happiness." She smiled. "If you can't find happiness in Paris, where can you find it?"

Nick Savage's bare buttocks moved up and down with increasing lust as he made love to the cute brunette actress in the bedroom of his Park Avenue maisonette. Nick, who at twenty-four was the youngest of Johnny and Rachel's four children, was known to his friends because of his amatory excesses as "the naked Savage." It was certainly true that this tall, good-looking young man caused women to swoon, and the actress he was laying, whose name was Trixie, was crazy for him. When they both had come, with loud grunts from Nick and ecstatic "Yes, yes, yesses" from Trixie, Nick got off the bed and said, "You'd better scram now, baby. I've got some business people coming over for a drink. But I'll take you out to dinner tomorrow night. You pick the place. Gotta take a shower now, so I'll see you."

He went into the bathroom as Trixie started to put on her clothes.

Twenty minutes later, after Nick had put on his tux, he opened his front door to admit his older brother, Cesare, who was carrying a suitcase.

"Cesare!" Nick exclaimed, his face lighting up. "It's great to see you. Come in."

"I brought you a present," Cesare said, indicating the suitcase. "And who was that cute little trick I saw come out this door as I got out of my taxi?"

"That's Trixie, my aspiring Sarah Bernhardt."

Cesare laughed.

"Nick, you're a worse goat than I am. Where'll I put the booze?"

"Take it into the living room."

Nick closed and locked the door, which was his own private entrance to the side street off Park Avenue. Nick, who was a great athlete but not a great scholar, had flunked out of two colleges before finally getting a B.A. so that he wouldn't break his mother's heart. He was working as a teller at Johnny's bank. Now he followed Cesare into the living room of his six-room apartment. Cesare was taking bottles of wine and whiskey from the suitcase and placing them on Nick's bar.

"Fresh off the boat," he said as his younger brother joined him at the bar. "The best booze in town. So, what have you been up to, besides screwing every woman in New York?"

Nick laughed as he gave his older brother's arm an affectionate shove. Nick thought Cesare was the most glamorous man he had ever known, and the smartest. He had helped tutor him to get his degree. Nick truly adored Cesare.

"Aw, not much. Slaving away at the bank, as usual. The old man gave me a big Christmas bonus: a hundred dollars. The old bastard's tight as a tick with money."

"Tell you what," Cesare said, taking his wallet from his coat. "Here's five hundred bucks. Go blow it on some gorgeous dame, and when you've run through this, there's more where that came from."

He pulled five hundred-dollar bills from his wallet and held them out. Nick looked at the money.

"Aw hell, Cesare, that's terrific of you, but I can't take money from my own brother."

"Why not? Here: take it and no arguments. What's a big brother for? Now let's open one of these bottles and get a load on. I've had a busy day and need to relax, and who is there better to relax with than my own kid brother?"

He gave Nick's shiny black hair an affectionate Dutch rub.

"What the hell do you put on your hair, axle grease?" he said, wiping his hand with a handkerchief as Nick laughed and opened a bottle of Scotch.

"Yeah, I buy it at a gas station. So, Cesare, when are you going to tell me where you get all your dough? I mean, I'm jealous as hell. I slave away at the bank earning peanuts, and you live like Rudy Valentino. You're a real man of mystery. Come clean: is it true what they say? That you're a bootlegger?"

He filled two shot glasses with whiskey. Cesare smiled.

"And what would you say if it were true?" he asked.

"I'd say, hot damn! My brother's a goddamn bootlegger! That's great!"

"Do you mean it, Nick? You wouldn't be ashamed of me?"

"Ashamed? Why would I be ashamed? You know I've always thought you were the best at everything, and I'd assume you were the best bootlegger. Cheers."

The brothers clicked glasses. Cesare eyed Nick as he sipped the excellent whiskey.

"Well, little brother, it's true," he said. "I am a bootlegger—of sorts—and there's a helluva lot of money in it. But I'd appreciate your not telling anyone else in the family—especially the Old Man. If he knew, he'd probably turn me into the police."

Nick was looking at his brother almost worshipfully.

"A bootlegger," he said. "Gosh, Cesare, that's about the most exciting thing I've ever heard. And don't worry: I'd never rat on you. You're not only my big brother: you're my best friend." He finished the shot glass and refilled it. "By the way, Bro, when's some lucky debutante going to break your heart and lead you to the alter?"

Cesare stared sadly at his shot glass.

"I haven't any heart left to break," he said quietly. "What heart I had got broken long ago in Rome."

PART EIGHT

BEATRICE AND THE FASCIST

29. UNLIKE HER YOUNGER SIBLINGS, BEATRICE SAVage was a rather shy and bookish person whom her mother was beginning to worry might end up an old maid. While Beatrice was an attractive girl with her mother's dark hair and a good figure, she certainly wasn't a beauty like Brook; and her lack of interest in fashion or trends, as well as her retiring personality, made her something of a social dud. Nor did it help that she was nearsighted, so that she had to wear rather thick glasses to see well.

But what Beatrice lacked in superficial charm, she more than made up for in intellectual achievement. She had a first-rate mind, had graduated third in her class at Vassar where she also starred on the field hockey team, and was fluent in French and Italian. After graduating, she rather surprised her parents by renting an apartment on Irving Place and devoting herself to social work with the desperately poor on the Lower East Side. While her mother admired Beatrice for her concern for those less fortunate— certainly, in Rachel's opinion, Beatrice behaved much more admirably than her younger sister, Brook—still at the time for a young woman in Society to devote her full time in the slums was not quite *comme il faut*. And by ignoring the usual round of Society dinner parties, teas, and balls, Beatrice was doing her best, unconsciously or not, to discourage a prospective husband. When her parents urged her to accept invitations, or invited her to parties at their house in the hope of attracting a possible suitor, Beatrice somehow always found an excuse not to go—she was either "busy" or "ill." While Rachel clung desperately to the hope that one day she would finally fall madly in love, her step-father, Johnny—who was as fond of Beatrice as he was cold to her brother, Cesare—accepted the fact that she would probably end up an old maid, and a rather eccentric one at that. After all, she was thirty-four years old. Her youth was almost gone.

The one romantic facet of her personality was her passionate love of Italy, and she found time to take several trips to that sunny land a year, staying in Rome with her grandparents, Fiammetta and Justin, at their palazzo. While New York Society bored her—she found it trivial and artificial—inconsistently enough, she found Roman Society rather interesting; the fact that so many of the families of this ancient city had been important for centuries, many of them having Popes and Cardinals in their family trees, fascinated her. Rome's glorious history, as well as its architecture and culture, held a glamour for Beatrice that New York's comparatively brief history and its money-mad culture lacked. She felt at home in Rome the way she had never felt at home in New York, and each visit reinforced her love of the place. It got to the point where Rachel said, rather sadly, to Johnny: "Rome may be our last chance to find Beatrice a husband."

In the autumn of 1922, Beatrice sailed for Italy yet again, and after landing at Ostia traveled the short distance to Rome where, as usual, she stayed with her grandparents. Fiammetta was not unaware of Beatrice's situation: she not only had many letters from Johnny, but she had seen with her own eyes how unaccomplished her granddaughter was in the art of flirtation. And, as she had had a hand in Cesare's ill-starred romance with the unfortunate Antonia Barberini, she now privately decided it was time for her to take a hand in the lackluster love life of his sister. To welcome Beatrice back to Rome, she gave a dinner party the second night of her stay at the palazzo and, perhaps rather unsubtly, invited a number of the most eligible bachelors in the city. She spent a good deal of time arranging the place cards, and took care to flank Beatrice with the two men she thought were the most eligible, one being a Prince Chigi, and the other being a young doctor named Bruno Vespa. An hour before the guests arrived, Fiammetta knocked on the door of Beatrice's bedroom.

"Yes?"

Fiammetta, who was wearing a stunning evening gown of silver lamé and her famous rubies and diamonds, opened the door. "It is I, dear," she said, coming in. "I wanted to see what you're wearing tonight."

"It's my best dress, Grandmomma, but I'm sure you won't like it. You never do like my clothes."

She was standing in front of a full-length mirror. She had on a brown dress trimmed with black that was woefully out of fashion and as seductive as a burlap bag. Fiammetta looked at it with obvious lack of enthusiasm.

"Well, my dear, brown has never been one of my favorite colors, but I suppose it will do. I don't suppose I could talk you into using some lipstick? Just a little. All the young women are wearing it now."

"I know, but I'm old-fashioned. If people don't like my face as it is, it can't be helped."

"You have a lovely face, Beatrice, but we all can use all the help we can get. As you can see, I've started wearing it, though at my age it does seem a bit of a lost cause."

Beatrice smiled and hugged her.

"Grandmother, you're still the most beautiful woman of all."

"You're sweet, my dear, but I have mirrors. I used to lie about my age, but there comes a time when one simply throws up one's hands and gives in to the inevitable. Now, I've put you between two very charming and attractive young men, and I do hope you'll make an effort to make conversation. I know small talk bores you, but do try."

"I'll do my best, but you know I'm not very good at chitchat."

"I know, dear. But this young Bruno Vespa may surprise you. He's a doctor—a very good one, I'm told—and he spends two afternoons a week working at a charity hospital, so I thought you two might have something in common, considering your work in the slums."

"Yes, he does sound interesting. Thank you, Grandmother."

"His family is a very old one, quite distinguished. Quite rich, I might add, which never hurts. Now, I know you'll do me a favor and not wear your glasses."

"But I can barely see without them . . ."

"The others won't know that. You have beautiful eyes, but glasses somehow spoil the effect."

Beatrice sighed and took off her glasses.

"Oh, all right."

"Charming." Fiammetta smiled and kissed her cheek.

Fiammetta's *sala da pranzo* was one of the most spectacular rooms in Rome, a city filled with spectacular rooms. The ceiling soared to forty feet, and on it was a Tiepolo allegory depicting the deification of the sixteenth-century ancestor of her first husband, Count Sigismundo di Mondragone, a well-known sadist and torturer. Count Sigismondo, supported by a number of winged angels, soared through puffy clouds toward a burst of light in the middle of the ceiling, presumably God Himself, while choruses of chubby cherubs sang and trumpeting angels tooted their horns in glory. It was all terribly theatrical, more than a bit ludicrous, and totally wonderful.

But this was only part of the show. The walls were pale pink marble, interrupted by a series of pink-veined marble pilasters crowned by gilt Corinthian capitals, and fronted by a number of elaborately carved gilt rococo tables on which Fiammetta's superb collection of silver plate was displayed: chargers, vases, epergnes, and what have you embossed with the Mondragone coat of arms and polished to reflect the gleam of a thousand candles. A long mahogany table, capable of seating forty, filled the center of this cavernous room; on it, yet another set of epergnes, vases, and candelabra was placed, this in vermeil, the vases bursting with great floral displays, the epergnes groaning with luscious fruit. Twelve bewigged footmen in yellow livery served the thirty formally dressed guests. Beatrice had seen this fabulous visual feast before; but tonight, without her glasses, it all was a big blur.

"Is something wrong with your eyes?" asked the bearded young man sitting to her right, Prince Baldassare Chigi. "You're squinting."

"Oh, it's just that I broke my glasses," she lied.

"Ah. Well, if I can help you in any way, please ask."

"Thank you."

Beatrice was in agony, her normal shyness being reinforced by her inability to see anything clearly farther than five feet away. Unable to think of a single thing to say to the handsome young prince, she cut into her *vitello tonnato*, praying to God that this evening would soon be over. Flouting all the rules of good manners, she didn't even bother to say a word to the young man on her left to whom she had been introduced by her grandmother. However, she was dying of curiosity to speak to Bruno Vespa; she simply couldn't think of an opening gambit, and she cursed herself for her inability to make small talk. Finally, Vespa solved her problem by speaking to her.

"Your grandmother tells me you do social work in New York?" he said.

Beatrice abandoned her *vitello tonnato* to look at him. He was a good-looking young man with black hair, blue eyes, clean-cut features, and skin that had been ravaged by terrible acne, giving his face the look of a lunar landscape.

"Yes," Beatrice said, unable to pursue this opening gambit. Say something! she thought. Anything! But her shyness sent her back to her food.

The big room buzzed with conversation as minutes dragged by like hours. Finally:

"Have I offended you?"

She almost jumped. She turned to look at Bruno.

"Oh . . . no . . . I'm so sorry . . ."

"I thought perhaps I offended you by asking about your social work?"

"Oh no, not at all . . ."

"You didn't seem to want to talk to me."

She was dying of embarrassment.

"It's just that I'm . . . well, I'm a terrible conversationalist. I just never can think of anything to say, so I end up saying nothing. I'm so sorry."

He smiled at her.

"Well, I'm not exactly Oscar Wilde. Would you prefer me to shut up?"

"Oh, please no. Please: let's talk. I'll do my best not to be boring."

"And I'll do my best not to bore you. If I may say so, it strikes me as rather unusual that a girl like you would be doing social work. How did you get interested in it?"

"Well . . . I just . . . I mean, there's so much terrible poverty in New York, and I wanted to try and do something to help those people. I mean, the slums are just horrible . . . And most people really don't care, so I try to care a little extra to make up for the . . . indifference."

"I admire you for that."

"Oh, I don't do it for admiration! I suppose I'm really rather selfish, because I do it . . . well, it makes me feel good to do it."

"And I admire you for saying that. It's very honest. Few people who do charity work admit to themselves that they do it for their own pleasure."

"Well, I don't think 'pleasure' is the right word."

"No, probably not."

"My grandmother told me you work several days a week at a charity hospital."

"That's right. I do it not only to help, but because one sees quite unusual medical cases from time to time. So you can see that I'm not entirely altruistic myself. I try to improve my professional knowledge."

"I . . ."

She cut off her sentence, cringing with embarrassment.

"You started to say something?"

One of the footmen removed her plate, giving her a breather. Speak to him! she screamed at herself. Say what you want! He's really very nice!

"I don't suppose it would be possible . . . I mean, I've seen most of the touristy things in Rome, but I've never seen a charity hospital. I don't suppose . . . Oh, I'm so terribly inarticulate . . ."

He looked at her rather tenderly.

"I'll call for you at ten tomorrow morning."

She almost burst into tears of gratitude.

The hospital was on the edge of Rome and it was run by nuns. Beatrice followed Dr. Vespa as he made the rounds of the immaculate wards, stopping to talk to each patient, most of them extremely elderly. Beatrice was touched by the personal tenderness Bruno exhibited to these poor old people; she was even more touched by the obvious affection these people had for him. When they had finished and were driving back into Rome in his Fiat, she said to him, "I can't thank you enough. It was so very interesting, and you're so wonderful with them! I almost cried at how thrilled they were to see you! Oh, how I admire you!"

Bruno turned and smiled at her.

"I thought you were inarticulate," he said.

"Oh, but I am."

"That sounded very articulate to me. You know, you're a very pretty woman. But could I ask you a rather personal question?"

"Of course. I mean . . . if it's not too personal."

"Well, last night you had on lipstick and weren't wearing glasses. But today, there's no lipstick."

"Oh. Well, my grandmomma made me wear lipstick last night. I think . . . well, I think she's trying to catch a man for me. It's all a bit embarrassing."

"Why?"

"Well, I'm my family's old maid. It really doesn't bother me, but poor Grandmomma . . . well, she was a great beauty in her day and I think romance is very important to her."

"It's not important to you?"

She blushed slightly.

"Well . . ." She forced a smile. "I'm afraid I don't know much about romance."

"Perhaps it's time you learned. Would you like to have lunch?"

She looked at him with surprise.

"Oh, you mustn't feel you have to be nice to me . . ."

"I don't. I want to take you to lunch, period. Will you?"

She gulped, still staring at him as if he were from another planet.

"I'd love to," she said honestly.

"Bea, darling, you look different!" exclaimed Brook two weeks later as she picked Beatrice up at the Gare de Lyon in Paris. "You're wearing lipstick, and your clothes are so smart! What's happened?"

Beatrice, who did indeed look different, blushed as her sister's chauffeur took her luggage and headed down the train platform. "Well, Grandmother took me shopping," she said. "She's always said I have no interest in clothes, which used to be true . . ."

"But it isn't now?" Brook interrupted as she took Beatrice's arm. Brook, as always, looked smart with a fur wrap around the shoulders of her suit. But Beatrice the frump looked just as smart in a gray wool suit and a snappy hat. Though she wore her glasses, her face had been definitely improved with the addition of lipstick and some eye shadow.

"I've sort of gotten more interested," Beatrice said. "I mean, I'm hardly a clothes horse, but I feel better."

"And you look so much better! But there must be a reason. Let me guess: you're in love!"

Beatrice blushed.

"You're a witch. Yes, I am. Oh Brookie, I've met the most wonderful, sweetest man! I never thought I'd ever fall in love, but I have, head over heels, just like in books, and I've never been so happy! And he's asked me to marry him! Look." She pulled off her suede glove to reveal a diamond and sapphire ring. "Isn't it beautiful?"

Brook stopped to examine it.

"Oh, it is! Bea, I'm so happy for you! No, I'm not: I'm wildly jealous, but oh, well: come on, let's go home and you'll tell me all about him."

Brook had taken a two-year lease on a stone town house on the Avenue Foch that had been built at the turn of the century by a successful perfume manufacturer in a handsome Louis XVI style. As Brook's black Hispano-Suiza limousine pulled up in front of the house, the chauffeur jumped out to open the rear door and the two sisters went into the house. "Graydon's talking now," Brook said as they came into the stone entrance hall, "babbling in English and French. It's amazing how children pick up different languages so quickly. He has a nice French nanny named

Chantal who speaks French to him, and I speak English. How's everyone in Rome?"

"Grandmother's fine, but Grandfather Justin is beginning to show his age. He's well into his seventies now, you know."

"Yes, I know. Come on: I'll show you your room. You can freshen up, then we'll have a little cocktail before lunch in the library and you can tell me about your big romance."

"Oh, I never drink during the day."

"Well, I'll have a cocktail. You can have tea or whatever. I even have Coca-Cola."

The library was an extraordinarily handsome room paneled in walnut and filled with books Brook never bothered to look at. When Beatrice came downstairs, having changed out of her traveling suit into a simple black dress, the lush sounds of Rachmaninoff's first piano concerto were pouring out of a Victrola as Brook, a martini in hand, twirled in slow, dreamy turns around the room. When she spotted her sister, she turned off the music, then smiled and came over to kiss her.

"I can't tell you how pleased I am to see you, darling. I hope you'll change your mind about only staying three days?"

"Oh no, I have to get back to New York."

Gaspard, Brook's butler, appeared with a Coke on a silver salver, which Beatrice took. Then Brook flopped into a leather sofa, patting the cushion beside her for Beatrice to sit on, which she did.

"Now, tell all. What's his name?"

"Bruno Vespa, and he's a doctor."

"Bruno: what a wonderful name! It sounds sort of overbearing."

"Oh, he's not at all. He's a very gentle man. I went with him to a charity hospital he works at two days a week, and it's so wonderful to watch him treating his patients. They absolutely adore him!"

"A charity hospital? You mean, he treats them for free?"

"Yes, which I admire so much! He really cares for them, and most of them are so old and poor . . . I mean, he's really a sort of saint!"

"What's the saint look like?"

"Well, he's six feet and weighs about a hundred and eighty pounds. He has a nice build and black hair and the most wonderful blue eyes . . . I think he's very handsome, though he does have rather bad skin. He told me when he was a teenager he was painfully shy because of his acne."

Brook finished her martini and got up to go to an English butler's tray where a silver shaker rested amid several glass. As she refilled her glass, sticking in a tiny onion, she said, "Well, he sounds wonderful, darling. And when's the wedding going to be? And where?"

"Grandmother volunteered to give it at her place in Rome, which we've agreed to. But now there's so much trouble in Italy, we're not so sure what to do."

"Trouble? Oh yes, I've been reading about it in the papers. All the strikes, and the Black Shirts—what do they call them?"

"Fascists. It's from the word *fascio,* which means a political group. Apparently, practically every town in Italy has a *fascio,* and they can get a bit ugly. You know, they beat people up and force their enemies to drink castor oil."

"How charming." Brook returned to the sofa, sipping her drink.

"But a lot of people think they're the only thing that can save Italy from anarchy. I don't pay much attention to politics, but Bruno admires this Mussolini person, who's their leader. He's from Milan and has a newspaper. A bit of a rabble-rouser from what I can gather, but Bruno says he's a terrific orator. Well, we'll see. But enough about me. Tell me about yourself. Are you happy here in Paris?"

Brook sipped her gin.

" 'Happy'? What an odd word. Yes, I suppose I'm happy enough. But you know Parisians will never accept Americans—at least until they've lived here twenty years."

"Are you having any romances?"

"Plenty of dates, not much romance. I think dear old Alex, that bastard, may have killed romance for me forever."

"Why?"

"Oh Bea, don't you think I'm haunted by what happened to that poor young man, Lance Fairfax? He lost his life because of Alex's twisted hatred of me. I can't help but think the whole thing was my fault, my irresponsibility, and every time I want to fall in love, something holds me back. I wonder if I'm not some sort of a curse! I don't want to hurt people and I'm terrified that I may if I get too closely involved with someone. So I just sort of drift." Tears welled in her eyes. "Oh God, now I'm going to get a crying jag."

"If you ask me, Brookie," her sister said, "you're getting too closely involved with gin."

Brook shot her an angry look as the butler appeared in the doorway.

"*Madame,*" he announced, "*est servie.*"

30. THE FIVE-MAN BLACK JAZZ COMBO IN THE COR-ner of the living room of the Park Avenue duplex penthouse was playing "The Birth of the Blues" as almost fifty guests, dressed formally, milled about drinking the best bootleg booze and puffing on endless cigarettes. Cesare Savage was hosting a cocktail party to celebrate the completion of his ten-room apartment overlooking the city, and the weatherman had been kind: it was a balmy, early-autumn evening, pleasant enough that the guests, if they wished, could go out on the spectacularly planted terraces and enjoy the city's skyline above which a trillion stars twinkled against ebony velvet, like a jeweler's box. A dozen white-jacketed waiters passed trays of champagne and canapés, while three full bars had been set up in strategic places as oases for the thirsty.

The crowd was what the tabloids had begun to call "café society," a much looser, younger mix than the old society with enough shady characters to make it irresistibly spicy to Park Avenue and Fifth Avenue types bored with city and country clubs. That Cesare was the host gave it enough legitimacy that the more daring debutantes had clamored for invitations; Cesare of course was "Society," but by now it was no secret that he was somehow involved in bootlegging and making a fantastic fortune doing it. Even his mother knew by now. And even though Cesare had told her over and over that he was not breaking the law—which was technically true—and that he was only doing what respectable businessmen like Joe Kennedy and the Bronfmans were doing, he had come perilously close to a permanent rupture with Rachel who, no matter how much she loved him, shuddered at the thought of gangsters.

But while none of his family was present, his date was Amanda Chatfield, a stunning brunette right out of the Social Register, who happened to be crazy about Cesare, a fact he was well aware of and exploited for his own purposes: if he was good enough for Amanda Chatfield, he was good enough for anyone. Cesare, dashing in his well-cut tux, stood by the entrance to the apartment greeting guests with Amanda at his side. This has got to be the best night of my life so far, he was thinking. I've got New York eating out of my hand.

The penthouse was causing comment, for it was decorated in a daring new "modern" style. Cesare had hired a young French decorator from Paris who knew where the wind was blowing in the most rarefied corridors of that world; he knew that the International Exposition of Decorative Arts, originally intended to open in 1915, then postponed by the war and later financial troubles (which would finally open in 1925), was where the future trends lay. Thus he had been able to jump-start the art deco look that a few years later would be the rage, and the walls of the huge living room were lacquered white, with black-lacquered panels interrupting the snow. Guided by his sister, Brook, in Paris, who was well up on the art scene there, Cesare had bought a big Picasso for one wall, and a Matisse for another. Sleek modern sculpture was in evidence everywhere, and the furniture was all modern with a vengeance, with brightly colored woven rugs on the marble floor. For a generation raised in late Victorian and Edwardian clutter, this brazenly modern apartment was like a glimpse into the future. To Cesare's intense satisfaction, everyone was impressed, if not bowled over.

By nine o'clock, the crowd had begun to thin as the party-goers left, in various stages of drunkenness, to go to their favorite speakeasies for dinner.

"Come on," Cesare said to Amanda, "let's go to the Purple Parrot and get something to eat. All this party food leaves me ravenous. I'm ready for a steak."

What he didn't tell her was that he had found out something about his partner, Arnold Rothstein, and he wasn't happy. He also didn't tell her that beneath his dinner jacket was a revolver.

"We've got a couple of movie stars here tonight," Arnold Rothstein said as Cesare and Amanda came into the Purple Parrot a half hour later. The speakeasy was packed with drinking customers and, on the small stage, a sleek chanteuse in a slinky white satin dress was singing "Melancholy Baby." "Mabel Normand is at table five, and Gloria Gilmore is at table eight with her new boyfriend, Jesse Breen, the Wall Street plunger."

Cesare looked across the smoky room at the table near the stage where blond Gloria Gilmore was drinking with a balding middle-aged man.

"Gloria's old boyfriend used to be my father," Cesare said.

"No kidding?"

"Take Amanda to our table, will you? I want to meet Miss Gilmore."

"Sure, kid. I guess her Hollywood career is pretty washed up, but they say Breen is crazy for her, and judging from the rocks she's wearing, he's spending big bucks on her."

"Good for Gloria. I'll join you in a moment, Amanda."

Cesare made his way across the room to Gloria's table.

"Excuse me, Miss Gilmore?" he said. "My name's Cesare Savage. I think you're acquainted with my stepfather, Johnny Savage?"

Gloria, who was in fact dripping diamonds, looked up at him.

"You mean, Old One-Leg?" she said. "Sure I'm acquainted with him, the bastard. He walked out on me when I really needed him. So you're his son?"

"Stepson. Hello, Mr. Breen. Cesare Savage here—don't get up."

He held out his hand but Breen said, "Sorry, I never shake hands with strangers. No offense: germs, you know. Everyone's got germs. I've heard a lot about you, Cesare. Can I buy you a drink?"

"My pleasure, sir."

Cesare took an empty chair between Breen and Gloria, who was looking as glamorous as a movie star should in a white beaded evening gown that showed off her natural assets to advantage. After Breen had summoned a waiter and Cesare ordered a Scotch on the rocks, he said to Breen: "By the way, Mr. Breen, I'm looking for a little action in the stock market, but I don't have a broker. I don't suppose you'd be interested in representing me?"

Breen, who had a long, thin face and rather beady eyes, sucked on his cigarette as he pulled a business card from his wallet.

"Give me a call, Mr. Savage," he said. "I'd be pleased to do business with you. Any stock you're particularly interested in?"

"Yes, there's one I'm extremely interested in."

"Which is that?"

"The Savage Bank."

Breen's eyes narrowed with interest.

"You fascinate me, Cesare," Gloria said. "Are you thinking of running Johnny's stock up?"

"Perhaps. Or down. Or both ways."

Jesse Breen chuckled.

"I'm beginning to sniff something very interesting. I'll be looking forward to your call."

"Arnold, the word around is that you're swindling me," Cesare said an hour later. He had parked Amanda with a bottle of white Burgundy and requested a meeting in Arnold Rothstein's private office at the rear of the speakeasy. Arnold lit a cigarette and exhaled.

"Kid," he said, "I don't like to hear this kind of talk from my partner."

"I don't either. But what I'm told is that you're taking the premium grade hooch from my yacht, then diluting it with rotgut and selling it five to one on the market. I don't like this, Arnold. This wasn't our agreement. I don't mind bringing in good stuff, but I do mind selling it to the public under false pretenses. And I don't like being cheated."

Arnold Rothstein flicked his ashes as he looked at the two goons who were standing behind his desk, one of them being Little Hymie Weiss.

"So," he said, "assuming what you say is true, what do you intend doing about it, Cesare?"

"I intend to insist that either you stop this, or you cut me in as an equal partner, fifty-fifty."

Arnold smiled.

"You have a fine moral standard, Cesare. As long as you get your cut, you don't care what you do."

Cesare shrugged.

"Maybe."

"And what if I get nasty? What if I say to you, go to hell? I really don't need you, Cesare. My operation is so big that if I lose your Cuban connection I'm still going to do quite well."

"I know that. But why lose anything? Listen, Arnold, we're making a fortune. We've got a really terrific operation going here. Why the hell screw it up? Why should we be fighting each other when we're doing so well? It doesn't make any sense."

Arnold Rothstein sucked on his cigarette, looking at Cesare sitting across the desk from him.

"All right, you have a point. I'll cut you in, fifty-fifty. But, Cesare, the profits are so enormous diluting the hooch, it's crazy not to do it."

Cesare nodded.

"Fine. But you might have told me about this up-front."

31. THE CHÂTEAU WAS SITUATED IN A WOODED park near Versailles, and as Brook's car pulled up the gravel drive in front of it she thought the two-story building with the slate mansard roof and the shuttered windows was classically simple and beautiful. The invitation for a week-end had come from Count Maurice de Belleville, who had telephoned Brook at her Paris home and introduced himself as an old friend of her mother's. Now she got out of the rear of the Hispano-Suiza and walked across the gravel to the front door of the stone house as her chauffeur carried her suitcase behind her. On such a lovely autumn day, with the leaves beginning to turn, the thought of a Saturday night out of Paris in the country was agreeable, to say the least.

The door was answered by a retainer in a white jacket, who took her suitcase from the chauffeur, then led her through the entrance hall to a salon where Maurice came to kiss her hand. She had met him once before in New York and remembered how handsome he was. He was a tall, white-haired man, looking very much the country squire in a tweed jacket.

"When I heard Rachel Savage's daughter was living in Paris," he said, "I couldn't resist meeting you. And how is your beautiful mother?"

"She's quite well. How long ago did you know her?"

"Ah, more years than I like to think about. It was in England, back in the last century when your mother and I were still young. I fell quite hopelessly in love with her, and I flatter myself that my love was reciprocated. Unfor-

tunately, there was a problem about our religions. I was—
and am—Catholic, and of course your mother was Jewish.
The irony is that my second wife, who died last year, was
Jewish. So I lost the opportunity of being your father. Now,
please come outside and meet my son, Bernard. Then we'll
have lunch."

He led her to French doors that opened onto a charming
stone terrace where a round table had been set for a meal.
Standing by the stone balustrade was a tall young man,
quite slim, with thick, wavy golden hair. He was wearing
a blue blazer and white duck trousers.

"Ah, Bernard," his father said, "this is Mrs. De Witt
who's moved to Paris from New York. As I explained,
she's the daughter of a very dear old friend of mine."

Brook came up to the young man, whom she thought
was one of the most beautiful creatures she had ever seen,
and extended her hand.

"How do you do? My name is Brook."

Bernard stared at her for a moment. Then he kissed her
hand.

"I'm very glad to meet you," he said in excellent English.

"And now," his father said, "lunch. I hope you like turbot?"

"I love turbot," Brook said, sitting down on the white-
cushioned wrought-iron chair.

The first course of the lunch was an unusual beet, orange,
and fennel salad, followed by the turbot cooked in a delicious cream and wine sauce, all served with fine white
wines.

Maurice de Belleville was congenial and a good talker,
but Bernard remained mostly silent. Brook became aware
that he was looking at her when he thought she wouldn't
notice. Since he was sitting opposite her, she tried to get
him to talk several times. But aside from his telling her that
he was an archaeologist and that he had worked on a dig

in Egypt the previous summer, she couldn't extract much more information from him.

After lunch, Maurice took Brook riding through his park.

"Tell me about Bernard," she said as their horses meandered through the trees. "He seems terribly quiet."

"He's a bit shy around people he doesn't know."

"He's so terribly good-looking, he must have dozens of girlfriends."

"So far, he doesn't seem particularly interested in girls. By which I mean he's very bookish. I think he's quite normal, so I suppose someday he'll come home to tell me he's madly in love and wants to get married."

"I'm sure he'll find someone wonderful."

"I hope you're right. I found someone wonderful years ago—your mother—but was foolish enough to lose her. I've regretted it ever since. But knowing you eases the hurt."

After dinner that night, where they were joined by two other couples, neighbors of the de Bellevilles, a few games of bridge were played and then Brook, who was tired, excused herself and went up to her bedroom to take a bath and go to bed. After putting on a white silk nightgown, she turned out the lights and went to the two French doors that led out to a narrow wrought-iron balcony overlooking the rear of the building. A full moon was out, and the château's gardens with their several fountains and classic statuary seemed magical in the moonlight. She was about to turn to go back inside when she saw someone standing on the terrace below looking up at her.

It was Bernard.

When he saw her see him, he hurried inside.

What an odd young man, she thought, going back into her bedroom. She got in the big bed with the thick white duvet and quickly fell asleep.

Something woke her up a few hours later—was it a noise? Rubbing her eyes, she sat up to see someone standing in the open French doors, silhouetted by the moonlight.

"Who's there?" she whispered, terrified.

"Please . . . I didn't mean to wake you . . ."

The figure came into the room and she realized it was Bernard. He was wearing the same white slacks he had worn at dinner and a white shirt, open at the collar. He came up to the bed.

"What are you doing in here?" she whispered.

"I . . . please don't tell my father, he'd be furious at me, but I wanted to be near you. I meant no harm . . . You see, the balcony goes all the way across the back of the château and my bedroom is next to yours and . . ." He took a deep breath. "I couldn't help myself. I wanted to look at you, be near you . . . you're so beautiful . . . But I'll leave now, I won't bother you again."

"No, wait," she whispered. "Stay a moment. I'm very flattered, Bernard, but I'm a bit older than you and I have a child. I think you're wasting your time with me."

She could see enough in the moonlight to see that he was trembling. Slowly, she reached out her left hand and took his, squeezing it a moment.

"Don't be afraid," she whispered. "I hope we can become friends in time. I think you're a very nice young man. Really."

He raised her hand to his mouth and kissed it.

"I want to be more than your friend," he whispered. "I want to be your lover. And I will be . . . soon."

He kissed her hand again. Then he released it and went out on the balcony to disappear into the night.

Dear me, she thought. I think Bernard has finally fallen in love.

Then she remembered Lance Fairfax, and a sense of

dread came over her. She would have to leave first thing in the morning before Bernard's apparent fascination for her became something more obsessive. He was too sweet, too vulnerable, and she was cursed. If something happened to Bernard like what happened to Lance, she could never forgive herself.

I must never see this young man again, she thought.

But when she went downstairs in the morning for breakfast, she was informed by Bernard's father that he had gone into Paris for the day. Rather relieved that the situation seemed to have resolved itself, she had breakfast, then informed her host she couldn't stay for lunch after all, that she had been informed by her nanny that her son was sneezing and she wanted to see whether she should call a doctor. After breakfast, she called her chauffeur, who had spent the night at the château; and after her luggage was in her car, she thanked Maurice and started back to Paris.

Maurice is so nice, she thought, and Bernard is so sweet. I mustn't do anything to hurt them.

At the same time, she felt slightly disappointed that she hadn't been able to see Bernard one final time.

When her Hispano-Suiza got back to the Avenue Foch, she was surprised to see Bernard walking slowly back and forth in front of her house. When he saw her get out of her car, he stopped pacing and stared at her.

"Bernard, what are you doing here?" she asked, coming up to him.

"I'm waiting for you," he said simply.

"But how did you know where I live?"

"I looked you up in my father's address book. I want to take you to lunch. Will you have lunch with me? I know a wonderful little restaurant near here . . ."

"It's too early for lunch. Bernard, what are you trying to do? Well, we can hardly talk here, on the sidewalk. Come on inside the house."

She went to her front door, taking her key from her purse, and opened it as her chauffeur took her luggage from the car. She went inside, followed by Bernard and the chauffeur. When he was inside the entrance hall, he looked around.

"It's odd," he said. "For some reason, I thought your house would be more American, but this looks very French."

"It is French," she said. "I rent it, and everything in it. I hope you're not disappointed?"

"Oh no, it's very beautiful. Do you like jazz?"

"Yes, why?"

"I guess all Americans like jazz, don't they?"

"I suppose there are some who don't. Anyway, let's go into the living room—or, salon, as you call it—and talk."

She went into the adjacent salon, took a cigarette from a malachite box, and lit it. She turned to see Bernard watching her. He was wearing a light gray suit.

"You're not going to scold me, are you?" he said.

"I don't know *what* to do with you. I left your father's house because I was embarrassed about what happened last night. And now, here you are again. I don't want your father to think that I'm chasing you, or something worse."

"What could be bad about my loving you?"

"Bernard, you hardly know me. And as I said last night, I'm older than you, and I have a child . . ."

"Is there someone else?" he interrupted anxiously.

"No, there's no one else."

"Well, then." He smiled. "You'll come to love me soon enough. May I see your child?"

She hesitated.

"Yes, why not? Let me call the nanny."

She put her cigarette out in an ashtray and went across the room to an ormolu desk and pressed one of three buttons on a small box. "He may be having a nap."

"You are so beautiful."

"Bernard, please . . . you're embarrassing me. Talk about something else."

"What else is worth talking about except love?"

"You're not in love with me, you're just infatuated, like some teenager. I'm very flattered, but this will pass in time."

"I don't want it to pass. I could look at you all day."

"Madame rang?" came a voice from the doorway.

"Ah, Chantal. Is Graydon napping?"

"Yes. He's been asleep for about fifteen minutes."

"Well, then, don't wake him," Bernard said. "I can meet him some other time."

"No, wake him," Brook said. "Bring him downstairs."

The nanny curtsied and left the room.

"Why are you waking him?" Bernard asked.

"Because perhaps when you see the reality of the situation, you'll stop this foolishness."

He came to her, took her right hand, and raised it to his lips.

"You're laughing at me," he whispered. "And I know I'm saying foolish banalities. But perhaps love is banal."

"But you don't love me . . ."

"You're wrong, my darling. Oh, so wrong. I've never been in love before, so I know what has hit me. When I first saw you yesterday, I fell in love. It's that simple, that trite. And to me, that beautiful. You've changed my life in one instant, Brook. My life will never be the same from now on."

She looked into his gray-blue eyes. There was no denying his sincerity.

"Mama, why did you wake me up?"

The boy's voice was rather petulant. Bernard turned to

see a beautiful child standing in the doorway, his one hand holding the nanny's, his other wiping his eyes sleepily. The boy, who had curly brown hair, was wearing a nightgown and was barefoot.

"Chantal, you should have put on his slippers," Brook said, coming over and picking Graydon up, giving him a kiss. "Darling, this nice man wanted to meet you," she went on, carrying him to Bernard. "That's why I had you wakened. Graydon, this is Count Bernard de Belleville."

"How do you do, sir?" the boy said, yawning as he stuck out his small hand, which Bernard shook.

"I'm honored to meet you, Graydon," he said. "And you're a fine-looking young fellow."

"Thank you, sir. Mama, may I go back to bed now?"

"Of course, darling." She kissed him again, then handed him back to Chantal, who took his hand and led him out of the room.

"He's adorable," Bernard said. "And he looks a little like you."

"He looks more like his father. I just pray he doesn't turn out like him."

"Why?"

"It's a long story, and not a pretty one. But perhaps you should hear it. Yes, you should know about me, see about my flaws. Maybe you won't be so much in love with me when you realize I caused the death of a fine and innocent young man." She looked at her watch. "It's close enough to lunch. Let's go to the Crillon. I love the food there. I could use a drink, and I'll tell you the story of my life."

"So there you have it," she said an hour later as she sat opposite Bernard in the elegant restaurant overlooking the Place de la Concorde. "A rich, spoiled woman looking for thrills caused the death of a young man who might have been the great writer he dreamed of being. I'll never forgive myself, just as I'll never forget Lance Fairfax. So you can see that I'm dangerous to know."

She ordered her third martini.

"But you couldn't have known what your husband was going to do," Bernard said. "You should feel no guilt."

"That's kind of you to say, but I do feel guilt. You should keep your distance from me, Bernard. You're a sweet young man, and I don't want to bring you bad luck."

He took her hand. She was feeling the effects of the gin to the extent that his face swam slightly in her eyesight.

"My father is going to London tomorrow for a week," he said. "I'll be all alone at the château—even the servants are taking a vacation. Come out and stay with me."

"Of course I won't. What if your parents found out?"

"They won't. Please say yes. Please give me a chance to make you love me."

She closed her eyes a moment.

"You don't understand, do you?" she whispered, reopening her eyes.

"Understand what?"

"Understand that the reason I'm trying to run away from you is that I think I'm falling in love with you."

32.   TWO DAYS LATER, AGAINST HER BETTER JUDG-
ment, she left Graydon in Chantal's charge and drove out to Versailles for lunch, giving in to the repeated phone pleas of Bernard. So far, it had been a lovely fall, and on this day the weather continued to please, being cool with cloudless skies an azure backdrop to the autumnal leaves'

splendor. When the car reached the château, she got out, telling her chauffeur to go have a leisurely lunch and pick her up later in the afternoon. As the Hispano-Suiza turned around on the gravel drive, she started walking to the door of the building, which had been opened and in which Bernard was standing. He was wearing a white chef's toque on his head, an open white shirt, and a white apron. Despite her nervousness about coming there, she couldn't help smiling.

"Are you opening a restaurant?" she asked.

"Chez Bernard. Best food in the neighborhood, and the prices are cheap. Welcome, dear lady."

"Are we really alone? And are you really cooking lunch?"

"After you eat my cooking, you're going to appreciate what a true prize I am. And yes, we're really alone. As Baron Scarpia says when he finally gets Tosca alone in the second act, 'At last!' "

"I hope your intentions are a little better than Baron Scarpia's."

"And I hope you're not intending to stab me, as Tosca did him."

She looked suddenly sad.

"Oh no," she sighed. "I'll never hurt anyone again in my life."

"I've upset you," he said. "How stupid of me. Come in. It's such a lovely day, I thought we could eat out on the terrace again. And I've prepared a fantastic meal for you, starting with oysters, the food of love."

He took her hand and kissed it.

"Bernard," she said, "I didn't come out here to be seduced."

"Then why did you come out here? For lunch?"

She looked troubled.

"I don't know," she sighed. "I suppose I . . ." She looked at him, at his marvelous face, his thick golden hair curling out from under the chef's hat. "I wanted to see you."

He put his arm around her and led her inside the house. "No more than I wanted to see you."

He had gone to such infinite pains with the lunch that she was as touched as she was impressed. He had laid the small table on the terrace with a beautiful blue and white cloth from the south of France and set it with morbidly cheerful china from Nevers decorated with hand-painted slogans and logos of the French Revolution—"My family was on the wrong side," he said with a smile as he seated her.

"You mean, they got guillotined?"

"Several, yes. The others fled to England."

In the center of the table was a small vase filled with multicolored chrysanthemums. With the soft tinkling of the fountains in the garden, the setting was infinitely delightful. He wheeled out a cart on which were various dishes and a wine bottle in a silver bucket.

"Belon oysters," he announced, placing a plate in front of her, then filling her blue-glass wine goblet. "Arguably the best in the world."

"Bernard, can't I do something? Can't I help?"

"Absolutely not. If you so much as budge from that chair, you'll be sent to the guillotine."

"In that case, I'm glued."

After he had served himself, he removed his toque and sat opposite her, spreading an oyster with his fork and holding it up.

"Do you know anything about the sex life of the oyster?" he asked.

"Absolutely nothing. It never even occurred to me they had one."

"Ah, such divine ignorance. The fact is, the oyster reproduces himself, or itself. The oyster is a man half of the year; then it gets very milky and becomes a woman and voilà! Baby oysters."

"I don't believe it."

"It's true."

"Well, it saves a lot of money on dates."

At which point, they both laughed.

"How did you get interested in archaeology?" she asked twenty minutes later after he had served the roast chicken slathered in garlic, salt, butter, and rosemary that was one of the most delicious things she had ever put tooth to—not to mention the accompanying *pommes frites* that, she reflected ruefully, would probably put five pounds on her.

"I've always been fascinated by mysteries, and what greater mysteries are there than the mysteries of the past? To me, a *roman policier,* or whodunnit, is of minor interest. I don't particularly care who murdered Lady Vivian, or whomever, at the house party. But to discover the tomb of Queen Hatshepsut! Now there's a thrill! If things work out, I may be going back to Egypt in a few weeks to work with Howard Carter and Lord Carnarvon at a dig near Luxor."

"That does sound thrilling. I've always wanted to go to Egypt and see the Pyramids."

"Then why don't you come with me?"

He said it so matter-of-factly, she was a bit stunned.

"Well, I don't know . . . I mean, does one just dash off to Egypt?"

"Why not? It's fascinating. And romantic. There's nothing more beautiful than to stand in front of the Sphinx on a cool desert night and look at the stars over the Pyramids. Then one truly gets an idea of eternity and what life and death are all about. Not to mention love."

She took a sip of the delicious dry white wine.

"You tempt me," she said. "You really do tempt me."

"Excellent. I hope to continue to tempt you. I hope to be the apple in your little Garden of Eden."

"Or the snake."

He smiled.

"The same thing."

She took another bite of the chicken, eyeing him across the table.

After a truly wonderful crème brûlée, he served a demitasse and they sat opposite each other on the terrace in silence, sipping the strong coffee, as a late-summer bee slowly buzzed around the bouquet of mums.

"I feel so much at peace here," Brook finally said. "It's so odd: all my life I've been looking for—what? Thrills? Love? Excitement? Fulfillment? Sex? I suppose I've had it all, at least to some extent. But right now, just sitting here with you enjoying this coffee, I feel, I don't know . . ."

"Happy?" he suggested.

She smiled at him.

"Yes. Happy. How simple and uncomplicated. And how silly everything else in life seems when you think that having lunch in a beautiful garden with a man you like can make you feel so wonderfully happy. I thank you for this, Bernard, with all my heart."

He smiled at her. After a moment, he reached out his hand and put it on hers. She had been physically attracted to him from the start; but now, his touch ignited a fire inside her. Yet it was different from the desire she had felt for other men: she had, after all, desired Alex De Witt, and her desire for him had blinded her to what had turned out to be his odious personality. Now, while she desired Bernard, there was more to it than mere lust, as powerful as that could be. There was a sweetness to this young Frenchman that had been totally lacking in Alex. It was, she thought, the difference between a raw red wine and a full-bodied Burgundy.

After a while, a breeze began to blow.

"It's getting a bit chilly," he said. "Shall we go inside?"

"I'll help bring in the dishes . . ."

"Forget the dishes," he said softly, and yet there was a hint of an order in his voice. "I'll clean up later."

He stood up, still, holding her hand. She was almost mesmerized by him. She also stood up, coming around the table to him. He ran his hand over her hair, but made no attempt to kiss her, which made her desire him even more fiercely. He led her across the terrace to one of the French doors leading into the salon. They went inside, closing the door behind them.

The château was silent. They looked at each other a moment. Then, so very lightly, he leaned his face toward hers and put his mouth on her lips. She felt his tongue give her lips an exploratory lick, as if he were tasting her. Then he took her in his arms and pressed her toward him, kissing her with increasing passion.

"I adore you," he whispered. "Say you adore me."

"Yes," she whispered back. "I do. Oh Bernard, let's be sensible about this . . ."

"Why?"

"I'm afraid . . . so afraid I may hurt you . . ."

"Nonsense. If I get hurt, it will be my fault, not yours. Come."

Taking her hand again, he led her across the salon to the entrance hall toward the spiral staircase leading to the second floor. She stopped.

"No," she said. "It's too soon. Let's wait . . ."

"My darling Brook, when we're eighty years old—if we make it—we'll look back on this day and say, why in God's name did we waste one precious moment of our youth? People who wait end up dead."

He picked her up in his arms and started up the stairs.

She said nothing, relaxing in his strength, adoring the moment, anticipating what was to come. At the top of the stairs, he carried her down a hallway and pushed open a door with his foot. He took her into a large, airy room overlooking the garden, much like the room she had slept in the previous Saturday. There was a large antique bed with a white cover. He carried her to the bed and gently placed her on it, leaning over her to kiss her again.

"What a perfect afternoon," he whispered.

Then he straightened and began unbuttoning his shirt. She watched as he took off his clothes, fascinated by his lithe body. When he was naked, he climbed on the bed beside her and began unbuttoning her blouse.

"You're very lazy," he whispered. "You should have been getting undressed. Now I'll have to do it for you."

When they were both naked, he began making love to her, licking her breasts, her neck, her ears, her eyes, then her mouth.

"God," he groaned, "I'm like a dog in heat."

"What lovely heat," she whispered. "Oh, Bernard, I've never been so happy in my life."

"Will you come to Egypt with me?"

"I'll go to the moon with you."

"Then let's see some stars on the way."

On Halloween of 1922, the Black Shirt Fascists began their much-threatened march on Rome. From all over Italy, enthusiastic young Italians converged on the ancient capital, encountering little or no resistance by a government that was enervated by months of labor strikes, a staggering economy, and a lack of leadership and national direction. While the leader of the Fascists, thirty-nine-year-old Benito Mussolini, was not quite as enthusiastic as his followers—Mussolini vacillated about the march until the last moment—when it actually began, he accepted what he considered was his destiny with the same fatalism that would mark his extraordinary career until, twenty-three years later, he would be machine-gunned down by a garden wall near Lake Como and his bloody corpse hung upside down over a filling station in Milan.

Within a week, he was dictator of Italy.

The enthusiasm for the new regime was so widespread that Bruno and Beatrice decided they could now move forward with their marriage plans. Fiammetta, who was not one to lose time, set the date for the twentieth of November; and even though she had fought with the Catholic Church in the past, she had so reconciled herself to the Vatican that she got the Pope himself to agree to conduct the ceremony, and there was no religious problem because Beatrice was already a Catholic. In Fiammetta's palazzo, as in almost every princely palace in the city, there was what was called a throne room that was used to receive His Holiness on the occasion of his visit. In Fiammetta's case, the throne room was on the *piano nobile* of her vast palace, a tall room with walls covered with green silk and a gilt throne on a small dais that was turned to face the rear wall except when the Pope was actually present—which in Fiammetta's case hadn't happened since the year 1823.

On the happy wedding day, a crowd of over a hundred of Italy's aristocracy gathered in the throne room, the men wearing white tie and tails with sashes and medals, the women in long dresses wearing a king's ransom in jewels, most of them sporting diamond tiaras that blazed in the sunlight that streamed through the upper windows. Rachel and Johnny had come over from New York for the wedding; Brook and Bernard were there, on their way to Egypt, Brook acting as her sister's matron of honor. As a string quartet struck up the wedding march, Johnny started down the aisle with his daughter; and everyone who had known Beatrice before almost gasped with astonishment at how lovely she looked. Under her grandmother's direction, Beatrice had been fitted with a white satin wedding dress that had a twenty-foot train and a matching veil. Fiammetta had hired Rome's leading hairdresser to make her face and set her hair; and although Beatrice had argued about wearing her glasses—she claimed she would trip on the way down the aisle without them—Fiammetta had threatened to throw her glasses out the window if she wore them. So Beatrice gave in, promising to try not to squint.

The result was that she made a beautiful bride.

On their honeymoon at St. Moritz, Beatrice was told by her new husband that he had just joined the Fascist Party.

33. "I JUST GOT A CABLE FROM NICK," JOHNNY SAID as he came into his suite on the *Mauretania*. After leaving Rome, he and Rachel had gone to Paris on the Train Bleu, spent a week shopping, then went to Calais to catch the magnificent ocean liner back to New York.

"I hope it's not bad news?" Rachel asked. She was seated at a vanity putting her makeup on preparatory to going to dinner.

"I'm afraid it is. Nick says there's a raid under way on the bank stock. Someone has bought over a hundred thousand shares over the past week."

"But, darling, isn't that good news? The stock must be rising like a skyrocket."

"Yes, the stock is up ten points since last week. But I don't think this is mere stock manipulation. I think this is someone who wants a seat on the Board of Directors."

"Who?"

"The raid's being handled by a stockbroker named Jesse Breen. Nick says the word on Wall Street is that Breen is buying the stock for his older brother."

"Who's Breen's older brother?"

"No, I mean Nick's older brother."

Rachel, who was looking glamorous in a silver satin evening gown, turned to look at her husband.

"Cesare?" she asked.

"Cesare."

Looking troubled, Johnny eased himself into a flame-stitched chair.

"But why? I don't understand . . ." Rachel said.

"I do. This is his revenge against me, whom he's hated all his life. I've had him checked out and the money he has made has been from bootlegging. He'll bring his dirty millions into the Savage Bank and destroy its good reputation—or what's left of it since apparently everyone but us knew he was nothing better than a common criminal. Who knows? Maybe he'll try and boot me out and put himself in."

"Oh darling, I can't believe that!"

"I think you'd better start believing."

"Johnny, for years you've had these morbid fantasies about Cesare. After all, you can't deny that he saved Brook in that horrible mess—if it hadn't been for Cesare, she might have gone to jail!"

"I'll admit that, and I'll admit I've had morbid fantasies about him. But in this case, I think we have to consider the worst."

Rachel, who had given in to the trend and had her hair cut short with bangs on her forehead, giving her a surprising resemblance to the beautiful flapper movie star, Louise Brooks, turned around in her chair to look at her husband. Her elegant hands, on which she wore several magnificent jeweled rings, squeezed nervously.

"I'll talk to him," she finally said. "I'll find out what he's up to. He won't lie to me."

"I hope you're right. But be extremely careful. From what I hear, your beloved son has become an extremely dangerous man."

She looked startled.

"Dangerous?" she said softly. "What in the world do you mean?"

"I haven't wanted to tell you this for obvious reasons, but the word around town is that he carries guns. It's even said he's killed people, but I don't know if that's true."

Rachel winced slightly.

"I simply can't believe it. For all his faults, Cesare isn't a killer."

"When you do business with crooks, you eventually become a crook." The ship took a sharp roll to starboard. "We'd better go into dinner while I still can navigate the decks. The Captain told me he's expecting bad weather soon." He stood up. "Unfortunately, I fear this family is expecting bad weather soon too, dammit."

On the afternoon he sent his father the cable on the *Mauretania*, Nick Savage left the Wall Street office of the family bank and took a taxi uptown to the Racquet Club where, as was his custom two afternoons a week, he played court tennis for an hour, then did ten laps in the pool. After showering and dressing, he taxied to his maisonette on East Sixty-third Street and Park Avenue, where he changed yet again into his dinner jacket. Shortly before eight, he took another taxi to Fifth Avenue where he picked up his date for the evening, twenty-three-year-old Edith Rhinelander, then they went on to The '21' Club for cocktails and dinner.

After dinner, they succumbed easily to the latest rage in trend-mad New York by taxiing uptown to the Cotton Club in Harlem, at Lenox Avenue and 142nd Street, where they listened to Duke Ellington's Orchestra and the newest sensation, Bessie Smith from Chattanooga, who wowed the all-white crowd with her renditions of " 'Tain't Nobody's Bizzness If I Do" and "Down-Hearted Blues." Actually, the rage to visit Harlem had started the year before when a superb all-black musical called Shuffle Along had become a smash hit on Broadway. This had been followed by other black shows such as *Liza, Runnin' Wild*, and *Chocolate Dandies*.

At three in the morning, after necking in the backseat of the taxi for twenty minutes while the driver watched the meter climb, Nick brought Edith to her doorman, then went home. While he was searching for the key to his private door of the building, the main door-manned entrance of which was around the corner on Park, a black Buick pulled up behind him. The back door opened and two men jumped out. One grabbed Nick from behind while the other smashed a blackjack on the back of his head.

After they hauled unconscious Nick into the backseat, they slammed the door and the driver pulled away, heading uptown on deserted Park Avenue into the night.

Rachel was undergoing a bad case of seasickness on the last night of the *Mauretania*'s voyage to New York when Johnny came into their first-class suite. She could tell from the look on his face that more bad news had come.

"Nick's been kidnapped," he said.

"Oh no . . . oh my God . . ."

"I just got a cable from the bank. A ransom note was delivered this morning. They want a million dollars."

"Does anyone have any idea who kidnapped him?"

"The police haven't an inkling."

Rachel started sobbing.

"First Cesare, now this . . . Johnny, it's too much! I don't think I can take any more . . ."

She started gagging. Hurriedly, she got out of bed and went across the elegant stateroom to the bathroom, where she went inside and slammed the door.

Johnny heard her retching into the toilet, and his heart went out to her. He knew that Nick Savage was, in her mind, still her baby boy, the love of her life.

When Nick regained consciousness, he found he was tied to a wooden chair in a small, dark bedroom that stank of poverty. One window above the brass bed blinked depressingly from a neon sign across the street that read "Kelly's Bar, Open All Nite." Nick's head ached from the blow. His wrists were tied behind him, and his ankles were tied to the chair legs. A filthy rag gagged his mouth.

After a moment, he tried to test the ropes binding his wrists, but it was useless: they were tied tight, so tight, in fact, they were cutting off the circulation to his hands, which were tingling with numbness. Then he tried to chew through his gag, but that didn't work either. Sweating with fear, he began to grunt.

After a moment, a door opened and a man entered. He turned on a ceiling lightbulb and came over to Nick. He was a tall gorilla in a cheap suit. He looked at Nick a moment, then grinned, revealing a gold tooth.

"Hey, Mr. Wall Street rich kid," he said. "You don't look like you're enjoying yourself. In fact, you look downright miserable. You miserable, boy? Huh?"

He reached down and patted Nick's curly brown hair. Then he slapped him so hard he knocked his chair over on its side. Nick groaned as his head bumped the floor.

"Hey, rich kid," the man said, kneeling beside him, the grin on his face even wider. "Sorry about that. Why, I wouldn't mean to hurt you, would I? You're our ticket to a million bucks, kid. Then we'll be rich like you, you get it? Maybe we'll buy us a big apartment on Park Avenue and get our names in the Social Register. Can you imagine that, rich kid? Why, I wouldn't hurt you because one day soon I may bump into you at the opera or at some fancy dinner party. So I'm gonna be nice to you, rich kid. Real nice."

He kicked him in the stomach, hard. Nick oofed with pain. Then the man leaned down and picked him up, righting the chair. Nick stared at him as he reached out and pinched his right cheek.

"You're real cute, rich kid. I hear they call you the Debutante's Dream. Real cute. Hope to God your parents are cooperative. I'd hate to blow your brains out."

Giving him a friendly little pat on the cheek, he went back to the door, turned the light out, and left the room, closing the door and leaving Nick alone in the dark with terror.

The neon light of Kelly's Bar blinked drearily on and off through the rest of the horrible night. Finally, daylight began creeping through the city and the neon was turned off. As the city outside came to life, Nick sat agonizingly in his chair, wondering what his fate would be.

He had lost all sense of time as the morning dragged on. But at what must have been around ten o'clock, he heard voices in the next room, followed by two gunshots and brief screams.

Then silence.

As Nick stared at the door, it suddenly opened and Little Hymie Wiess came in, carrying a gun. He looked at Nick, then stuck the gun in an armpit holster and pulled a jack-knife from his pocket. Coming over to the chair, he quickly cut Nick's wrist ropes and removed his gag.

"Who are you?" Nick gasped when the gag was removed.

"A friend of your big brother, Cesare," Little Hymie said,

kneeling down to cut the rope on his ankles. "I just rubbed out those two punks in the next room who kidnapped you—the third guy we took care of an hour ago in an alley."

Nick, in a daze, was rubbing his right wrist.

"Cesare sent you?" he asked unbelievingly.

"That's right. He said, 'Nobody fucks around with my family.' " Little Hymie straightened and pulled a wallet from his jacket. "This is yours—they took it from you. Come on: I'll drive you home. If you're squeamish, don't look at the bodies in the next room. I really messed them up."

He handed Nick the wallet. Nick stood up from the chair, his joints stiff from his prolonged imprisonment.

"So Cesare saved me?" he said. "What a swell brother I have! I'll never forget this."

"Yeah, Cesare's an OK guy."

Little Hymie opened the door.

"Remember what I told you," he said. "There's blood all over the place. I don't want you tossin' your cookies or anything."

"Don't worry, I can take it. Frankly, the way they roughed me up, I'll be glad to see them dead."

"These guys aren't just dead: they're wiped out."

He went into the next room. Nick followed him. The two kidnappers were sprawled on the floor, blood all over their faces where they had been shot. As much as Nick hated them, he winced as he looked at the corpses.

Cesare, with his streak of narcissism, had installed in the master bedroom of his Park Avenue penthouse a huge bed with a mirrored headboard and, above the bed, a mirrored ceiling so that he could watch himself making love. Which was exactly what he was doing with a redheaded showgirl named Wendy when he heard the house phone ring.

"Who the hell could that be?" he muttered, checking the

clock on his bed table. It was five in the afternoon.

"What lousy timing!" Wendy grumped in her squeaky voice. "I was about to explode."

"I know what you mean," Cesare said, getting out of bed and walking across the room, his erection jiggling merrily. He picked the house phone off the wall.

"Yes?" He listened a moment, frowning. "Okay, send her up."

He hung up and hurried across the room to start putting on his clothes.

"Who is it?" Wendy said, watching him from the bed.

"My mother. Get dressed and get out of here . . . Use the servant's entrance in the kitchen. And for God's sake, don't let her see you!"

"Well, it's not as if I'm dirt," Wendy said, getting out of bed. "You treat me awful, Cesare. Sometimes I think all you're after is sex."

"That's a distinct possibility. Sorry about this, sweetheart. I'll call you tonight after the show." He blew her a kiss as he pulled on a shirt, tucking it into his trousers.

Five minutes later, looking cool and well dressed, he opened the front door of his apartment. Outside, in the small elevator vestibule, was Rachel, looking elegant in a smart black coat trimmed with fox.

"Mother!" Cesare exclaimed, opening his arms to hug her. "What a happy surprise! Why didn't you call me?"

"I was afraid you wouldn't ask me to see your new apartment, which I'm dying to see. Besides, I wanted to thank you in person."

"Thank me for what?"

"Oh, darling, don't pretend you don't know! For saving Nick from those terrible hooligans."

"Oh, that." He grinned and kissed her cheek. "Well, I couldn't let them hurt my kid brother, could I? Come on in. Now that you're here, I'll give you the grand tour—

though I'm afraid you may not like what you see. This is pretty modern for your tastes."

He led her inside, closing the door. Rachel looked around at the sleek art deco living room.

"Cesare, it's lovely!" she said.

"Really? You like it?"

"Well, you know I happen to be your mother, but I'm not an antique yet. Of course I like it. It's new and exciting—exactly what a young man like you should have."

"That's wonderful! I'm thrilled you like it. Here: let me take your coat . . ."

"No, I can only stay a moment. I'm meeting your father in a half hour to go to a meeting of the Philharmonic."

"Stepfather. Since when did you get interested in the Philharmonic?"

"If you were still a member of the family, you'd know that I've been a patron for five years now."

He looked at her thoughtfully.

"You don't consider me a member of the family anymore?"

"How could I? I hardly ever see you. You never write me and hardly ever phone. You might as well be back in Cuba as far as I'm concerned."

Cesare went to a table and took a cigarette from an onyx box. He lit it with a solid silver lighter. After he exhaled, he turned to her.

"You know why I stay away," he said. "I don't consider myself a criminal, but I know your husband does—and I suppose the rest of the family too. I've made a fortune for myself, Mother, and I'm not ashamed of one damned penny of it. But I know what you think of me and I stay away so as not to embarrass you."

"Isn't it a bit late to worry about embarrassing me? Oh, Cesare, there were so many ways you could have gone, so many wonderful things you could have done with your life! I would have done anything for you, anything to help you, but what did you ask me to do? Finance your becoming a bootlegger. How demeaning. How deceitful. How low." She sank into a chair and began to cry. He put out his cigarette and came over to her.

"Please, Momma," he said softly. "I know I've disappointed you, and I'm sorry for it. But I'll soon be out of this business, and you won't have to be embarrassed any longer. Why, I've bought a lot of the bank stock! I'm a respectable businessman now: you can be proud of me!"

She pulled a handkerchief from her purse and wiped her eyes.

"My God," she said softly, "you really believe that, don't you?"

"Of course I believe it. Look at old man Rockefeller! How do you think he got to be the richest man in the world? Everybody knows Standard Oil was founded by strong-arm methods. You don't get rich being a sweetheart."

"But you were already rich," she said.

"I wanted to make my own money. So maybe bootlegging isn't exactly a profession that gets medals from the Chamber of Commerce, but what the hell. There are a lot of crooked lawyers and doctors. I honestly am proud of what I've done. And look at Beatrice! She's married a damned Fascist, and from what I read in the papers they're nothing but a bunch of hoods who've taken over a whole country."

She sighed, shaking her head.

"Oh Cesare, why can't I be angry with you? Your father says you're my Achilles' heel, and I suppose he's right. You're a devil, but a devil with charm. And I do appreciate so much how you helped with Brook and now with Nick. I like to think that . . . well, that we all really are still a family and that we all love each other, the way families should. Even families with a Fascist—and Bruno isn't very active in the party."

He leaned down and hugged her.

"I love you," he said. "And I love Brook and Nick and Beatrice."

"Love your father too," she implored. "Please: for my sake. Let's all be one happy family again."

He released her and straightened.

"That's asking me to go further than I can," he said coolly. "At least, for the time being. But if he offered me a seat on the board of the bank, well then, things might be different."

She looked at him, surprised.

"A seat on the board? Is that what you want? Is that why you're buying so much stock?"

"Yes, why not? Listen, Mother: Johnny Savage is a good banker, by which I mean he's slow and steady and hasn't bankrupted the damned place. But he's also old-fashioned. He has no ideas, no flair! Everybody on the Street knows that the Savage Bank is slipping, that it isn't the power it was fifty years ago. The place needs new blood, and why not me? You say you want us all to be one big happy family again—all right, you can make it happen. Talk your husband into giving me a seat on the Board—God knows I have enough stock now to deserve one—and I'll bury the hatchet with him."

Rachel studied him awhile.

"Would you," she finally said, "give up this terrible boot-legging business?"

"Absolutely. It's getting to have too much competition anyway, and a real ugly element is getting into it. Not that it was filled with saints to begin with."

"Oh Cesare, if I could only believe you . . ."

"Believe me! I'm one hundred percent honest when I say I'll give it up." He knelt beside her and put his arms around her. "And I'll tell you another secret," he added, lowering his voice. "I've got another reason for wanting to be 'respectable,' if being a bank officer will make me that. I'm in love."

"You are? With whom?"

"Amanda Chatfield, Grosvenor Chatfield's daughter."

Rachel's face lit up.

"But she's charming!" she said in a delighted tone.

"Don't you think a charming girl could fall in love with me?" he said, laughing.

"Oh, I didn't mean that . . . Oh Cesare, that's wonderful!"

"And I'm thinking of asking her to marry me. But I have a funny feeling her father wouldn't be too thrilled about her marrying a bootlegger, so this could solve everything, couldn't it?"

"Yes! Oh darling, I'm so completely thrilled . . ."

"But you have to get my stepfather to put me on the Board to make it work."

"Oh yes, I see that . . . I'll do it!" She stood up and Cesare rose next to her. "Your father may not like it at first, but I'll wear him down. Oh, this is the best news I've heard in ages! I'm totally, completely thrilled!" She put her arms around him and hugged him. "Oh Cesare, I do love you so. Whatever differences we've had in the past let's put behind us. From now on, we'll be . . . everything will be perfect!" She gave him a kiss, then checked her watch. "It's late . . . I must be going. I'll start working on Johnny tonight."

"Wonderful! Here, I'll show you to the door . . ."

He went with her back to the door.

"I never thought this could turn out so wonderfully well," she said as he opened the door. "You've made me very happy, darling. Thank you."

Giving him another kiss, she went out and rang for the elevator.

"Good-bye, Mother," he said.

"Good-bye, darling. And I love your apartment."

"I forgot to give you the tour . . ."

"Another time. We'll bring all the family."

As the elevator door slid open, she blew him a kiss and got inside.

Cesare closed the door and leaned on it a moment. A smile slowly creased his mouth.

"It worked," he said to Arnold Rothstein an hour later as he joined him at his table at the Purple Parrot. "It worked like a bloody charm. Damn, sometimes I'm amazed at how clever I am. My mother's going to get me on the Board of the bank."

Arnold chuckled as he lit a cigarette.

"Cesare, you're a sly dog, I'll admit," he said. "So your mother doesn't suspect that you had your brother kidnapped so you could 'rescue' him, quote unquote?"

"She doesn't have a clue. By the way, did you give our kidnappers a bonus? Hymie said the fake blood from the so-called bullet holes was as good as in a movie."

"Yeah, I gave them a hundred bucks extra apiece. I also gave them an introduction to a Hollywood producer I know. Starving actors will do anything for a part. By the way, maybe we should think about getting into the movies? There's lots of money to be made in Hollywood."

"Maybe we will, A. R. After I get control of the bank, the sky's the limit on what we can do."

"You think you can handle your stepfather?"

"Sure. I've handled him all my life. He's a pushover. Buy me a drink, A. R., and let's toast going legit. With me at the bank and you running this town, we're going to have a merry time of it. A real merry time."

"It's as beautiful as you said," Brook exclaimed as she stood with Bernard de Belleville in front of the Sphinx outside Cairo. "And as romantic. Oh, Bernard, I'm so glad you brought me here."

The young couple had been driven out from Cairo in a horse-drawn carriage. Above them, the night sky was strewn with stars.

"If you consider that this is one of the oldest man-made structures on earth," Bernard said, "and yet, as old as it is, it is nothing compared to the age of these stars."

"Which makes us newborn babies."

"Exactly."

He smiled at her, then put his arm around her waist and leaned over to kiss her. Their guide, a pith-helmeted Egyptian assigned by their hotel, Shepheard's, stood by watching the couple as the driver held a torch.

"And speaking of babies," Bernard went on, "I would very much love having a few with you. Legally, of course."

She looked at him in the torchlight.

"Is that a proposal?" she whispered.

"It sounds like one to me, but I suppose I could do better." Holding her hand, he got down on one knee. "My dearest Brook, here, in front of the Sphinx—who, by the way, is watching us, I'm sure—I ask you most humbly to be my wife and live with me the rest of our lives."

"I won't even hesitate. I accept."

He stood up and took her in his arms, kissing her.

"Oh Bernard," she whispered, "I'll never, never hurt you. We're going to be so happy."

The guide, standing nearby, applauded.

"In all my years bringing people out here to the Sphinx and the Pyramids," he said, "I've never seen any of my clients make a proposal. Congratulations."

Two days later, Bernard was present when Lord Carnarvon and the archaeologist Howard Carter opened the tomb of King Tutankhamen. The tomb had not been opened for 3,300 years. "I see wonderful things," Carter mumbled as the first rays of his torch glittered off the golden funerary artifacts within.

Rachel was so thrilled that her daughter was marrying a Jew who happened to be the son of Maurice de Belleville that she decided to throw a wedding to remember, and Johnny agreed, feeling his beloved Brook had finally met someone with whom she could settle down. Thus, at each window of the facade of the Fifth Avenue house shone a crystal candelabra with four lighted candles. Eight huge torches illuminated the entrance to the mansion, before which limousines pulled up to disgorge their beautifully dressed passengers. The guests climbed the great staircase while twenty musicians played lush Viennese melodies, the musicians dressed in red uniforms, and the stairway decorated with palms, roses, and greenery. At the top of the stairs, the guests went down a rather mysterious corridor, lighted only by the torches of valets in red suits and powdered wigs until they arrived at the dining room, where the tables were all "placed" with cards that indicated each seat. As a string orchestra played Strauss waltzes, the guests took their seats in the enormous dining room, which was decorated with orchids, roses, and carnations. They proceeded to devour a menu that included a consommé Aurélie, mousseline de sole Mahenu, canard à la Madrilène, salade Clarinda, soufflé glacé Agénor, Château Lafite-Rothschild, Moët & Chandon, and Château d'Yquem. Beatrice and Bruno came from Rome, and Hemingway and Hadley from Paris for the occasion.

Rachel was especially pleased not only to see Maurice again after so many years and to have her family united with his, but also because Bernard's mother had been Jewish. The wedding ceremony was conducted by a rabbi.

How ironic, Rachel kept thinking. I lost Maurice because I was Jewish, and now my daughter is marrying his son, who is Jewish. I'm so sorry Mother didn't live to see this. She would have been so happy.

Brook and Bernard honeymooned at Claridge's in London. Rachel had arranged a meeting for them with Lord Lionel Rothschild. This Lord Rothschild was the one to whom, in 1917, Arthur Balfour had addressed the now-famous Balfour Declaration in which Balfour, then the Foreign Secretary of England, had pledged the backing of the English government to the "establishment in Palestine of a national home for the Jewish people," albeit muddying the waters by adding "it being clearly understood that nothing shall be done which may prejudice the civil and existing religious rights of existing non-Jewish communities in Palestine." This ambivalent attitude on the part of England had caused so much trouble in Israel—then known as Palestine—that after the Great War, the English had taken control of the country militarily.

Brook's interest in the ancient country had been piqued by her mother and her own trip there. And she found out that Bernard was a passionate Zionist on his own, with an additional interest in the archaeological ruins in Palestine. Thus, the newlyweds met with Lord Rothschild, the distinguished gentleman considered at the time the de facto head of the world Jewish community.

This meeting was to lead Brook and Bernard into a fulfilling future.

Cesare was wearing an elegant black silk dressing gown trimmed with silver braid when he opened the door of his Park Avenue penthouse to admit his mother.

"Mother!" he exclaimed with a smile as he hugged and kissed her. "You're looking as beautiful as ever. No: more so."

"You're sweet, Cesare, but I'm not feeling very beautiful," Rachel said as she came into the art deco living room. "In fact, I'm feeling rather wretched."

"Are you sick?"

"No, I'm fine."

"Let me get you something."

"No thanks. I can't stay very long, and I'm afraid you're not going to like what I have to say."

She took off her coat and sat on a chair. Cesare frowned.

"It's your husband," he said softly. "Johnny One-Leg."

"I've had a terrible row with him. It's been one of the worst fights we've ever had—and believe me, we've had plenty in this long marriage. I used every argument I could think of . . . I finally simply pleaded with him. But he is adamant: he won't put you on the Board of the bank. He doesn't want you to have anything to do with the bank."

"That bastard."

"Darling, don't call him that . . ."

"He's that and worse. He's hated me all of my life, but by God I'll get him in the end!"

"You might as well hear all of it."

"There's more?"

"Yes. He told me he's writing you out of his will. You won't get a penny of his money. Of course, you'll get money from me, but . . ."

"I don't want his damned money!" Cesare yelled. "I've made my own money! And I don't want his damned bank, either! I saved Brook's ass and I saved Nick, and this is the way he pays me back? To hell with him!"

He picked up a heavy crystal ashtray and threw it with all his considerable strength at one of the French doors leading out to the terrace. The ashtray crashed through one of the windowpanes. Rachel stood up, a look of shock on her face.

"Darling, please," she said, "I know you're angry, but

time can settle this somehow. I'll continue to work on him . . ."

"No! Forget it! I appreciate what you've done for me, but I don't want you begging him for favors for me. To hell with him! If I never see him again in my life, it'll be fine. But I'll tell you something, Mother: I won't forget this. Someday he's going to crawl to me for mercy."

"Cesare, stop talking that way!" she said angrily. "You sound like some condottiere out of the fifteenth century!"

"Yes, that's what I am," he said, clenching his fists. "I'm an Italian condottiere who's hungry for vengeance. I'll get him! You'll see!"

"Cesare, you're also Jewish and my son. Jews seek healing, not vengeance."

His dark eyes seemed to flash fire.

"The best healing," he said softly, "is death."

She looked frightened.

"Surely you don't mean that?" she said. "Oh, my darling son, take those horrible words back! Don't break my heart!"

His handsome face turned stony.

"I don't retract one syllable."

She came up to him and slapped his face, hard.

He instantly slapped her back.

"Cesare!" she cried, anguish on her face. "Oh, my God, Johnny's right: you've become a monster. Or maybe you always were!"

Bursting into tears, she ran to the door of the apartment and opened it. She looked back at her son, tears rolling down her cheeks.

"You'll have to change, Cesare," she said. "Otherwise, you'll never see me again."

And she left the room, closing the door behind her. Alone, Cesare sank into a chair, buried his face in his hands, and burst into tears.

34. AT AROUND FOUR O'CLOCK IN THE AFTERNOON of June 10, 1924, a thirty-nine-year-old Socialist member of the Italian Parliament named Giacomo Matteotti left his house in the Via Mancini in Rome. It was a small street that joined the Via Flaminia and the Lungo Tevere Arnoldo di Brescia. A large seven-seater automobile pulled away from the curb at the opposite side of the street and started toward Matteotti as he started on his way to the Parliament building. The rear door of the car opened and two men jumped out and grabbed Matteotti, who was a tall, dark man who had been attacking the Fascist Party in Parliament. After a brief struggle, the men pulled Matteotti into the car and slammed the door. The car roared away, but Matteotti managed to throw his special railway pass as a Member of Parliament out of the window.

One of two onlookers on the street picked up the pass, which had Matteotti's name on it. The other managed to get the license number of the car.

Matteotti was stabbed to death in the backseat of the car. His body was found two months later in a forest twelve miles outside of Rome.

But as soon as it was reported that Matteotti had disappeared, a great uproar arose across Italy that threatened to bring down the two-year-old dictatorship of Benito Mussolini.

✸

"Well, Bruno, what are you going to do now?"

The speaker was Fiammetta, who was sitting at the head of a table in the garden of the villa she and Justin had bought before the war outside the charming town of Todi, north of Rome. It was a warm summer day, and a white-jacketed servant was passing a tray of tempting cold antipasti. Bruno and Beatrice were also at the table, as was Justin. The latter, looking stooped with age, was seated in a wheelchair. The patriarch of the Savage clan had suffered a mild stroke the previous month and was partially paralyzed, though he could still use his hands. Birds chirped in the trees; Fiammetta's white borzoi, a magnificent animal, was curled on the grass at her feet dozing in the lazy summer warmth.

"Do about what?" Bruno asked, sipping the chilled Pinot Grigio from a Venetian goblet.

"Oh, come now: what is everyone in Italy talking about? The murder of Signor Matteotti. Or are you going to tell me the Fascists didn't kill him?"

Bruno, who was wearing a white suit, looked rather uncomfortable.

"No one knows for certain whether he's been killed," he said. "He's simply disappeared."

"Yes, after savagely attacking Mussolini in Parliament. Do you think he's taken a summer vacation?"

"I don't know what to think. Can we change the subject?"

"What would you prefer talking about? The weather? The weather is delightful. There is nothing more to be said about the weather. So: what if it is proven that Mussolini ordered his murder. What would you do? Stay in the Fascist Party?"

"Grandmother," Beatrice said, "please: can't you see Bruno doesn't want to talk about it?"

"Of course he doesn't. I'm forcing him to take a moral position, which nobody likes to do, particularly at lunch on a nice day. But we're a prominent family in this country, and as long as a member of this family is a member of the Fascist Party, it gives the appearance that we condone the regime. Up to now, while I haven't particularly liked the Fascists and their strong-arm methods of getting their way, I haven't disliked them enough to do anything about them—not that an old lady like me would have much influence anyway. But now, if it's true that they orchestrated this murder of the one man with guts enough to stand up to them, well then we all have to do some rethinking, in my opinion."

Bruno was staring at a fly on the white tablecloth. Finally, he said, "I take it you're hinting that I have to do something to save the family honor?"

"I'm merely suggesting, dear Bruno," Fiammetta said. "You're the only man in the family able to do anything. My poor darling husband"—she reached over and patted Justin's hand—"has been invalided, and besides he's an American. Of course, we could do nothing, which would probably be the smartest thing in the short run, at least. But it seems to me that if you resigned from the Fascist Party, that would send a signal to the country that we find this murder repugnant."

Bruno tore his eyes away from the fly and faced his wife's formidible grandmother. What a magnificent old woman! he thought. And dammit, she's right!

"If I resign from the party," he said aloud, "they could make life uncomfortable for Beatrice and me. And you, for that matter."

She shrugged.

"What could they do to a woman my age? Cancel my next face-lift?"

"When you totally run a country as Mussolini runs Italy, there are dozens of ways to make life uncomfortable. Tax records, for example. They could charge you with tax evasion."

Fiammetta chuckled.

"They could charge every Italian with tax evasion, and they'd be right," she said.

"You can laugh, Grandmother, but they're ruthless and they have the power. They could confiscate your properties."

"Let them. They cost a fortune to maintain anyway. Justin and I could move to Paris or go back to New York, for that matter."

"Not if they took your passport. I'm not saying any of this could happen, but it might. I won't disagree with you: I think this Matteotti business is an outrage, and if the regime gets away with it, then Italy is in for some bad times in the future. But I know enough about the Fascists to know that if we do anything against them, no matter how inconsequential, we will be opening a nasty can of worms. And with Beatrice expecting, it's a rather difficult time for us to be taking political stands."

Fiammetta looked at Beatrice, who was in her second month of pregnancy.

"Well, perhaps you're right," the old lady sighed. "And I suppose it's easy for me to talk morality when most of my money is in Switzerland. Perhaps I should just shut up. Perhaps we should, in fact, talk about the weather."

The young servant, who was standing beside the table holding the salads and whose name was Guido, had listened to the conversation most carefully.

The next morning, which was a Monday, Bruno drove back to Rome, leaving Beatrice in Todi with her grandparents. It was much cooler in Todi than in the capital. Arriving at his small villa set in a lovely garden on the Via Appia Antica outside Rome, he changed, then went into Rome to his office.

That night, he returned to his villa and ate alone, his

dinner having been left in the refrigerator by his cook, Maddelena. After eating, he went outside into the garden to smoke a postprandial cigar; it was a hot night, but a slight breeze was stirring. As he sat smoking, not for the first time did he mull over the conversation held the day before at Todi, nor for the first time did he wrestle with his soul about leaving the Fascist Party. He had joined the party two years before, thinking the Fascists were the only hope for stability in Italy and believing they would carry out the reforms they had promised. But, like most governments, they had reneged on most of their promises. In his heart, he knew he should resign. But he was only too well aware of the consequences if he did.

He was about to go upstairs to bed when he heard a knock on the front door. He went through the house and opened the front door. Outside was a black car. Two men in black shirt Fascist uniforms were standing at the villa door.

"Dr. Vespa?" one of them asked.

"Yes."

"You will come with us."

Bruno looked confused.

"Why? What is this all about?"

"You will ask no questions. Come with us."

The two men pulled guns from their coats. Then, with their free hands, they grabbed Bruno's arms and started taking him toward the car.

"Wait!" he cried. "Let me close the door to the house . . ."

They ignored him. Opening the rear door of the car, they pushed him inside, then climbed in beside him as a driver started the engine. The car roared off into the night, down the Appian Way toward Rome.

Twenty minutes later, it stopped. Bruno was hustled out of the car into a dark stone building he recognized as one of the Fascist police barracks. He was taken to the basement into a windowless room illuminated by a single bulb hanging from the ceiling. Beneath the bulb was a small wooden table and a wooden chair. Three other Black Shirts were standing in the room. One of them was smoking a cigarette. Now he said, "Put him in the chair."

Bruno, tense with terror, was pushed across the room and forced into the chair.

"What's this all about?" he said. "Don't you realize I'm a party member?"

"Yes, of course, Dr. Vespa, and we want you to remain one," the man with the cigarette said. As Bruno's eyesight grew more accustomed to the darkness of the room, he could see that the man, who wore a civilian suit, was rather young, rather fat, and rather balding. "We know about your lunch conversation yesterday at Todi."

"What lunch conversation? What are you talking about?"

"Come now, Doctor. Let's not play games. It was suggested to you by your wife's grandmother that you should resign your party membership as a signal of your disapproval of the regime's handling of the Matteotti affair. You quite wisely pointed out that such a move could cause grave problems for you and your family—problems with the government, I mean. Have you changed your mind on this point?"

Bruno squirmed uncomfortably as he looked around the room. It was difficult to see the Fascists' faces because they were standing outside the pool of light caused by the ceiling bulb. He didn't know if it was his imagination, but he could almost feel their eyes boring into him.

"No," he said. "I haven't changed my mind. I am a party member in good standing."

"Excellent. But to impress upon you the foolishness of changing your mind, if you ever do, we have decided to give you, Doctor, some medicine. There will be no charge. This is free, a gift of the government."

He snapped his fingers. One of the guards stepped forward and put a large bottle of slightly yellow liquid on the table, along with a large spoon.

"Being a doctor," the man with the cigarette went on, "you of course know how healthy castor oil is for one. It is a cathartic, a laxative. It cleans out the bowels. We want to send you home clean through and through, Doctor. So we will give you a treatment of castor oil. It may cause you to be a bit smelly, but there you have it: no treatment is perfect."

Again, he snapped his fingers. Bruno was grabbed from behind by two of the men and his mouth was forced open by a third. Another man opened the bottle of castor oil and filled the spoon, forcing it into Bruno's mouth. He almost gagged as the stuff went down his throat.

They gave him a moment to catch his breath, then they forced another spoonful into his mouth. Then another. And another.

By the time the full bottle had been forced down his throat, he had lost all control of his bowels. It was the most degrading experience of his life.

"It must have been that young Guido," Fiammetta said two days later as again the family convened in the garden behind the villa outside Todi. Bruno, who had recovered from the nauseating experience of the castor oil, had driven back up to tell them what had happened to him. "There was something *louche* about him from the first. He was always listening too intently. Most servants pay no attention to what's being said. I'm sure he was spying for the local Fascists. Dear God, what is our country coming to when you can't even trust the servants?"

"Did you fire Guido?" Bruno asked.

"No, he left the next morning. Didn't even give any notice, he just disappeared. Well, we shan't have any more political conversations in front of the servants." She looked around the garden to make sure they were unattended, which they were. Then she looked again at Bruno. "And so those thugs in Rome decided to intimidate poor dear Bruno."

Bruno, who had not eaten in forty-eight hours to recover from his nausea, was now gingerly forking his pasta.

"They didn't intimidate me," he said slowly. "Far from it. They were fools. Before I could go along with them, even knowing that they're nothing but thugs. But now? Now I hate them. Now I will fight them . . ."

"No!" Beatrice interrupted. Then she looked startled at her unusual fierceness of tone. Her hands trembling, she took off her glasses. "I'm sorry," she went on, "but I didn't leave America to become involved in Italian politics. I don't care two figs about politics! I love you, Bruno, and I want us to be happy and live in peace. I want our children to be happy and live in peace. It's terrible what they've done to you, but you were right the other day. If we defy them, they'll just make all our lives more miserable. They could send you to the Saint Antonio Prison where I hear they beat people to death and then say they committed suicide by banging their heads against the wall! I've even heard they put political prisoners in iron boxes with an air tube and lower them thirty feet below the sea, leaving them there in the dark, totally alone, until they go crazy! So yes, we may all hate them: but we'll hate them in private. Publicly, we'll remain out of it, totally out of it."

Silence as several bees buzzed around the wine goblets. Then Bruno said, "You realize what you're saying, darling. You're saying that we must all be dishonorable."

"Yes, I know that. I don't care! I'm a wife and about to be a mother, not a saint." She turned to Fiammetta. "I know you'll probably despise me for saying that, Grandmother, but that's how I honestly feel. I love Italy, but not enough to disrupt my family."

Fiammetta sighed as, next to her, Justin dozed in his wheelchair. She waved away a fly.

"I don't despise you," she said. "For all my brave talk the other day, I agree with you, I suppose. We're all so damned comfortable, who wants to be uncomfortable? But I wonder if keeping quiet will be enough in the long run. Well: Bruno needs to regain his strength. Let's talk about something else. Have you read any good books lately?"

The literary conversation, perfunctory at best, lapsed shortly later as the lunch continued in gloomy silence. Then, the distant whine of a siren was heard, growing louder.

"What's that?" Bruno asked with a touch of alarm.

"Probably an ambulance," Beatrice said.

The siren was now so close its shriek blanketed any possible conversation, clawing the warm summer air like some savage beast. Then, when it seemed in front of the villa, it stopped.

"They're coming here," Fiammetta said.

"Do you suppose it's the police?" Beatrice said, now as alarmed as her husband.

Then, as suddenly as it had stopped, the siren began again, except this time it diminished in sound. After a moment, one of Fiammetta's white-jacketed servants who had been in her employ for years came out of the house bearing a white envelope on a small silver salver. He came up to Bruno.

"This just arrived from Rome, sir," the servant said.

Bruno, looking confused, took the envelope.

"Who delivered it?" he asked.

"A Black Shirt on a motorcycle." He turned to Fiammetta. "May I clear, madame?"

"Later," Fiammetta said, indicating for him to go back inside the house, which he did. "Well? What is it?"

Bruno had opened the envelope and pulled out what looked like a formal invitation.

"It's an invitation for Beatrice and me," he said, "from the Foreign Minister. We're invited to the Palazzo Chigi tomorrow night for a reception honoring the Swedish Ambassador."

"There must be some mistake," Beatrice said. "Either that, or it's some sort of trap . . . Yes, it must be a trap . . ."

"I'm not so sure," Fiammetta said. "They're clever, these thugs. They've used the stick on Bruno, now perhaps they're using the carrot."

"But we couldn't possibly go! Not after what they did to Bruno!"

"No," Bruno said quietly, "we will go. They wouldn't dare do anything to me at the Foreign Office. It would be like arresting someone inside the Vatican. Besides, I'm curious to find out what they're up to."

"They want us in their camp," Fiammetta said. "If they can't bully us, they'll seduce us. How very clever."

Construction of the Palazzo Chigi had begun in 1562 and over the years it had become one of the grandest palaces in this ancient city. Acquired by the government in the nineteenth century, shortly after Mussolini assumed power he decided to move his Foreign Office from its traditional seat in the Consulta Palace to the Palazzo Chigi, mainly because of its central location at the corner of the Corso and the Piazza Colonna. Fashions might have become much more casual since the war, but in high diplomatic circles pre-war protocol still obtained and Bruno was wearing white tie and tails as they entered the ancient palace, which, in the midsummer heat, was decidedly uncomfortable. "I bet the Swedish Ambassador wishes he were back in Stockholm," he mumbled to Beatrice, who was wearing a mauve evening gown and jewels borrowed from her grandmother (she had put her glasses in her purse at Fiammetta's insistence).

After entering the palace, they were directed by lackeys to the *piano nobile* where the reception for the new Ambassador was being held, most of the guests wishing the evening would be quickly over so they could get out of town. Bruno's thoughts were on the "entertainment" the Fascists had given him a few nights before in the police barracks; but as he passed down the receiving line shaking hands and bowing to the highest-ranking Fascists in the government, he maintained the old Italian *bella figura,* refusing to let these street hoodlums in fancy dress know what he was thinking.

The reception was being held in the ballroom of the palace, an enormous space decorated in elaborate rococo style, and tailcoated lackeys were passing trays of champagne and canapés to the elegant guests.

"One would think," Bruno said to Beatrice as he sipped the excellent champagne, "that our fine-feathered Fascists had graduated from the best universities in Europe instead of Castor Oil College. I wonder why they invited us. I feel like a fish out of water."

A few minutes later, he found out. A tall, distinguished-looking man in white tie and tails came up to him and extended his hand.

"Ah, Dr. Vespa," he said. "I'm delighted you could come on such short notice. I am Dino Grandi."

"Yes, I recognize you from your pictures in the paper. This is my wife, Signora Vespa."

Grandi, whose manners were quite elegant, smiled and kissed Beatrice's hand.

"I am delighted to meet you, signora," he said. "But I owe both of you my most profound apologies. I learned only yesterday of the unfortunate incident at the police barracks. Believe me, this would never have happened if I had known about it. Sometimes our police behave over-zealously. I have disciplined the officer involved who will not make such a stupid mistake in the future, I can guarantee you. I hope you will accept my apologies for this unfortunate business?"

Bruno looked uncertainly at Beatrice. Then he turned to Grandi, who was one of Mussolini's closest advisers.

"Mistakes can happen, Signor Grandi," he said. "I can only hope that the government will abstain from such crude tactics in the future. All Italians, myself included, want to respect our government, not fear it."

"Well said, Dr. Vespa, and these are my sentiments exactly. We all have much to do in Italy, much building. While we need strong government, it must always be tempered with compassion. I have heard of your work in the charity hospitals, and I greatly admire you for what you've done. If you would give me the honor of coming to my office tomorrow at, say, eleven-thirty, I would like to take you to lunch and discuss your future."

"My future? I'm not sure what you mean."

Grandi smiled.

"You have much to offer to Italy, and Italy has much to offer you. Until tomorrow, then?"

"Yes . . ."

"Excellent." He turned to Beatrice and again kissed her hand. "I'm delighted to have met you, charming signora. You are as lovely as I've been told."

Bowing again, he melted into the crowd, charming the diplomats and their wives with unctuous suavity.

"Well, I'll be damned," Bruno muttered. "I think he's actually going to offer me a job!"

"They want me to be Minister of Health!" he exclaimed the next afternoon to Beatrice after returning from Rome to the villa on the Appian Way. "Grandi took me to this sumptuous lunch at the Excelsior Hotel—he really throws money around, I suppose he has a limitless expense account—and went on at great length about the Duce's dreams of giving excellent health care to every Italian, no matter how poor."

"Do you think they mean it?"

"Who knows? Talk is cheap, of course, but Grandi is very enthusiastic about the whole thing, and I must admit his enthusiasm is rather catching."

"Bruno, you mean you accepted?"

"No, not yet, but I told him I'd think it over. The man really is most charming, and if they're serious . . . Beatrice, they'd give me huge amounts of money to build clinics and new hospitals . . . It would be like one of my oldest dreams come true!"

"But, darling, we've all agreed they're crooks! And look what they did to you. I mean, Grandi can apologize till the cows come home, but still and all it seems to me that's the true version of Fascism: forcing castor oil down your throat."

"Yes, I know, but . . . this castor oil is different! And maybe they're going to force it down the throat of Italy, but if it works, how wonderful it would be! I mean, you know enough to realize how bad most medical facilities are in this country. This is an opportunity to correct all that!"

"Yes, I see what you mean. Then, are you going to accept?"

Bruno went to the sideboard to pour himself a Bacardi and soda.

"Yes," he finally said, "I think I will accept. It's too great an opportunity to pass up. Isn't it odd? A few days ago, I was saying I hate them. And now . . ." He took a sip of the drink. "Now I'm joining them."

Beatrice came over and kissed him.

"Darling," she said, "I know that if you think it's right, then, it is. I just hope . . ."

"What?"

"That we have no regrets later on."

PART NINE

THE GREAT
SHOPPING SPREE

35. "Congratulations, Nick," Cesare said to his younger brother. "You're finally tying the knot. Valerie Hawthorne's a lucky girl."

"I'm the lucky one," Nick said. They were drinking at the crowded bar of The '21' Club on a cold November evening in 1926. "Valerie's a great girl. I want you to be my best man, Cesare."

Cesare stirred his martini with the toothpicked onion.

"Well, I'm flattered, Nick, and I thank you. But I don't think that would be such a good idea. I assume your father is going to be at the wedding, and I don't want to be in the same room with that bastard. You know he cost me my wedding. When he wouldn't put me on the Board of the bank two years ago, Amanda's old man nixed our marriage. Said he didn't want his daughter marrying a bootlegger."

"Oh, come on, Cesare, isn't it time to bury the hatchet between you two? Mother's certainly hoping it is. She's told me often that she's just sick about the split in the family."

Cesare shrugged.

"Well, I'm sorry about Mother, but the split is there. He hates me and I hate him. By the way, how are things at the bank? Is he paying you well?"

Nick chuckled.

"Oh, sure. I haven't had a raise in two years."

"How do you get by?"

"Barely. Mom and Dad are paying for our honeymoon, and Mother gave me the money to buy Valerie an engagement ring. But it's going to be rough going at first."

"But Valerie has money, doesn't she?"

"Nah. I mean, her old man makes a good living as a lawyer, but they're not rolling in dough. That's our one big problem: Valerie has expensive tastes. But we'll manage."

"Are you in the market?"

"Nope."

"Hey, come on, Nick: Wall Street's on a roll! Get in the market and make yourself a bundle. Then you can tell Johnny One-Leg to stuff it."

"Well, I would if I had any money. But ..." He shrugged.

"Hey: you're my kid brother. You shouldn't have to worry about money. Tell you what." He reached inside his jacket and pulled out his wallet. "Here's a thousand bucks, part of my wedding present to you. And I'll get you another nine thousand tomorrow. Plus, I'll tell you where to invest it in the market. You listen to me, and this ten thousand will be fifty thousand in two months."

Nick stared at the wad of hundred-dollar bills. Then he slowly shook his head.

"Cesare, that's swell of you, but I can't take it. I mean, that's a fortune. I already owe you for saving my life from those hoods."

Cesare shoved the money into his hand.

"Take it," he said. "What are brothers for?"

"Well ... gosh, thanks ..."

"Maybe you can do a favor for me someday. Now: when can I meet Valerie? I've seen her picture in the Society pages, she looks like a real stunner."

Nick was putting the cash into his wallet.

"Oh, she's gorgeous. Beautiful red hair and a great body. Let's all have dinner together one night."

"Tomorrow night at my place. By the way, does she know about your reputation with women?"

Nick blushed slightly.

"I don't know," he said. "I mean, she knows I'm called the Debutante's Dream. She thinks it's sort of funny."

"How about that other nickname? The one your infamous sex life has earned you?"

"You mean 'the naked Savage'?" He laughed sheepishly. "No, I don't think she's heard that one."

"Then we won't tell her. Anyway, tomorrow night at my place. Say, seven-thirty." He got off the bar stool and put a twenty-dollar bill on the bar.

"I really can't thank you enough about this gift, Cesare."

Cesare patted him on the back.

"As I said, maybe you can do me a favor someday."

Valerie Hawthorne was a redheaded flapper right out of *Flaming Youth* and the cartoons of John Held, Jr. She loved to Charleston, drink bootleg booze, smoke endless cigarettes, gossip with her girlfriends on the phone, use all the latest slang, read movie magazines, and smooch in the backseat of racy cars. Although she was crazy about Nick, she was grimly hanging on to her virginity until the wedding night: she wasn't *that* wild. A twenty-four-year-old graduate of Vassar, she also loved to shop. When, the next night, Nick brought her into Cesare's penthouse, she took one look at the fabulous living room and said, "Gee, this place is the bee's knees!"

"Cesare, this is Valerie. Valerie, my big brother Cesare."

Valerie, who was wearing a fur-trimmed coat over a lime silk dress with a skirt three inches above her knees, shook hands with the suavely tuxedoed Cesare, and gushed: "You're the first bootlegger I've ever met! I just think bootleggers are the bee's knees!"

Cesare chuckled as he shook her hand.

"I'm actually an ex-bootlegger," he said. "Now I'm into investing."

She looked around again.

"Well, you certainly must be good at investing because this apartment is . . ."

"The bee's knees," Cesare finished for her. "Let me take your coat. Nick, you know where the bar is. Arthur will make you a drink."

"I just love giggle-water!" Valerie exclaimed, taking off her coat. "At Vassar, we used to get high as kites."

Nick, who was wearing a tux like his brother, crossed the big room to the bar where a young man in a white jacket was standing.

"A martini, very dry," Nick said. "Valerie, what do you want?"

"Is there any champagne?"

Arthur the bartender nodded.

"Here's the other nine thousand," Cesare said, coming up beside his brother and handing him an envelope.

"Cesare, I'm not sure I should accept this . . ."

"It's my gift to you: you can't turn it down."

"Well . . ."

"Take it."

He did.

"What's this funny painting?" Valerie asked as Nick brought her the glass of champagne. She was standing in front of an oil in a fancy gold frame.

"That's my Picasso," Cesare said.

"Oh yes, I've heard of him." Valerie took a sip of her drink. "He's Spanish, isn't he?"

"That's right."

"It's sort of an ugly painting, isn't it?"

Cesare rolled his eyes.

"It grows on you."

Valerie giggled.

"Like a tumor." She sipped more champagne. "I don't like modern art," she went on, "but I love this apartment! Oh Nicky . . ." She put her arms around his neck and kissed him. "I want to live like this! Tell me we're going to have a big apartment and fancy clothes and furs and jewels and big, flashy cars . . ."

"Sure, honey," Nick said, kissing her back.

"Nick's going to be very rich," Cesare said with a slight smile as he put his hand on his brother's shoulder. "I'm going to make him rich. Oh, by the way, Valerie . . . I bought you a little trinket today." He pulled a slim black velvet box from his dinner jacket and handed it to her. "A getting-to-know-my-new-sister-in-law present."

Valerie set down her champagne glass and took the box, opening it.

"Oh!" she gasped. Inside was a diamond and sapphire bracelet. She lifted it up and stared at it, twirling it around slowly. The diamonds flashed in the light. "Oh, it's beautiful! I love it! Oh, thank you, Cesare!"

She threw her arms around him and hugged him.

"Oh Nicky," she exclaimed, "I adore your brother! He's . . ."

"I know," Nick said, "the bee's knees."

"I'm crazy about Valerie," Nick said to his older brother three months later. "But I can't stop her spending."

The two brothers were once again at the bar of The '21' Club.

"What does she buy?" Cesare asked.

"Everything! Clothes, hats, shoes . . . she's got something like fifty pairs of shoes, she's a shoe fetishist, she has so many shoes there's no more room left in her closets. She made me buy a weekend house out in Locust Valley, and then of course I had to buy a car. And not just any car, she wanted a Cadillac." He sucked nervously on a cigarette. "I tell you, I can barely keep up with my payments, and now she wants to buy a bigger apartment. She hates my little maisonette and says rich people should own their apartments, not rent them. What she can't seem to get through her head is that I'm not rich, I just have rich parents." He shook his head sadly and ordered another dry martini.

"Can't you say 'no'?" Cesare said.

Nick looked sad and lowered his voice.

"When I do, she locks me out of our bedroom."

"There are always other women."

"Not like her. She's great in bed, Cesare. She drives me crazy. It's the best sex I've ever had and I've had plenty."

"Well, you must have made money off those stocks I told you to buy? They've all gone up."

Nick looked guiltily at his brother.

"I sold them," he said.

"No. Oh Nick, why the hell did you do that?"

"I needed the money!"

"Why didn't you get a loan from the bank?"

"Father wouldn't approve it. He said we're living too high off the hog. You know how tight he can be."

"Then go to Mother."

He shook his head again as the bartender placed a new drink in front of him.

"He told me not to. Apparently she made you a loan a few years back which made him furious."

"Sure, but I paid her back with interest. Look: how much money do you need?"

"Well . . ." He took a sip of the martini. "The apartment Valerie wants to buy is priced at forty thousand, and I'll need fifty percent as a down payment. That is, if I can get a mortgage somewhere."

"Forget mortgages." He pulled a checkbook from his pocket, then a pen. "Look: I'll loan you fifty thousand dollars. That way, you can pay cash for the apartment and have ten thousand left over to give you a little elbow room."

"Cesare, I can't accept it."

"Why not? What are brothers for? You can pay me back whenever with three percent interest."

"Well . . . are you sure?"

"Sure I'm sure. Johnny One-Leg, that old fart, is going to die someday and you'll be a rich man. You're as safe an investment as Radio Corporation stock."

"Well, if you put it that way . . . I mean, three percent is awfully low interest . . ."

Cesare was writing the check.

"You're my brother," he said. "I'm not going to gouge my own brother. There." He tore the check out, waved it twice to dry the ink, then handed it to Nick. "Now stop worrying."

Nick looked at him with relief.

"You're so damned good to me," he said. "I wish to hell there was something I could do for you."

Cesare lit a Régie cigarette with a gold Cartier lighter.

"Well, actually, there is something," he said, exhaling a cloud of Turkish smoke.

"Anything, Cesare. Anything."

"As Assistant Cashier of the bank, you must know what the investment department is doing on the market."

"Of course."

"Well, if you could keep me informed of any large moves they're making, it would be a great help to me in terms of my own investing. If you see what I mean."

Nick frowned.

"Well . . ."

"I mean, if it bothers you, forget it."

"If the old man ever found out, he'd kill me."

"Why would he ever know? Besides, it's all in the family. I mean, if the old bastard had brought me into the bank as I wanted, I'd have known firsthand. This way, I'll know secondhand. And I could give you a percentage of the profits."

Nick finished his second martini and ordered a third.

"Well," he said, "it's not illegal. So why the hell not?"

Cesare smiled and squeezed his brother's shoulder.

"What are brothers for?"

It had been said of stockbroker Jesse Breen that when he was gambling on Wall Street, he was thinking of screwing; and when he was screwing, he was thinking of gambling on Wall Street. Born forty-seven years before on a farm in Massachusetts, he went to work at an early age around the State Street market in Boston. He had a phenomenal talent for figures and could do mathematical calculations in his head faster than most people could do on paper. At the age of fifteen, he became a quote-marker on a blackboard at Paine, Webber. After the office closed, Jesse would stay on playing the bucket shops, which were essentially stock casinos where you could bet on stock movements without actually owning the stocks. He had nerves of steel and terrific gut impulses. He was also very superstitious with a great respect for the occult: he would bet on a stock according to whether a friend's cat had a litter of kittens. In Atlantic City on vacation one day in 1906, he wandered into a brokerage house and sold a thousand shares of Union Pacific stock short. When the broker questioned this in view of a current bull market, Jesse tripled his order. The next day, the San Francisco earthquke hit and Union Pacific shares plummeted, making Jesse a fortune. So perhaps he had good reason to believe in the occult.

Breen, who was almost totally bald, had a half-dozen residences around the world, owned a yellow Rolls-Royce and a yacht, and wore a sapphire ring on his little finger. He abhorred physical contact with men to the point of refusing to shake hands unless he knew you well. He had an alcoholic wife (perhaps understandably on her part) and went through mistresses with abandon. He had been with Gloria Gilmore for almost six months, which for him was a record of durability.

Despite the fact that he was one of the best-known personalities on Wall Street, he had a mania for secrecy. His penthouse office atop a fifteen-story building on Central Park South was unmarked and the elevator attendants were instructed to claim they had never heard of him. He had a burly bodyguard named O'Casey who refused entry to anyone without an appointment. However, O'Casey knew Cesare. And he greeted him with a smile one morning a week later when he came into the reception room of the penthouse.

"Himself is expectin' you," O'Casey said, opening a second door. Cesare went into a room with a great view of Central Park. Jesse was seated at a desk holding a dozen telephones, one of which he was talking on. There were two ticker tapes, and a large blackboard covered with stock quotes. Jesse gestured to a chair in front of the desk. Cesare sat down and waited till he hung up.

"Savagecorp is buying a hundred thousand shares of General Motors tomorrow," he said to Jesse. "That should send G. M. stock up a couple of points at the very least, so buy me twenty thousand shares."

Savagecorp was the "security affiliate" of the Savage Bank. While it was illegal for banks to sell stocks, they could—and with increasing frequency were—setting up affiliated companies that could deal in stock transactions. Moreover, they could legally do two astounding things: sell the bank's own stock, and not publish earnings statements as the banks themselves had to do. As the great bull market of the twenties began to roar, these security affiliates became gold mines. Obviously, the advantage of insider knowledge, as Cesare was getting from his brother, was the key to the mint.

Furthermore, big customers like Cesare were allowed to buy on "margin," meaning he only had to put up twenty-five percent of the stock value. In essence, Cesare was making millions on nothing.

But so were countless others.

After Jesse had placed the order—and bought ten thousand shares for himself—he hung up the phone and smiled.

"We're going to have to do something nice for your brother," he said.

Cesare stood up.

"I'll take care of my brother," he said. "And I'll take care of my stepfather. In fact, I'm going to mop up Wall Street with my stepfather."

That evening, Cesare had just sat down to dinner in his penthouse when Arnold, his butler-cook-valet, came into the dining room and said, "There's a Miss Gilmore downstairs. She wants to see you."

Cesare, who was wearing one of his natty suits and a red silk tie, stood up. "Send her up. And hold dinner."

"Yes, sir."

Cesare went back into his living room. When the doorbell rang, he opened it. Gloria Gilmore, wearing a smashing white cape trimmed with white fox fur, was standing outside.

"Jesse's dumped me," she said. "Will you buy me a drink?"

"Sure. Come in."

She came into the penthouse, taking off her cape. Beneath it she was wearing a short dress of silver bugle beads. She tossed the cape on a chair.

"I suppose," she said, "I should be mad at the big lunk, but I knew his reputation. Apparently, I retired the cup by hanging on to him for six months. God, men are such pricks. Present company excluded, of course." She gave him a dazzling smile as she opened her silver purse and pulled out a gold cigarette case. When she removed a cigarette, Cesare came up to her and lit it with a silver table lighter he had bought at Tiffany's for $500.

"Who's his new girlfriend?" he asked.

She exhaled.

"Some chorus girl named Wendy Gaines."

Cesare laughed.

"What's so funny?"

"Wendy Gaines used to be my girlfriend."

"This is beginning to look like a game of musical beds."

"Isn't it. What'll you drink?"

"A bourbon on the rocks."

"Coming up." He went to the bar and poured a drink, which he brought to her. "I was about to sit down to dinner. Want to join me?"

She took the drink and smiled.

"I was hoping you'd ask me," she said. "I was feeling terribly lonely. It's not a nice feeling to be all alone in this big city."

"Something tells me you won't be alone for long, Gloria."

She took a sip of the bourbon.

"You know, I was really fond of your stepfather," she said. "Even without a leg, he was a great lover."

He took the glass out of her hand and set it on a table. Then he took her in his arms and kissed her mouth, hard.

"Never," he said softly, "mention my stepfather again."

"Are you in some sort of competition with him?"

"Let's call it a duel to the death, and I'm going to win." He took her hand. "We'll have dinner later. I'm going to show you how a two-legged Savage makes love."

He led her into his bedroom and turned on the lights. She looked around.

"I like the mirror above the bed," she said. "Do you watch yourself making love?"

He took off his coat.

"Of course. You get twice the kick."

She laughed as she unbuttoned the back of her dress.

"I think life with you is going to be fun, Cesare. And you know something?"

"What?"

"I've wanted to go to bed with you since I first laid eyes on you at that speakeasy."

Cesare smiled. "Sometimes dreams come true."

36. THE PARTY NICK AND VALERIE GAVE THAT WARM

June night was to celebrate the purchase of their new mansion on Long Island's tony North Shore, and in later years it would be remembered as one of the wildest parties ever given during those wild years of the twenties. Almost one hundred of the popular young couple's friends came in black tie and evening gowns, many bringing bathing suits as well because the invitation had included "Midnight Dip in the Pool Optional." Valerie had hired the North Shore's best caterer and Nick had hired Paul Whiteman's jazz orchestra to play under the huge white tent set up by the pool, the tent being illuminated by big round Japanese-style lanterns lit by an electric power line that had been dug under the lawn from the main house for the occasion. Around the wooden dance floor twenty round tables had been set up, each seating eight; in the center of each table was a big white wicker basket filled with fresh flowers in soft pastels accented by gorgeous pink peonies. Outside the main tent, a smaller cooking tent had been set up where five cooks were preparing the dinner of barbecued roast beef, cold poached salmon with green sauce, two different kinds of potatoes, a variety of fresh vegetables, and tossed salad. Meanwhile, as the guests gathered at twilight for cocktails on the lawn, two dozen waiters in white jackets passed around trays of canapés while three different bars set up beneath the towering trees of the estate that had once belonged to Alex De Witt and Brook were besieged by thirsty guests. Fine wines and champagnes protruded from big ice-filled tubs on the grass.

"Oh Nick," Valerie gushed as she surveyed the scene from the rear terrace, "isn't it all the bee's knees? And aren't you glad we bought this beautiful place? I think it's got to be the biggest, most beautiful house on Long Island! Don't you think everyone's just pea-green with envy?"

"Maybe," Nick said a bit nervously. "Of course, my father thinks we're crazy to have bought such a big place."

"Oh pooh, why shouldn't we have it? Brook lived here, why shouldn't you? And when Alex De Witt was killed in that drunk driving accident, I knew it was meant to be that we buy this." The orchestra under the tent struck up a big *ta-dah!* chord. "Oh, goodie, they're starting the water ballet. This is going to be something!"

As the guests holding their drinks turned toward the pool, which was lighted, six bathing beauties in tight suits came out of the house and ran to the side of the pool. The orchestra played "All I Do the Whole Day Through Is Dream of You" and the girls began a wild and crazy Charleston as they sang the catchy tune. At the conclusion of the song, they all dived into the turquoise water as the band segued into a dreamy "Remember." The girls swam in circles and then performed an intricate water ballet, which was a huge hit with the guests.

After they had returned to the house, a dinner gong was struck and the guests filed to the edge of the tent where the buffet had been set up. It was all going splendidly, but Nick was too nervous to thoroughly enjoy himself.

He knew what all this was costing, and once again he had been forced to go to Cesare to borrow money.

By midnight, when most of the guests were loaded, those

who had brought bathing suits went to the pool house to change and jump in for a boozy swim.

But Nick, who was drunk, lived up to his nickname of "the naked Savage" by running out of the pool house buck naked and jumping into the pool with a howl and a cannonball splash.

He was the hit of the evening.

"I read about your party in the Society pages," Johnny said the following Monday morning. He had called Nick into his office at the bank. "You made quite a splash—so to speak."

"Um, yes," Nick said, squirming uncomfortably. He didn't remember his infamous skinny-dip, but the North Shore's telephone lines had burned with people discussing it. "It went very nicely."

"A party like that must be very expensive." Johnny watched his younger son from his desk chair.

"Yes, it wasn't cheap. But Valerie wanted it."

"Did you ever hear of a Frenchman named Nicolas Fouquet?"

"No."

"He was in charge of France's finances under Louis XIV. He was a very clever and ambitious man, and he built a beautiful château outside Paris called Vaux-le-Vicomte. It still stands today, your mother and I have seen it. At any rate, when the place was finished, Fouquet decided to show it off, and he threw a big party in the summer of 1661 and invited the King. This was a serious mistake, because the king was so jealous when he saw what Fouquet had built, he began to investigate his finances. Three weeks later, Fouquet was convicted of stealing from the Treasury and was sentenced to life imprisonment. An interesting story, wouldn't you say?"

Again, Nick squirmed slightly.

"I guess. I'm not much on French history."

"Perhaps you should read more of it. Where are you getting all this money, Nick? I know you paid over a million dollars for your house, because it was in the papers. You don't have a million dollars. Plus you bought an expensive apartment . . . if you weren't my son, I'd start investigating your personal finances. But since you are my son whom I love very much, I'm asking you to tell me."

"I've done very well on the stock market."

"Ah. So you play the market?"

"Like everybody else."

"I see. Do you think it's quite proper for you, as an officer of this bank, to be playing the market?"

"It's not illegal."

"No, that's true. But you have an unfair advantage because you know what Savagecorp is buying and selling. Or are you going to tell me you haven't used this information to your advantage?"

Another squirm. Beads of sweat appeared on his forehead.

"You don't have to answer me," his father said. "I can see you have by the look on your face. Nick, I can't tell you how disappointed I am in you. As you say, what you've done is not illegal: it's worse. It's dishonorable. From now on, I'm giving instructions that you are to be kept uninformed of Savagecorp's stock transactions."

"But, Father—!" Nick exclaimed.

"I have nothing more to say to you. You may go."

"No, I won't go! I'm your son! You and Mother have all the money in the world—why should Valerie and I not be able to live the way we want? It didn't bother you when Brookie lived there . . ."

"Nick, I don't want to discuss it further."

He stood up.

"But you have to! Valerie has expensive tastes! I can't ask her to live like some housewife . . ."

"Valerie's tastes are your problem, not mine. Go."

"No!" he yelled.

"Get out!" Johnny yelled back.

Nick, his face white, his hands trembling, looked at his father. Then he turned and left the room.

"What am I going to do?" Nick almost blubbered that night as he drank his cocktail in Cesare's penthouse. "The old man yelled at me . . . he yelled! Oh, it was terrible, Cesare. Terrible."

Cesare, who was wearing one of his elegant bathrobes, this one scarlet with gold trim, lit another Régie. "I think giving that party last weekend wasn't the wisest thing to do," he said.

"I know, but Valerie wanted it."

"Uh-huh. So. You're not going to be able to give me any more stock tips. You didn't tell Johnny One-Leg you were passing the information to me?"

"Oh no. Your name didn't even come up. Father just thinks that I was using the insider information myself."

"I see." He inhaled on the cigarette and blew out smoke. "You owe me a lot of money, Nick."

Nick pulled a handkerchief from his pocket and blew his nose.

"I know, Cesare. You've been so swell with me, and you've made me a lot of money. But Valerie spends it as fast as it comes in." He shrugged sadly. "She just won't stop shopping. It's like a disease with her. I don't know what to do."

"Get her pregnant."

"She doesn't want kids now."

"I don't care what she wants, get her pregnant. That'll keep her home more, and when you have kids, it will soften old Johnny One-Leg up. There's nothing like grandchildren to make older people go gooey."

Nick went to the bar and poured himself another martini.

"Well, maybe you're right," he said.

"I know I'm right. But to get back to the money you owe me. It's almost a half-million dollars now. That's a lot of money, Nick."

"I know," he groaned. "I don't know what to do about it."

"Don't you? In that case, you're not using your imagination."

"What do you mean?"

"You're the Assistant Cashier of the bank. You have access to the safety deposit boxes. Now you can't tell me that there aren't dozens of those safety deposit boxes that are never opened. Old widows leave their stocks and bonds—sometimes even cash—in those boxes for years. A lot of them probably forget they even have them."

Nick, who was by now a little drunk, looked at him with bloodshot eyes.

"What are you getting at?" he said.

Cesare shrugged.

"You could 'borrow' some of those unused bonds and raise money on them. Put the money in the market under my guidance, triple your money, then pay me back and replace the bonds. No one would ever know."

Nick blinked at him.

"But that's illegal! That's embezzlement!"

"Not if you don't get caught." He put out his cigarette. "Think about it, Nick. It seems to me you don't have much choice."

"I have to have time . . ."

"Of course. Take all the time you want. I'm not trying to pressure you into anything. After all, what are brothers for? But I want my money back by New Year's. With interest. Or I'll have to take the loan papers you signed to old Johnny One-Leg, and he's not going to be very happy with you, Nick."

Nick, his face sweating, stared at him.

"You wouldn't do that?" he whispered.

"Of course I don't want to. But I'd do it if I had to."

"Guess what?" Gloria Gilmore said as she tossed down a Scotch on the rocks. "I'm pregnant."

Cesare, seated across the table from her at the Purple Parrot speakeasy, stared. "You're kidding."

"No I'm not, Love-Lumps. I missed my period again, so I went to the doctor this morning. I'm two months pregnant, and the daddy, darling, is you. So, what happens now?"

Cesare thought awhile. Then he smiled.

"Well," he said, "I guess I have to make you legal."

"Is that a proposal?"

"Sounds like it to me. I'll go buy a ring in the morning."

"Hey, wait: I don't want any Justice of the Peace in New Jersey wedding. I want the real thing. And I want your family to be there."

"Are you out of your mind? My mother wouldn't come within a mile of you! In case you might have forgotten, she hates your guts."

Gloria fumed for a moment.

"All right," she finally said. "I suppose I can't expect her to come, and she probably wouldn't let Johnny come, either. After all, that could look a bit ridiculous, under the circumstances. But I want your sister to be there! The one who's a Countess."

"Brook? Oh sure. As a matter of fact, why don't we get married in France?"

Gloria's face lit up.

"Oh, I like that! My movies always did well in France!" She frowned. "A helluva lot better than they did here."

"Then we can go to Rome for our honeymoon and you
can meet my other sister."

"The one who's married to a Fascist?"

"That's right. He's the Minister of Health."

"That sounds like fun. Oh good, Cesare! Let's do it—
and soon, before I get too big. I wouldn't want people
snickering at the wedding."

"I'll start making the plans tomorrow with my travel
agent. Hey, waiter!" He signaled to the nearest waiter.
"Bring us a bottle of champagne, the best in the house.
We're going to get married!"

"Cesare, you can't marry this woman!" Rachel exclaimed
the next morning. After he had telephoned the news of his
upcoming marriage to Gloria to his mother, she had taken
a taxi to his apartment. Rachel was as worked up as Cesare
had ever seen. "You can't disgrace this family!"

"Mother, she's carrying my child!" Cesare said. "Do you
want me to sire a bastard?"

"I'd much prefer that to having you marry this cheap,
vulgar woman . . ."

"Mother, please. You're talking about the woman I
love."

"You don't love her, Cesare. This is just part of your
lifetime battle with Johnny, to make him look ridiculous by
marrying his former mistress. And how does it make *me*
look? After everything I've done for you over the years,
how could you cover me with dirt by marrying this awful
woman?"

"Mother, I don't think you've given Gloria a chance.
You're not being fair."

"Fair? She's nothing but a whore!"

"That's simply not true."

"It is true! She's slept with so many men, if she had a
reunion they'd fill a hotel! I can't believe you'd do such a

thing. You could have any woman in New York—why would you marry this one?"

"Nevertheless, I am."

She was sitting in a sofa. Now she looked at him for a moment, hurt in her eyes.

"How I've loved you," she finally said. "How I've fought for you, covered for you, rationalized for you. And over the years, you've betrayed me. Well, Cesare, this is the final straw." She stood up, taking her purse off the sofa cushion. "If you marry this woman, I'll disinherit you. I know you're rich in your own right, but you may think twice about losing forty million dollars."

"You won't disinherit me, Mother."

"Oh yes I will. I've reached the end."

"No you won't. Because if you do, I'll tell the police that your beloved Nick has embezzled over half a million dollars worth of bonds from the bank. And he will go to jail."

A stunned look came over her face.

"You can't be serious," she whispered.

"I'm afraid I am. Nick is in very serious trouble."

"I knew it," she said, sinking back down into the sofa. "Valerie spends money like a drunken sailor . . . I feared this might happen . . . But how do you know?"

"Because I have the bonds he embezzled. Nick owes me a fortune. I put up the money for his apartment, I loaned him the down payment on his mansion out on the North Shore, and he has to pay me back."

"I'll pay you back."

"No, you won't. And it won't alter the fact that Nick has embezzled."

"Why have you done this? So you could control Nick?"

"No. So I could control the whole family. And now, Mother dear, I think you had better talk to your beloved husband about inviting me onto the Board of Directors of the bank. Otherwise, there's going to be a very nasty scandal."

Again, she stood up, putting her purse under her arm.

"I said a moment ago that you betrayed me," she said. "Now I'll change that. You've betrayed us all. Johnny has been right all along. You're as amoral as your father."

"My father wasn't a murderer!" he shouted, losing his cool.

"Oh yes he was. He admitted it to me on his deathbed. I never told you because I was trying to protect you from the ugly truth. Your father was a murderer whose only re- deeming features were his good looks and his charm. Un- happily, you remind me exactly of him. Which is probably why I've loved you so deeply. But not anymore, Cesare. Not anymore."

She walked to the door and let herself out of the apart- ment.

"You bitch," he whispered to himself. "I'll get you for that. I'll get you all. Once I'm on the Board of that bank, I'll destroy it." He raised his voice to an angry shout. "I'll bring down *all* the Savages!"

He swung his fist at the crystal lamp, knocking it over onto the floor where it smashed into a thousand shards.

The black 1925 Buick roared around the corner of West Fourth Street and Sixth Avenue. A man with a face that a chorus girl would later describe as looking like "Bing Crosby with his nose bashed in" leaned out the back win- dow and fired his tommy gun at a truck labeled "Myers Plumbing Supplies." It was ten-thirty in the evening, and the man was an up-and-coming gangster named Dutch Schultz. As the gun screeched, bullets sprayed the plumb- ing supply truck, instantly killing the driver. An outrider beside the driver was also killed, but another man in the rear of the truck started firing back at Schultz's Buick.

The plumbing supply truck, which was actually carrying fifty cases of bootleg whiskey owned by a rival mobster named Owney Madden, swerved out of control as its dead driver slumped over the steering wheel. The truck careened into an all-night deli on the west side of the avenue, crashing through the plate-glass window and hurling the gunman in the rear halfway to the back of the deli where he smashed into the sharp edge of the fan over the hamburger stove, cutting off his head.

In the Buick, which was roaring downtown, Dutch Schultz, whose real name was Arthur Flegenheimer and who had grown up in a Jewish section of Harlem, put his tommy gun on the floor and lit a cigarette.

"Take me to Pier Twelve," he said to the driver in front of him. "I'm going to a sailing party on the *Mauretania*."

Schultz, who was known to have a hair-trigger temper and who had endeared himself to the homosexuals of Manhattan by saying in public "Only queers wear silk shirts," was wearing a rumpled tuxedo he had rented for five dollars for the night.

It was the first time he had ever worn a dinner jacket.

"When she was born in 1907," said Franklin Delano Roosevelt, "the *Mauretania* was the largest thing ever put together by man . . . she always fascinated me with her graceful, yachtlike lines, her four enormous black-topped red funnels, and her appearance of power and good breeding."

"It was a beautiful thing all told," wrote Theodore Dreiser. "Its long, cherry-wood paneled halls . . . its heavy porcelain baths, its dainty staterooms filled with lamps, bureaus, writing desks, washstands . . . The little be-buttoned call-boys in their tight-fitting blue suits amused me. And the bugler who bugled for dinner! That was a most musical sound he made, trilling the various quarters gaily, as much as to say, 'This is a very joyous event, ladies and gentlemen; we are all happy; come, come; it is a delightful feast.' "

This queen of the Cunard Line, the most popular ocean liner of its day, was longer than the Great Pyramid was high and burned a thousand tons of coal a day, her gaping furnaces attended by a "Black Squad" of 324 firemen and trimmers. This Grand Hotel with engines was a hodgepodge of decorational styles: the grand staircase was paneled in French walnut with carved pilasters and capitals, the writing room and library were Louis XVI with gray sycamore panels highlighted in gold and ivory. The main lounge and ballroom were eighteenth-century French, the main dining room was Francis I, the smoking room was fifteenth-century Italian, and the Verandah Café was modeled on the Old English Orangery at Hampton Court. For all that, the ship, according to its advertisements, was supposed to remind one of "a stately British country home." The *Mauretania* was the ship of choice of Society "swells" and movie stars, which was why Dutch Schultz wanted to see it, one movie star in particular: Gloria Gilmore, whose blond pulchritude had turned on his teenage hormones eating popcorn in the Biograph.

At the moment, Gloria and Cesare were posing on the main deck of the *Mauretania* for a dozen reporters, Gloria giving her most sensuous movie star smile as the flashbulbs popped.

"Is it true," one reporter asked, "that you and Mr. Savage are getting married in France?"

"We're already married," Gloria lied. "But it was only a civil ceremony. We're going to have a church wedding in Paris. I'm really very religious."

"Hey, Gloria," yelled another reporter, "was your father-in-law at the wedding? He's an old friend of yours, isn't he?"

Gloria shot a nervous look at Cesare, who was wearing a camel's-hair coat over his tux.

"My stepfather," he announced with a straight face, "had a cold and couldn't come to the ceremony. It was just me and Gloria"—he smiled at her and took her hand—"and we're very happy and very much in love."

"Are you going to be doing any more movies, Gloria?" called a third reporter.

"I'm through with acting," she announced. "From now on, I'm just going to be a housewife."

She smiled as the flashbulbs turned her twenty-carat diamond engagement ring into a solar eruption.

"No more questions, fellows," Cesare announced, "and no more pictures. I'm throwing a little sailing party in our suite. Thanks."

"Are you serving any of your bootleg booze?" said one reporter.

"I'm not a bootlegger, and we're serving lemonade. We're good law-abiding citizens." He ignored the snickers. "Good night, fellows."

He led Gloria into a midship passageway as the reporters outside continued to pop their flashbulbs.

"Do you think they believed us?" Gloria asked. "I mean, about already being married?"

"Who cares?"

"I about died when they mentioned your father."

"You'd better get used to it. And he's my stepfather."

Cesare had booked the biggest suite on the ship for the crossing to Europe, and when they reached it the cabin was already filled with guests drinking booze served by a white-jacketed steward. When Cesare and Gloria came in, the crowd cheered. Arnold Rothstein came up and pumped Cesare's hand.

"Congratulations," he said. "Can I give the bride a kiss?"

"Sure, why not?"

He kissed Gloria as Cesare greeted his fellow guests, taking a highball from the steward.

A few minutes later, Rothstein took him aside.

"There's a kid that works for me who'd like to meet you. His name is Dutch Schultz. I took the liberty of asking him to the party, because he told me he'd never been on an ocean liner. Do you mind?"

"Of course not, A. R."

"He did a job for us about an hour ago. He took care of one of Owney Madden's trucks. He's a little rough around the edges and has a hot temper, but he's dependable. Got balls of steel." He turned to Dutch Schultz, who had just come in the cabin and was looking around with wide eyes. "Hey, Dutch, come over here. This is Cesare Savage."

The Bing Crosby look-alike shook Cesare's hand.

"Glad to meet you, Mr. Savage," he said. "Can I meet your wife? I've never met a real-live movie star."

"Sure. Gloria?"

He signaled to Gloria, who came through the crowd. "I want you to meet one of the boys, Dutch Schultz. He's never met a movie star."

Gloria smiled as she shook Schultz's hand.

"And what do you do, Mr. Schultz?" she asked.

Schultz looked at Rothstein and smirked.

"I drive trucks," he said.

"How interesting," Gloria said sniffily. "I've never met a truck driver."

Schultz's face darkened.

"Hey," he snarled, "you don't have to high-hat me, lady!"

"She wasn't high-hatting you," Cesare said.

"Oh yeah? I didn't like her tone. She looked at me as if I was dirt. Besides," he added, turning on Gloria, "I've read about you in the movie magazines. You've slept with everyone in Hollywood—including this asshole's father!"

Cesare grabbed him and slugged him so hard he fell back against the bar, then slid down on the deck.

"Get this jerk out of here," he ordered the steward. The latter reached down to take Schultz's arm. Schultz, as swift as a cobra, pulled a gun from inside his jacket and aimed it.

"Don't touch me," he said.

The steward, looking terrified, jumped back as Schultz got to his feet. He turned to Cesare.

"You've just made a big mistake," he said quietly. Then he put his gun back in its holster and walked out of the cabin.

"Well," Cesare said as he picked up a new drink, "nothing like a little excitement to make a party."

The other guests laughed, albeit rather nervously.

"I don't know whether to roar with anger," Johnny said, "or cry with shame and disappointment."

He was slumped in a chair in the drawing room of his Fifth Avenue house. With him on this chilly evening were Rachel, who, after much deliberation, had told him about Nick's embezzling of the bonds, and Nick and Valerie, both of whom looked nervous, if not, on Nick's part, panic-stricken. "Nick, how could you have been so foolish? How *could* you? Didn't you see the consequences of what you were doing?"

"It was Cesare!" Nick blurted out, taking a nervous drink of his highball. "Cesare, that rat, that damned, slick rat . . . He sucked me into a situation where I had to do something! I trusted him! And he made it all sound so easy and simple . . . I could borrow the bonds, use them to raise money, then return them later on . . ."

"I don't excuse Cesare!" Johnny said hotly, straightening out of his slump at mention of his stepson's name. "And I see the whole damned plot now! It was clever—damned clever—and it worked because you two were weak and greedy! You're as much to blame for this disaster as Cesare!"

Valerie burst into tears.

"Oh Father, please don't be mean to us . . . I'm trying to give you a grandchild now so you have to be nice."

Johnny sighed and shook his head.

"What has this family come to?" he said sadly. "What silly fools we must look like to the outside world!"

"The outside world is never going to know the truth," Rachel said in a firm tone. "We're going to work this out some way in private."

"How?" Johnny said. "How in God's name can we do anything? Cesare has the bonds, and he and . . . and his new wife are in Europe on their honeymoon. He's got our hands tied."

"Not if we give him what he wants," Rachel said.

"Never!" Johnny yelled. "I won't put him on the Board of the bank! He's a thief! He'll ruin everything! Listen: I have good information that he's still connected with Arnold Rothstein and, despite his malarkey about being an ex-bootlegger and an investor, has leased out his yacht to other hoods who are still bringing in the illegal liquor from Cuba and he's still making enormous profits off it! How could I reward a bootlegger with a seat on the Board of Directors of the bank? It's inconceivable!"

"Johnny, we have no choice!" Rachel said, standing up. "Unless you want to see Nick in jail for embezzlement! If we don't do what Cesare wants, he'll go to the police with the bonds! Listen, darling, you were right about Cesare all along—I can see that now. You were right and I was wrong, because I loved him—as Shakespeare said, not wisely but too well. I've been as foolish as everyone else, and Cesare has been the clever one. But what does that matter now? We have to give him what he wants!"

"Mother, couldn't the police charge him with embezzlement?" Nick said, drinking more of his highball.

"Of course not," his father snapped. "He'll say he had no way of knowing they were taken from the bank. *You're* the embezzler."

"Oh God," Nick wailed, getting up to go to the bar and refresh his highball. "It all seems like some horrible nightmare!"

"Stay away from that bar!" his father ordered. "You're beginning to drink like a fish."

"I just want a little refresher . . ."

"No! Put that glass down! I have yet to make up my mind what to do with you, but I certainly don't want to have to deal with your drunkenness as well as your embezzling! And you, Valerie." He turned to her. "I'm putting you on a strict budget. Your shopping spree is at an end."

She burst into tears.

"What'll I do?" she wailed.

"You'll stay home and read good books."

"Oh, that sounds so boring!"

"Nevertheless, that's the way it's going to be. Perhaps some of this is my fault because I was too lax with both of you in the past. But I trusted you, Nick. In my love for you, I couldn't imagine you would do anything so thoroughly dishonest as embezzling, so I turned a blind eye to the way you were spending money. Buying that mansion on Long Island and that vulgar party you gave . . . it was only then that I began to see something had to be seriously wrong, and of course there was. You were giving stock tips to Cesare. Oh God, my son, if you knew how much I loved you, the great hopes I had for you . . . and now, you've destroyed my trust in you. And what can I do with you? Leave you at the bank? How can I? I don't *trust* you anymore!"

Nick sat down and now he burst into tears.

"It was all Cesare's fault," he sobbed.

"Yes, we can all blame Cesare," Rachel said. "But he

saw how to play on our weaknesses: my blind love, Valerie's passion for spending money, Nick's easy morality . . . even your hatred of him, darling," she added to Johnny. "He was smart enough to see that your hatred made you vulnerable to him. Since you couldn't stand thinking of him, you were essentially blind to him and he worked around you. So, here we stand, the great Savage family, naked to the world, weakened by our own folly. But as the mother of this family, I can tell you one thing: my son is not going to jail."

There was a silence except for Nick's and Valerie's sniffing. All eyes were on Johnny.

"My pride," he finally said, "won't let me do it."

"Darling," Rachel said, "I love you with all my heart. But it may be too late for pride. We have to give Cesare what he wants. We have to make him a director of the bank."

Tears slowly formed in Johnny's eyes.

"What," he finally whispered, "will my father think? What would your father think? They were such honorable men. That it all could end like this."

"Your father was a pirate, my father had many faults, and the Rothschilds started out as peddlers who got rich by means similar to Nick's. I could even make a case that what he has done is no better nor worse than what the first Rothschild did during the Napoleonic wars when he borrowed the Hessian prince's fortune to make his own. The point is, we're in a corner now, but we have to survive. Survival is the important thing! Besides, we still control the bank. The Directors are all our friends. What can Cesare possibly do?"

"I don't know," Johnny said in a despondent tone.

"And also, Cesare's been clever, it's true. But it's time he made a mistake."

Johnny looked at her thoughtfully.

"Perhaps," he finally said, "you're right."

Ten days later, Cesare and Gloria were married in Bernard and Brook's house on the Avenue Foch, Cesare's old friend Hemingway as the best man. At the reception, Hemingway got roaring drunk and Cesare was somewhat surprised to see that success had hardened him. Somewhere along the line, he had lost that boyish charm that had seemed so natural when they had been together in Italy. In fact, Hemingway was rather full of himself.

Then Cesare and Gloria went to the Riviera for a two-week honeymoon. As they lounged at a seaside restaurant in Nice, lunching alfresco at umbrellaed tables with Cole Porter, Gerald and Sara Murphy, the American expatriates who had made the south of France fashionable in the summer, roly-poly Elsa Maxwell and Coco Chanel (to whom Brook had introduced them), Cesare received a telegram from New York. After opening it and reading it, he turned to Gloria and said with a smile, "I've been offered a seat on the Board of Directors."

"Oh darling," Gloria gushed, giving him a hug, "congratulations!"

"I've won! I've beaten Johnny One-leg! I've won!"

He hugged her, thinking, I've done it! I'm on top of the world! And I've avenged my father! How sweet success tastes! How wonderfully sweet!

Part Ten

Incident at Repulse Bay

37. THE YOUNG MAN RODE DOWN THE POLO FIELD
on his pony, swung his mallet, and hit the ball, sending it
into the goal. It was a brilliant June afternoon in 1928 at
the Hong Kong Polo Grounds near Happy Valley racetrack,
and the crowd of well-dressed Chinese on one side of the
field cheered and applauded as the English, on the other
side, remained glumly silent. The seventeen-year-old scorer
was named Lance Wang, he was captain of the Hong Kong
Dragons and the son of General and Madame Wang. He
was considered the best polo player in the Far East, where
polo was a passion among those who could afford it.

As the beautiful young girl on the English side stared at
him through her binoculars, she thought Lance was the
most exotically handsome young man she had ever seen.
Her name was Nora Manderville, and she was the daughter
of the Governor of Hong Kong, Sir Neville Manderville.

"Momma," she said to Lady Elvira Manderville who was
standing next to her, "aren't the Chins coming to the ball
tonight?"

"Yes, of course," Lady Manderville said. She also was
watching the action through binoculars. "The Chins being
the most important Chinese on the island, they naturally
would be invited to the first ball at Government House
where Chinese and English will mix." She put down her
binoculars and looked at her seventeen-year-old daughter,
who was wearing a light white dress and a small white hat
with a dashing white plume. "Your father is making history
of a sort tonight, you know, my dear. It's time we English

began to lower the barriers of racial prejudice. I'm very proud of him."

"Yes, I know," Nora said, bored by the idea of making history. "Lance Wang is staying with his grandmother, isn't he?"

"Yes."

"So he'll be at the ball?"

"Oh yes. He was sent an invitation, and he accepted."

"Excellent."

Nora's binoculars were still trained on Lance.

"Didn't he just graduate from Eton?" she went on.

"Yes. I'm told he did very well, and he's going on to Oxford."

"How very interesting."

Nora, who had soft blond hair cut in fashionable bangs and the loveliest peaches-and-cream complexion, felt her heart thumping.

"How very handsome you look," Julie Chin said as she came down the staircase of her house on Victoria Peak overlooking Hong Kong and its magnificent harbor below. "Now, you must remember to dance with your cousin Isabel. Her mother tells me she's very shy, and you must be gallant."

"Yes, Grandmamma," Lance said. He was standing at the foot of the staircase in the great hall of the imposing mansion. He was wearing a well-cut white dinner jacket, and his jet-black hair was brushed cleanly back. Already six feet tall, he had the wiry physique of his father, General Wang, who had kidnapped his mother, Jasmine Chin, so many years before, and who was now military attaché to Generalissimo Chiang Kai-shek, the new leader of the Republic of China, in Nanking. Lance really didn't like Nanking, which was a fairly grubby provincial town although it was the republic's new capital. Lance much preferred

Hong Kong, which, while it was itself a bit dowdy and provincial compared to London, Paris, or New York, still had many attractions for a young man with smashing good looks and a fortune to boot. Plus, Hong Kong had polo. And polo, at least at his age, was Lance's life.

He kissed his grandmother's cheek. Julie, who was now seventy-three, still was a handsome woman; and in her Western-style silver ball gown, the suite of diamonds and emeralds, including a splendid tiara, that her late husband had bought her decades before, and the pink-edged-with-pearl-gray sash of the Order of the British Empire slashing diagonally across her from her right shoulder to her left waist, she looked as imposing as Queen Mary herself. The honor had been granted her in 1921 by King George V for her heavy financial contributions to hospitals and other charities in Hong Kong. The Chin hong had, over the years and under the inspired direction of Julie and her son Edgar, developed into one of the economic powerhouses of Hong Kong, Edgar having branched out from the original department stores into real-estate development, investments in industry and shipping, and banking interests. The Chins were one of the richest families in Hong Kong, and Julie was the undisputed grande dame of Chinese society on the island. This daughter of a Chinese pirate and Justin Savage had come a long way from her childhood as a prisoner-hostage of the rascally Dowager Empress in the Forbidden City in Peking.

"You look beautiful yourself, Grandmomma," Lance said, offering her his arm.

"Flatterer," she said with a laugh. "I'm an aging wreck, and I know it. But I love to hear your lies. Come, my Prince Charming: let's go to the ball. It's an important evening for Hong Kong."

As her Chinese majordomo opened the front door, bowing as he did so, Lance and Julie went out into the pleasant twilight to climb into her silver Rolls-Royce and be driven up the hill to Government House, which was ablaze with light for this gala evening.

The Hong Kong that Tim and Julie Chin had come to so many years before had had as its major mode of transportation man-drawn rickshas with occasional animal-drawn carts and wagons. Now, in the Age of the Charleston, there were so many cars, taxis, buses, motorcycles, and trucks clogging the streets of Hong Kong that the Chinese complained bitterly of these "coughing, stinking dragons," causing strict traffic laws to be passed. (One unfortunate American flour merchant named Howard Werschul got two months hard labor for "wanton and furious driving.") Even so, driving in Hong Kong was still an adventure.

Government House stood on Upper Albert Road opposite the beautiful Botanical Gardens and not far from military headquarters and the Anglican cathedral. By the time the Rolls was near enough to see its lights, Lance and his grandmother could hear the Governor's military band playing on the lawn outside the neoclassical mansion, pillared all around, with a porte cochere and a handsome pair of guardhouses. It had a spectacular view of the harbor below, and for the amusement of the Governor and his guests there were five tennis courts, three grass and two asphalt. Once, in the 1880s when the British Empire was at high noon, the Governor's servants wore long blue gowns and white gaiters and wore pigtails so long they almost reached the floor. Now, with the British Empire slowly sinking in the west (though only the more prescient English realized it at the time), the servants wore smart white jackets more in keeping with 1928. Two young servants held the Rolls-Royce's doors for Julie and Lance, bowing snappily as they emerged and started toward the front door, where yet more servants bowed them inside. While the Empire might be in decline and Noel Coward might be tweaking its nose with songs like "Mad Dogs and Englishmen," worldly cynics like Coward and Maugham still vied for invitations to the

Empire's many Government Houses girdling the globe where the aging Empire, crippled by strikes at home and anti-Imperial stirrings abroad, still managed to put on a damned good show. And just to remind visitors who still had "the upper hand," the entrance hall was flanked by two life-size, gold-framed portraits of the sovereigns, King George and Queen Mary, in all their bejeweled splendor. Julie, who was one of the few Chinese to have been to private receptions at Government House, had seen it all before. But Lance, who, because of his English public school education, thought of himself as English as if his bright brown eyes hadn't been slightly slanted and the skin on his high cheekbones hadn't been slightly yellow, felt a thrill that would have pleased Queen Victoria.

"I say," he whispered to his grandmother, "it's rather impressive, isn't it?"

"They do it better in India," his grandmother replied tartly. Julie, despite her Order of the British Empire, had experienced enough of British anti-Chinese racism that she was no great fan of the Empire. She had seen the signs in the Shanghai public parks proclaiming "No Chinese or Dogs Allowed."

Because of the importance of the evening—the first official mingling of the races—except for the most extreme bigots on both sides, everyone who was anyone in the colony was at Government House, and the place was jammed, the men mostly in white dinner jackets and black ties, the women in plumes and jewels with evening gowns that were several years out-of-date from what was being worn in Europe and America. The crowd moved slowly toward a great pillared hall the height of the house where Sir Neville Manderville, his wife, and his daughter were standing in a receiving line, the Governor in full summer fig, and Lady Manderville in a rather severely cut, if handsome, white evening gown, wearing her jewels, tiara, and sash of the Order of the British Empire. The passing guests curtsied

and bowed as the band outside played slightly out-of-date
show tunes like "Tea for Two" and "I'll See You Again."
The protocol for these official functions was as out-of-date
as the show tunes, but the mystique still pertained that the
Governors and Viceroys of England's far-flung Empire
were the representatives of the monarchs and were to receive the same bows and curtsies as if the King and Queen
themselves had been there.

When Julie and her grandson reached the Governor, Sir
Neville, who was a tall, imposing man thirty pounds over-
weight, was particularly gracious. After speaking for a moment to Julie, he turned to Lance and smiled. "Well," he
said, "this young man needs no introduction. What a splendid show you put on this afternoon at the polo ground.
What a horseman you are, sir! Even though you beat us, I
extend my congratulations."

"Thank you, Sir Neville. You're very kind."

"This is my wife, Lady Manderville . . ."

Julie curtsied and Lance bowed.

"And my daughter, Nora."

Lance looked at the lovely young creature in the pale
peach chiffon evening gown with the string of seed pearls
around her slender throat. My God, he thought, what a
beauty! She's a dream!

Nora extended her hand and smiled.

"I, too, watched you this afternoon," she said. "It was
very thrilling."

Lance shook her hand.

"I . . . uh . . . thank you," he blurted out.

Then, as the band segued into "Deep in My Heart, Dear,"
he followed his grandmother into the hall that was rapidly
filling up with guests taking glasses of champagne from
passing waiters.

"Grandmother," he said, "she's lovely. The daughter, I
mean."

"Yes, isn't she?" Julie said, taking a glass of champagne.

"Very sweet and pretty. The mother's a bit of a bore, but her father's all right, doing a decent job as Governor, and I certainly admire him for having the guts to hold this ball tonight, bringing everyone together. It's long overdue, of course, but there you have it: the English move like glaciers." She took a sip of the champagne, which was icy and good. She saw Lance looking back at Nora. "Taken your fancy, has she?"

"Well, yes . . . I mean, do you think I'd dare ask her for a dance? I mean, she being the daughter of the Governor?"

"Of course. She's probably dying for you to ask. You're the best-looking male in this place, believe me. But don't get any fancy ideas."

"What do you mean?"

"Well, the Mandervilles are very grand and the title goes back to the Crusades or something, but they're poor as church mice. Of course, out here all the English live like lords because help is cheap. But once they get back home to England, they can barely pay the gas bill."

"All I'm thinking of is to ask her to dance."

"Oh, I daresay. But I just thought I'd warn you. You're a prize catch, my dear, and the jewel in my crown. You know, I suggested to your mother to name you Lance after my first husband, whom I loved so much. And I'm going to make sure you get the pick of the crop one day, not some second-rate bureaucrat on a pension."

Again, Lance looked back at Nora. "I don't know anything about girls," he said. "I've never even kissed one! And you've practically got me married off."

She smiled and patted his cheek.

"I'm just an old woman looking after those she loves. But remember one thing, Lance. She's English. You're Chinese. It's good that we all can come together here tonight— that's a step forward. But for the really important things in life like love and marriage . . . stick to your own kind."

"Grandmother, you're a terrible snob!"

"When you've been snubbed by Anglos and Americans as many times as I have in my long life, it becomes a distinct pleasure to put the shoe on the other foot."

The band outside started playing "Always."

"Isn't the full moon beautiful?"

The question was asked by Nora, who had come out on the terrace where Lance was standing, looking at the harbor lights below. He turned to look at her.

"Yes," he said. "It's such a beautiful evening."

"Are you staying long in Hong Kong?"

"No, just a week with my grandmother. Then I'm going to Shanghai to spend two weeks with my parents, who have a house there as well as Nanking."

"And then?"

"Well, Shanghai in the summer is pretty ghastly. Terrible heat and humidity, you know. So I'm going to the south of France where a classmate of mine has invited me to stay at his parents' villa for two months."

"Oh, that sounds very romantic."

Lance smiled.

"Yes, I suppose it is. They have a yacht. I like yachting very much. Do you?"

"I don't know much about it." Nora leaned on the stone balustrade as a slight breeze blew her blond hair. The band was playing a Strauss waltz. "Waltzes are so old-fashioned," she said, "but I still love them. Do you?"

"Yes."

She turned to him and smiled.

"Then why don't you ask me to waltz?"

Lance stared at her a moment. Then he offered his arm.

"Would you care to waltz?" he asked.

"I've been waiting for you to ask me."

The beautiful young couple went back into the ballroom.

"I so admire your parents," Nora said as Lance twirled her around the crowded dance floor.

"Oh? How so?"

"Well, I'm very much for Chiang Kai-shek, and of course your father is very close to him. I mean, I think they are the best hope for China in the long run. And your mother is so wonderful, doing all that work for the charity hospitals in Nanking. It must be rather dreadful, living in Nanking."

"It's awful. But my mother is very dedicated."

"I admire her for that. And she's so very beautiful."

"Thank you."

"I've seen her photographs in the rotogravure. She has the most exquisite beauty."

"Yes, you're right. I sometimes look at her and just sigh."

Nora smiled.

"What if I told you I look at you and just sigh?"

"You couldn't possibly. I have a hawk nose, like my father's, and I'm far too skinny."

"Lance . . . may I call you Lance?"

"Please. If I may call you Nora."

"Oh yes. Lance, you are the most beautiful man I have ever seen."

He stopped waltzing in the middle of the dance floor, surrounded by other couples twirling to the infectuous beats of Johann Strauss.

"You can't be serious?" he said.

"Oh, but I am."

"But I'm Chinese."

"So what?"

Lance looked at her a moment. Then he took her in his arms again and began twirling around the dance floor.

"What are you doing tomorrow?" he asked.

"Nothing."

"Would you like to go on a picnic?"

"Oh yes, I adore picnics. Where?"

"Well, I don't know. How about the Botanical Gardens? At the monkey cage?"

"That sounds fun. When?"

"Noon. I'll bring everything."

"Oh Lance, that sounds wonderful!"

"You don't . . . I mean, you can go without a chaperone?"

She giggled.

"I know we're all terribly provincial here in Hong Kong, but we're not that provincial. Yes, I can go all by myself."

"Then I'll see you tomorrow."

"I'm looking forward to it."

"So am I."

Lance stood in front of the big iron cage, stuck his thumbs in his ears, and wiggled his hands at the monkey before him, making a face. To Nora's delight, the monkey made a face back at him. Then Lance hunched over, dangled his arms almost to the ground, and jumped up and down, making grunting noises. Nora laughed when the monkey did the same.

"You should be in the movies!" she exclaimed as Lance came over and sat on the blanket he had laid on the grass.

"The monkey should be in the movies," he said, reaching into the wicker basket and pulling out a sandwich. "Do you like ham sandwiches, cucumber, or cold chicken?"

"All three. I'm starving."

"And I have some potato salad. My grandmother's cook makes terrific potato salad."

"Wonderful. I love it."

As Lance prepared a plate for her and Nora opened a jar

of pickles, he said, "Tell me about yourself. Do you go to school here in Hong Kong?"

"Oh no. Mother sent me to her old school in England, Chilton Manor. I graduated just last month."

"Are you going on to college?"

"No. My father doesn't believe in college for girls."

"He doesn't? That's terribly old-fashioned."

"Yes, I know."

He handed her the plate and gave her a napkin rolled around a knife, fork, and spoon.

"Can't you talk him into it?"

He poured her some iced tea from a Thermos.

"Well, the truth is," she began, rather tentatively, "my parents don't want to spend the money for tuition."

"Really? I'd think a college education is worth the money."

"Well, it would be if I were a boy. Then I'd probably go to Oxford, where my father went. But you see, after I was born, my mother couldn't have any more children and Father had desperately wanted a boy. So he's rather bitter about me. I mean, he loves me and is very kind. But I know it hurts him that I wasn't a boy. So I'm almost like the Chinese, who treat girl babies rather like dirt."

Lance looked into her eyes.

"I can't imagine anyone treating you badly," he said.

"Oh, Father doesn't treat me badly."

"Anyway, I'm glad you're not a boy."

She smiled, looking at him almost adoringly.

"Right now," she said, "I'm very glad I'm a girl."

In the distance, opposite the Excelsior Hotel, they fired the noonday gun. Its noise echoed around the hills and across the azure harbor filled with ships, ferries, and yachts.

"Do you have any boyfriends?" Lance asked.

"Oh yes. Dozens. Men just fall at my feet."

"I bet they do. Anyone in particular?"

"No. And I was just joking. Men really don't fall at my

feet. I think they're rather intimidated that I'm the Governor's daughter. And of course, the English boys are all looking for someone rich, and they know my family doesn't have any money."

"How could anyone think about money when they look at you?"

"They do, believe me. This potato salad is delicious."

"Want more?"

"I shouldn't. I'll get fat as a pig. But yes, please."

She held out her plate and he spooned more salad onto it. In so doing, his hand accidentally touched hers. They looked into each other's eyes for a moment. For a moment, there was electricity. Then she put her plate back on the blanket. She was wearing a white blouse and a dark blue skirt, with a wide-brimmed straw hat.

"I like your hat a lot," he said.

"Oh? Thank you. It's local. I bought it on Cat Street." She giggled. "It was probably stolen. Mother says everything sold on Cat Street is stolen, but the best bargains in Hong Kong are there." A bee buzzed around her hat. "Is something wrong?" she asked.

"I beg your pardon?"

"You were staring at me."

"Oh . . . I'm sorry. I was just daydreaming."

"Tell me your dream."

He looked sheepish.

"If I did," he said, "you might slap my face."

"Is it something shocking?"

"Well, rather."

"Tell me."

"No, really, I can't. You see, I'm very awkward around girls. I actually don't know many."

"I can't imagine that girls wouldn't chase you like absolute mad."

"Well, you're very kind, but you see in England, I'm . . .

well, you know. The English girls think I'm some sort of a freak."

"Because you're Chinese?"

"Yes. It doesn't bother me, I guess."

She placed her plate to one side, got on her knees, and crawled across the blanket to him. Then she put her arms around him and kissed him on the lips.

"There," she said. "I certainly don't think you're a freak. I think you're the most wonderful boy I've ever met." She crawled back to her place and held out her plate. "May I have another cucumber sandwich?"

He stared at her, almost in a daze. Then he crawled across the blanket to her and put his arms around her, kissing her with all the passion in his young body. Her straw hat fell off her as he gently leaned her down on the blanket, kissing her. Her arms tightened around him. After a long moment, he released her.

"I'm crazy for you," he whispered.

"And I'm mad for you," she whispered back. "Absolutely mad. The first moment I looked at you, I thought . . . Oh God, I can't tell you what I thought."

He ran his fingers over her cheek.

"Tell me."

"I thought, 'That's the man I want to be my first lover.' Isn't that shocking?"

"No. I'm flattered. And it doesn't bother you that I'm Chinese?"

She smiled, looking into his eyes.

"I'm crazy," she whispered, "for Chinese food."

He kissed her again, and she responded to him with all the hunger in her body.

"You see," she said after a moment, "I had a grandmother who was terribly wicked. 'Mad Lady Manderville' they called her, because she was rather promiscuous with men. And of course sixty years ago, if you were as loose

as she was, one simply had to be mad. It just wasn't done.
I think I must have inherited her blood."

"Are you mad Nora Manderville?"

"I think I must be. Look at me! Throwing myself at you
wantonly, and I only met you last night. I'm sure this will
all end badly."

"It doesn't have to. We'll make sure it doesn't. We'll be
careful. But, Nora, for the first time in my life I'm in love."

Tears formed in her eyes as she looked up at him. Then
again she threw her arms around him and kissed him.

"Oh Lance," she whispered, "this is the most beautiful
day of my life. And I love you. I love you so much it has
to be good, doesn't it? A feeling this wonderful can't possibly be bad."

"How can love ever be bad?"

The two young lovers lay in each other's arms staring
up at the cloudless sky and the hot sun.

"Where did you go today?" Sir Neville Manderville asked
that evening as he, Lady Manderville, and Nora ate in the
dining room of Government House. "Cook says you
weren't here for lunch."

Two ceiling fans hummed softly as they twirled, causing
the flames of the candles in the silver and crystal hurricane
lamps to flicker slightly. Sir Neville had, as usual, dressed
for dinner in a white dinner jacket. Lady Manderville wore
a long pale green chiffon dress. Her silver hair was bobbed.
She looked at her daughter.

"Answer your father, Nora," she said.

"I went shopping." Nora spooned her cold watermelon
soup.

"Why didn't you tell Cook you wouldn't be here for
lunch?"

"It slipped my mind, I suppose. I'm sorry."

"That's very unlike you, Nora. Please see that it doesn't happen again."

"Yes, Father."

Silence as a white-jacketed Chinese servant removed the soup bowls and another served the first course of prawns. After the servants had left the big paneled room, Nora said, "No, that's a lie. I didn't go shopping. I went on a picnic with Lance Wang, and it was the most wonderful picnic of my entire life."

Her parents, sitting at opposite ends of the big table, stared at her. Then her father put down his fork.

"Do you think that was wise?" he asked.

"Why? What's wrong with it?" Nora said defiantly.

"Darling," her mother said, "Lance is a very nice boy, a very handsome boy, and he comes from a wonderful family. But he's Chinese."

"Of course he's Chinese. What's the difference?"

"You know what the difference is," her father said. "And you're the Governor's daughter. For you to have any social contacts with Lance Wang is totally out of the question."

"Oh Father, that's ridiculous!" she exclaimed hotly. "And I'm amazed to hear you, of all people, say that! After all, you were the first Governor to mix the races here the other night, which was a wonderful thing. I'd think you'd be the last person in the world to object to my seeing Lance."

"Well, you think wrong. As Governor, I have to carry out the policy of the Colonial Office, which is to relax the barriers between the whites and the other races. And I believe it is a good thing. But for my own daughter to . . ." He hesitated. "Did he make advances to you?"

She laughed.

"I made advances to him," she said. "I behaved like an absolute hussy, and I don't care who knows it! I'm crazy for him. And if you want to know more, he's taking me tomorrow to a tea dance at Repulse Bay."

"Nora!" her mother exclaimed. "I can't believe what I'm hearing!"

"Nora, you will forget this madness!" her father snapped. "You know full well Chinese aren't allowed at the Repulse Bay Hotel! You will call this Lance up and politely decline his invitation. Tell him you have a cold. I'm very fond of his grandmother and I think he's a fine young man so I don't want to hurt either him or Madame Chin. But you will decline his invitation."

Nora threw down her napkin and stood up, her blue eyes flashing angrily.

"I will not!" she exclaimed. "And if you want to know the whole truth, we're madly in love with each other. So you both had better start getting used to it!"

She ran out of the dining room.

"Dear God," her father muttered.

"What can we do?" Lady Manderville asked anxiously.

Her husband shook his head.

"I don't know," he said. "But we must stop this. God knows what may happen if Lance tries to get into the Repulse Bay."

"It's in her blood! It's Mad Lady Manderville all over again!"

Her husband stood up.

"I'll call Madame Chin," he said, starting out of the dining room. "She'll stop him. She's the last one to want an incident."

"The Governor called me," Julie said that evening as she and her grandson enjoyed a sundowner on the verandah of her house. "He says you're going to take his daughter to a tea dance tomorrow at the Repulse Bay Hotel."

"That's right," Lance said, sipping his gin and mango juice.

"You know they don't allow Chinese in the hotel."

"Yes, I know. But I seriously doubt they'd keep out the Governor's daughter. And Nora won't go in unless they let me in."

Julie drummed her fingers thoughtfully on the arms of her high-backed wicker chair.

"So you're making a sort of political statement with what is just a date?"

"It's no political statement. It's just that we want to go to the tea dance, and why shouldn't we be allowed to?"

Julie sipped her drink a moment. Then she smiled slightly.

"Exactly," she said. "Why shouldn't you? Go and have a wonderful time."

Lance looked at his grandmother and also smiled.

"I thought you didn't want me to get involved with Nora?" he said.

"Oh well, I was being rather silly, wasn't I? You're both far too young to think about marriage. And meanwhile, have a good time. It should be rather interesting to see what happens at the Repulse Bay."

"Let's just hope we don't get repulsed."

38. THE REPULSE BAY HOTEL ON THE SOUTH SIDE OF the island was a dowdy but rather endearing Victorian building with a renowned view of the eponymous bay between Aberdeen and Stanley. When Nora and Lance arrived in a taxi the next evening at seven, its small string orchestra was already playing on the bay-side terrace and couples, mostly young, were dancing to "How Deep Is the Ocean?"

"Well," Lance said as he paid the cabbie, "here goes."

"There won't be any trouble," Nora said. She was wearing a pretty lemon-yellow silk dress with matching shoes. "Everything will go well."

She took his arm as they went to the front door where a Chinese doorman in a rather resplendent uniform looked uncertainly at Lance, who was wearing his white dinner jacket.

"So sorry, sir," the doorman said, "but Chinese not allowed in hotel."

"Do you know who I am?" Nora asked.

"Oh yes, missee. Very pretty daughter of Governor."

"This gentleman is my guest."

The doorman gulped slightly, then opened the door, bowing as they went inside.

"You see?" Nora whispered. "There was no problem."

"So far."

They walked through the hotel lobby, garnering startled stares from the clerks and guests, to the entrance to the verandah with its wicker chairs. An English maître d' met them. He, too, looked nervously at Lance.

"Good afternoon," Nora said with a gracious smile. "We'd like a table for two."

Beads of sweat appeared on his brow.

"Yes, of course, Miss Manderville. However . . ."

"One with a view, if that's possible."

"Yes. But your friend is not permitted."

"Why not?"

"He is, um, Chinese."

"Yes, I'm aware of that. But he is my guest."

The two dozen or so dancing couples on the verandah beyond had stopped and were staring at the little drama. Now the orchestra stopped playing, and an odd silence descended on the scene. The maître d', in a sweat of uncertainty, did nothing. Finally, Nora said, "I'm waiting for my table."

One could almost hear him gulp. Now he took two large menus from a pile on a table and said, "Follow me, please."

He led them around the dance floor as the guests stared. When they were halfway around, a tall, strapping young man with curly blond hair left his girlfriend and stepped in front of Nora and Lance, who stopped.

"Hello, Reggie," Nora said. "Do you know Lance Wang? Lance, this is Reggie Alford, one of my friends."

Lance extended his hand.

"How do you do?"

"Nora," Reggie said, "why are you doing this? You know the rules."

"The rules are being changed."

"Not this rule. I'm sorry, Wang, but you're not allowed here. Please leave."

"No. I like it here," Lance said.

"Don't make me force you."

"Try."

"Reggie," Nora said angrily, "you're being a bore. Now stand aside. I want to go to my table."

"Nora, he's not bloody well supposed to be in here!" Reggie shouted. "He's a bloody Chink!"

"He's my guest!" she shouted back.

"I don't care! He has to go!"

He gave Lance an angry shove on the shoulder. Lance slugged him on his chin so hard that Reggie fell back onto a table, then crashed to the floor, where he lay dazedly rubbing his jaw.

"Now," Lance said to the maître d', who looked ready to faint, "show us our table, please."

They followed him to a table near the edge of the verandah, where they were seated. "I think we should have some champagne," Nora said to Lance.

"I agree. A bottle of champagne. Veuve Clicquot, if you have it."

Reggie had gotten to his feet. Now he started whispering

to some of the other male guests, who nodded their heads. Couples started quietly walking toward the door. Others who weren't standing on the dance floor got up and followed suit. Within minutes, Lance and Nora were the only guests left. Nora turned to the orchestra leader, who was standing at a loss what to do.

"I believe you're hired to play music," Nora said. "We want to dance."

Nodding rather numbly, the conductor turned to his musicians and raised his baton. They started playing "Tea for Two." Lance stood up.

"Would you like to dance?" he said.

Nora smiled and stood up.

"I'd love to."

He twirled her onto the dance floor.

"I thought that went rather well," Lance said.

"It was ghastly, and Reggie is an ass. But don't worry: they'll come back sooner or later. And we've just made a little bit of history."

"I think there's going to be hell to pay."

"Probably, but I don't care. Did anyone ever tell you you dance divinely?"

"No."

"Well, you do. And I adore being in your arms." She put her cheek on his. "In fact, I adore you."

After Lance had taken her home to Government House, she kissed him good night, saying, "You were magnificent. I loved it when you hit Reggie. He deserved it, the stuffy idiot."

Then she got out of the taxi and hurried to the front door as Lance told the driver to take him to his grandmother's house.

When Nora let herself in, her father was waiting for her.

"They phoned me from Repulse Bay," Sir Neville said.

"The hotel manager. He told me what happened, and he was furious. He said all his customers left except you and Lance, and it cost him hundreds of pounds!"

"I don't feel in the least sorry for him. He should have changed the rules long ago, just as you changed them here."

She started past him, but he took her arm.

"Nora," he said in a low voice, "what is this madness? Do you realize what you're doing here?"

"Of course I realize. I love Lance Wang, and where I go, he goes."

He grabbed her shoulders and shook her.

"You don't love him!" he said angrily. "I won't allow you to love him!"

"Father, you're the one who's mad! Lance is a fine human being! Oh, you should have seen him tonight when he hit Reggie Alford! I was so proud of him, I wanted to shout!"

"Do you realize what you're doing to me? When the Colonial Office in London hears that the Governor of Hong Kong's daughter is causing scenes in one of the best hotels because of her Chinese boyfriend, they may bring me back to London! Is that what you want? To disgrace your own father?"

"Of course not. You yourself said it's the policy of the Colonial Office to lower racial barriers here. I'd think you'd congratulate me."

He groaned and let her go.

"Dear God," he said, "how could this be happening?"

"There's nothing wrong with what's happening!" she insisted. "We love each other! It's the most beautiful thing that's ever happened to me! Why don't you admit that what you're really afraid of is that I'll marry him and give you half-caste grandchildren? And believe me, if he asks me, I'll say yes."

She walked past him and started up the stairs to her bedroom. Her father went into the living room and poured himself a stiff drink.

"What can I do to stop this?" he muttered to himself as he drank the whiskey. "What?"

When Lance got out of the taxi, he paid the driver, then started walking to his grandmother's house, which was dark except for a few lighted windows on the second floor and a light by the front door. Lance was halfway to the house when Reggie Alford and five other young men stepped out from behind some bushes. They were carrying cricket bats.

Lance stopped as they started toward him.

"You bloody Chink," Reggie said softly. "You're going to be sorry about tonight."

"We don't want Chinks in our hotels," another young man said. Lance recognized him as having been at the Repulse Bay that evening.

"Except as waiters and busboys," said a third.

"Or people who clean the loos," said a fourth.

"That's what Chinks are," Reggie said. "Bloody servants. And don't you forget it."

He swung his cricket bat. Lance grabbed it and jerked it out of his hands.

"Do you think this is a fair fight?" he said, holding the bat in an attack position. "Six of you against one bloody Chink? Why don't we make this fair? Three of you against me."

"We like our odds better," one of them shouted, swinging his bat as two other also attacked. Lance fought them off, but he was hopelessly outnumbered. When they all were hitting him, he went down on the ground, unconscious.

They beat and kicked him for almost five minutes. Then, bravely, they ran into the night.

39. PO LING, ONE OF JULIE'S HOUSEBOYS, HEARD the scuffle and ran out of the house to find Lance's bloody body on the grass. Horrified, he stooped to make sure he was still alive. Then he ran inside the house and called an ambulance, excitedly telling his mistress when Julie came downstairs in a bathrobe.

"Lance!" she cried, hurrying out of the house to kneel beside her adored grandson.

He was taken to the Tung Wah Chinese hospital where it was discovered he had a concussion, numerous cuts and bruises, two broken ribs, and had lost two teeth.

"He's badly hurt," the doctor told Julie, who had hurriedly dressed and followed the ambulance. "But I think he'll be all right. Do you have any idea who did this to him?"

"I have an idea," Julie said, and her tone was grim.

That afternoon, dressed in one of her most elegant pink cheong-sams, Julie had her chauffeur drive her up the Peak to Government House where she had made an appointment with Sir Neville. She was escorted into his office, where he stood up and came to kiss her hand.

"We must talk," she said.

"I agree. Please sit down, Madame Chin. Would you like some tea?"

"No thank you."

Julie sat down in a chair before the Governor's desk. Behind him, open windows gave a wonderful view of the harbor below.

"You have heard what happened to my grandson," she said after Sir Neville had sat down at his desk.

"Yes. I regret the incident deeply. And my daughter is practically hysterical. When she saw Lance at the hospital, she burst into tears and hasn't stopped crying since. Has he come out of the coma yet?"

"Not yet, but we hope soon. When he does, he will be able to name his assailants. What do you intend doing to them?"

"We'll prosecute them, of course."

"You know who they will be."

"I have an idea."

"If these young men turn out to be from the Repulse Bay Hotel, and if they are brought to trial before an English jury, do you think they could possibly be convicted?"

Sir Neville pulled a handkerchief from his coat and mopped his forehead. It was an extremely hot day and fans were twirling, but the Governor's sweat was more from nerves than humidity.

"I'll be honest with you, Madame Chin," he finally said. "As much as it pains me to say it, I'm afraid the answer is 'no.' "

"And you are right. This incident at the hotel that your daughter and my grandson caused is like a powder keg. We must do everything in our power to prevent it from exploding."

"No one is more aware of that than I, Madame Chin. But to be frank, I'm not quite sure what to do."

Julie remained silent for a moment. Then she said, "You realize that presently there are about four thousand five hundred Britons in Hong Kong surrounded by seven hundred and twenty-five thousand Chinese. What do you think the long-term result of this situation will be?"

"I of course cannot speculate on that officially."

"Then speculate unofficially."

The Governor looked even more uncomfortable.

"Well, someday . . ." He shook his head. "I really can't discuss that subject."

"Then I'll discuss it for you. We Chinese are becoming richer and more powerful by the day. We soon will control almost all the businesses. It is inevitable that with power and money will come control. Now, do we—the English and the Chinese—want to have two totally separate societies on this small island?"

"No, not in the long run. Which is why I opened Government House to both races."

"Exactly, and it was a wise decision on your part. But the Chinese will not stand for long to be excluded from places like the Repulse Bay Hotel. Surely you can see that?"

"Let me say that my daughter sees it, and perhaps she has a clearer view of the situation than people of my generation."

"A very diplomatic answer. What I am getting at is that I'm thinking of telling my grandson when he comes out of the coma not to name the people who attacked him. I'm going to send him off to Shanghai, as was already planned, and then he's spending the rest of the summer in the south of France."

"But why would you do that?"

"Because if he names the attackers, they will be brought to trial and be acquitted. But the trial in itself will exacerbate the tensions already on the island. So it is better not to have the trial. Rather, we should encourage what is already existing, as I see it."

"What is that?"

"The love between your daughter and my grandson."

The Governor stiffened.

"That is something I'd rather not discuss."

"But we must. I know how you feel, Sir Neville. You don't want your daughter marrying a Chinese. I feel the same way, except the other way around. I would much rather that my grandson marry a Chinese girl—in fact, I have several already picked out. I have my little list, as Koko says in *The Mikado*. But perhaps we are both wrong. For if my grandson married your daughter sometime in the future, what better symbol could there be of the new Hong Kong that is bound to emerge?"

"It's out of the question."

"Would you rather see them elope?"

"Of course not."

"I hesitate to bring up the matter of finances, but I will remind you that my grandson will one day be an enormously rich man. He stands to inherit something more than thirty million pounds sterling."

She was secretly amused by the startled expression that came over the Governor's face.

"Is that possible?" he said softly. "I knew you were rich, but . . . *that* rich?"

"That rich. Think about it, Sir Neville. Your grandchildren might be half-castes, but they would be extremely rich half-castes." She stood up. "It's something to consider, isn't it?"

The Governor stood up.

"I hope, Madame Chin," he said, "that you don't think I could possibly be bought?"

She smiled.

"Of course not, Sir Neville," she said. "You are an honorable man and a gentleman. But . . ." She shrugged slightly. "As we say in business, everything has a price. I can see myself out. Good day, Sir Neville."

After she had left the office, the Governor sat down and once again mopped his brow.

He whispered to himself, wonderingly: *"Thirty million pounds?"*

PART ELEVEN

THE DAY AMERICA CRASHED

40. ON NOVEMBER 4, 1928, ARNOLD ROTHSTEIN was shot in the stomach at the Park Central Hotel in Manhattan over the nonpayment of a poker debt he claimed had been "fixed." He was rushed to a hospital where he died a few days later, refusing to tell the police who had shot him. His funeral was a big affair: A. R. was still the best-known gangster in America, although Al Capone was rapidly catching up. His father, who had disowned him so many years before, old Abraham Rothstein, stood by the grave wearing a prayer shawl, for the second time saying Kaddish for his son.

Cesare Savage did not attend the funeral. But Cesare knew what the F.B.I. was just getting an inkling of: Rothstein, foreseeing the inevitable repeal of the wildly unpopular Prohibition, had gotten into drug trafficking, importing large amounts of illegal drugs from pharmaceutical plants in Europe, in particular France.

Cesare had liked Arnold Rothstein and admired his flashy style, some of which he had copied for himself. But Cesare's peculiar morals, which permitted him to bootleg without batting an eye, drew the line at drugs.

Besides, he was having too much fun—and success—on Wall Street to bother with crime these days.

And, after all, a Director of the prestigious Savage Bank could hardly be expected to attend the funeral of a common gangster. Not to mention the father of two adorable twin sons, Mark and Sebastian Savage, who had been born six months after he married Gloria Gilmore.

"I'm a family man now," he told friends at '21.' "Respectable. Solid."

His friends snickered behind his back, but as long as Cesare bought the drinks, they smiled to his face.

Of course, Cesare's newfound respectability was just a front. Behind the facade, he was up to many of his old tricks and quite a few new ones. Shortly after Rothstein's funeral, he bought from the estate control of the Purple Parrot speakeasy. And it was into A. R.'s old office in the rear of the building that, one cold night in late November, his club manager, Bill Hayes, came with some news.

"Boss, there's a cabaret agent from the Morris Office outside named Mo Levine. Do you know him?"

"I've heard of him. What's he want?"

"He's got a new singer he wants you to look at. She's a stunner."

"Then let's look at her. Send them in."

Cesare, wearing his dinner jacket, was sitting at A. R.'s old desk smoking a cigarette. One of the attractions to him of owning the Purple Parrot was the show business angle of it. As Johnny had once been bitten by the movie bug, Cesare was bitten by the Broadway bug. He had invested in several musicals, losing most of his money in the process (he had turned down an opportunity to invest in *Show Boat,* saying, with monumental lack of foresight, "Who wants to see a show about darkies on the Mississippi?"). He thought that owning a nightclub would give him a more hands-on approach to the talent; and with Cesare's sexual appetite, the expression "hands-on" had an obvious double meaning.

The door opened, and a short man in a flashy suit with a bowler hat on his balding head and a cigar in his mouth bustled in.

"Mr. Savage," he announced, "I'm Mo Levine, and I want you to meet the hottest little ticket to hit New York in years: Tempest Shaw!"

He whipped off his bowler and pointed to the door. A

tall blond in an extremely tight gold dress insinuated herself into the office. She smiled at Cesare, who removed the cigarette from his mouth and drank in the splendors of her flesh. She really was extraordinarily beautiful.

"Is Tempest her real name?" he asked.

"Of course not."

"Can she sing?"

"Like Marilyn Miller, only better. Just listen."

Mo crossed the office and sat down at an upright piano, where he played a brief introduction. Then Tempest began singing "Embraceable You." Her voice was throaty and pure sex.

As she was singing, Gloria came into the office. She stood at the door, watching Tempest, then watching her husband watching Tempest.

When Tempest was finished, Cesare put out his cigarette.

"Very nice," he said. "In fact, sensational. Have you worked anywhere else?"

"In Chicago," she said as Gloria came around the desk and put her hand on her husband's shoulder. She was wearing an ivory silk dress.

"I don't like 'Tempest,' " Cesare was saying. "It's too obvious, too cheap. I'd like something more subtle. Would you change your name for me?"

She smiled seductively.

"I'd do anything for you, Mr. Savage," she said.

"I'm Mrs. Savage," Gloria said in an overly sweet tone, with a bitchy smile. "We're not going to like each other, are we?"

The singer looked at her.

"Probably not," she said.

"Amber," Cesare said. "Amber Shaw. I like that: it sounds warm and sweet and sensual. Mo, bring her back tomorrow night and we'll work out the details. Good night, Amber. I think you've got a great future."

"Good night, Mr. Savage."

She smiled at him. Then, giving Gloria a cool look, she followed Mo Levine out of the office.

"You know, darling," Gloria said, running her hand over his slick, black hair, "I'm getting a little bored with being jealous of your protégées, if one could distinguish that piece of trash with the word."

"Then don't be jealous. It's only business, and you have to admit she sings well."

"Why do I suspect she uses her throat for other purposes?"

"Don't be vulgar. Why did you want to see me?"

"You are my husband. I thought it might be amusing if we had dinner together for once. The happy little family, so to speak."

"Of course. Let's go out and get a table."

He stood up when Bill Hayes came back into the office. He looked rather flustered.

"Boss, Dutch Schultz just came in. He wants to see you."

Cesare looked troubled.

"Is he alone?"

"Yeah."

"Send him in."

Gloria, who had been perched on his desk, stood up as he opened the middle drawer slightly, revealing a gun.

"Is there going to be trouble?" she whispered, rather anxiously.

"Probably not, but it pays to be safe. You go on out and get a table. Order me a shrimp cocktail. Get some champagne."

"Darling, I'm scared. I remember what happened on the *Mauretania*."

"Don't worry. I can handle it. Go on now."

She hurried out of the office. A moment later, Dutch Schultz came in and closed the door. He was wearing a dinner jacket, one slightly better cut than the one he wore the night he wiped out Owney Madden's booze truck.

"Good evening, Mr. Savage," he said in a not unfriendly voice. "Your wife's looking as gorgeous as ever."

"Thank you."

"I hear you have twin boys?"

"That's right. Mark and Sebastian."

"Congratulations."

"What can I do for you?"

"I hear you've started an investment trust, something called the Eagle Fund."

"That's right."

"Could you explain it to me? I'm sort of dumb when it comes to investments."

"Certainly. Take a seat." After Schultz had sat down, Cesare said, "The idea's really very simple. It was something that came over from England after the war. People buy shares in the investment trust. Then we, the management, use our knowledge of the market to invest in a lot of different stocks—stocks that we think are good investments. Naturally, not all stocks go up. But this way, when you invest in our trust, you're protected. If one of the stocks we've invested in goes down—call it stock A—you have stocks B, C, D, and so forth still going up, which lessens your risk. And, as I said, you have the advantage of our insider knowledge of the market. The trusts have gotten very popular. A hundred and forty trusts were formed this year alone."

"It sounds like a good idea."

"We think it is. Here." He opened another drawer and pulled out a brochure. "Here's some literature on it, if you're interested."

"Yeah, I am interested." He took the brochure and looked at it a moment. Then he stuck it in his pocket. "I also hear you're not all that choosy about who invests."

Cesare shrugged.

"Money is all we're interested in, not where it comes from."

Schultz leaned forward and lowered his voice.

"I hear there's a lot of money coming in from your old friends, if you know what I mean."

"I know what you mean. I won't deny it. As I said, I'm only interested in the money."

Schultz grinned, showing a gold tooth.

"Then you'll take my money?"

"With pleasure. How much are you thinking about?"

"A hundred grand."

Cesare looked impressed.

"I'll have the stocks issued tomorrow. What name should I use?"

"Arthur Flegenheimer. That's my real name."

Cesare jotted it on a notepad.

"Why don't you come by tomorrow night and have dinner with me? Bring me a check, and I'll have the stocks for you. Dinner will be on the house, of course."

"Hey, that's real swell of you, Mr. Savage!"

"Call me Cesare."

"Yeah, Cesare." He stood up and reached across the desk to shake hands. "I guess we sorta got off on the wrong foot that night on the ship, but maybe we can be friends."

"Why not?"

"Too bad about Arnold, wasn't it? Getting shot like that over some dumb poker bet. A swell guy like that! A real shame."

"It's a rough world."

"Yeah, it sure is. Okay: see you tomorrow night. What time?"

"Oh, about eight o'clock?"

"You got it."

After Schultz left the office, Cesare closed the gun drawer, stood up, checked his image in a mirror, straightened his bow tie, and slicked his hair, then went out into the speakeasy that was, as usual, packed solid and filled with smoke. Four chorus girls were on the small stage

Charlestoning to a jazzy rendition of "I Want to Be Loved by You and Nobody Else but You."

As Cesare made his way through the crowd to Gloria's table, he thought the good times would keep rolling forever.

This was the best of all possible worlds.

Four mornings later, Glenda O'Brian, Johnny Savage's long-time secretary, came into Johnny's office at the Wall Street bank and said, "Your stepson's here and wants to see you."

Johnny, whose hair was turning gray, sighed.

"This means trouble. All right, send him in."

A few moments later, Cesare came into the paneled office looking, as always, well dressed and debonair.

"Good morning," he said. "I won't take much of your time. I wanted to speak to you about Nick."

"Take a seat, Cesare. What about Nick?"

"At the Directors' meeting last night, you mentioned wanting to promote him to a vice presidency of the bank. Do you think that's wise, all things considered?"

He had taken a seat in front of Johnny's desk.

"Exactly what do you mean?" Johnny said warily.

"Well, of course when I turned over to you the bonds that Nick had improperly taken from those safety deposit boxes—I won't use the word 'embezzled,' which has an unpleasant smell to it—the bonds were returned and nothing more was said about it. You kept Nick on as Cashier of the bank, which I must say seemed to me rather peculiar, considering the fact that he had broken the law, although we covered up for him."

"Listen, Cesare: Nick took those bonds because of your suggesting he do it!"

"Well, that may be so, but still and all I didn't embezzle—I suppose I have to use the word—he did. As a major stockholder of this bank as well as a Director, I find it amazing that he was allowed to stay on in a position of trust. And now, you want to promote him! I'm sorry, but as fond of Nick as I am, I have to object to this most strenuously."

"What do you suggest doing?"

"I'd fire him. I would have fired him last year when it happened."

Johnny's eyes narrowed suspiciously.

"What are you up to now, Cesare?" he said quietly.

" 'Up to'? Not a thing, except trying to protect the integrity of the bank."

"I find it appalling that you have the nerve to use the word 'integrity.' However, I'll grant you Nick made a terrible mistake—egged on, as he was, by you. But since then, he has behaved most honorably, and I have no desire to punish my son for something that was caused by you. Besides, if I fired him, he'd be ruined. I won't do that to my son whom, with all his faults, I still love."

"You may not have any choice." Cesare pulled a folded piece of paper from his pocket and tossed it on the desk. "That's a photocopy of a document I had Nick sign before I returned the bonds he embezzled. It's a full confession. I told him to shut up about it, which he has. But now? Well, to safeguard the bank, unless you fire him I'll have to turn this over to the police."

Johnny, looking stunned, unfolded the paper and quickly read it. Then he looked up at Cesare.

"Why are you doing this?" he said quietly.

"To safeguard the bank."

"Baloney. You're up to something in your usual twisted way."

Cesare stood up.

"I see no reason why I have to be insulted," he said. "If Nick isn't out of this bank by noon tomorrow, I'll go to the police."

He started toward the door.

"Damn you!" Johnny shouted after him. "Goddamn you, you rotten bastard! What I'd do to get you out of my life!"

Johnny, his hand on the doorknob, turned and smiled.

"Why Father dear," he said, "I've never heard you use such bad language. I'm shocked."

He opened the door and left the office.

That night, Amber Shaw made her debut at the Purple Parrot. Cesare stood at the back of the room smoking a cigarette as the lights dimmed and a spot hit the stage. Then Amber came out. She had cut her blond hair in a fashionable shingle style and was wearing a long black dress cut very low in the back and as low as possible in the front, held up by two thin straps with a big black bow on the left shoulder. The bottom of the skirt was cut in a sort of flame style and lined with scarlet. She looked breathtaking.

The speakeasy fell silent as she started singing the new torch song, "Why Was I Born?"

When she finished, the crowd went wild. Cesare smiled. His instincts had been right: a star was born.

A half hour later, after Amber left the stage, Cesare started to go into his rear office when he was grabbed from behind and wrenched around. It was Nick, and he was drunk. He started to slug his half brother, but Cesare grabbed his wrist.

"What the hell's wrong with you?" he snarled.

"You bastard! You dirty, rotten bastard! You got me fired!"

And he burst into drunken sobs.

Cesare put his arm around him.

"Come on," he said, leading him to the door to his office. "We'll have a drink . . ."

"I don't want a drink from you!"

"Yes you do." Cesare signaled to a nearby waiter. "Bring us a bottle of Scotch." Then he took Nick into his office and closed the door. "Come on, sit down. Pull yourself together."

"Why did you do it, Cesare?" he sobbed, sinking into a sofa. "Why are you out to ruin me? What did I ever do to you?"

"Nothing, Nick, and I'm not trying to ruin you. I want to help you."

"Stop bullshitting me. A great way to help me! Getting me fired . . . You made me sign that damned confession, and now I can't get a job anywhere, and Valerie's hysterical . . . I don't know what to do . . ."

Again, he broke down, drunkenly sobbing his heart out. The waiter handed in a bottle of Scotch, and Cesare poured two drinks.

"Here, Nick," he said, bringing him the glass. "This'll make you feel better."

Sniveling, he took the glass and drained it in one gulp.

"I need money, Cesare," he slurred. "Valerie's spending hasn't slowed down . . . Oh shit, I'm so damned miserable . . ."

Cesare refilled his glass.

"You have nothing to worry about, Nick," he soothed. "There's an easy way to solve all your money problems."

"Oh, sure: embezzle! Thanks a lot for that one!"

"No, no: you have something to sell, and I'm willing to pay a lot of money for it. I mean, a lot."

Nick looked at him as he sipped the whiskey.

"What are you talking about?" he asked.

"Your bank stock."

"I don't own any bank stock."

"But you will, when the old man dies. You and Brook will inherit a huge hunk of bank stock. Now, I'm willing to pay you a million dollars cash . . ."

"How can I sell what I don't own? Besides, the stock's worth a helluva lot more than that . . ."

"I'm not talking about buying the stock. I'm talking

about buying your voting rights in the stock. Sell me your voting rights in perpetuity. I'll give you a million bucks and you'll still own the stock when the old man dies."

Nick looked confused.

"But why would you do that? I don't get it. Besides, the old man's perfectly healthy. He could be around for years!"

"Fine. That's my problem. But meanwhile, you've got your million dollars, which ought to solve all your money problems for a long time."

Nick frowned as he finished the whiskey.

"I don't understand you, Cesare . . ."

"There's nothing to understand," he said, refilling his glass. "Look." He set down the bottle and pulled an envelope from his pocket. "I had my lawyer draw up this agreement between you and me. Don't read it now, you're drunk. But take it home, read it, let your lawyer read it, then bring it to me and sign it and I'll give you a check for a million dollars. Could anything be simpler?"

"No, I guess not . . ."

Cesare inserted the envelope in Nick's coat pocket.

"Just keep it a secret between us. Okay?"

"I guess . . ."

"Now have a final drink, and I'll put you in a taxi and send you home. Everything's going to be wonderful, Nick. Believe me: everything. You'll see."

An hour later, Nick stumbled into his new apartment on East Seventieth Street to be met by Valerie in a bathrobe.

"Nick!" she exclaimed. "Good God, you're drunk as a skunk. Where've you been?"

"Went to see my old buddy, Cesare," he slurred, weaving into the living room that Valerie had decorated in lavish style.

"Your old buddy? Cesare, that rat?"

"Cesare, that rat. Except he may have saved the day for

us. Look at this." He pulled the envelope from his pocket and tossed it to her, then went to the bar to pour himself yet another drink. Valerie opened the envelope, pulled out the document, and hastily read it. Then she looked at her husband.

"A million dollars?" she said. "He'll give us a million dollars just for the voting rights to the bank stock?"

"Thass right," he slurred. "Crazy, isn't it? Do you think we should do it?"

"Oh, Nick, a million dollars!" she exclaimed ecstatically. "Just think what we could do with that much money!"

He turned from the bar and shook his finger at her.

"Valerie, you gotta stop spending . . ."

"Oh, we'll be careful, of course, but . . ." She ran to him and hugged him, almost knocking the drink out of his hand. "Oh Nick, let's do it! Who cares about some silly old voting rights to stock we may not have for another twenty years? Let's take the money now, while we're still young! A million dollars! Oh, it's a miracle!"

41.   THE BRAND NEW, BLACK, FOUR-DOOR CADILLAC sedan roared down the country road on Long Island.

"How fast are we going?" Johnny asked his chauffeur from the backseat.

"Sixty-seven miles an hour, Mr. Savage," the chauffeur said.

"God, it rides like a dream! Let's take her up to seventy-five. The salesman told me this thing can go to eighty-five, but I'll settle for less. How does it handle?"

"Fine so far."

"Okay, let's go faster."

The chauffeur pressed the accelerator. The speedometer needle slowly climbed past seventy, then seventy-two . . . three . . . five . . .

"We're going seventy-five, Mr. Savage."

"Excellent! Well, I'd say this is one damned fine car . . ."

He was interrupted by the chauffeur blowing the horn.

"Goddamn—!"

A farm wagon had pulled onto the road from a side lane to the right. The chauffeur slammed on the brakes as he turned to the left.

"The brakes!" he screamed. "They're not working—!"

The Cadillac crashed into a tree at sixty-seven miles an hour. The chauffeur was hurled through the windshield and was killed instantly.

Johnny Savage, who was seventy years old, was hurled over the front seat where he crashed into the dashboard.

"It's a miracle he's alive," Rachel said to her daughter, wiping her eyes. It was a week later. Brook had taken the first boat from France when she heard the news of the accident, her husband being on a dig in Palestine. "His back was broken in two places, his hip was fractured, one shoulder dislocated, his jaw broken . . . He'll be in the hospital for weeks, and the doctors say he may be paralyzed the rest of his life. Oh Brook, it's so terrible. Your poor father has suffered so much as it is, having lost his leg . . ."

Again, she broke down. They had returned from the hospital where Johnny was in traction, unable to speak, and now were in the drawing room of the Fifth Avenue house. Brook hugged her mother.

"But what caused the accident?" she said. "Wasn't the car new?"

Rachel nodded.

"I'm not even sure it was an accident," she said. "Your father can still write with one hand. He wrote on a notepad that the brakes had failed. Well, I wondered how in the world the brakes could fail on a car three days out of the showroom, so I had the car—or what was left of it—examined. The mechanic told me it looked as if the brakes had been tampered with."

"But what does that mean?"

"It means someone tried to murder your father."

Brook frowned.

"But who? Why?"

"Who has hated your father all his life? Who stands to gain most if he's dead? Cesare."

Brook slowly stood up.

"I can't believe that," she said. "I know Cesare's done some bad things, but murder? That doesn't seem possible. Why, just two weeks ago he sent me a check for fifty thousand dollars for the children's hospital Bernard and I are building in Tel Aviv. I can't believe someone who could be that kind and generous could try to commit murder."

"Well, believe it. Cesare is a monster, but he's a complicated, clever monster. Of course, I can't prove it. I'll probably never be able to prove it."

"But what could be his motive?"

"He got Nick—that poor, foolish son of mine—to assign him his voting rights in Nick's bank stock. All it took was for my poor darling Johnny to die, and Nick would inherit the stock. Then Cesare could vote Nick's stock and his own, and he would have a majority of the stock and would control the bank. Somehow, I feel this is all my fault."

"Mother, don't be silly. How could it be your fault?"

Rachel wiped her eyes again.

"I brought Cesare into the world."

Brook hugged her mother.

"You mustn't think that," she said, kissing her cheek. "You've been the most wonderful mother to all of us, and if Cesare has gone bad, it's not your fault. But listen, Mummy: such wonderful things are happening in my life! Can I tell you about it, or are you too worried about Daddy . . . ?"

"No, tell me. I could use some good news."

"Well: you know how all my life I've been searching for something to give my life some meaning?"

"Yes?"

"Well, I've found it. I mean, first it was sex, which turned out to be not so great after all. Then I found love with Bernard, which was so wonderful that it makes sex by itself seem, well, like second-rate in comparison."

"I tried to tell you that when you were younger."

"I know, but you have to live these things to really understand them. And now it's our children's hospital in Tel Aviv, which is all thanks to you, because you got me interested in Palestine and you sent us to Lord Rothschild and . . ." She sighed happily. "Well, I just can't tell you the thrill we're getting from building this place. It's going to mean so much to the children of Tel Aviv, and it's so thrilling to be part of a new nation . . . well, it's not a new nation yet, but someday it will be. Anyway, it's remade our lives, we're happier than we've ever been, and so much of it is thanks to you. So, if you're disappointed in Cesare, one of your children has turned out blissfully happy and fulfilled: me."

Rachel smiled.

"Darling Brook," she said, "that makes me very happy to hear. I used to worry so much about you because you seemed so shallow and aimless . . ."

"Oh, I was."

"But now, you've turned out to be worthwhile. That makes me feel extremely good."

Cesare's tongue slowly licked Amber Shaw's left nipple, then her right. Amber, stretched naked on the bed of a Plaza Hotel suite, purred with pleasure.

"You certainly know how to make a girl happy, Mr. Savage," she said.

Cesare, who was also naked, smiled.

"Don't you think it's time you called me Cesare?"

"All right, Cesare. I like that name. It's got a sort of bite to it."

Cesare moved up her body and licked her right armpit.

"Isn't it odd?" he said. "I find armpits extremely erotic. I sometimes wonder if it's a sort of perversion."

He licked her left armpit.

"If it is a perversion, it's a fun one," Amber said. "What other parts of the body do you like?"

"I'm extremely partial to the ass."

"Yes, I like asses too. Especially your ass, Cesare. You have a wonderful ass."

"What an intellectual conversation this is."

She giggled.

"It's kind of hard being intellectual when you're buck naked."

"You have a point."

"What if your wife finds out about us?"

"She won't."

"Don't be too sure. She looks like she could be real mean."

"Uh-huh. I can handle her. I'm going to go in, now."

"Don't you use a rubber? I don't want to get pregnant!"

"I'll pull out in time."

"But won't you be awfully frustrated?"

"There are other orifices in the body."

"Cesare, honey, I think you have a real dirty mind."

"That's a distinct possibility."

The doorbell rang.

"Shit."

Cesare got off the bed and went to the bathroom to put a towel around his waist as Amber covered herself with a sheet.

The doorbell rang again.

"Coming!" Cesare crossed the room. "Every time I'm about to have some fun, someone interrupts," he grumbled.

He unlocked the door and opened it. Gloria came in, giving him a shove in the chest.

"Now, I couldn't guess who's in that bed!" she said, biting every syllable.

"How did you get here?" Cesare gasped.

"I followed you from the Purple Parrot. Well, well: isn't this a charming scene? Little Miss Tonsils from Chicago, as I live and breathe. And my faithful husband."

Cesare had closed the door.

"Gloria, let's not have a scene we'll regret . . ."

"So she's only business?" Gloria exclaimed. "Hah! Your kind of business! Get your clothes on, lovey. You're coming home with me. In case you've forgotten, you've got a goddamned family! And you—bitch!" She turned to Amber, who was sitting up in the bed. "You can pack your bags and go back to the Chicago slum you crawled out of!"

"Don't call me a bitch!" Amber yelled.

Gloria ran to the bed.

"I'll call you whatever I goddamn please!"

She grabbed her arm and pulled Amber out of the bed, where she fell on the floor. As Amber screamed in rage, the two women started hitting each other with their fists. Cesare, a bemused expression on his face, lit a cigarette and leaned against the mantel watching the wrestling match. The two women rolled over and over on the flowered carpet, yelling, pounding each other with their fists, tearing at each other's hair. Finally, Cesare put his cigarette in an ashtray, went over, and grabbed Gloria's arm, pulling her off Amber.

"All right, ladies," he said, "time-out. We don't want the management tossing us all in the street."

"As for *you*," Gloria puffed, jamming her fist into his genitalia causing Cesare to howl and double over, "give that baseball bat of yours a vacation! I'll wait for you downstairs in the bar." She went to the door, opened it, and looked back at Amber, who had gotten to her feet and was half hiding behind Cesare. "And keep your hands off my husband—bitch!"

She slammed out of the room.

42. BY 1928, EVEN THE ITALIANS WHO DIDN'T LIKE Mussolini and Fascism were resigned to the regime, preferring it to the alternative, which was the chaos of the years preceding the march on Rome. But while Mussolini cunningly softened the outward appearance of Fascism, he was quietly tightening the grip of Fascism throughout the country, imprisoning or firing those who opposed him. Even sports were not excused. Under a 1927 regulation, all sporting clubs were put under the control of the Fascist Party; the Party Secretary was appointed an honorary football referee and presented with a golden whistle.

A year later, any pretense of democratic government was abandoned when Mussolini dissolved the Parliament and vested all power in himself and something called the Grand Council, which was under his thumb.

These events were troubling Bruno and Beatrice Vespa more and more. In private, they bemoaned the drift toward absolute dictatorship and crushing of personal liberties: hundreds of Italians, including the future Prime Minister Alcide de Gasperi, were imprisoned for attempting to flee the country. Even more, Bruno was increasingly disillusioned with his role as Minister of Health. "They promise me everything, and give me nothing," he complained to Beatrice. "And the corruption! Money melts away! Funds that were supposed to go toward building hospitals and clinics end up in the pockets of the politicians. It's a scandal."

Yet the pleasantness of their private life, their joy in their daughter Gabriella, and the usual inertia of life prevented them from taking any action. Not to mention fear. Action of any sort that could be construed as being against the regime meant imprisonment.

Meanwhile, Mussolini's prestige at home and abroad rose to new heights. Foreigners as diverse as Winston Churchill and George Bernard Shaw hailed him as the greatest statesman of the day. And his international reputation reached its apogee early in 1929 when he signed the Lateran Treaty with the Vatican, which ended the decades-old war between the Pope and the Italian government and created the Vatican State. While the 500,000 square yards of the Vatican was not a very good real-estate bargain for the Popes, who once had owned most of central Italy, still it brought peace to both sides and was considered a coup for Mussolini, who had spearheaded the negotiations.

To celebrate the signing of the treaty, a reception was held at the Palazzo Chigi. And while Beatrice had come to loathe these governmental functions, Bruno told her they had no choice but to attend since Mussolini himself was going to be there—which was unusual because Il Duce generally disliked these events as much as Beatrice. Consequently, they dressed up in full fig and drove through the dreary, rainy February night to the Palazzo Chigi where the cream of Roman society was gathering to pay hommage to the all-powerful little man with the jutting jaw and piercing black eyes who had dazzled the world with his climb to power.

Mussolini, like other politicians before and since, was a notorious predator with women—he was known to step out of his huge office in the Palazzo Venezia into a small anteroom, drop his pants, and indulge in a five-minute quickie. Thus when he saw Beatrice, whom he had never met, he whispered to Dino Grandi, the host for the evening, "Who's that good-looking woman in the green dress?"

"That's Beatrice Vespa, Dr. Vespa's American wife."

"Ah yes. Introduce me. Then take Vespa aside and give him the bad news. Do it gracefully. He's been complaining a lot lately, and I don't want him out of sorts tonight."

"Yes, Duce."

Grandi, who looked distinguished in his tails, came up to the Vespas and kissed Beatrice's hand.

"How lovely you look tonight, signora," he said. "The Duce had asked to meet you. If you'll come with me?"

He led her through the crowd to Mussolini, who was also wearing white tie and tails. The blacksmith's son from Romagna could be charming when he chose, and tonight, basking in his glory, he was, by his standards, positively effulgent. He kissed Beatrice's hand and began a quiet conversation with her as Grandi made his way back to Bruno.

"The Duce finds your wife charming," Grandi said, taking a glass of champagne from a passing waiter.

"I hope I don't have to worry?" Bruno said.

Grandi smiled slightly.

"In olden days, to be the King's mistress was considered a great honor."

"But this is 1929."

"Of course. Oh, the Duce told me to tell you that we're making some changes in the budget."

"Now what?"

Grandi laughed.

"My dear Doctor, you're an alarmist. And you mustn't look so grim. People might think that you weren't one hundred percent with the regime in this, its finest hour."

"What cuts are you making now?"

"Well, you know that our defense expenditures have been higher than we estimated—because of the Duce's admirable intention to make Italy as strong as any nation in Europe—and so we've had to trim certain areas. I'm afraid your plans for the clinic in Naples will have to be postponed for a while."

Bruno got red in the face.

"Dammit, Grandi, you know how important that clinic is! It's much more important than two more tanks for the bloody army!"

Grandi's eyes grew cold.

"Keep your voice down, and for God's sake keep your temper under control," he said softly. "I probably shouldn't have told you here, but the Duce commanded it. There will be no arguing: the budget cuts are made. And I'd watch your behavior. We know more than you think about your true feelings about the regime. And you may take that as a warning."

He left him, melting into the crowd. Bruno, his temper sizzling, grabbed a glass of champagne and drank half of it down in one gulp.

"I've had enough," he said to Beatrice an hour later as they drove home from the Palazzo Chigi. "They've postponed the clinic in Naples, where it's desperately needed. Grandi told me it was because of the army budget, but I don't believe it for a minute. It means the money's going into somebody's pocket—probably his."

"What can you do?"

"I can resign."

"Oh darling, we've gone over this so many times. You know if you resign there'll be hell to pay."

Bruno drove through the rain in silence. Finally, he said, "What did the Duce say to you?"

"He asked me about America and what Americans

thought of him. The man's a total egocentric monster."

"What did you tell him?"

"That many Americans admire him, which is true, unfortunately. And then I think he made a sort of halfhearted
pass at me."

"What do you mean?"

"He told me that anytime I wanted anything from him,
I could come to his office at any hour and he would see
me immediately. Well, you know what that means. All
Rome knows what games he plays there in his little room
to the side."

"The man's a swine."

"True, but he's our swine. We're stuck with him."

"You wouldn't think of going there?"

"Darling, how could you even say that? You're driving
too fast."

"Sorry."

When they got home to the villa on the Appian Way,
they went inside for a nightcap.

"You know," Bruno said, "I feel as if I'm living in a sty.
I mean, everything about this regime is dirty. What would
you think of leaving Italy? I mean, permanently."

"Isn't that a bit out of the question?"

"No. There's a conference in Paris next month of world
health organizations. I've been invited to speak. We could
go to Paris and never come back. What would you think
of that?"

She didn't answer for a moment.

"What about Gabriella?" she said.

"We'd take her with us, of course."

"And my grandparents?"

"I wouldn't think they'd do much to them. I mean, your
grandfather is ninety. And I don't think they'd dare do anything against your grandmother; she's too popular in Italy."

"Well, how would we live?"

He shrugged.

"I'm a good doctor. We might even go to America. The point is, I'm sick of the lies, the corruption, the fear . . . I want to live free, and unfortunately that's something you can't do in Italy today."

She took a deep breath.

"All right," she said. "I'm with you."

He came over and hugged her.

"I love you," he whispered. "I'll love you even more when we're out of this sink pit."

"We have a lot of planning to do."

"For God's sake, don't say anything over the phone. I wouldn't be surprised if our phones are tapped."

"It's that bad?"

"Perhaps. Grandi gave me a warning tonight. It was polite enough, but it was a warning."

"Grandi knows."

It was three days later. Bruno had come home from the office in a foul mood.

"What do you mean? They won't let us go to Paris?"

"Oh no. We can go to Paris—that's fine. But we have to leave Gabriella here with the nanny. The man's clever—I'll give him that. He senses how dissatisfied I am."

"Then what can we do?"

Bruno went to the bar to prepare his usual martini. After he had stirred the gin and poured two drinks, he took one to Beatrice. He sipped the drink, then said quietly, "We're going to escape."

Four days later, Bruno and Beatrice parked their Fiat on the Via delle Botteghe Oscure and walked a half block to a basement photographer's shop. Bruno was carrying a black attaché case. They rang the bell, and the door was opened by a thin young man.

"My wife and I want our pictures taken," Bruno said.

The photographer, who had a large mole on his chin rather like a male witch, stood aside.

"Come in."

When they were inside, Bruno pulled a card from his pocket and handed it to the photographer.

"We were sent here by this gentleman," he said. "How much do you charge for false passports?"

The photographer gave him a sharp look, then pulled a black shade down over the door's window.

"A hundred thousand lire, cash."

"All right. We want Austrian passports in the name of . . ."

"Wait a minute. Let me get a pad."

After the photographer had a pad and pencil, he said, "Go on."

"Anton Gruner—that's me, obviously—and my wife, Frieda."

"Address?"

"Rainerstrasse 16, Salzburg."

"You don't look very Austrian."

"I have blond wigs in this case."

"All right, put them on and sit over there. I'll take your pictures. But first, the cash."

Bruno pulled a wad of money from his jacket and counted out one hundred thousand-lire notes, which he gave the photographer. Then he pulled a blond wig from his case, a false mustache, and a pair of glasses, all of which he put on in front of a small mirror. Then he sat in a chair in front of a white screen and had his picture taken while Beatrice put on a blond wig with braids. When she had had her picture taken, the photographer said, "You can pick up the passports tomorrow at noon."

"Excellent."

When Bruno and Beatrice had left the shop, the photographer picked up the telephone and called the police.

Count and Countess Bernard de Belleville—for Brook had insisted on using Bernard's title; she knew it had influence—got out of the open Rolls-Royce to inspect the progress of the construction of the children's clinic they were building on the outskirts of Tel Aviv. Inspired by their talks about Zionism with Lord Lionel Rothschild in London, as well as the investments made in Palestine for Jewish settlements by the enormously rich Baron Edmond de Rothschild, as well as her own mother, the young couple had become increasingly enthusiastic about the prospects of Jews settling in the former Turkish colony. Brook and Bernard had decided they should make a contribution themselves. They bought ten hectares of land near a lush orange grove that had been planted in the 1890s by money donated by Baron de Rothschild, hired a local architect to draw up the plans, and, at the end of 1928, began construction of the clinic that would have a hundred beds, with state-of-the-art medical equipment and a staff of ten doctors and twenty nurses. The hospital, fully funded by and named after Count and Countess de Belleville, was half-finished. The architect led Brook and Bernard around the construction site under a hot Mediterranean sun. They were thrilled with the progress.

"It's like a dream coming true," Brook said to her husband as they started back to the city. "I've never been so happy."

After they had returned to their hotel in Tel Aviv, the concierge handed them a telegram, which Bernard opened.

"Good God," he said softly.

"What's wrong?"

"It's from your mother in New York. Bruno's been sentenced to five years in prison!"

"Your husband, signora, is a good doctor but a very bad escape artist." The speaker was Dino Grandi, who had come to Fiammetta's palazzo on the Corso to meet with Beatrice and her grandmother. "Faking the passports was clumsy at best. And to disguise yourselves as Austrian tourists was laughable. The whole thing was a farce. Unhappily, it is a farce that carries a high price."

"The farce was the trial!" Beatrice exclaimed. "If it could even be dignified with that name!"

"Your husband is well known in this country," Grandi said suavely. "For him to try to flee the country demonstrates a disregard for the laws of Italy that amounts to treason. You are lucky we didn't prosecute you, as well, signora. But the Duce was merciful."

"Why are you here?" Fiammetta asked. "I assume you didn't come to pay a social call?"

Grandi smiled.

"Well," he said, "I have always wanted to see your beautiful palazzo, Comtessa. And since you have never invited me, I decided to invite myself. You don't much like Fascism, do you?"

"Shall I lie?"

"You don't have to. Your support has always been lukewarm, at best. While other families of your financial resources have contributed generously to the party, you have never given one lira. This strikes me as not only unpatriotic, Comtessa, but rather foolish. I would advise you to reconsider your position, especially now, with Dr. Vespa in prison. The Regina Coeli is not a very pleasant place to spend five years. As much as we try to improve sanitation, the prison is very old, and there are, alas, vermin. The prisoners are allowed only one shower a week. In the winter it gets quite cold, and in the summer unpleasantly hot. And then, there are the other prisoners. They are not exactly the kind of people a person of Dr. Vespa's background would be used to. It is said some of the prisoners force others to commit perversions . . ."

"Stop!" Beatrice cried out. "For God's sake, stop!"

She burst into tears.

"What do you want?" Fiammetta said icily.

"Of course, Dr. Vespa's incarceration could be made more pleasant. It is possible, under certain conditions, his prison term might be reduced—"

"How much?" Fiammetta interrupted.

"If, Comtessa, you could consider making a donation to the party," Grandi said, "we could begin negotiations. In the meanwhile, I will bid you charming ladies good day."

He bowed, then left the room. When he was gone, Beatrice sobbed, "Oh, God, I hate them all! They're pigs!"

"Yes indeed. Well, my dear, we'd better face the harsh facts: this is going to cost us a lot."

The negotiations went on for one week. In the end, Beatrice paid the equivalent of one million dollars, borrowed from the New York bank, and Fiammetta deeded her palazzo to the Italian government on the occasion of her death.

Bruno's sentence was reduced to six months.

43. AT TEN O'CLOCK ON THE MORNING OF THURSday, October 24, 1929, a young man named William H. Crawford leaned over the gallery in the New York Stock Exchange and tapped a mallet to a gong, thereby starting trading on the Exchange on a day that would literally change the world and live in infamy as Black Thursday.

The market had been having a bad week. On the previous

Saturday, a half day of trading had lost in a few hours what had taken the market months to gain—certainly an indication that the great bull market of the twenties was finally losing its breath. The next Monday, the twenty-first, was another bad day. The stock volume was the third greatest in the history of the Exchange, which caused the tape to be an hour and forty minutes late. Tuesday had started with a stock rally, but it petered out in the afternoon and stocks headed south again.

The next day, Wednesday the twenty-third, millions of nervous investors began selling. A new record of six million shares were traded, and the tape was 104 minutes late at the close. With margin rates as high in some cases as ninety percent—meaning people could buy stocks putting as little as ten percent of the money down—brokerage houses who had lent this "call money" began nervously calling in the margin accounts, demanding cash. By Wednesday evening, people who kept up with Wall Street—and millions did—were uncomfortably aware that the next day, Thursday the twenty-fourth, might well be catastrophic unless a miracle of stock buying happened—and there were eternal optimists who thought the miracle might occur.

The bull market had been roaring for years. Everybody in America talked about the stock market, even those who weren't actually in it. Tipsters flourished: the story went that Joe Kennedy decided to get out of the market when his shoeshine boy gave him a stock tip. Everybody seemed to know what stock was currently hot, and the general belief was that the Dow-Jones average would go "on to heaven," in the words of the famed astrologer Evangeline Adams. The square-jawed Miss Adams had eerily foretold the 1923 Tokyo earthquake, the death of Rudolph Valentino, and the length of Lindbergh's transatlantic flight to within twenty-two minutes of its actual duration. From her studio over Carnegie Hall, she issued a newsletter about the market that went out to twenty-five thousand subscribers who breathlessly read her reports of the influence of Mars on General Motors stock, or that the position of Pluto in Aries meant that General Electric was a good buy. America was in the grip of market madness. Everybody, except fools, was going to get rich.

Thus, on the morning of the twenty-fourth the focus of America was on Wall Street, and the floor of the Exchange was crowded with over a thousand traders, the usual number of traders present on the floor being around 750. Within moments of the opening gong, twenty-thousand-share blocks of General Motors and Kennecott Copper were ordered sold. This was almost unheard of: huge blocks of stock were usually traded later in the day, when the market's movement had been gauged by the seller.

These sellers obviously wanted out, fast. It was a bad sign.

President Herbert Hoover and his wife Lou were on a special presidential train returning to Washington from Louisville, Kentucky, where he had made a speech; earlier that week, the Hoovers had celebrated the fiftieth anniversary of the development of the electric lightbulb in Detroit with the bulb's inventor, Thomas Edison, and his great admirer, Henry Ford.

On a train going from Baltimore to New York was fifty-four-year-old Winston Churchill who for the first time in years was out of a job in English politics. Churchill was in America on a book and lecture tour, raising some much needed money. At the time, Churchill was wildly out of favor with the English, being blamed for many of the things that were going wrong in Great Britain. He had even written his wife that he was thinking of getting out of politics permanently.

In Germany, a youngish political orator named Adolf Hitler was pretty much at the nadir of his fortunes, his Nazi Party's membership ebbing, and Hitler himself mentioned, if at all, as the butt of jokes. The Depression that would be caused by Black Thursday would put him in power in a few short years.

By ten-thirty that morning, the selling had become a tidal wave and the stock ticker was already fifteen minutes late. In the first half hour of trading, the volume was an incredible 1,676,300 shares—almost as much in a half hour as there was on a normal trading day.

Panic began to cast its shadow over the great city.

By the close of the market at three that afternoon, Cesare knew he was in serious financial trouble. Standing by his ticker tape in his penthouse—which was hours behind the market due to an unprecedented volume of almost thirteen million shares traded that day—he realized with quick calculations that his Eagle Fund investment trust—or mutual fund as it would later be called—had lost over half of its value. His personal fortune of ten million dollars was also cut in half. But Cesare, with his usual gut instinct for survival, realized that there were fabulous opportunities for those with any nerve or cash left to reenter the market and gobble up the tremendous bargains that would be available the next day. He was ready for a fight, perhaps the fight of his life.

It was then that Gloria came into the apartment.

"I've been at the hairdresser," she said. "Everyone's saying the stock market crashed."

"Everyone's right," Cesare said, coolly lighting a cigarette.

"Have we lost money?"

"Only about five million bucks."

"Dear God! I need a drink."

"I could stand one too."

"I'll fix us a martini."

The phone rang. As Gloria took off her hat and coat and went to the bar, Cesare picked up the phone.

"Cesare, what the hell are you going to do?" It was Dutch Schultz. "The Eagle Fund fell on its ass today."

"It'll go back up."

"Says you. What the hell are you going to do to get my money back? I've lost a half million goddamn dollars!"

"We've all lost, except a few bears and Joe Kennedy. But the market will go back up again. In fact, I'm going to be buying tomorrow. There'll be fantastic bargains . . ."

"You're going back in to buy?" The gangster was screaming. "Are you fucking crazy?"

"Dutch, you knew the market's a gamble . . ."

"You know what I do to guys that double-cross me? I kill the bastards! If you lose any more of my money, you'd better watch your goddamned ass!"

He slammed the phone down. Cesare hung up and took a drag on his cigarette.

"Who was that?" Gloria asked, bringing him the martini.

"One of my customers," Cesare said suavely. "You remember our old friend Dutch Schultz."

"That piece of garbage. Was he upset?"

Cesare smiled.

"You might say. He threatened to kill me."

As Gloria stared at him, he stirred the onion in his martini, then took a sip.

To Rachel Savage's joy and amazement, her husband slowly recovered from the terrible automobile accident. Although he was in the hospital four months and would be confined to a wheelchair the rest of his life, still, for a seventy-year-old man, the recovery was astonishing. And by September of 1929, he was able to return to work at the bank—perhaps not the best time, historically, to return to Wall Street. But Johnny had been leary of the great bull market for some time, and the bank's portfolio, under his guidance, had reduced its position in the market so that the great crash of Black Thursday left the Savage Bank, unlike many of its competitors, in a healthy position.

But Johnny, like Rachel, was convinced the car crash that had so nearly killed him was no accident, but rather the work of Cesare. He told Rachel that this time, Cesare had gone too far, to which she agreed, and that he was hiring a private detective agency to investigate Cesare's dealings in the hope of being able to uncover enough evidence to bring legal proceedings against him—something the police had either not been able to do or had quietly been bought off to ignore. Rachel was saddened to think that her own flesh and blood would become the target of an investigation launched by her own husband.

But she also agreed to it.

And the night of Black Thursday, when hundreds of thousands of Americans were trying to figure out how much they had lost in the market crash that day, Johnny came home to tell his wife a piece of good news about another kind of crash.

"They've found the guy who worked on the brakes of the Cadillac the day before it crashed," he said. "And he's willing to testify that Cesare paid him to do it."

Rachel didn't say anything for a moment. Then: "Does this mean he'll go to jail?"

"Yes. We'll turn this over to the District Attorney, and Cesare will be prosecuted for attempted murder."

Rachel sighed and sank into a chair. Her husband watched her.

"I know what you're going through," he said quietly. "I won't do it if you don't want me to."

She looked at him with tear-filled eyes.

"No," she finally said. "As much as it hurts me to say this about my own son, he's gone too far, and he might have killed you. He must be brought to justice."

The day after Black Thursday, Friday the twenty-fifth of October, Wall Street began to look better. There was heavy trading, but stocks remained for the most part steady, though there were a few losses. The general wisdom was that there had been a terrible crash the day before, but that things were coming back to normal and Black Thursday had been an aberration. Cesare plunged heavily in, buying what he thought of as "bargains," certain that he could recover the ground his Eagle Fund had lost the day before.

What most of the Wall Street "insiders" didn't know was that in the rest of the country, manufacturers, frightened by Black Thursday, had begun revising their production quotas downward for November and December. Approximately two hundred thousand people were fired.

There were a few suicides. Winston Churchill, walking the streets of the financial district, actually saw a man jump to his death from the top of one of Wall Street's office buildings.

The next day, Saturday the twenty-sixth, the selling began again. Only the fact that it was a half trading day prevented a disastrous slide.

The weekend was tense. Cesare, outwardly cool, was actually terrified. But he said nothing to Gloria, and spent a half hour Sunday afternoon playing with his sons in their nursery.

Monday, the twenty-eighth, was horrendous. From the opening bell, stocks went into a downward spiral, quickly losing all the money that had been made the previous Friday and plunging into uncharted depths. General Electric fell forty-eight points, A.T.&T. thirty-four, Westinghouse another thirty-four. Monday's market losses were greater than the entire proceeding week. Even on the gilded North Shore of Long Island, where Whitneys, Phippses, Vanderbilts, Morgans, and Spreckles lived in mammoth mansions with private golf courses and solid gold doorknobs, a feeling that something was *very wrong* began to take root.

Even Cesare's cool facade began to crack. When Gloria told him she wanted to go to Europe to shop, he actually screamed at her, "You stupid bitch, don't you realize we're in trouble?"

Gloria burst into tears and locked herself in the bathroom.

The next day, Tuesday the twenty-ninth of October, 1929, the Roaring Twenties screeched to a horrible halt. It was the worst day ever experienced on the New York Stock Exchange. In the first half hour of trading, an unheard-of three million shares were dumped. In the five hours of trading, eight billion dollars were swept away, the equivalent of half the federal government's debt expenditures for the entire year. There was frenzy on the floor of the Exchange, and thousands of people outside gathered on Wall Street, aware that America was going to hell in a handbag.

Even the astrologer Evangeline Adams, who had predicted that the market would recover, evidenced a monumental lack of trust in her own predictions by telling her broker to sell everything she owned.

"Nick, darling, you know how much I love you," Valerie Savage said to her husband as they came downstairs in their Georgian mansion on the Gold Coast of Long Island for cocktails.

"Yes, I know," Nick said. "And I love you. What's wrong?"

Nick went to the bar to make a batch of sidecars. He knew his wife well enough to realize that when she told him she loved him out of the blue, there was trouble.

"Well, you were so terribly smart to stay out of the market," Valerie said, lighting a cigarette. "I mean, thank God you have foresight after the mess today on Wall Street."

"You can say that again. The one good thing that's happened to us this god-awful year is that we don't have to worry about the crash."

"Well, sweetie, perhaps we have to worry a *teeny* bit."

Nick stopped shaking the silver cocktail shaker and looked at her.

"What do you mean?"

"Well, you know, everyone at the Creek Club is in the market, and all the girls on the golf course talk about it all the time, not to mention the girls in my bridge club and the mah-jongg club, and, well, *everybody*. So I took a little money out of the bank to put in the market to surprise you. And I was doing terribly well until this past week . . ."

"What do you mean, you took a little money out of the bank? How much?"

"Now, I don't want you to get mad . . ."

"How much?" he screamed.

She burst into tears.

"A half million dollars," she sobbed.

Nick stared at her.

"A half million . . ." he gasped. "That's almost all the money we have!"

"Well, you were so stubborn about not buying stocks, and all my girlfriends told me I was foolish not to be in the market, and I was doing so well until recently and . . ."

"What's left?" he managed to choke out.

"My broker told me a half hour ago it's all gone."

Nick leaned over the bar and buried his face in his arms. Then after a moment, he straightened and wiped his eyes.

"I'm so terribly sorry, Nick . . ." Valerie said tentatively. "But apparently everyone's broke, so why don't we just shrug if off and have our cocktails?"

"No." Nick unscrewed the top of the cocktail shaker and poured the contents into the sink. Valeria looked confused.

"What are you doing?"

"We're going on the wagon."

"Oh, darling, don't be silly . . . this is no time to stop drinking! God, if anything, it's time to get stinking drunk! And then we'll go upstairs and I'll make you forget all about this. You know I always do."

He set down the shaker and came around the bar.

"There are going to be a lot of changes made," he said. "Up till now, I've blamed everyone but myself. It was Cesare's fault I embezzled the bonds, it was your fault for spending like a drunken sailor . . ."

"Don't blame me for what's happened! I mean, I suppose a little of it's my fault, but . . . Besides, your parents still have plenty of money. It's not as if we're dead broke . . ."

"I'm not going to ask my parents for one red cent. From now on, I'm going to make my own money. And I'll do it too. I've got a good head on my shoulders. Sure I've made lots of mistakes; but I'm going to show the world that Nick Savage is not just another half-drunk rich kid. And the first thing we're going to do is sell this house."

"Oh no!" she cried. "I love this place! And what will everyone say?"

"I don't give a damn what they say. If there's any lesson to be learned from the past few crazy years, it's that when you become obsessed by money, money possesses you. Well, that's over now—and thank God for it!"

Cesare Savage stood by the brick parapet of his penthouse terrace and stared down at the street nineteen floors below.

It must be easy, he thought. At least it would be quick. Just climb over the parapet and jump. Then a few seconds of falling, and then . . . what? Oblivion? Hell? Heaven? Well, probably not Heaven, in my case. But it would be easy and quick.

He sipped his dry martini and averted his eyes from the street below to the lights of the city he had come to love. It was a chilly night. He was dressed in his tuxedo. He was to meet Gloria at the Purple Parrot for dinner in a half hour, but he wasn't hungry.

It had not been a good day, to say the least. The crash had wiped him out. But even worse, as if the gods had decided to really punish him in a grand slam manner, two detectives had come to the apartment that morning with a warrant for his arrest on a charge of attempted murder. His lawyer had managed to raise bail money on the penthouse, but at ruinous interest rates, and he would have to put the penthouse up for sale. And after the market crash, who would want to buy a Park Avenue penthouse? Who could afford to buy it? As Eddie Cantor had said when John D. Rockefeller had commented that he and his son had faith in the economy and were buying stock, "The Rockefellers are the only people who have any money left." Cantor, like Cesare and millions of others, had lost everything in the crash. It had been a great party, but America was broke.

Cesare finished the martini and set the glass on a table. Then he leaned both hands on the parapet and looked down.

So quick.

So easy.

And, probably, painless.

"Mr. Savage?"

He almost jumped with surprise. He turned to see Nellie, the nanny, standing in the open French doors leading to the living room.

"Yes?"

"Mark is sneezing. Should I give him some aspirin?"

"Oh . . . yes, I suppose."

"Will you be going out soon?"

Cesare turned to look at the parapet again.

What am I, a coward? he thought. Only cowards and fools jump. I'll beat this yet. I'll beat everything. I'm Cesare, master of the world. They can't put me in jail. I'll get my millions back somehow.

"Yes, I'm meeting Mrs. Savage for dinner. I'm leaving now, as a matter of fact. Good night."

He started back into the penthouse.

"They're good little boys, aren't they?" he said to the nanny, who went back into the living room in front of him.

"Oh yes, sir. They're little angels."

"You'll kiss them good night for me, please."

"It will be a pleasure."

He put on a camel's-hair coat and a top hat in the foyer. Then he took the elevator down to the street.

"I'd like a taxi, please," he said to the doorman.

"Yes, Mr. Savage."

They both went out on the sidewalk, Cesare waiting by the front door of the building as the doorman stood at the curb, looking for a taxi. Cesare looked down at the pavement. He shuddered slightly as he thought of what might have been lying there, sprawled on the cement, if he had jumped.

A black car parked down the street started up, its headlights blinking on. As it rushed by the building, a machine gun jutted out of the back window. Cesare was dead before he even heard the chatter of the gun or felt the bullets pierce his chest.

"Thanks for the stock tips!" Dutch Schultz yelled out the window as the car roared down Park Avenue into the night.

The doorman, who had thrown himself onto the sidewalk as the gun started firing, now picked himself up.

"Mr. Savage!" he cried, running over to Cesare's body.

But Cesare, lying faceup in an expanding pool of blood, didn't answer.

"It's funny," the old man in Rome whispered. "Here I am at death's door, and I'm not even scared. Don't you think that's funny?"

The speaker was Justin Savage, the ancient patriarch of the family, who so many years before had set sail on his father's clipper ship for China. He had been severely weakened by a series of strokes, so much that his body was almost totally paralyzed, though he could still mumble; the doctors had told Fiammetta he couldn't possibly last out the day.

"It's not funny, darling," Fiammetta said. She was sitting

next to his bed, holding his right hand. "It just means that you're very brave, as always."

"Do you believe in the afterlife?"

"Oh yes, Justin. I've fought the Church over the years, and I still think that there are many rascals in it and it's often wrong. But I've never doubted that it's right about what happens after we die."

"Huh. I've doubted. But I suppose now I'd better start believing. What if I run into that wicked bastard, my half brother Sylvaner?"

"Oh darling, he won't be in Heaven. I'm sure he's in Hell."

"With about half the rest of the people I've known." His eyes closed and he was silent. For a moment, she thought he had died. Then he whispered: "I'll miss you, Fiammetta. But maybe we'll end up together after all."

"Oh yes, sweet Justin. I'll be with you—probably very soon. And we'll be together forever."

"Do you think we'll fight?"

She smiled, though there were tears running down her cheeks.

"Oh, I'm sure. It wouldn't be any fun without fights, would it?"

"We've run a good race, haven't we?"

"I think so, yes."

"And our children have come out pretty well, with some glaring exceptions, like Cesare. That's the important thing, isn't it? Children. Family."

"You're so right, my darling."

He fell silent again, and his breath began wheezing slightly. Fiammetta nervously looked around at the nun who was standing behind her and who had been nursing him. Then she heard him mumbling, and she turned back to him.

"What did you say, darling?"

"It's odd," he whispered. "I see a light . . . a bright light . . . There seems to be someone there . . . He's holding out a hand to me . . . Or is it a she?"

Then he became silent.

The nun reached down to feel his pulse.

"He's gone," she said.

In Hong Kong, Lance Wang and Nora Manderville were married in Government House. Although some were shocked by the interracial marriage, most people in the colony applauded the beautiful young couple who were so happily in love. Afterward, at the reception, Sir Neville Manderville danced the first waltz with Julie Chin.

"Well," he said with a smile, "it all turned out nicely, wouldn't you say?"

Julie smiled back.

"It's a very happy ending."

In Rome, Dr. Bruno Vespa was let out of the Regina Coeli prison. He was met by his wife in their car. Beatrice was crying as she embraced her husband, who looked pale and had lost twenty pounds.

"Darling, I'm so happy to see you again," she sniffed.

"I love you."

When they had returned to the villa on the Appian Way, Bruno said, "Someday, in some way, I'll pay them back."

They all came to Cesare's funeral. Even Johnny, in his wheelchair. Rachel, swathed in a black veil, stood beside him as the priest read the service for the dead. Then there were Nick and Valerie. And Brook who was thrilled to be pregnant; she had insisted on coming to her half brother's funeral. After all, Cesare had saved her from a jail term—perhaps even the electric chair. Her adored husband, Bernard, Comte de Belleville, was in Tel Aviv overlooking the children's hospital they were building. Brook and Bernard were desperately happy, awaiting the birth of their first child. And there was Gloria with Nellie the nanny holding the twins, Mark and Sebastian, who cried as the chilly autumnal wind swept over the cemetery.

Afterward, Rachel tossed a rose onto the coffin. Then she came over to Gloria and took her hand.

"Let's bury the past with Cesare. He did some terrible things, but he was my son. I want you to know that I consider you part of my family. And Mark and Sebastian are my grandsons."

"That's kind of you to say, Mrs. Savage," Gloria said.

"Please: Rachel. We must all make a new beginning. When you have an opportunity, I would like to take you to lunch and discuss, among other things, your finances. I want to help you."

"Rachel," Gloria said, "you are a real lady."

And she meant it.

As Johnny and Rachel drove back into Manhattan, Johnny thought of the eight-year-old Cesare who had sliced the sleeves of his coats off so many years before.

"The tragedy is that Cesare was at war with himself and hatred won. No matter what he did to me," he said, taking Rachel's hand, "and God knows he did plenty, I hope he rests in peace."

Rachel leaned over and kissed his cheek.

"And may we have many years of happiness ahead of us," she said. She smiled. "You know, I've been very happy with you all these years, despite all our problems and fights. And yes, we've had fights, God knows. But it was all well worth it, Johnny Savage. Well worth it. And I still love you very much. Oh, it's a different kind of love than it was at the beginning. But it's much richer now."

"Yes," he said softly, "I would never have thought this when I was young, but love gets better as it gets older."

Rachel leaned over and kissed his cheek.

"And may we have many years of happiness ahead of us," she said. She smiled. "You know, I'm still crazy about you."

The End

AUTHOR'S NOTE

The old Waldorf-Astoria Hotel, where the Bradley Martin ball took place, was at the site of the present Empire State Building.